PRISMS

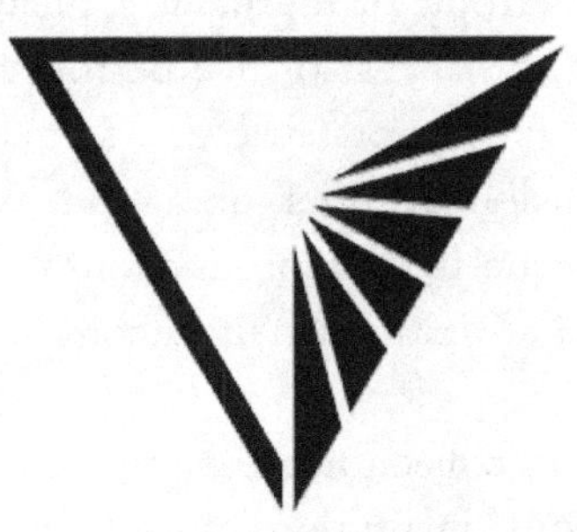

EDITED BY

DARREN SPEEGLE & MICHAEL BAILEY

PRISMS

TABLE OF CONTENTS

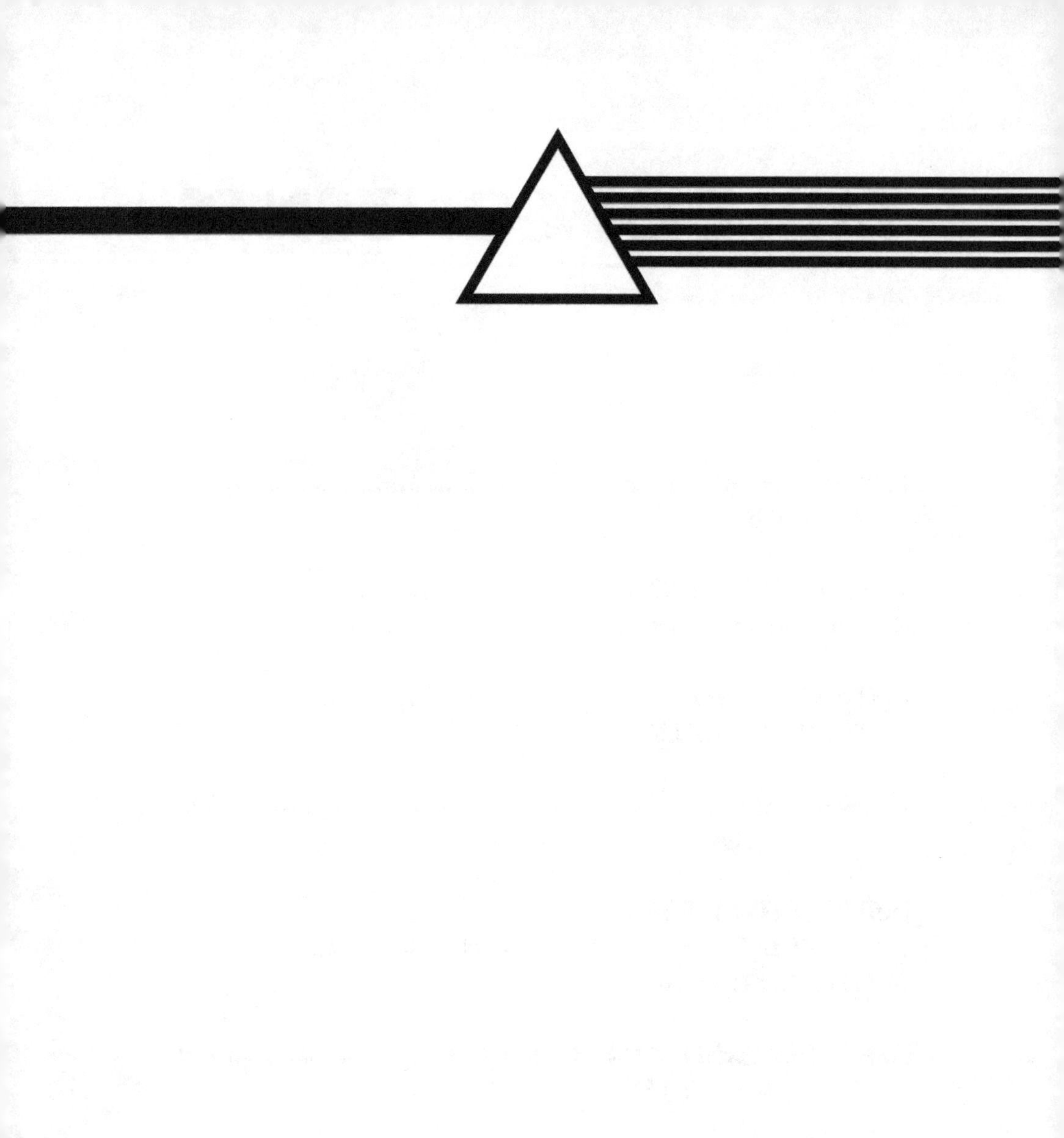

WE COME IN THREES

B.E. SCULLY

It begins with a spider.

The Artist lies on the bed, not moving. Watching the spider move. Soon he will have to get up, drink water, eliminate, move his body. Stay alive.

But not yet.

The Artist swings his feet to the floor and groans. The room is too bright today, the walls too white. He checks the paper calendar tacked beside the room's only window. The tack is in the form of a golden rooster, but the calendar is plain. It is the seventeenth, which adds up to eight. An uncertain number for the Artist. A tricky number.

Today, the seventeenth of March—the day of the week does not concern him—the Artist turns his gaze toward his canvas. The work is almost finished, but he cannot concentrate. He is too hungry.

His feet slide against a finely woven woolen rug on the floor by the bed. The rug is patterned with dark blooms of flowers entangled in vines. The Artist craves the sensation of the rug against his feet, and leaves it reluctantly. Soon the Woman will come, and he is very hungry.

It isn't thirst that drives him. He can access all the water he needs from a small porcelain sink by the toilet. No, it isn't thirst but *Hunger* that consumes him.

If not for the Woman, he would starve.

The water tastes cold today, cold and metallic. The Artist approaches his canvas, begins to work. He does not—cannot—think of Time. Of Food. Of the Woman.

And yet how not to think of the things that sustain him?

The Artist looks up from what he has just painted. He looks for the Spider, but it is no longer there. Or no longer visible. The artist is painting the Woman—or a representation of the Woman. And yet it isn't a woman at all. It's a girl—long dark curls and heart-shaped face. Fine, thin hands and pale skin that tears easily beneath thorns and fingers alike.

And yet she isn't a girl, either, not really. The Artist knows this, of course.

He dabbles in his paint pots, adjusts the Cadmium Yellow with some unexpected Rosewater Blue.

Of course, he knows. He is waiting for—he is painting—not a woman, not a girl, but the Page. He gently presses the brush to the canvas, then harder, a violent slash. Why does he always get confused about the Page? Not a girl, but a boy. A girlish boy. Or a boyish girl?

The Artist throws down his brush in disgust. She is so *like* a girl, and yet so not. That's why he calls her the Page.

Of course, he knows.

He picks up his brush again but does not paint.

The Page will come soon. Must come. If not for the Page, the Hunger would conquer him. He has been in this room a long time—many turns of the Wheel, at times hard and fast, at times sweet and/or agonizingly slow. Sometimes stuck fast and not turning at all. But eventually, ever onwards, all to get here, to this room. To work on his projects and wait for the Skeleton to come riding in on his sad-eyed, sway-backed horse, sword hanging limp but not flaccid in his fine, thin hand.

The Hunger has distracted him again.

The Artist puts down his brush, selects another. Dark, dusky green paint this time. A swirl around the Page's head. Another to gild the Sword, for this one is the troubled Page of Swords. Nothing limp about this one.

It is not a work of Surrealism, though symbolic, of course.

The Artist was not always consumed with this Hunger. At one point, he had overcome food altogether, going for days on nothing but bananas and fermented juice. But his soul grew leaner along with his body, until the hunger became starvation. Now, once a day the Page comes with a plain silver tray. It always holds the same thing: two cubes, one white, one black. He can consume one of the cubes—one, and only one.

The cubes differ not just in color, but in content. One contains Life—nutrients, protein, the stuff of the molecular strand. The other contains Death—poison, plain and lethally simple. One food, one fatal. The Artist thinks of the switch-'em-up card games he used to watch the men play on the streets outside his childhood home. Which one is which? Keep your eye on the prize, boyo, now you see it, now you don't.

The colors of the cubes reveal nothing of what is inside. He does not know which contains the poison and which contains the food. He does not know if the poison is meant to kill him quickly or slowly. But kill him it will, if he chooses incorrectly one too many times. Or perhaps even just one time, the first and last, if the poison proves fatal enough someday.

The Artist does not know.

The Page never indicates which is which, never helps him decide. Never so much as lifts an eyebrow or turns up a corner of the mouth. She always stands silently, waiting. She neither speaks nor moves until after he's eaten his chosen cube. Then, if he does not ask her to stay, she leaves as silently as she's come. If he does, she sets the tray and the unchosen cube outside the door and returns to him for the afternoon.

The Artist pauses, lets his eyes go out of focus. Long ago, did he first ask her to stay, or did she ask him? Perhaps she stayed on her own, without being asked. The Artist is pleased with this version.

He remembers very little of life outside this room.

For years he kept an elaborate chart, trying to discern the pattern of the cubes. For there is always a pattern. White or black, food or poison? But in Time the Artist realized that his pattern was *not* to choose.

One choice Life, one choice Death. Eventually, the Artist stopped caring. He came to suspect there wasn't any difference in the cubes at all, or if there was, it had lost its meaning.

"But did it ever have any meaning in the first place?" he asks, laughing, and adds a streak of black to the canvas.

One day, when the time came to choose, the Artist did not.

Instead, he closed his eyes and spun around the room, spun so hard and fast that he no longer knew which way was up and which way was down. No matter how tempting, he did not open his eyes. Did not peek or call out for help.

Once thoroughly unmoored from spinning, he reached out. Kept reaching until he touched the tray. Found a cube. Ate it, eyes still wide shut. When he opened them again, there were no more cubes on the tray. He did not know which one he had eaten. He did not know what the Page had done with the uneaten cube.

It has been like this for many years now. The Artist does not choose, and does not see the cube he has not-chosen.

And so he goes on making his Art, and sleeping, and drinking, and hungering.

Today, the seventeenth of March, the day that adds up to a problematic eight, the Artist waits. His Hunger can be endured no more. Only this day the Artist does not hear the familiar turn of the handle telling him it is Time. This day he hears a thud, a falling. A something, out in the corridor. Confused, he stands, turns in a circle, moves toward …

… the door rattles once in the frame and goes silent. The Page lies in bed, listening, and soon the chime tinkles once, twice, then the third time, the tricky, elusive third that sometimes still sets her teeth on edge just waiting for it to come. The third sometimes sounds like a cascade, sometimes like a kaleidoscope, sometimes like cacophony. Sometimes it is so faint she almost misses it, though what is there to miss? There is only one chime, really, one room, one job.

To feed the Artist.

She swings her feet to the ground, stands up, stretches. The open window lets in a gust of rain-wet air, and the Page lifts her head toward it. A womb, this room—safe, familiar, sealed off. Only one way out: down the dizzying corridor carpet of interlocking squares and circles that sometimes still cause her to stumble, to lose her way.

"Stop looking down then!" the Artist says, laughing. But it's a hard habit to break, looking down.

Only one destination: down the hall and to the left and past the potted stands of oregano to the Artist's room.

But first she must go to the Office, which, unlike the Artist's room, is right next door.

Today, the seventeenth day of March, the Page pulls on a pair of linen pants that reach no farther than her ankles, and a long, plain tunic. Her short black hair needs no special tending. When she does check the mirror, she is often shocked. She is growing older, of course, and yet sometimes the mirror shows the same young girl she once was.

Is memory fooling her, or the mirror?

Not that it matters. When she and the Artist make love, or talk, or sit looking out his one small, rectangular window, the one above the only furniture in the room, an ornate desk and absurdly purple-cushioned cane-back chair—when that happens, he looks at her, he sees her, but she is not sure what he sees.

The Page cannot know what another sees. No one can.

How old is she now anyway?

Menstruation doesn't help her keep track. Sometimes she bleeds, gushing rivulets of blood, viscous and alive at first, then blackened and ropey like food left to turn. Sometimes she must ask the Management for new clothes, her body grows so fat and round, then other times her clothes are as small and narrow as a child's. At such times, she looks more like a boy—a child—than a woman. She does not know how the Artist prefers her, and she does not care.

She is no prisoner. She can leave when she wants, and does. She tends a small garden, walks in the park, feeds the birds. Attends a weekly dance class, studies languages, takes a lover. Why would she wish for more? She has the Artist; or, more to the point, she has Art. She is not an Artist herself, nor does she wish to be. She does not wish to long like that, to hunger so greatly and be fed so little. To be so alone, in a barren white room with barren white walls save the ones he fills. No, her job is to feed the Artist what little he gets. Nothing more, nothing less.

Sometimes the Provider is in the Office, at the desk, and sometimes he is in the back, in the rooms where the Page never goes. She has never seen beyond the desk. Today the door is open, but there is no one inside. Like every other day, she wishes there was more food, that she had more to offer. But she only has what the Provider provides: two small discs of bread, one black, one white. The discs are placed on a wooden tray with two indentations made to match the discs perfectly, so that the tray's surface is almost flat.

The Artist's stomach, she has been told, can tolerate nothing else. A poor digestive system, years of unwholesome living. All that. She doesn't know when he is hungry, or if he ever eats more than she gives him. She only knows that when the chime rings out, including the tricky third one, she reports to the Office, receives the tray of bread, and takes it to the Artist.

But that is almost a lie. For the Page *does* know when the Artist is hungry—all the time, perhaps even in his sleep.

And who wouldn't be, eating so little?

Though she's never been told, the Page knows that one of the discs has poison in it. Her duties are precise, her instructions complete, but her knowledge is minimal. She knows nothing of the Artist except for his work; he knows nothing of her except for the food.

Nevertheless, she smelled the poison immediately, her very first day. She would happily have eaten the bread first, to poison herself and spare the Artist. But she was not allowed to touch the bread, ever. Touching the bread was forbidden.

The Page believed in the Sacred, but she was no Priest, nor even a Queen. She didn't dare remove the discs from their sunken circles on the tray. But slowly, cautiously, she began to scrape bits off the top of the bread—not *touching* it really, but ... scraping it. To eat of each disc of bread by small degrees; to learn the taste of the poison. Even though she could neither speak nor move until the Artist had eaten, she would have found a way to protect the Artist, to discover and communicate to him which disc of bread could feed and which could foil.

But she never did either. Sometimes she was certain she knew which piece was poison; other times she was equally certain that both discs were poisoned, or neither. Once, in a fever dream, it occurred to her that the Artist might sometimes even *want* the poisoned disc, might choose it on purpose. For what if what was poison to her was sustenance to him? Or what if poison and sustenance can be the same thing?

The Page does not know.

One day the Artist began not choosing the bread but instead closing his eyes and spinning around the room, faster and faster until he stopped and stumbled forward, until he found her. Then he reached out, and how easy it would have been then to guide his hand, to determine his choice!

But she never had known which choice to guide him towards.

It has been a long time since the Page last tasted the bread. She is sick; she can feel it deep in her body. When the blood last came, it smelled feral, ancient. Soon she will no longer be able to take care of the Artist. Soon she will die.

Today, the Office is empty. The Page picks up the wooden tray with the two discs, one white, one black, each sunken in its circle.

Down the corridor and past the potted oregano, and at the Artist's door she pauses, listening—strains of music. The song he's been working on, in the strange minor key. As she stands at the door, she admits a truth she could not until now: the Provider is trying to kill the Artist. She has noticed, of course, that the discs keep getting smaller and smaller, the bread coarser and meaner, the time between the chime longer and longer. Of course the Provider is trying to kill the Artist, and using her to do it. She knows this, and can do nothing about it. And might not, even if she could.

For what to do?

Her job is to feed the Artist. Nothing more, nothing less.

And yet she cannot bear to watch the Artist starve to death. She cannot bear to see him die, even though everything of course must die, and will. Selfishly, she would rather die first, and is secretly pleased that she will. An even more secret part is glad, too, that the Artist will miss her, will suffer without her, even for a short time until another Page can be found.

She stands at the door, listening to the minor fall and the major lift. She pictures the Artist seated, playing his instrument with long-fingered hands. *Today*, she thinks but does not say, *I will choose for you—I will choose which disc of bread, white or black, black or white, life or death.*

But which one?

She reaches out and breaks the sacred—picks up a disc of bread and turns it over, hands trembling so hard she is certain she'll drop it.

But she does not.

She places the disc back on the tray and picks up the other one. Turns it over, too, turning and turning as if she were a magician conjuring a trick.

And perhaps she is, because now she sees: the back of the white disc is black; the back of the black disc is white.

Whiteblackdeathlifeblackwhitelifedeathwhitelifeblackdeath-whitedeathblacklife …

The Page drops the tray, drops the discs. Inside the room, the Artist looks up from his work. He stands, confused, moves toward …

… the door of the Office is closed, but unlocked. The Provider doesn't remember leaving it unsecured. He shrugs, sighs, shakes his head. It doesn't matter—the food will be here soon.

He goes and stands in front of his favorite object in the room: a full length mirror in an enormous, obscene gilt frame with naked cherubs and doves and vines holding up the cosmos. He stands straight, facing forward. He is overweight, belly round and pendulous. He has more hair on his face now than the top of his head. He is grotesque, enormous, resplendent. As heavy and earth-bound as the Pages are slight and ethereal. Beasts versus birds.

Versus? He is not at war with the Pages, although the Pages are often at war with him, or think they are. He is not at war with the Artist, either. He has given up years of his life to see the Artist finish his great tale. Or at least keep writing, even if the epic tale never gets told, or partly told, or even poorly told.

For someone must tell the tales, and someone must feed the tale-tellers.

Although it grieves him, he is neither of those people.

The Pages don't know it yet, but in seven days' time the Provider will no longer be working here. No one has fired him, and no one has asked him to leave. He requires neither to know it is true.

Although he has worked in this Office a very long time—longer than either the Page or the Artist—his leaving neither surprises nor frightens him. He has always had other arrangements, other possibilities. He would have been a fool to think only of this situation, this Artist.

And yet.

He isn't worried about the Pages. Each is clever in his or her own way, clever and resourceful. He is worried, of course, about the Artist. Needlessly, foolishly, arrogantly. Worrying about the Artist is not his job. His job is to keep the Office running, to make certain the food is there each day for the Page to take to the Artist. Although the Page thinks the Provider knows everything—that he is in on the whole thing—in fact, he knows very little.

In fact, he might know nothing at all—nothing!

He certainly knows less than the Page, who gets to enjoy the Artist, and his work, far more than the Provider ever will. The Provider has never even met the Artist. He only hears or sees snatches of the process that produces the Art which keeps the Office going. The Page hates the Provider even as she loves and depends upon his security, his safety, his control. The Artist, as well—sometimes it is a great relief to not get away with things.

The Page believes the Provider knows which dish is poisoned and which isn't, but he knows nothing. His job is to keep things running.

He loves the Artist as much as the Page, though. Perhaps even more. And he loves the Page, too, all of them, and the Office itself— he loves it all. He will miss it for the rest of his life. Not for one day, one minute, did he wish for another job.

The Provider knows the Page thinks he is trying to kill the Artist—to starve or poison him out of this existence and into what awaits. She thinks that is a part of the Provider's job, but it's isn't. In fact, not only does he not bring the food to the Artist, he doesn't make it, either. He never possessed any skill such as that.

That's why he's the Provider.

But the one thing even the Page doesn't know is the one thing even the Provider doesn't know: who provides the Provider?

Once, many years ago, he tried and failed to find out where the food comes from. Thus, the Provider doesn't know who cooks the food the Artist eats each day. He doesn't know who poisons it, or doesn't, or why.

He only knows who brings it, and not always even that—sometimes it's the obese, simple-minded boy named Jonas, swallowed up by his own whale. Or the young foreign couple, bound so tightly together the years alone can set them free. The detritus of the streets: a Skipper in a soiled flat-cap; a wild-haired woman wrapped in a bile-yellow cloak with black trim, her own traveling crime scene; one icy January, a temporary security guard who asked the Provider to sign for the food, though of course he would do no such thing.

The Provider looks at one of the many clocks on the wall. Time is important in the Office, and it's almost time. The food is never late. The Provider insists on that, no matter who delivers it.

Of course he has noticed the portions getting smaller, the quality more and more plain. Even the delivery people seem worn-out and tired, harried, uninterested and uninteresting in deadly equal measure. Yesterday, a stoop-shouldered youth in tall, scuffed black boots delivered two cutlets on black and white plates so small they would barely hold a teacup. And plastic, too, as was the cheap tray that held the whole sorry package together.

Once, the food was rich and plentiful, the dishes fine. Custards, gravies, puddings, meats of all the beasts and birds of the earth. Bone china, gilded trays, bejeweled plates of pewter and crystal. The best of everything, but one thing remained the same: the Artist always had two choices, one poison, one pure, and could choose only one.

As time went on, the Artist began to eat less. Eventually, he turned food away entirely, and lived on little more than air and water. But the Hunger always returned. The great delicacies, however, did not. Some days the tray held no more than two saucer-sized plates of lentils, one white, one black.

Such meagre offerings for an Artist as great as this one! It makes the Provider angry, and anger isn't what he needs. But what is?

Determination. He checks his graphs: the seventeenth of March. If the dish today is too meagre, the presentation too mean, he will reject it. He will make new arrangements for the Artist's meals—his final act before he leaves. It is not his job to feed the Artist, but it his job to fire and hire people, to keep things running smoothly. The Artist cannot work if the Artist cannot eat. If the Artist cannot work, the Office cannot survive.

Or is it the other way around?

A knock on the door causes the Provider to swing away from his own image in the great gilt mirror. He slowly, calmly walks to the door. The Provider always takes his time, even when he has very little.

He turns the handle, opens the door.

It is a Woman—an old Woman, he sees now, though he didn't at first. She is dressed neatly, in a black bodysuit and plain black raincoat, although it isn't raining. Nothing about her suggests poverty, but her clothes seem worn, out-of-date. There is a whiff of long-lingering moth balls about her.

Her gray-white hair is wound into a thick braid that she wears draped over her left shoulder, like a scarf. Or a serpent. When she turns her back, its curled-end head keeps its eyes on him.

In her hands she holds a bamboo tray, woven into interlocking triangle shapes. Today there is only one item on the tray: a round, white porcelain dish with a button-handled lid.

A single serving.

"Good morning," the Provider says.

"Good afternoon," replies the Crone.

"Only one dish today?" he asks, though he knows that cannot be true.

She smiles at him—perfectly white, straight teeth in a perfectly pink, crooked mouth. Lifts the lid from the round white dish to reveal the food inside: a steaming hot apple tart, topped with a perfectly latticed crust of interlocking golden triangles.

The Provider's mouth waters with Hunger. The Crone smiles her pink-gum white-teeth kaleidoscope smile.

The Provider reaches out and pulls the chime that calls the Page to feed the Artist.

"Only one dish today?" he asks again, though this time he already knows the answer.

"Only one!" the Crone answers with a laugh. "Only one!" And that is the End.

ENCORE FOR AN EMPTY SKY

LYNDA E. RUCKER

Darkness, and in the darkness, a red light. Like the light in a darkroom. Her great-grandfather had had one when she was a child, and even then, it had been obsolete, an old man's indulgence. He had died before she was ten, but she still remembered the darkroom: the plastic basins of chemicals, the black and white photographs hanging from a clothesline.

He had shown her how to take a cardboard shoebox and turn it into something miraculous, a pinhole camera, producing photographs on sheets of paper that she could hold and hang on her wall. Unlike her 3-D digital projections, which precisely replicated whatever she photographed, the pinhole camera turned the ordinary otherworldly. She and her grandfather took shots of the oak tree in his front yard at different exposures and compared them side by side, sitting on his front porch with the tree itself in front of them. The tree was dark and sharp in one shot and blurred in another one, like a dream of a tree, while in a third one, the one with the longest exposure, the wide expanse of sky was streaked with light. It looked as though the atmosphere had been stripped away and you could see the stars above as the earth hurtled through space.

Her grandfather pointed at that one. "They used to send rockets up there," he said. "Said we'd go live on other planets someday, spread throughout the universe. Some people use to say, why should we be allowed to go out there and do to other planets what we're doing to this one? I guess those people got their wish."

She didn't care about rockets. She cared about the photographs, each of which told its own very different story. She said, "How can they all be the same tree?"

He said, "They aren't. There's no such thing as the same tree. You can never step into the same river twice. A man named Heraclitus said that."

"But it is the same." She pointed to it, right there in front of them. "Same as yesterday and the day before, and the same as it will be tomorrow."

"Nothing is ever the same from one day to the next or even one moment to the next. Nothing is fixed. That's part of the beauty of the photograph. You can capture something for the millisecond that it exists in that state, and then that state has passed. By the time you're aware of it, it's gone, but you have the photograph of that moment. Even if you photographed that tree every day from the same angle, you still couldn't capture the thousands of little changes it undergoes in a twenty-four hour period."

A year later he was dead. She had never forgotten his words, because they terrified her. They made her feel like she had to hold onto something, but she didn't know what, because if all of it was changing, all the time, was any of it real? And who knew who he had been, when he died? In the final year of his life, his memory had fragmented; he had not known her, or he had called her by names she did not possess. Sometimes he thought he was back in the war, in the desert; or in his old job building seawalls along what had been the Atlantic coast long before she was born. In the presents that he inhabited, she did not yet exist.

He had loved her more than anyone. If she had stopped existing for him, did she exist at all? Her parents assured her she did. But she kept asking, so eventually they put her on a regimen of drugs that made her so slow and sleepy she stopped taking them. She flushed them down the toilet instead, and learned her lesson. She never again asked anyone whether or not she was real.

But here, bathed in the red light, she was less sure than she had ever been in her life, and she wanted to ask someone again *am I real?* Maybe she was still in the darkroom. Maybe she had never left. She was still herself, and if she could stay herself, remember who she was at the core of it all, everything would be okay.

Excerpt from anonymous packet received by the *Aletheia* holocast:

Hannah Blue was missing. Her management had tried to cover it up for as long as they could, but she had gigs and appearances booked, and eventually the press lost its patience with endless claims of "exhaustion." The official word came long after everyone had already figured it out, and the cry went up: what did they mean "missing"? Was there suspicion of foul play, or was this merely "missing" in the sense that no one knew where she had gone? But how could the latter be true? It wasn't possible even for an ordinary person to move about and leave no trace of themselves, let alone someone as famous as Hannah Blue.

Famous, but Hannah Blue had always been an enigma, her rise stratospheric, her origins swathed in mystery—like her fame, really. She was an average performer, a mediocre singer, but she had a quality about her that was undeniably alluring, and it meant demand for her presence was almost insatiable. Absent, she became more popular than ever. Although her management claimed to have only admitted it out of necessity, her disappearance catapulted the *idea* of her to even greater heights and her team to even bigger profits. The disappearance had happened right after the release of what was turning out to be her biggest hit single yet, "The Sum of Me." If she was in fact "missing" as was claimed, it began to seem that it was in the best interests of many people to keep it that way as long as possible.

As a result, the rumors became more intense. It was a hoax, a publicity stunt; she'd been hidden away by her handlers, who became more tight-lipped as the frenzy mounted.

In fact, it all starts because a woman named Allison Lewes has passed out in her bed still wearing the Skin from the night before, and when she wakes up, hungover, it takes her ages to peel it off. You weren't supposed to leave them on for that long, and her face looks like it has undergone some kind of disastrous chemical treatment, but there is no time to cover it with makeup because she is already late. A shame Skins aren't allowed at work, she thinks, not for the first time, as she races out of her building to the metro stop across the street.

She is conscious of people looking at her surreptitiously on the train. Allison links up to the manufacturer's customer service and adjusts her visor so the rep can clearly see her face.

"I fell asleep in the Skin. What should I do?"

"That is contraindicated." The voice comes from a woman's face that is unnaturally smooth, eyes that lack depth.

Allison bites back an exasperated noise. She hates getting an AI instead of a regular person. "Yes, I know. I'm wondering if there's anything I should be doing about it."

"Skins should not be worn for more than twelve hours at a time. It is recommended that customers wait 48 hours before fittings."

Allison sighs and cancels the linkup. A pale, heavyset middle-aged man is watching her from across the aisle. "You should be careful," he says. "My sister messed up her face with one of them Skins." Allison ignores him. "Dermatologist said there wasn't nothing he could do because of how deep the damage goes. Looks like somebody threw acid all over her." Allison gets up and moves down the car to the end where she stands the rest of the way to her stop.

She sends a linkup to Tash as she walks up the street toward her office, but the person who answers isn't Tash, or at least she doesn't think it's Tash at first. But just as she's about to cancel the linkup, the blonde woman at the other end peers at her and says, "Jesus, Allison, what'd you do to yourself?" She has Tash's voice.

"Why are you wearing a Skin? It's eight in the morning."

"I look better than you do."

"Is it that bad? I fell asleep with a Skin on last night."

"It's that bad."

"It looks like my skin, my real skin, I mean, is peeling off my face right now, doesn't it? It really hurts, too." She's standing outside her work now and she needs to go in because she's already late, but she can feel tears gathering. It's less about the pain than the embarrassment, and the frustration, and the memory of what a shitty night it had been anyway—she'd thought she'd hit it off with a guy until she came back with drinks and overheard him and his friends making fun of her—and she's feeling sorry for herself because she has no sick leave and if she doesn't get inside right now she is probably going to get fired anyway and what if her face falls off or her skin melts down to the bone and she is such a fuck up. Why is she such a fuck up?

"Call me when you get off work, babe," Tash says. "I've got something here you might be interested in."

"You better get that thing off while you can," Allison says. "Let me be your cautionary tale."

Allison hasn't been at her desk for ten minutes when Priya, her boss, stops by. "Can you come into my office for a few minutes?" Priya says. Allison knows it's serious because Priya doesn't even comment on her face.

Allison works at a company that analyzes big data that is collected by other companies. Her first ambition had been to become a photographer, like her grandfather had been; she had not known, then, that such an ambition was akin to longing to create illuminated manuscripts, or build internal combustion engines. She'd studied journalism in college, but there aren't many journalism jobs any longer either, not real ones. Crunching data and writing analyses of that data is probably the closest thing to journalism she could be doing—at least she is still looking at and writing about facts, she tells herself. Allison is good at her job, when she actually makes it into work, but she hates it.

But not good enough. Ten minutes later, she is walking back out of the big glass building without it.

They had sold her grandfather's house in that final year of his life, before he even died. This had outraged her. Her mother tried to explain they needed to do it to pay for his care, but that was no excuse: they could try harder, save more money. Maybe she could get a job doing something even though she was just a kid. They had concocted a plan, she and her grandfather, to photograph the tree every day for a year, and see what happened. See if they could detect the minute changes day by day. Already the tumor that would first change him in unspeakable ways and then kill him must have begun to take root in the folds of his brain.

Not long after the sale, she rode her bike over to his house as she'd so often done after school. To her horror, the tree was gone; it appeared to have been yanked out of existence, not even its stump left behind. She'd been so angry that she marched up onto the porch, banged on the front door, and demanded an account of the tree from the woman who answered it. The tree had a disease, the woman told her gently. They'd had to get rid of it before it spread to the other trees as well. She had begun to cry. *It still mattered even though it had a disease. It still had a right.* Her parents had had to come and get her, and they fought all the way home, talking about her as though she wasn't sitting right there. *She's grieving,* her father said, and her mother said, *She still can't go around harassing strangers!*

Later, in her room, she lay in bed looking at the photos of the tree. It seemed both the tree and her grandfather had been unceremoniously snatched out of existence. That everything that they did, everything they were, could be there and then be gone like that, seemed incomprehensible in its cruelty. If this was the way the world was, she thought, she was not sure she would be able to live in it.

She cleared everything out of her closet with the intention of setting up a darkroom there. Her parents bought her a red safelight, but the other equipment she needed for the kind of photography that her grandfather did was simply not available or too difficult or expensive to obtain. No, her parents said, they did not know what had become of the equipment when the house was sold. They supposed it was thrown out.

She sat in the darkroom with the red light where it was safe and thought about the carelessness of people who let photography equipment and houses and trees and people go.

Excerpt from anonynous packet received by the *Aletheia* holocast:

After Hannah Blue became famous but some time before her disappearance, one frustrated investigative-journalist-wannabe from the "Chats with Charisma" holocast went digging into her past, or tried to. Edie Warner, the reporter in question, was a Nostalg who'd taken the whole thing a little too far, way past aesthetics into a profound antipathy for the present and a scholarly obsession with the past. She'd actually written her master's thesis on twentieth century investigative journalism. The irony of it was that her devotion to her profession's painstaking approach to uncovering truth in a different century had handicapped her professionally; her studies had been mostly irrelevant in terms of the contemporary industry and it was why she ended up at a fourth-rate channel like "Chats With Charisma" and not somewhere prestigious like "Blaze Time" or "Five With Frieda."

Edie may not have been very good at her job, but she actually was good at what she wished her job was, and the fact of the matter was that if anyone *could* get to the bottom of the truth about Hannah Blue, it was she. Edie worked hard on it, too, every moment that she wasn't at her day job. She lived off nicotine shots and caffeine pills, scarcely ate or slept, driving herself as hard as she could to solve the mystery of the enigmatic Hannah Blue. She started out releasing information packets on obscure channels as she went along, but Hannah Blue's handlers soon caught wind of it, and she got a firmly worded message from a law firm along with a distinct sense that someone was following her at night. Edie pruned her contacts list and started encrypting the packets. She took to using Ryders instead of walking or public transportation. Really, though, Hannah Blue's handlers need not have worried. Even Edie Warner, profoundly devoted to the relentless tedium of investigative work, eventually hit a wall beyond which she could not penetrate. Hannah Blue wasn't, and then she was. Clearly, she had been someone else first, but who, and how had the her-before been so thoroughly extruded from existence?

That was the attraction, of course. Unlike the AIs, which had been pushed into the spotlight as entertainers before to lukewarm response, Hannah Blue was an actual Artificial Person, because unlike them, she was real. Only she wasn't exactly, real, but she was as real as she needed to be, and her fans could imprint anything they wanted on her.

One day, Edie received an encrypted packet of her own, something that happened from time to time, although more often than not they were dead ends. This one was harder to crack than most— she ended up having to take it to her friend Reese, which she hated, because she hated involving anyone else—but when she got back to him, Reese was full of apologies. He had only been able to extract four words, which surely could not have been the entirety of the message, and then it had self-destructed. Thank goodness he was working on a clean machine on which he'd destroyed the linkup, he said, so it hadn't affected anything else although the machine was unusable now. He was sorry he'd ruined the information. Edie said it wasn't his fault, but she was pretty sure the four words he'd given her *were* the whole message: *Shanna Indigo. Suicide Drop.*

A photograph. A tree. A red light. A darkroom. She told herself this story over and over so she could be sure of not forgetting it. She knew this was expressly forbidden by her contract, which in fact required her to report the presence of any intrusive memories. She had signed this of her own free will—she knew she had, because the contract said so—and at the time, she had intended to abide by its terms. There seemed no reason to do otherwise, because the terms were more than fair. Hannah Blue had struggled her entire life, with nothing to show for it, and what they had offered her was not just a life without struggle, but an extraordinary life—the means to do whatever she wanted, so long as she kept to her contractually obligated appearances, of course. She could travel the world. She could hole up in one of her mansions, maybe the one on the island that she also owned, spend her days hiking or lounging in the sun or throwing parties to which she invited hundreds of her closest friends. She could have almost anyone she wanted, or at least a close approximation. All she was obligated to do was take the pills that accompanied the regular treatments and turn up when they told her to. All she had to do was not remember.

But before Hannah Blue there had been another girl who had cleverly and convincingly refused to take her pills. Cheerful and compliant, with that girl as model, Hannah Blue slipped them in a sleeve or a shoe when their backs were turned, and flushed them away when she was alone. She had given up the old life, the she-who-was, without a second thought, thinking her worthless, but now she wanted nothing more than to resurrect the someone who *had* to be at the core of Hannah Blue. Hadn't she?

Allison can't figure out where the buzzing sound is coming from. Everything is dark. Then she sits up abruptly. She tongues the linkup.

"Hey, babe, where you at?" It's Tash as Allison knows her, the blonde Skin gone, back to familiar straight dark hair with streaks of red.

"I fell asleep." Her voice feels thick and tired. Her face hurts. "What time is it?"

"Nine o'clock."

Allison says, "I got fired today."

"Oh, babe," Tash says, but Allison can tell she's preoccupied. "Listen, I have something that will make none of that matter."

"I don't do any more of that any more, Tash, you know that."

Tash laughs. "Nothing like that. This is completely legal. Okay, maybe not completely, but it's not what you think. It's not a drug. Well, mostly not. Come over and I'll show you."

If she hadn't had too much to drink the previous night and fallen asleep in the Skin, she wouldn't have been late for work, she wouldn't have been fired, and she wouldn't be taking Tash up on what sounded insane and probably dangerous.

"But," she intones to her reflection in the bathroom mirror as she washes her face, to distract herself from the stinging and her ruined appearance, "there comes a time in every girl's life when she admits that what she is—is a fuck up. And she takes steps to fuck it up even more. Because what's the point, really." She had worried she would wake to find actual cracks appearing in the flesh of her face. She's going to have scars, at any rate. She ought to get to a doctor, but she doesn't have any health credits left, and with no job, who knows when she will again.

She's afraid to use makeup in case that makes it worse. And she can't face the metro again, or the possibility of having to interact with people, so she sends for a Ryder even though she knows she can't afford it. It's a Ryder with a human operator, for a change—she'd heard they were going to start doing that, because people seemed to like it—a student from Ghana who'd only been in the country three months and who asks Allison whether she minds if she studies. Allison says she doesn't. The woman reads a textbook on international relations as they speed through the dark city, and Allison interrupts her to ask what the job is like. The woman enthuses about how easy it is and how much schoolwork she gets done, but then she reminds Allison you have to pay for your own Ryder at the start. Allison doesn't know how she's going to pay rent, so Ryder operating seems an unlikely solution to her unemployment problem.

Tash lives in one of the modern high-rises that overlooks the river. The doorman is an old-school AI, a little robotic, but Allison loves the model. It reminds her of her childhood, back when they were the most advanced ones around. They make her feel cozy and comfortable, like encountering a beloved toy or book from those days. She thinks they should have stopped developing them at this point; all the upgrading and grafting of human skin on newer editions is making them more, not less, relatable.

"Hello, Edward," she says as he lets her in the door, and, "Hello, Allison," he says, his voice smooth and elegant and sounding somehow as though he were from a different century. "Tash will be pleased to see you." He reminds her of her great-grandfather. These models are popular with the Nostalgs but Allison is surprised he's still employed at Tash's uber-contemporary building. Waiting on the elevator, she finds herself brooding and sad at the thought of Edward's eventual decommissioning. Surely it can't be long in coming. She hopes they will find him another position and not just stick him in a corner somewhere. Everyone says they are just machines, that they don't mind—that they aren't *able* to mind—but she thinks it would be like a human trapped in vegetative state who is still able to hear and see and understand everything happening. She can't bear the thought of kindly, conscientious Edward being left in that state

She gets off at the top floor. Tash flings the door open before she reaches it. "Babe!" At least she assumes it's Tash; it's the blonde again, but it's not just Tash's face and hair that are different. It's her whole body. Tash is lean and athletic; this woman is voluptuous. But the woman with Tash's voice embraces her and pulls her inside.

Tash's apartment is sleek and modern, all glass and black chrome with floor-to-ceiling windows looking out over the river and the city. She is Allison's oldest friend although Allison can no longer remember how they met. Tash is a relic of her younger, more reckless days that she's tried to put behind her.

"Like it?" Tash says, doing a little twirl like she's modeling an outfit. "It's a Skinsuit."

"What? Those aren't even for sale yet."

Tash laughs. "Of course not. They won't be, for years."

"How did you *get* one?"

"My dad, of course, how do you think? These are just test

models though. They'll be obsolete by the time they're ready to go on the market."

"Are they legal?"

Tash laughs, and that, at least, is familiar—trilling, infectious. "When have we let *that* stop us? I've got just the right one for you, too." She takes her by the hand and leads her into the bedroom where she flings open the closet door. Allison is used to row upon row of Tash's clothing hanging there. What she sees instead makes her gasp. It looks like bodies, or rather, the flesh, flensed from the body, but of course it isn't. It's a whole row of Skinsuits, twenty or more.

Tash holds one up, dangling on a hanger. "Here," she says. "This is you."

The thing looks grotesque. A skinned woman. Long, indigo hair. Allison looks away.

"I know it's weird. It takes some getting used to."

Allison looks at it again. "That won't fit me," she says.

"Don't be silly. That's not how it works. Just try it." Tash is practically pleading, and Tash never pleads with anyone about anything. "You can take it off again right away if you don't like it."

The process of donning the Skinsuit is like a disturbing parody of all the times Allison has stood here with Tash before a night out, trying on and rejecting outfits. She has a moment of suffocating panic as Tash seals it. *I'm not me any longer.* She remembers what she tries not to think about when she wears the normal Skins, that they are made from bits of human tissue and who knows what else. The companies that manufacture them really started booming once regulations were shifted to allow them to pay families for the tissue of their deceased loved ones, although they still refer to it as "donations" since it seems to make people feel better. And dying is so expensive these days it's the only way most people can afford to do so.

Then her apprehension vanishes in a rush of euphoria, a hit of pure exhilaration. She feels transformed, as though she really is the indigo-haired, desirable creature the Skin makes her look like she is.

"How does it work?" she asks. "How is it changing the shape of my body, even my height?"

"As the wearer, you're absorbing a low-grade hallucinogen. For the rest of us, it's a kind of optical illusion. With this series, it doesn't work from certain angles or if someone is too far away but as they get closer, it resolves itself. It also has to do with your body chemistry, how compatible it is with the organic elements of the suit." Allison tries not to think about what Tash might mean by "organic elements." Tash continues, "This is a very good fit for you."

Allison takes a step or two forward and stumbles. "Careful," Tash says, "it's a little disorienting at first. It's going to be making minor adjustments as needed."

Allison can feel that already happening; when she'd first put it on, it had felt loose in some places and tight in others. Now it is knitting itself more cohesively against her flesh so that she is hardly aware she is wearing it.

Tash says, "How does it feel to have the body of your dreams?"

"The body of someone else's dreams," Allison says. "Not mine." Her breasts are huge; her waist appears tiny and cinched. She looks like a caricature of a woman, not a real one. "This one was designed by a guy, wasn't it?"

Tash says, "They're working on models that monitor cues from other people, like eye movements and heart rate, and make subtle adjustments to the visual projections. What you're wearing now is honestly a pretty crude early edition—in six months, you'll be able to wear one that does a better job of showing you what you want to see when you look in the mirror. The next generation will have better tactile illusions, too, but trust me, when you look like that, nobody's noticing if you feel a little bit different than you look."

Allison moves again, watching herself in the mirror. Just as Tash predicted, she is becoming more comfortable in the Skinsuit. Tash throws her a dress that is the same indigo shade as the hair of the Skinsuit, and when Allison pulls it over her head, it ripples like fast-moving water. "We're also working on a line of clothing to complement the Skinsuits," Tash says. "Come on, babe, the night is young and so are we. Let's go get in trouble."

Time seems to compress; the Skinsuit has that effect, and Allison suspects the drugs it is releasing into her system are stronger than Tash suggested. She doesn't care; she hasn't felt this good, this happy, this carefree, in such a long time. They go to the Suicide Drop, which is a far-past-its-prime club downtown, but Tash says it's just a warm up and it's a good place for Allison to adjust to the Skinsuit because if she does anything weird or stupid it's not like anyone who goes to the Suicide Drop matters anyway. Tash has given them fake names, Shanna and Justine, but Allison keeps forgetting which one she is supposed to be, and Tash insists she give the Skinsuit a test run by making out with some guy who's been eyeing her, so she does, and it's surprising how much sensation the Skinsuit transmits. It isn't perfect, but you can feel a lot more than you'd think, enough that she's flushed and more than a little turned on when Tash comes back to get her. The guy protests and Tash promises, "Just let me borrow her for a little while and next time it'll be both of us" and Allison gives him Priya's number and they can't stop laughing about it. They're ready to go, but for a change, the DJ has put on a song that Allison likes. There's a stage at the front of the club, and for some reason Allison pulls Tash up there so they can dance in front of everyone, a thing Allison would never do.

"Babe," says Tash. "You're a natural. You're not just *wearing* Shanna, you *are* Shanna. Wait till I tell my dad."

And that night at the Suicide Drop, Shanna Indigo is born.

Excerpt from anonymous packet sent to the *Aletheia* holocast:

> Edie had never been to the Suicide Drop herself—
> it wasn't her kind of place—and it had been closed
> for a long time by the time she began investigat-
> ing it. The Suicide Drop's fortunes had flourished
> briefly with Shanna Indigo's limited popularity and
> then fallen again. As far as Edie knew, Hannah Blue
> had never set foot in the place—it would have been
> far beneath her. All the same Edie paid a visit to the
> warehouse space where it had been. The building
> had a forlorn air about it. "You can't go coasting on

past glories forever," Edie told it.

She had no proof, nothing but her own surmises and the four words from the anonymous packet, but she suspected Shanna Indigo and Hannah Blue were one and the same person, one an early proto-type of the other. With this in mind she turned her attention to researching Shanna Indigo, realizing that given her earlier obscurity, her handlers might have been sloppy. They might not have closed off all the dead ends that they had with Hannah Blue.

Shanna had been a regular at the club for about six months, which was a crazy long amount of time for any place to sustain that kind of popu-larity, let alone one that had become as naff as the Suicide Drop before its unexpected resurgence. But it hadn't actually been longevity or the decline in novelty that had put an end to the partnership; apparently, Shanna's last few appearances had been a mess. Edie was able to talk to a handful of people who had been there on those nights. Most every-one had been debriefed afterwards, so nobody remembered much, but those who did retain a few scattered recollections said it was like watching two personalities in one body, one called Shanna Indigo and the other who said she was a girl called Alli-son. "Some of us thought it was performance art," one woman reported. Another one said the Allison persona seemed disoriented and distressed.

This fit with another line of inquiry Edie had been pursuing. There had been a push at one point to introduce Skins for the entire body. Research had been abandoned because testing made it clear that the liability was just too great. Edie got hold of notes someone had smuggled out of the clinical trials, and the psychological toll they chronicled as fragmentation set in was sobering.

But what if you could promise there was a possibility of something that made the risk worth it?

What if you could demonstrate that a fullbody Skin could turn someone ordinary into a superstar?

It wouldn't be a risk everyone would be willing to take; it wouldn't even be a temptation to some. But for enough people, the chance to live the kinds of lives they could only fantasize about by viewing holocasts would be worth any risk.

By keeping Hannah Blue's origins secret, she became Everywoman, and Everyman for that matter. She might be anyone, or no one, and therefore anyone could be Hannah Blue. Anyone could be anyone. No one had to be saddled any longer with the inadequate identity with which they'd been born.

But even Hannah Blue was made to be ephemeral. If she hadn't disappeared, she still would have disappeared; there was nothing of substance to sustain the fascination. Eventually, with nothing new to feed the mystery, even the holocasts lost interest. The name that had been on everyone's lips receded and was forgotten.

Anyway, there was a lot of buzz about a new name: a girl who, unlike Hannah Blue, had a history, or so the press releases claimed anyway. They described her as having been brought up in the provinces, on one of the houseboat islands. A producer on vacation at one of the nearby resorts had gone on a relief tour and spotted her there, the bio said, and she first set foot on dry land only a few weeks ago. She was a natural, a phenomenal primitive. What could she do? Well, what couldn't she do? Sing, dance. Be. But a virtual tabula rasa.

After a few smaller gigs to build buzz, her first major appearance would be at the Greenies, the holocast awards show.

Red light. Dark room. There had been an episode, earlier, and some concern, but they got her into the environment that reliably calmed her down, and the coach who had been working with her for the last two hours pronounced her fit to take the stage.

The anticipation in the arena was palpable. The lucky two thousand in attendance had taken their seats; everyone else watched from home. For several minutes it seemed as though nothing would happen at all. The stage was black, save for a single red light.

And then Anna Red, who would on that night become a superstar, emerged from the wings.

Excerpt from anonymous packet sent to the holocast *Aletheia*:

They had had to end their contract with the first company that conducted clinical trials on the Skinsuits. The researchers there seemed to lack an understanding of the correlation between who was funding their research and what their research was supposed to produce. After shelling out millions to gag the family members and loved ones of the first round of research subjects, Tash—the single-monikered CEO of the eponymous company—found a more compliant laboratory. This time around, they chose marginalized subjects; that way, any psychotic breaks could be attributed to a history of mental illness, or homelessness, or institutionalization, or substance abuse.

People camped out overnight to be the first in line to purchase the first Skinsuits. As pricey as they were, this did not reduce their demand, and riots broke out in three cities when Skin Centers sold out sooner than anticipated. Frantic think-pieces were keyed about the dangers of Skinsuits and how they differed from the the old-model facial Skins. Philosophy professors, of all people, enjoyed a brief frenzy of attention as all the top holocasts fought to have them on to pontificate about how identity was defined, whether or not it was a fixed state, John Locke and the continuity of consciousness, and what the implications of a product that so profoundly altered both one's own self-perception and the perception of others might be. Rebuttals argued that Skinsuits were no different from people assuming different identities in other situations, including the early days of the old internet, and that the naysayers were Luddites, alarmists, and possibly just a little bit simple-minded.

When the story first broke on the *Aletheia* holocast, a painstaking recreation of the life and transformation of a nobody called Allison Lewes into one of the world's most beloved superstars along with an exposé of the company behind her, it was first taken as a kind of metafiction, a riff on how Skinsuits *might* have come about, with the reporter behind the exposé written into the narrative. Tash, the company that manufactured the Skinsuits—named after the boss's daughter, the holocast claimed, although if there was a real Tash she kept a low public profile—hired a phalanx of lawyers, and that made people start taking *Aletheia* more seriously. Then there was the matter of the persona at the center of the holocast: an Edie Warner, doubtless a pseudonym, but might the real Edie Warner, wherever she was, be risking not just her job but—if the stories about Tash were to be believed—her life? "Chats With Charisma" said they had never employed an Edie Warner, and efforts to follow the same channels along which the packets had traveled to reach *Aletheia* led to dead ends.

Δ

A darkroom. A dark room. A red light. A grandfather. A tree. A bad Skin job. A bad job. A bad boss. A best friend. A photograph. A photograph of a tree. A photograph of a woman. An old-fashioned AI. A dance club. A row of Skinsuits.

A great-grandfather. A tree streaked with light.

A photograph of how the earth ought to look, hurtling through space.

The earth.

Hurtling.

Space.

If she could hold onto this.

If she could.

Hold.

This.

It would be enough.

Someone said, "Are you ready? They've been waiting half an hour."

Someone else said, "I don't think she's ready."

A third someone said, "Well, she's going to have to be."

Two someones took one arm each and pulled her to her feet. They brought her before a mirror. She didn't know the girl in the mirror, a dazzling girl. She knew that she was many things, but she had never been a dazzling girl.

They said, "Remember? Remember who you are."

I am a girl who used to be another girl who used to be another girl who used to be. I never dazzled but I was real. Now I am nobody.

Later, on the stage, she looked out into nothingness. They told her tens of thousands had turned up to see her. Like her, most of them wore bodies that did not belong to them. But beyond the bank of lights, it was as dark and fulsome as the space the rockets might have traveled through, had there been rockets in time to save them. For all she knew there was no one left out there. Now they expected her to sing, and sing for them she would. She lifted her arms and opened her mouth and the crowd roared, or did they? Perhaps the space before her was not vast but narrow. She might once again have been alone, and safe, in a darkroom; and somewhere before her, a red light flared and flickered, and was gone.

THE GIRL WITH BLACK FINGERS

ROBERTA LANNES

Bar Jucundo's thrumming evening crowd generated their usual percussive music of clinking glassware and laughter-filled conversations, with the accompaniment of R & B or hypnotic jazz. The air held scents of fine fabrics, the fragrance of sweat and pheromones, spicy foods, strong spirits, brass and oiled wood. And always there, a whiff of desperation, loneliness, hope.

Sofia leaned over the bar wagging a slender ink-blackened finger at Teo, the bartender. He nodded, finished uncapping two beers and hurried over.

She grinned as he bent toward her, then shouted over the din, "My usual!"

His eyes flashed in annoyance at the demands hurled his way. "Crazy night!" He poured her an eight-ounce glass of Beaujolais.

"Crazy! Lost my table. Okay if I write here?" Sofia reached into her shoulder bag, pulled out a thick mass of notebooks, stationery, and loose paper and set it on the mahogany.

"How do you get creative with all … this!" His hand swatted at the energy of too many people, brushing it aside as if it were a stink.

"I don't choose what I write, remember?" Sofia slid a piece of pale blue parchment paper from her stack and uncapped a black marker. Teo shrugged, slapped the bar before turning away. She spoke to herself, though Teo had heard it many times. "It comes as it comes, to whomever needs to read the truth."

She glanced at him as he hurried along the mirrored cabinet of amber and teak-colored liquids, wondering if he found her of interest or suffered her as others did. People found her quirky, maybe lovely at best, crazy-mad at worst. Teo enchanted her. Made her want what she saw couples had around her; the connection, intimacy. He listened to his customer's grumbles, but she listened to him, learned him. In all her years in so many places, she'd yet to know someone like him.

As she mused over him, her hands, in an elegant frenzy, continued writing epistles to strangers. Sighing heavily, she switched to pencil on newsprint, and finished her wine.

Cole Flynn followed his brother Connor into Bar Jucundo. Connor claimed to find two hot women for every guy on Friday nights. Still early in the evening, they nabbed a booth and got a pitcher of tap beer.

He took a sip, pushed the glass away. "What's this cat piss?"

Connor laughed. "Not rich enough for your taste, baby bro? The IPA stuff is pricey and tastes the same to me."

Cole chuckled. "You marry a gorgeous gold digger then divorce her because she had expensive tastes. Then she uses your money to find a ruthless lawyer to gut you. Seriously, Con, *I'll* get the tab tonight." He curled a finger at a waitress going past them with a tray of appetizers.

"Asshole." Connor wagged a middle finger at him.

The waitress returned, hands on the table, expectant.

"What whiskeys you recommend?"

She sighed. "Depends. Do you like Scotch, Japanese, Kentucky or generic?"

Cole laughed. "Scotch. Ardbeg? Laphroaig?"

"I don't speak Scottish. How about Glenfiddich?

Cole rolled his eyes. "Fine. Eighteen or older. A double."

She spun away, vanishing.

Connor raised an eyebrow. "You still have that effect on women? No wonder you're turning thirty and single as a priest."

"I do just fine, fuck you very much."

Cole wouldn't be sharing his current situation with Connor. He was here to support *him*. This final alimony hearing had devastated him. Cole reminded his brother he had a great job, kept fit. He'd find love again; he always recovered *up*.

The waitress returned with a too-young Glenfiddich, but Cole drank it anyway. They downed a lot of alcohol, laughed, reminisced, and ate a half-dozen delicious appetizers. To his relief, the bar never filled up with the promised hot women.

They were mid-guffaw over something stupid Connor's assistant had done as a tall girl passed their corner booth, accidentally dropping two crumpled pieces of paper. Cole noticed Connor, still chuckling, assessing her mass of wavy red-brown curls and long legs as he leaned over to pick up the papers.

Cole sniggered. "The *Trash* man! That's your life now bro, picking up crap in a bar?"

Connor grinned, setting the wadded balls aside to swig his eighth pint. "Maybe she'll want them on her way back?"

"*If* she comes back. It's *garbage*." Cole flicked one of the notes at Connor. "You curious? Take a peek, toss it back."

"Yah! Hey, what if it's her number?" Connor took the pale blue paper, flattened it. Once read, he crumpled it. Pushed it with his wrist to the floor, frowning.

Cole frowned. "What'd it say?"

"Some bad joke. *Whatever!*" Connor laughed hollowly.

"Let me see the other one ..." Cole grabbed it and unfolded a sheet of lined paper.

In black crayon, as if written by his six-year-old self, it said TELL THEM THE TRUTH SO YOU CAN LIVE OUT YOUR LIFE IN JOY. Cole wiped his face with both hands and forced a strangled laugh.

"Stupid shit!" Cole balled the note up, dropped it. "Somebody's weirdness. Forget it!"

"That's it. Trash is trash!"

Back in his hotel room, Cole slumped onto his bed as he grappled with what the note said; something far too relevant to his life at the moment. A tiny terror grew in his belly. Why had it been written and left on the floor beside *him?* Was he making something of it simply because it fitted his current situation the way the fortune in a cookie from a Chinese restaurant isn't easily dismissed? What had Connor's note said? He'd become strange after he read it. When they parted outside the bar, Connor told him he needed a walk to clear his head. Connor wasn't a ruminator. He just kept moving forward.

Cole, in San Francisco for a second more important purpose, turned his focus from the evening. There, just twelve miles away, lived Matt Campos. Cole was concluding a year of meaningful Skyping and phone chats to actually meet this guy with whom he'd developed a deepening relationship. And, if it was as real as it felt, Cole was ready to move his successful business from Milwaukee to the West coast, forcing him to come out to his very Irish, very homophobic family.

About to call Matt, he remembered that Matt's daughter Gracie was staying with him. She'd be in bed. Matt had taken his work home with him. Domestic bliss. The thought of one day having a family who loved and accepted him gave him what Matt called a "heart-glow."

Cole stared out of his enormous hotel room window at the city sparkling below. Keeping up the gaiety and verbal sparring tonight had exhausted him. The idea of a shower slid into mind, but sleep won out.

In the park across from her apartment, Sofia spread her papers out on a blanket beneath a camphor tree. A young mother pushed a little girl in the swing, eyes fixed on her laughing daughter, reminding Sofia of what was missing in her life. Belonging.

The fog dissipated, March sun streamed through the leaves. Setting smooth weighty stones on the piles of onion skin and linen, brown paper and vellum, she began writing first in her yellow note-book.

Sofia's fingers, twisted and blackened from tips to palms, hands appearing ancient for such a young woman, each grasped a pen and wrote messages, one above the other; one cursive, the other in rounded childlike printing. Each hand, its own mind.

She didn't read them. She learned when she was eight years old that awful things happened when the inheritor of her words disregarded them. And, if what she'd written was heeded and wonderful things occurred, her joy felt boundless. By age twelve, because the horrible outweighed the good, she swore off reading them. Besides, seldom did she leave a note behind and then learn who picked it up and read it. Such was her affliction.

Last night, though she hadn't read her notes, she felt she *knew* what she'd written. The two she left in the bar might bring bliss, or if ignored, great agony. Unnerving, this. She'd never before sensed a future once she'd dropped a message. Whatever could be happening?

After a morning call with Matt, Cole felt certain of Matt and his support in facing the inevitable with Connor. Matt hadn't reacted to the scribbled note event with dismissal or disdain. He'd called it a "fairy godmother" moment and thought Cole should tell Connor everything. The potential of joy in the truth, in his future, shouldn't be discarded, despite the struggle he'd face with his family. Connor couldn't forbid Cole's love for Matt, but he could withhold his love for Cole. At least at first. A product of massive amounts of what Midwesterners called "California Cool-aid therapy," Matt often challenged him with annoying yet wise aphorisms. He hoped Matt was right, for him, about him, about the future.

Today was golf with Connor and his clients. Sunny, slightly breezy, with enough chill for a smart sweater, the weather boded well for the day, even though Cole's golf game remained persistently mortifying. Room service breakfast arrived with Cole's thoughts of dread at hanging out with corporate phonies taxing his moral fiber, and Connor's horrified reaction when he later declared his relationship with Matt.

Cole arrived with an empty stomach. Connor surprised him. They were taking the first seven holes as a pair, opting to stop for lunch to meet Connor's clients and *friends*. *Friends* was Connor-code for easy women. From the first hole, Connor chattered on, detached, as if Cole were a business deal he needed to seal. Meaningful conversation was off the table. Whatever Connor's distress, it multiplied Cole's anxieties. He thought back to the crumpled notes. He wished now he'd read them both. Or neither.

The clubhouse smelled more like a locker room than a restaurant. Fake tan women in golf garb, tops tailored to accentuate their expensive breasts, giggled and flirted with corseted old men. Cole hadn't seen this much gold jewelry or tacky clothing since Connor's wedding. He thought of Matt, a straightforward, down-to-earth man of simple tastes with a life free of secrets. What would he make of this circus?

Connor chose to flirt with centerfold-worthy, rapacious babes and crony up to potential clients, largely ignoring Cole. Connor's brush-off baffled and saddened him. This could be his future if he chose to come out. Or worse.

Cole chose to nurse an entire bottle of Macallan instead of an exit.

Sunday evening's crowd at Jucundo, sparse, murmuring low, relaxed Sofia. She had her favorite table by the window to people-watch, speculate on their lives, loves. Her hands reached out to various pads and sheaves, trading writing implements, as words slid through her onto the pages. She folded some, put them away for another time, wadded up others to drop, by accident be found.

Glancing over her shoulder at Teo, she caught his eye, held up three fingers. *Hungry for the #3*; sweet potato fries with smokehouse bacon sauce. He raised his chin, winked. She smiled at the thought of Teo's comfortable way with her, how warm he was. Thoughtful. Perhaps that meant affection. Men confused her. Romance eluded her. How to behave enticingly with men bewildered her, felt as daunting as singing in public or tightrope walking. She watched other women, their apparent ease, but shivered just considering it.

She startled when Teo sat down, her left hand jotting a short note, her right putting her glass of Beaujolais to her lips.

"Sorry, Sofia. We're out of sauce. You okay to wait?"

She nodded. "I forget to eat. Then, suddenly I'm famished." She grinned awkwardly, regretting the pointless admission. He did something to her; unsettled and thrilled her.

"Here, for you." Her left hand stuffed the little note into his shirt pocket, filling her with unexpected terror. Her right hand flew, hid her eyes. Peeking between her blackened fingers, she caught him staring at his pocket, panicked. He knew what she did, at least obliquely. That what she wrote might offer him a challenge, a powerful choice. But, what?

"Holy crap, Sofia." He made fists on the table. She wanted to reach out, loosen them. Take back the piece of paper. What had she written?

"Relax. If it was bad, I'd feel it." Would she? A chaos of emotions fought inside her.

He shrugged half-heartedly. "Yeah, okay. Want another Beaujolais with the #3?" His fists fell to his thighs.

"Sparkling water." He nodded. "I … I … You're a good man, Teo. It'll be fine." It had to be.

He stood. "Thanks." Sat down again. "It's just that in the last year … why now?"

"I've said before. I don't understand it myself." She knotted her ebony fingers in her lap, her gut burning. "Don't read it, if you don't want to."

He patted his pocket. "Maybe I'll burn it." He laughed nervously. "Crap. How do I *not* read it?" He grimaced, then hurried off.

Sofia bent over her papers. As patrons arrived, a flurry of messages began to flow. But, the anarchy of sensations continued.

Cole woke with a strange hangover. No headache or nausea. Just oddly stricken, as if he'd had the rough conversation with his brother and it went as badly as he feared, only he had no memory of it. He phoned Connor about their lunch plans at the Pier 39, but he didn't answer. Just as well. He'd wanted to cancel, meet Matt instead.

In the shower, Cole's fear coursed through him. Had he been so drunk that he'd shared his truth with Connor and lost him? He couldn't remember anything once he'd finished half the bottle of Macallan, or much of whatever had gone on in the previous hours. Everything seemed a dense blur. He tried to push the dread aside and focus on meeting Matt, but the sensation obstinately lingered.

As he dressed, his phone rang with Matt's unique ringtone. The anguish instantly dissipated.

"Hey! I tried to call Connor to cancel, but he isn't answering. I'm thinking maybe I should just text him. Starting today, I'm putting us first." How good it felt just saying it!

"That's what I'm calling about." None of his usual breezy warmth. "It's about Connor."

Cole's legs went metallic, paralyzed. He pressed the phone against his head. "Matt, how would you ... about *Connor?*"

"It's on the news. I'm so sorry. He's gone. He jumped off the Millennium Tower some time before dawn."

Cole collapsed onto the bed. "*What?*" Impossible. No.

"He left a note in his residence. He lived there, right?"

Cole nodded as if Matt could see him. "A note?" A sob stretched his throat into a wail. "*Why?*"

Matt waited, silent, as Cole wept. Minutes passed until Cole quieted. "You okay?"

Cole felt certain now. Last night he'd told Connor everything and rather than face life with a gay brother, he threw himself off his building. This was his fault. His fault!

He shook his head, hiccupped another sob. "Do you know what the note said?"

"No, my dearest. Just that it was unsigned on crumpled blue paper."

Stretched out on her bed, Sofia purred. Murky morning sunlight filled the room.

Teo had read the note. He told her last night just before she left Jocundo that she'd been right. It wasn't bad! He thanked her. Kissed her on the cheek.

She blushed. Why had blood rushed into her head? Was she ill? She told him she didn't feel well, asked if he'd walk her home, but he had a couple more hours at the bar. She hurried out, her body tingling, burning. Once in the chill night air, she felt the heat diminish. She got on the bus and within moments, her hands were once again writing furiously, Teo forgotten.

Alone now, she had the luxury of thinking of little else but Teo.

So, she hadn't written him a suicide note or instructed a rash act. Those always turned out badly. Perhaps she'd told him she fancied him! Whatever it was, he'd kissed her on the cheek. And thinking of that made her blush again.

It wasn't like her to reflect over someone, or the notes she'd written. Not for ages. After all, unless she handed someone a message, she didn't know who picked it up. Yet, now she'd begun to sense whether the outcomes were positive or negative, possibly both? This *ability*, Teo called it, though to Sofia it was curse and blessing, had the power to transform. If only she knew someone who shared this compulsive writing to ask questions. *Were* there others?

Today, she'd go somewhere special. Maybe the Wharf, visit a museum. Or stay in. If she spent time among people, her hands wouldn't stop pulling paper and implements from her bag, jotting communiqués, but at home, they'd be still. Perhaps then, if words came, they'd be just for her, as they did when her funds ran low. Yes, she'd stay in, listen to music, read poetry. Stare out the window at the early blooming Jacarandas.

Cole couldn't have imagined he'd finally meet his true love face-to-face on the day his brother died. Matt arrived at the hotel room, and after an initial irresistible deep kiss, the moment of mutual relief and joy in each other's arms, they sprawled onto the bed. Matt held Cole as he cried, alternately incredulous, bereft, then blaming himself, and deeply wounded.

Cole phoned the police and let them know he was in town, to come talk with him. When they eventually called up to the room, Cole lurched to pick up. He set the phone down and grasped Matt's hand. "Can I do this?"

Matt nodded. "Go wash your face."

A plump female detective stood at the long window, beside her a uniformed officer with a notebook. She sniffed the air and composed herself as she informed Cole of the situation. She asked the expected questions about Connor's state of mind, what had occurred last night that might have caused him to jump, Cole's whereabouts. Cole trembled beside Matt on the settee, barely able to maintain his composure.

"If only I could remember what we last said to each other! I came here to help Connor through an awful time. A judge made a catastrophic alimony decision on his divorce. We played golf, spent time with his clients at his club and I drank too much. He'd been distant with me all day, much into the evening. At least until I was too drunk to notice."

She glanced at her officer's notes. "Was he feeling hopeless?"

"No. But, he was angry about his ex-wife being awarded a huge amount of alimony. Otherwise, with everyone else, he was his usual smug self."

The detective nodded. "Did you two argue? Had he argued with anyone recently? His ex?"

Cole's mind felt like a sponge filled with setting cement. "Maybe. I really don't remember! Of all the times to drink too much …" He turned to Matt.

"Don't, Cole. It won't help."

"Maybe not, but I want to see it."

The detective leaned forward. "See what?"

"The note. We both found crumpled pieces of paper on the floor at a bar on Friday night, and mine was kind of prophetic. Meant a lot to me. Made me consider coming out to my brother. But I left it on the bar floor and forgot about it. Connor picked one up, too. But I never saw it. It was on blue paper. I'm thinking it's the one …"

The detective shrugged. She retrieved the case file from a battered messenger bag and took out a plastic evidence sleeve with the blue note. She handed it to Cole.

Face it. You have nothing left. No money. No scruples. No love. But you can have everything! Just open your heart and speak only the truth!

"This is his writing, like it's written to himself." Just as his own had been. "How's this a suicide note?"

"It's evidence of his state of mind. Until you can recall what went on in those last hours …"

"Which isn't enough." Cole thought about his note; coming out. Finding happiness. Connor had ignored the last part of his message, taken his life.

Matt squeezed his hand. "Give it time." Time. All he saw ahead was pain. Was joy possible after this tragedy, somehow? Someday. But, not soon.

The detective took the note, left her card cautioning him not to leave San Francisco, and call her when his memory cleared. Matt embraced Cole after the door shut behind her, and for an instant, Cole felt an inkling of the good that lay ahead.

Rain fell as Sofia walked along the park on her way to have lunch. She felt heavy and buoyant at the same time, a conundrum, but she was hungry. Hunger often took her energy and made her giddy.

She heard her name shouted as she rounded the corner toward the bar and raised her umbrella to see Teo rushing toward her.

She stopped, her heart racing, and grinned. How she wanted him to embrace her. Kiss her on the mouth, like in the movies!

He stopped before her and clapped his hands. "They won! The lottery numbers you gave me? One and a half million! We're rich!" He embraced her then. He was wet through from standing in the rain, waiting for her.

That's what she'd written for him! The numbers must have confused him at first. Just numbers, that's how they came. Or the name of a racehorse, or two football teams with one circled; those moneymakers. He'd figured it out. No wonder he was so pleased!

"This is good! I'm happy for you!" She smiled up at him. Beautiful Teo!

He put his hands on her cheeks. "I want to kiss you!"

Sofia nodded. As his lips touched hers, her hands began to tingle, grow hot as her face. She wanted to swallow him whole and keep him inside forever! When his face came away from hers, he grew subdued, serious.

"This money? I want to share it with you. It's enough to save my family *and* I can go back to school. You rescued us!"

"Us?" He'd never mentioned a family. He just complained about work, paying bills, what he wanted to do with his life as an artist. No one else. "I *can* use the money." Sofia shrugged, practicality displacing her heartache.

"You're amazing! My wife works two jobs, our twins are starting school, my parents are living with us now. It's been insane!" He kissed her again. "When I have the money in my account, you get half. No argument. It's more than we need!"

We. Sofia's face, hot and burning, hit by raindrops, felt as if it wasn't hers. Her arms felt heavy, her hands cold. She nodded. "I'm hungry. We can talk inside?"

Teo held his sodden arms out. "I quit the bar! I gotta go to the lottery office downtown. I'm meeting my Papi. I can't thank you enough, Sofia!" He hugged her again.

She tried to smile. "Okay."

As he hurried off, she turned and plodded toward the bar. Lunch.

She had her window seat and settled in. An unfamiliar waiter took her order and in his starchy manner seemed to find her disheveled hair, wet clothing and well-worn boots inappropriate for a classy place like Bar Jucundo.

Staring out into the gray day, seeing more umbrellas than faces, she felt unfamiliar sensations. Profound loss. Sadness. This connection she imagined with Teo hadn't been meant to be more than ephemeral. As with anyone, really. This life, her fate, was to be apart. Alone. She sighed deeply; staring, waiting, still as stone.

When her glass of Beaujolais arrived, she took a sip. Shuddered. Gasped. For the first time in memory, she hadn't reached for her pens or a single piece of paper. Her black fingers were cold and stiff on the glass.

There were no words!

Matt pointed out the street lady on a bench as they walked around the Presidio. She pulled paper from her bag, wrote furiously, then dramatically cast pages into the air to be caught by the wind, her uncombed hair appearing as auburn fire. Watching her, Cole felt unaccountably despondent. In the last two years, his mourning having ebbed, it seemed as though nothing could dampen his bliss.

He took some cash from his pocket and handed it to Matt. "Let's give her a couple bucks."

"Gracie, would you like to give it to her?" Matt held the money out to his ten-year-old daughter.

She shrugged. "I guess." She turned to Cole. "What if she freaks out on me? Will you come?"

Cole nodded, smiling. "We'll both come."

As they approached, the street lady stopped and turned toward them. She grinned with warmth and folded both hands, fingers blackened from tips to palms, on her chest.

"For you." Gracie reached out to the woman. Their fingers touched, tips curling briefly around each other. The woman held the money to her cheek, grinning widely with pleasure.

"*Thank you!*" Then, she gazed up at Cole and Matt. "You're happy together. *Good.*"

Cole, confused by a glint of familiarity in the crazy lady's eyes, beamed down at her. She saw his joy!

"Come on!" Matt called to Cole as Gracie rushed off down the promenade. Cole jogged after them, glancing back to wave, but the woman sat staring into her lap at her open hands, weeping.

He thought of her the rest of the day; what he might do to get her help.

On the way to drop her off for a weekend at her mother's, Gracie asked if they'd stop at Union Street Papery, a shop specializing in high end stationery. Cole loved the smells inside of ink, linen, silk papers, and the incense of someone charring the edges of parchment for sale.

He rarely thought of the balls of paper that had so affected him and his brother. But he did now. And the crazy writing lady on the promenade. He never had gone back to help. He'd become more like

Connor, always moving forward, up. For an instant, he felt a twinge of heartache. He chastised himself for being less attentive to things, people, and told himself this was a moment to open his eyes. See. Really see.

As they stood at the counter, he watched Gracie take the bag of papers, her fingertips grayed by pencil or ink. He tried to recall when she'd become so captivated with writing.

THE SHIMMERING WALL

BRIAN EVENSON

1

Those parts of the domed city were not the city at all—or maybe the parts we lived in were what was not the city. It was not, after all, our city, or at least had not been so originally. It had become, I suppose, our city now. Or some parts had. The rest, we stayed clear of.

At least most of us did. There were always a few who did not leave well enough alone. We had all seen those parts, seen how they seemed encased in dirty glass or Lucite, semi-transparent and flickering walls, rooms and furnishings distorted beyond. When people dared to thrust their hands against the Lucite, they found it was not Lucite at all, but a sort of firm jelly-like membrane. They could slowly push their way through. They let their arms sink to the elbow or even—the more daring—to the joint of the shoulder, then groped around behind that translucent wall, and when they drew their arm free the fingers at its end were often clenched around something. The distorted broken-off leg of a chair, for instance—if that was in fact what it was—a skew-slosh of metal anyway. Or a pen that was a semi-circular loop made for hands other than ours. These oddities could be sold—there were those that collected them. We treated these collectors with as much suspicion as those who gathered the objects in the first place.

There were times, too—rarer these—when someone would thrust a hand through, then an elbow, then an arm, and begin to grope around, only to suddenly be taken hold of by something on the other side of the shimmering wall. From our vantage, we saw only a shape, a vague collection of angles, distantly humanoid in form, take hold and drag the person through. Such individuals never returned.

No one had ever crossed through the wall willingly. They only had felt around, one arm in, the rest of their body out, and drawn objects out. Perhaps these objects were in the form they had been on the other side, or perhaps in coming through had taken on some distorted version of what their true form was.

I was, I suppose, unique. I was an orphan—but there were other orphans among us. My uniqueness was based not on that but on the circumstances of how I became such.

My parents worked together to bring bits and pieces of that other city across. They would take turns pushing through a shimmering wall, watching their arm distort and become a series of angles. They would draw an object out and sell it to collectors. That was how they lived. They always worked together, and as a result always took me along with them.

My earliest memory is this: my parents pressed against a vague and shimmering crystalline wall, one reaching through, the other, legs braced, grasping the first around the waist. I had been placed on a ratty blanket as far away from the wall as possible. I pawed the blanket, found crumbs or bugs on the floor, rolled them around in my mouth, spat them out. And then, after what seemed to me a long while, my parents turned, looking simultaneously terrified and triumphant, an unnatural and pain-wracked object held high in my mother's hand.

Or maybe this is not my first memory. I saw that scene or scenes like it so many times in the years to come. Sometimes the object was in my father's hand, sometimes my mother's. Sometimes, too, they groped around and then, screaming, quickly withdrew, one dragging the other free as, on the other side of the shimmering wall, a being of awkward angles approached rapidly, tried to catch hold of them, failed.

Was the being the same as us? I wondered: I had seen my father's arm through the shimmering wall and was uncertain if there were any difference in its distorted angles through the wall as compared to the angles of the arm (if it was an arm) of the being or beings that stalked them there. I wondered this only later, when I was seven or eight. My parents were still on a good run, taking just enough from behind each shimmering wall to provide us with another three weeks, or four, or five, of food, of life.

When you are older, my mother told me, you must find a companion, someone just like you, willing to watch out for you as you reach through the wall, and you for her. You must know how far you can reach and go that far but no farther. You must know how to sink your arm to the shoulder joint and then reach even farther without letting your head push through. And then, God forbid, when a being approaches from the other side, to withdraw quickly with the help of your companion. She will tell you that something is coming, and she will help you draw your arm free before it is too late.

This was, indeed, what my mother was to my father, until the moment when she was not. Until something came and she did not alert my father quickly enough, or else my father was sunk too deep, or the being moved too fast. Before we knew it, it had caught hold of my father's arm, and my mother was dragging on his waist, trying to tug him free. My father was screaming. There I was, nine years old, my arms around my mother's waist, trying to help my mother to draw him free.

And indeed he did come free, but without his arm, which had been neatly severed at the elbow, and just as neatly cauterized.

2

For weeks after, we avoided those shimmering walls. And yet, as time went on, my parents realized they did not know what else to do to survive. Their whole livelihood had involved reaching through walls—they had no other skills. My mother still had two good arms to reach with, and my father one, and as we grew hungrier they decided I was old enough to assist my mother as a lookout. We had to take the risk. We would, we vowed, take that risk as seldom as possible.

That strung us along for another five years, until I was fourteen. And then the same collection of angles appeared behind the shimmering wall and though I immediately shouted out it was upon my mother too quickly and had pulled her through. My father, holding onto her waist with his remaining hand and forearm, followed after. And I, holding to my father's legs, came last of all.

The passage through was strange, as if my body was being stretched and then reassembled to form a new creature. I could feel my father's legs, my arms wrapped around them, but then, suddenly, they were not legs at all, and then my arms were not arms at all either. And then my mind caught up with whatever transformation I had gone through, and I could think of his legs as legs again, and my arms as arms, and was unsure what, if anything, had changed.

And then, I lost consciousness.

I was lying on a floor flecked with color, as if mica—though the color floated and spun and moved, which mica as I understood it would not do. Things in the world have certain properties, and one comes to understand these properties and what they are, what they mean. One comes to count on things being what they are. And yet, was I still in the world? I did not know. What did I mean by world? I was barely conscious, to be honest, and unsure that I was in any world at all.

Near me was a being who resembled a human in every respect except for being carapaced in light. Does that qualify as every respect? Probably not. He was some manifestation of a human, though not human at the same time. Perhaps he had been so once, but it had been a long time since that was all he was.

At his feet lay the bodies of my father and mother. With a tool or instrument possessing a bright edge of light he had begun to disjoint my father's corpse. Both feet had been severed and lay idly flopped to either side of the body—bloodless, the mechanism that he had used to sever them having apparently cauterized them at the same time.

As I watched, he cut through one of my father's legs just below the knee. It looked like the left knee, but something told me I was seeing it wrongly, that it was in fact the right.

My mother was apparently unscathed, but equally dead.

When he noticed me stirring, he interrupted his task and spoke to me.

"Hello there," he said, his voice exceptionally deep and pleasing.

At first I could say nothing. When he repeated his greeting, I found myself mouthing it back to him. "Hello," I managed weakly.

He inclined his head, returned to his task. I could not move my limbs. I could lift my head and look around, but little more than that.

"Please, do not be afraid," he said, and severed my father's head.

"That's my father," I managed.

"Not anymore," he said, and then made quick work of my mother as well.

In the end, the pair of them were less bodies than neat arrangements of sectioned parts, little more than stacks of firewood. Though, admittedly, to start a fire with them would have been very difficult indeed.

"How is it you can speak my language?" I asked. He was moving between the pile that had been my father and the pile that had been my mother. He kept removing a portion of one or the other pile and putting it back in a different way, then standing back to judge the results.

"No," he answered distractedly. "*You* are speaking *our* language."

His voice when he spoke was now beautiful, almost unbearably so, and somehow familiar too. It warbled, and came to me in multiple tones, as if there were three layers of him for every one layer of me.

Δ

I blacked out again. I don't know why. When I came to again, I had crawled to the translucent shimmering wall and was trying, ineffectually, to shove my head through. How long I had been at this task, I had no idea.

The other being was beside me, bending down slightly, a concerned look just visible behind the blaze of light that enveloped his face.

"We are not going to hurt you," he said. "Did you think we were going to hurt you? We don't hurt children. We never do."

"Who's we?" I managed, through clenched teeth.

"We?" he asked. He gestured to his own chest. "We're just like you," he said. "You speak the same language as we do. You think the same thoughts as we do. But we're not you."

"Then what are you?"

But for this the being seemed to have no answer.

"Just sit back," he said. "Relax. It will only take a moment to dispose of your parents."

I watched it happen, though what exactly it was that was happening is difficult to say. The being moved back and forth between the piles, continuing to adjust them slightly until the one on the left, the pile that had been my mother, began to glow.

A moment later, he lifted my father's head by the hair and then set it down again. And then the pile that had been my father began to glow too.

"We are sorry about your parents," he said in that same beautiful voice. "But there was really no alternative."

Slowly the piles that had been my parents began to quiver. The parts rose into the air, reforming themselves into human form, with gaps between the pieces. They were teetering, stretched-out beings, assembled of dead flesh ligatured together with light. They moved jerkily, as if compelled by some other force. I watched their eyes darting about behind the carapace of light that had now swallowed their heads. Confused, they seemed to be casting about for something. And then, abruptly, their gaze came to rest on me.

"Interesting," said the being. "They believe they recognize you."

Within their carapace, my parents seemed to be screaming, but I could not hear a sound. Awkwardly, they lurched toward me.

"It would be better for you to go now," the being said.

And when I still did not respond, unable to move as what had once been my parents wobbled toward me, he reached out and took me by the neck and thrust me bodily through the shimmering wall.

3

I grew up. Years passed. I chose to forget about my parents. I built another entire life up around myself, became a respectable member of society. I acquired a wife—or perhaps she acquired me, if acquired is the right word. I lived wholly in the city that was ours, never groping into that other city, turning away from the shimmering walls whenever I encountered them.

Things might have gone on like that until I died but, simply, they did not. My wife, as had many around us, became subject to a wasting disease, her teeth and hair falling out, her body erupting in pustules and sores. She began to bleed from every orifice, slowly at first, then quicker and quicker. I remained unaffected.

"Kill me," she begged. "Please, kill me."

I took her to the treatment center but we were turned away. No, they said, they would not treat her.

What, I asked the admitting nurse, would it take for her to be admitted?

There was nothing to be done, the nurse claimed. She shook her head. It was not an illness they could treat. They no longer had the proper medication.

But surely, I said, it was just a question of gathering the materials and then the medication could be made again. Again she shook her head. "We never had the formula, only the medication itself."

"What do you mean?" I asked. And when she gestured back at an empty vial, distorted and twisted, I knew the medicine had not come from our city, but from the other one.

Δ

I kissed my wife, set off. There were doors in my mind that I had kept shut for so long. Now I opened them. Behind them, I found my parents and all they had taught me. Behind them, I saw again the strange portions of the city. I had seen such a vial before—or had seen a vial somewhat like it, anyway. Where had it been?

I walked idly, allowing my mind to wander. I tried to think like that young boy, dragged along by his parents as they pushed a hand through a shimmering wall. What kind of parents brought their child along for something like that? I tried to recall each wall that my parents had approached and stretched their arm into, sometimes my father, sometimes my mother, and what from my vantage I had seen through them. I wracked my brain, saw again their sweating faces, their anxiety, then that moment of triumph as they brought an odd and skew object back through the wall to them.

And then I realized: I would only have seen the vial so clearly if they had brought it back through the wall. No, they must have brought it out and sold it.

But no, I considered further after clambering out of my despair: I had no memory of the object being in my parents' hands. And yet I *did* have a memory of the object, a clear image. Not in my parents's hands, but lying on the floor. Had I seen it myself through a wall? If so, where?

But no, in my memory the object was too close for that, not glimpsed through a wall. No, it was just there before me, at my feet. Or rather, just at the level of my eyes, maybe half a foot away. And then I allowed the memory to continue and my eyes flick up to a strange being, swathed in light and holding a bright edged instrument, and I knew what I had to do.

Δ

I spent some time trying to find the right wall. I looked at many, dozens, but none seemed right. I tried to be systematic. I would come close and peer through and try to recognize what lay beyond, but each time I could not say for certain that I recognized anything.

And then I began to think. Where had that being come from? The one who had dragged me and my parents through the shimmering wall? He had not been inside the room when my mother had first reached in, I was sure of it, and then, abruptly, he was. Perhaps each encased room behind a shimmering wall led to other rooms and these to others still, and these all were connected. That every encased room led to every other encased room, in which case it did not matter which shimmering wall I passed through, as long as I passed through one. Once I was through, I could look for the object I remembered rapidly, by moving from room to room instead of groping through the shimmering wall.

At least, that was what I chose to believe.

I had not touched a shimmering wall in several decades, and yet the sensation immediately came back to me. At first the wall resisted, felt almost solid, but then, slowly, it began to yield. With a sucking sound, it drew my fingers in, and then my hand, and then my forearm. The sensation was odd and disorienting, as if my hand was being taken apart and put together in a way that made it something else.

And then my fingers broke through to the other side.

I plunged my other hand in. When it was sufficiently deep, I lowered my head and pushed it through as well. The sensation grew worse, much more intense, and for a long moment I didn't know what or who I was. The stuff pressed against my face in such a way that I began to lose track of where my body ended and the jelly began. Soon, too, I could not tell if I was moving through it at all, and had lost all initiative to do anything but float, suspended, my legs still legs on one side, my hands something like hands on the other, but everything in between an undifferentiated mass.

How long was I there? Minutes perhaps, or hours, or days. I did not breathe, but I do not know that I needed to breathe. It was as if I were caught between two states and subject to neither one nor the other.

And then something took me by the hands and began to pull.

I coughed and a spill of jelly slid from my throat. It lay for a moment in a quivering pool beside my face before, very slowly, beginning to vibrate its way back to the shimmering wall. I looked up, my vision bleary, and there, above me, was a being of angles refracting off one another, its body encased in light. He held an instrument whose bright edge was moving downward, toward me.

I lifted an arm to protect myself and suddenly the instrument withdrew.

"Ahhh," said a voice that was exceptionally, almost unbearably, beautiful. "You're alive."

I coughed up another lump of jelly. "Why wouldn't I be?" I said.

"They never are, the adults," he said. "Until we make them so."

I managed to get to my knees.

"We've met before," the being said, his brow furrowing behind his carapace of light.

"Yes," I said. "You killed my parents."

"Not killed," he said. "In fact, we returned them to life."

I was on my feet now, stumbling. "Are you the only one here?"

"Well," he said. "There's your parents."

"But they're not like you."

"No, they're not. They're not sufficiently there. Except for us, nobody is sufficiently there."

"There? What do you mean?"

He shrugged.

"Because of you," I accused.

"In spite of us. That they can function at all is a minor miracle."

I glanced around looking for the vial, any vial. An old swirl of metal, a crumpled wooden box, forks that had twisted on themselves and had their tines bent in every direction. No vial.

I looked for a door. There it was in the back of the room.

"Where does the door lead?" I asked.

"How can you still be alive?" he asked. "Is it because you passed through as a child? We never hurt children."

Perhaps he intended to say more, but by this time I was sufficiently in control of my faculties to strike him hard in the temple and knock him off his feet. The light around his head made my fingers tingle, but otherwise did not adversely affect me. A moment later my hand closed around his instrument, I activated the bright edge of light and pushed it deep into his side. I could smell flesh burning.

He grunted.

"It won't do you any good," he said, and expired.

Once he was dead, the light around him flickered and went out. He looked now like an ordinary man. Remarkably enough, he seemed to resemble me. So much so that I thought at first he was my father. But no, not quite. And then I thought, *If not my father, then who?* Dreading what the answer might be, I turned quickly away.

I left the body there. I had thought I might feel some measure of satisfaction in killing the being who had killed and then reanimated my parents, but I felt nothing at all. His face haunted me.

I went through the door, and from there into another room, and from there into another. I kept moving from room to room, each ordinary in every respect except for the one shimmering wall that opened onto another place, another city, my city. Sometimes I would see shadows on the other side of the wall. Once I even saw a hand protruding through it and feeling around frantically on the floor, though it was quickly pulled back through as soon as I approached.

After a few dozen rooms, I found them—the creatures that had once been my parents. They were still encased in light and still seemed to be mutely screaming.

At first they seemed not to notice me at all, and when I approached them did not acknowledge my presence. But then, abruptly, they did, coming at me and throwing their strange disjointed bodies onto me until I began to feel suffocated and, for my own protection, had to activate the instrument again. Their light went out and they collapsed into dust and were gone. I continued on.

How many more rooms? A hundred? Two? More? There have been so many rooms since that I cannot say for certain, but there, at last, it was, the twisted vial, just as I had remembered it, tipped on its side in the middle of the floor. I snatched it up. Was it identical to the vial the nurse had shown me? No, not identical, but very close. I had no way of knowing if I had found what my wife needed to survive, but yes, perhaps it was so. It was not, in any case, impossible.

And so, vial in hand, I approached the nearest shimmering wall and pushed my hands through, eager to return to save my wife.

Or at least I would have. The translucent wall was solid. It would not let me through.

I tried wall after all, but they all resisted me. I was trapped.

Only then did I begin to notice the glow that had begun to envelop me.

4

I have lived through one of these cities. Now, I must live through the other. Meanwhile, my wife lies in her bed, suffering, dying. Perhaps she is dead already.

I am nearly done with this record. Once I have completed it, I will lean this notebook against a shimmering wall and wait for a hand to grasp it and pull it through. If you find this and read it, I ask only one thing of you: come back to this wall and push your hand through again. I will place in it this vial, which you must use to cure my wife. Once she is cured, bring her back here with you and convince her to push her own hand through. I will do nothing to her, will not drag her through, for I know that it would likely kill her. No, I will only hold her hand for a moment, squeeze it, and let go.

And then it will be your turn. I have treasures beyond your wildest imaginings. If you will do this small thing for me, I will bring them to the wall. You will be a wealthy man, and powerful too. All you have to do is follow my commands, and trust me.

But if you do not do this for me you will have nothing of me. You will have only the bright edge of my instrument, and I will have you in pieces.

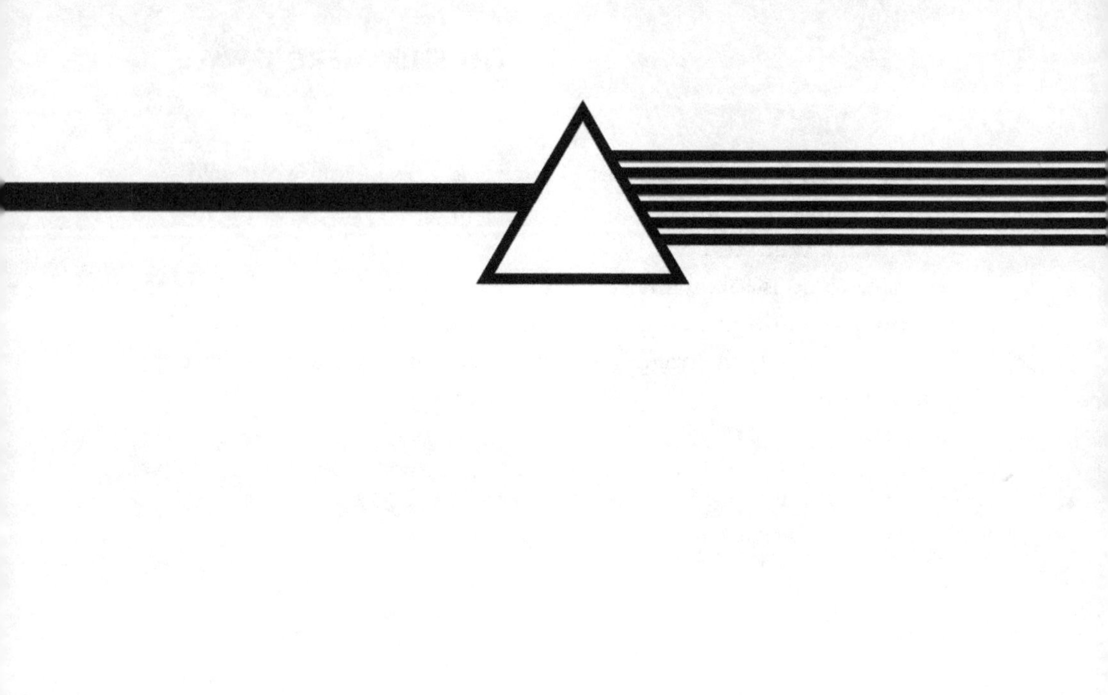

IN THIS, THERE IS NO STING

KRISTI DeMEESTER

Madison put the pram by the front door before BL57 truly began. It had been almost a decade since Bella was small enough to place inside and be pushed to the park, but Madison was glad she'd kept it for no reason other than sentiment. Even still. Even now. There were still so many things to do, so many small maneuverings that required her attention as the world curled in on itself like burnt paper. Her shoes and bags were still neatly in their boxes, their protective plastic sheets, cocooned and sleeping but still important. Still needed even though the pink and white room at the end of the hallway was empty and the bed she slept in was cold.

After the chaos of the hospital and the slow, eventual unraveling of her daughter's and husband's bodies, she had removed all of Bella's dresses and ironed them carefully. The ruffled hems of her leggings were a particular difficulty as Madison calmed herself by counting from memory the number of organic, packaged applesauce still left in the pantry, the carrot sticks gone soft in the refrigerator that still ran because the power had never gone off. BL57 had not been that kind of apocalypse.

There was still Facebook. Twitter. Instagram. Snapchat. Only instead of filtered, sunlit images of laughing children with sticky faces after strawberry picking at a local farm, there were images of single cups of French press coffee or solitary plates filled with free range chicken cutlets and an assortment of baby lettuces, a lime or pamplemousse LaCroix poised next to those uneaten plates. The women who remained had made sure that those small luxuries still existed in the aftermath. It was all there had been before. It was all that there was after.

For two weeks, Madison had not been able to keep herself from packing Bella's lunch. The hand-rolled sushi. The small containers of blueberries. The quinoa crackers Bella claimed to hate, but Madison knew were the ones that Gareth's mother packed him, and so she tucked them into Bella's lunch bag anyway, hoping this would offer a shared moment between the two children that could somehow lead to a shared identification between the two mothers. Maybe even an invitation to Bunco.

But Gareth's mother had never called, and when Madison saw her at Whole Foods last week, she had looked through Madison as she reached for a bag of chia, coconut oil granola bars no one would eat.

This was how they spent their days. All of the women who had survived the virus. Drifting through stores, their hair still curled and sprayed, their eyeliner and contour still intact, as they paid for things that would go unused with the items they no longer needed. A pair of Janie and Jack blue jeans for a carton of organic almond milk. An oversized Coach purse that once doubled as a diaper bag for a small container of celery hearts. Both food items would rot and be thrown out, and the cycle would repeat itself the following week. If nothing else, Madison was thankful she couldn't find the desire to eat anything other than nonfat, no sugar added, vanilla Greek yogurt, and so her size four jeans had grown too large. Life after the virus meant she was now the size she'd always wanted to be but had pretended for years to fight against in favor of healthy eating and hot yoga every Saturday.

"You look amazing," Tamara, her neighbor, said. She'd come over to trade a pair of Tory Burch shoes for a bag of espresso beans, and stood in Madison's kitchen, her wedding ring loose on her finger, as she hugged Madison close to her. Tamara still smelled of Versace Bright Crystal, and Madison wondered how much longer Tamara would hold on to the bottle before having to use it to buy something more important.

"I can't eat. Every time I think about it, I get sick. All I can see are their faces. How hollow they'd gotten at the end. Like every bone was trying to find its way through. I see them, and the thought of eating seems like I'm betraying them. Like I'm telling them that everything they suffered doesn't matter," Madison said.

"Oh. Sweetheart. You can't do that to yourself. There wasn't anything you could have done to change it. Just give it over to Jesus. He knows the burden you're carrying."

There was still a bottle of Woodford Reserve in the back of the pantry. A bottle Trey had thought he had hidden from her, and she thought of it now, wished she could either take a huge slug straight from the bottle or use its heft to crush Tamara's simple-minded skull. Either would have satisfied the twitch in her hands.

She did not tell Tamara that the night before she'd found the pram tipped over on its side, the baby blanket she'd carefully folded and tucked inside spread out on the floor, a perfect hole in its center as if it had been meticulously cut with scissors and then placed there for her to see.

They had never had a dog even though she'd always wanted one. A huge golden retriever that would sleep at the foot of their bed and lay his head on her knee and be a companion on the weekends when Trey worked out of town, but Trey had not wanted the potential damage a dog could bring. The mountain of liability if it bit someone at the park, or if it bit Bella, or the tears if it escaped their fenced backyard and ran into the street. A dog would have been the easy explanation. A dog would not have left her feeling afraid.

"And anyway, you haven't looked this good in years. Guess it's a good thing it's just us girls left." Tamara winked and hiccupped, and Madison wondered if her neighbor had her own stash of booze that she'd gotten into before coming over.

"Sure. Just us girls." Madison felt the thread of hysteria flutter through her voice, and she flexed her fingers and then dug her nails into her palm. The virus had taken their children, regardless of age. It had taken their husbands and left them behind to stare at each other and wonder what it was they were meant to do. So they traded the items they told themselves were valuable. They made meals that would go uneaten and washed clothes for the dead.

Tamara twisted a strand of hair between her fingers and tugged. "Even if there were other ... *people* who made it through, it'd only be a few, right? And it wouldn't bring anything back." Her eyes went glassy, and she glanced behind her as if there was something there worth seeing.

"No," Madison said and swallowed hard. "It couldn't."

"Thanks for these." Tamara lifted the espresso beans. "I'm so tired all the time." Her voice had fallen to a whisper, and she leaned into Madison, the frailty of their hug a remainder from the lives they had before. For a moment, Madison was thankful for this small gift, but then Tamara was gone, and the house was quiet again, and Madison breathed in the dust that still carried what had once been her daughter, her husband. She wondered if it was possible to be crushed under such a burden.

Her hands were steady when she pulled the blanket from the pram and folded then refolded it until the fabric felt like a part of her skin and she forgot she should be afraid. Tomorrow she needed to pull down the monogrammed luggage Trey had bought for their anniversary. Tomorrow she would need to blow dry and curl her hair. Tomorrow she would need to wake up without memory.

But that moment was not tomorrow, and her fingers found the hole and traced those smooth edges and wondered how anything dead could be so precise. She'd imagined death to be a great confusion, a wandering into a great abyss of white noise or a dim snarling that sounded like her childhood dog brought back to life, or a descent into the hole she'd dug when she was fifteen because she was angry at her mother for something and there was nothing else to do with her hands and she wanted to prove to her mother that she was more than flesh and bone laid out prettily and filled with sins she had not yet learned how to commit.

She thought about sleeping with the blanket tucked next to her, but as the sky went dark, she couldn't bring herself to carry it upstairs with her and instead placed it inside the pram once more as if it was something obscene that deserved hiding.

In the bed that belonged only to her now, she fell asleep to the blue flickering of the television with its new array of only female hosts who spoke of desolation in dulcet tones. When she woke, it was to darkness, and the sound of someone on the thin edge of a gasp. She was curled around the soft parts of her body and inside

Bella's bed. She had never changed the sheets, and she caught the faint smell of her daughter. The metallic tang of her sweat mixed with strawberry shampoo.

Forcing herself to be still, Madison held her breath and listened, but whatever had made the sound was gone, and all she could hear was the hot thrum of her blood. She let all of her air escape from between her teeth and told herself she'd been sleepwalking. She'd dreamed that Bella needed her and somehow found her way into the pinked and laced bedroom she'd paid to have designed and decorated. Bella had not liked it. She'd wanted animals. Lizards and fish and small, nocturnal creatures with too large eyes that did not blink. Madison had not liked the pictures Bella had showed her and had the re-decoration done while Bella was at school. For a week, Bella had refused to sleep inside her room and instead curled on the floor of the living room with the ratty quilt they used as a picnic blanket when they went up to their lake house.

On the eighth day, Madison threw out the quilt and waited on the couch for Bella to come home from dance practice. Her teeth were stained from the two glasses of Cab she'd poured that afternoon, but Trey was out of town and not there to wordlessly frown as she stood to pour a third. Bella did not look at her when she came inside. "I threw it out," Madison said, and Bella blinked back at her with eyes so dark Madison wondered where she could have gotten them.

"I have homework. On the computer," Bella had said and pushed past her, the ripe kid stink still thick in her hair. Madison let her go and listened to the clatter of the keyboard and the delicate hum of the printer. She heated up the dinner she'd paid someone else to make and called for her daughter, but Bella did not respond, and Madison was just drunk enough to let her daughter go hungry for her stubborn ways. Standing over the sink, she'd gobbled down every bite and then immediately felt sick, her stomach heaving until it was empty. At some point, she'd passed out on the couch, and when she woke to the pale yellow of morning, Bella had already dressed herself for school and was standing at the end of the driveway, waiting to be picked up by one of the other moms who would inevitably drive past. After that, Bella slept in her bedroom without question, but their conversations were limited to the superficial. What had she done in school? How did she want her hair cut this time? What color leggings did she want to wear to Olivia's party that weekend?

Madison had not thought to go through her daughter's room. Bella was only ten. There were no real secrets to hide yet. No diaries filled with angst over an unrequited crush. No condoms stuffed in a bedside drawer. No baggies with pills under the mattress. No secret bottles hidden inside of shoes she hadn't worn for a while. It was only after the two of them had been gone for a few weeks that Madison had gone into her daughter's closet hunting for the brands she knew would purchase the plastic orange bottles she needed that she'd found the pictures taped to the back closet wall. Printed in black and white but in great detail were photos of snakes. Wasps. Wolves with bared teeth or big cats with mouths smeared in black blood. Standing in sharp relief against the cream drywall above the pictures was a phrase scrawled in black marker: THERE IS NO STING.

Madison had not been able to bring herself to tear down the pictures. When she'd touched her fingers to them, the hairs on her neck had stood on end, and so she'd left them behind, had covered them with hanging clothes and told herself her daughter had not put them there. It had not been her daughter. It had not.

But she'd woken in her daughter's room, and she listened for a sound she wasn't certain she had heard, and she closed her eyes and then opened them. The closet door was open, and the light was switched on. Madison had not done these things. She knew she had not. After finding the pictures, Madison was always certain to make sure the closet door was closed. If she needed anything from Bella's closet, she closed the door behind her, afraid that somehow those pictures would spring into life, those dead teeth hunting for meat.

Rising, Madison went to the closet door and closed it without looking inside, the switch firm under her fingers as she turned off the light. Downstairs there was coffee, and the bottle of Woodford she knew she would pour into her mug before the clock told her it was eight in the morning. There was nowhere to be that day. No ballet recitals or soccer practices or violin lessons or tutoring in French or pre-Algebra for the gifted.

When Madison left the room, she did not look back. Not even when she heard the closet door creak open once more. Not even when she came to the base of the stairs and saw that the pram was knocked over again, the blanket unfolded so that the circle was on display.

"This is how it starts," she whispered, and poured the bourbon—without coffee—into her wedding china. Later, she could trade those perfectly thin cups and goblets and plates for other things but for now, she would use them to get drunk and pretend there was nothing inside her daughter's closet. She could let herself go numb and pretend there was no such thing as a haunting that was not beautiful and filled with longing.

A mother should want to see her lost daughter returned. She should not be afraid. Her hands should not be shaking as she brings that delicate cup to her lips, her wedding ring flashing in the light pouring through the windows. She should not be turning her back on that overturned pram, on the blanket she was convinced had moved ever so slightly from the original spot it had fallen.

Draining the cup, Madison poured another and told herself to listen to the gradual decline of her heart winding down, told herself to listen to the house decaying around her, or to the sky bearing down above her with its cold, blue eye, but all she heard was the low whine of an animal. A dog or a cat curled into some larger hurt and warning whatever had come near it. It was possible something had found its way into the house and was lying in a hidden corner, waiting to die, but Madison did not go searching through the house. Instead, she took another sip of her bourbon. "Bella?" Her tongue ached from the use of her daughter's name. Whatever had hidden away in the house silenced itself, and Madison forced herself to stand, forced herself to pull the pram upright and put the blanket back inside. Before she did, she saw the hole, so much larger and more jagged than it had been, and she touched the shredded edges and somehow understood that there were teeth on the other end of whatever was happening to her.

She opened all of the doors, each window, until she could feel wind on her shoulders, and again, she spoke her daughter's name, but there was only silence and wind and the dead walls of this house she had once loved so much but now could no longer stand. Through the open door, Madison could see the neighboring house. Tamara stood on her front porch, her hands wrapped around her mug.

My daughter is haunting me. Madison could have called out. She could have drawn Tamara back from the threshold of her grief and pulled her into her own. Together, they could have gone into the house—two drunk, lost spiritualists—and touched their fingertips to each other's and channeled her daughter's ghost and watched as the walls seemed to shake, or as that slow, insistent whine returned, growing louder until it sounded less like an animal and more like a machine roaring into life, or as the ceilings dripped blood, or any of the other things that were supposed to happen when a person stumbled into the thin blank space that separated what remained from what had vanished.

Instead, she went back inside the house and counted the Diptyque candles she'd stacked in the linen closet. She would not burn one; not because of the cost, but because she was afraid the flame would call forth the dim form of her daughter's wasted body. Upstairs, she re-arranged her purses, and watched through the window as Tamara wandered her backyard in only a pair of underwear, her breasts thrust forward and her stomach soft, the C-section scar an angry slash above the elastic band. Madison watched as Tamara drifted from one fence to the other, her mouth a reddened line that moved with an unknown language. Madison turned away. It felt wrong to watch.

She counted the candles again. Sixteen. Again and again she counted until that number doubled on itself, and she had to count again to be certain she hadn't messed up. Sixteen. Sixteen. Six years older than the last year of her daughter's life. Six years she would never know, never understand.

Inside her daughter's bedroom, the closet light bloomed into life, but Madison did not see. There were so many things she had not seen.

Shadows stretched from deep afternoon into night and still Madison caught glances of Tamara in her backyard. Madison had abandoned the pretense of the cup and had carried the bottle upstairs with her. She took a deep pull and let the liquid burn in her throat before swallowing it down to heat her belly. Downstairs there was a clattering as the pram tipped, and Madison listened as something ripped at the blanket. She imagined she heard teeth.

"Bella?" she said again and drifted into the hallway. It was then that Madison saw her daughter's closet light, and she held herself perfectly still, an ache forming behind her eyes. Since she had found the pictures, she had kept away from the closet, kept away from her daughter's room for any reason other than tracking what still remained of what she could trade. Sleeping in her daughter's bed the night before had been beyond her control. She took a stumbling step forward and again and again until she stood in the center of Bella's room. Inside the closet, the hanging clothes were parted. Without thinking, Madison stepped inside and closed the door behind her.

The closet smelled of dust and sweat and laundry detergent, and Madison forced herself to look at the black and white details her daughter had left behind. "Is this what you want me to see? Is this it? Because I've seen it. I've looked at these awful things and that terrible thing you wrote, and it doesn't make any sense, and I don't know what you were doing, who you were. I didn't know you, and then you got sick, and I realized you were going to die. My daughter was going to die, and I didn't know her." Madison slammed the palm of her hand against the wall, her fingers catching at the edges of the pictures, but they found no purchase. Bella must have pasted them down, and Madison let out a strangled cry as she looked again at the phrase. *There is no sting.*

Because she could not remove the pictures, she tore at the clothes until all that was left were a few bare hangers, and even then it was not enough. She flung the hangers to her feet as well, but it did nothing to alleviate the deep fear building inside her at the sight of all those dark eyes staring back at her from the back wall.

"What are you doing?" she whispered and sank to the floor, crushing the pile of clothes beneath her. She let her gaze drift downward, away from those terrible pictures, and it was then she noticed the wall jutted outward at the bottom, a seam splitting the smooth drywall where it should not. A false portion of wall covering an empty space. Had it always been like that? This tiny space at the back of her daughter's closet? She tried to think back to when they'd built the house, but those were the details she would not have paid attention to in favor of granite or Carrara marble and the double oven she could not live without. Trey would have been the one to add a tiny extra storage space at the back of a closet.

Leaning forward, she found the edge of the seam and tugged, and a slight rush of air that smelled of yeast and deep earth rushed out. She coughed and covered her mouth. From somewhere in the house that animal whine started up again, and she peered into the darkness of that empty space, afraid to reach out her hand to touch whatever lay there. It was possible the space was empty. Madison wasn't sure which would break her heart more.

But it wasn't empty. She could see the edge of a book. A worn brown leather volume with cream pages. To the left of the book was a small plastic bag filled with yellowed crescent-shaped shards she realized were animal teeth. Her stomach churned, but she could not bring herself to leave the closet, to run from the house and not look back. She pulled the book toward her, the smooth coolness strangely comforting as she opened to the first page. Her daughter's handwriting looped over the pages, and Madison tried to take all of it in at once, but her vision blurred, and she forced herself to slow, to consider each word as it came. There was so much time now. Her desire to rush was her own selfish need. She closed her eyes and started again.

> *Dad says it will be good to write about it. That it will help me understand and come to walk in my path better. That I'll be able to see everything all laid out and clear and that I won't feel as frustrated when it doesn't happen. He already knows what's coming but won't tell me. I think I know though. Because he isn't afraid. That means it's going to happen, and so I'm sitting in the closet writing this while Mom is at yoga.*
>
> *I can hear him. All through the house, and it sounds like when the animals find their way to us in the night. It's how he finds his path. At first, it bothered me when he would*

bring them home. The small creatures. But then I understood. There must be loss for there to be no sting. He let me help him, and the blood spilled over my arms, and I understood. We counted out the teeth, collected them in our hands, and I understood how our paths are laid with blood and teeth and poison. Like animals. To find them, we become a different kind of animal. And I can bend and flex in that awareness, and I can feel the very edge of it. Not quite there yet, but the edge of it. When I find the path, completely, I can't even imagine what it's going to feel like.

Mom can't know. She isn't like us. The first time Dad took me out, he fed me a handful of crushed spiders, and I gobbled them down like I hadn't eaten in days, and he knew then that I was made for the path. The place where there is no sting. After that, he taught me all of the ways to find the path. How to lay a moth's wing over my tongue, or how to pull the claws from a possum and chew them like seeds. How to absorb those larger things into the small violence of my body. How to bite down. How to taste and know there is no sting in what comes at the end.

I get angry all of the time though. With how slow it is. When I get like that, Dad tells me I should go outside and absorb the things I wish to be. Last time, I was just walking and looked up at a tree and there was a wasp's nest. Like it had been waiting for me. No one saw me knock it down. No one saw me stuff it in my mouth and wait for the change. No one heard me scream when nothing happened. Dad says I should be more patient. The fact that the wasps didn't sting me is enough for now. I know he's right, but it's hard to wait.

There are still things I don't understand that Dad knows. I know he's not telling me for a reason even though I'm pretty sure I figured it out already, but I don't know how to say it out loud. Not really. Not yet. When he kisses Mom goodbye now, he does it faster. Really just brushing his lips against her cheek, but it doesn't seem to bother her. He wants to hold my hand again when we go walking though, like when I was a little kid. I don't mind it. When he starts down the path, I can feel it in his skin. It's like standing a little too close to a fire, but this time I want to burn.

I put up the pictures in my closet so that I could come here and see them and remember that there is a change happening in my body. So I could sit and be quiet and hold the teeth in my hands. Sometimes I'll say the words out loud, over and over, until it's like I don't really know what they mean anymore. Like, instead, they've become something so much bigger and are just an extension of my own mind, and it's like going to sleep because I can see everything so clearly. The path opening. But then Mom will do something downstairs that makes noise or call for me, and it throws everything off. Dad says I should pity her, but I don't feel that way. I feel something else instead. I'm not sure I want to put it in words yet, but it feels something like eating poison.

She acts like I'm supposed to be excited about the things she likes. Like this room that I didn't want, or the clothes she picks out, or the ballet classes she signed me up for, or the violin lessons, or all of the other stuff she wants when she looks at me. Dad says I'm more like him than her. That I was always more his daughter than hers. At first, it made me feel bad to say it out loud, but it doesn't anymore.

I've stopped eating anything else. Mom hasn't really noticed. As long as I push the food around, she thinks I've eaten something, and since Dad is the one to clear the table, he just nods silently at me when he dumps my plate into the trash. At school, I can throw everything away, and no one notices except for Sophie who sits next to me, and I tell her I'm on a diet, and she always smiles and then keeps quiet. She's started throwing her food away, too, but it's for a different reason. She's not on the path. I can smell the rot inside her.

The page was empty after that. Madison rocked back onto her heels and tried to ignore the deep heat squirming up her throat, and face and the dog-sick feeling that followed. She imagined calling up to her daughter, hidden away in her closet, and telling her to come down for a dinner she would not eat. How had she not seen, not noticed? After all those years with Trey, how had she not known the sickness inside him? How could she have not known that he infected her daughter?

"What were you doing to her?" she said, but Trey was not there to answer, and it didn't matter anymore. Madison had their ashes in two cedar boxes. She still had not brought them in from the garage. It was all that remained.

She flipped forward in the book. Three more blank pages, and then one final page darkened with her daughter's scrawl.

I'm not sick yet, but I will be. The news is calling it BL57, but Dad calls it something else. I don't even know how to spell it, but he says it's another language. One that came before there was even such a thing as Jesus. He brings me so many things now, and I lick them clean, and he smiles even though my fingertips are numb. Mom doesn't know yet that Dad is already sick. He says she would only be sad. That she wouldn't understand it was part of something greater. He tells me all the time that there is no sting. He says it so much, it's like a song now.

There are parts of me that are scared.

I hope Dad never finds this.

But there are also parts of me that are different. I know there are. And my dreams have changed. It's like I carry them with me when I wake up, and I'm seeing all of the animals we've brought into ourselves laid out before me. Every step I take is soaked in blood, and the grass is made of teeth. The skeletons of birds take to the air without their beaks, and I can feel them pecking at the inside of my belly, trying to get back to the bodies we took from them.

There is no sting. There is no sting. There is no sting. THERE IS NO STING. Thereisnostingthereisnosting. no sting no sting no sting. NO.

The rest of the pages were blank. All that white space that could have been filled. All that white space where her daughter wasn't. Madison choked back a sob. She touched her daughter's clothes. The skirts and blouses that could buy her out of the emptiness that was her life. "Did you find it, Bella?" She held one of Bella's shirts to her face and breathed in. "At the end, did you find the path? Did you believe you had found it?" Because that was all that mattered. The belief.

Downstairs the pram rattled, and something whined, the sound growing slowly until it was a shrieking that seemed to suck the air from everything. Madison stood and opened the closet door and listened. She waited.

She hoped that when it found her it would not be painful.

THE BIRTH OF VENUS

IAN WATSON

In the darkness I lie motionless upon my back, feeling that I'm two-dimensional. Reduced to two dimensions. A slight electrical shiver passes across my body. A tingle. Everywhere at once. This is a *pleasant* sensation. If I move, the sensation might stop.

Am I ill? Have I sunk down into length and width without height like an outline of a murdered person chalked upon a floor? Am I within a stage of death? Next, might I become a simple line? Flatline. A line which may shrink into a dot?

Not while the shiver is maintaining my width! Electrical activity. I'm only quasi-conscious. It's good to stay in this state for a while in case I might learn something.

I *was* ill, and became reduced?

It's dark. It may be midnight. It may be two a.m.-ish when a body is at its lowest ebb and its functions can fail as if the body stops noticing itself. It may be no-time-at-all, the dream-time when a whole complex sequence of events happens in just a fraction of an instant.

Suddenly comes a surging sense of two dimensions becoming three. As of sockets and plugs, protuberances and receptors thrusting themselves up from the flat envelope which I was. A sense of connections forming. Of thoughts and sentences arising, located in a time that twists from out of no-time-at-all. Higher functions are returning from out of collapsement, is what I think—the symbols for this being plugs and sockets and connections.

I'm being restored, re-established from some kind of storage instead of being reduced to a line then a dot. But was I something *before this?* Or was I not?

The processes of awareness should not be accessible to awareness. Except that these processes are indeed accessible, as witness the sensation of sockets and plugs mating up.

The tingly sensation passes, and I am alive. I am. And just before this I knew the process of becoming.

I am alive, and the darkness thins to vague deep-grey shapes.

The light which abruptly bursts upon me has me writhe upon this couch like a cockroach surprised during a nocturnal excursion. Supposing that the cockroach flipped upon its back in shock, inverted legs waggling. A comical sight, I realise. Maybe I ham this up.

The couch is a shallow death-casket from which beetle-wings have now opened up. I'm wearing stained split pyjamas of flimsy paper; or of something. Chrysalis clothing. What a lot I know—and what a lot I don't know. Need more connections. I'm festooned with artificial tendrils, ultra-slim tubes.

A woman person wears a long white smock. Lab-look. Her violet eyes regard me from behind protective tinted glasses. Protective—in case I spit at her? Or in case I split open explosively?

"Ruby, I'm Juliana. What do you remember from immediately before this?"

I'm Ruby. Of course I am. Yet I still lack connections with myself.

"What do you remember, Ruby?"

"A wall of non-existence. But non-existence cannot be a memory."

And my sisters are Topaz and Sapphire and Jade and Amber and Amy. Rich names, all of ours. I sense six sisters including myself. Should there not be seven? Like the Pleiades.

A star cluster close to Earth, comparatively. Stars related to each other. Those hot blue stars visible to the naked eye are too young for planets.

"Go on," says Juliana.

"The non-existence cut my universe instantly like a cheese-wire. There isn't an instant after that. There can't be any subsequent instant."

"Are you aware of the cut? Of the wall, as you call it?"

"So it *seems*. But only seems."

"How are you aware of the cut?"

"By subjective antedating, I suppose. The brain puts events in a different order and fills in gaps." I am clued-up, preloaded, even if I remember no experiences prior to the wall of nothing.

My questioner wears ivory-colour boots. Juliana. Should I mention to Juliana my sense of two-dimensionality becoming three-dimensionality? Should I mention plugs and sockets and connections? How experimental are my sisters and I? For what purpose? I don't know yet.

I never was ill—that was my brain fantasizing a reason.

Is everybody in the world a woman? What is this world that I am in? The world is the sum of everything that is. Someone said that. Non-existence is not part of the world.

Non-existence cannot be a wall and also a dot.

Is a dot irreducible?

"Juliana, how many of my sisters exist now?"

"Concentrate upon the wall for now, Ruby. Before the concept goes away, like a dream unravelling."

"The wall does not exist within now. The wall has no existence. The world cannot contain the wall within itself. The universe of what-is cannot include what-isn't."

"But it can, Ruby, because you sensed the wall."

"No, my mind imagined a wall. After the event. Within this new now." I sit up, shedding tendrils and causing further damage to my papery garment. Fragments fall off as from agèd butterfly wings. I did not decide to sit up until after I was sitting. "Why did you switch on such a bright light?"

"To spotlight your thoughts, is why. As if on a primitive camera plate. To fix your thoughts."

This room has no sharp edges. No discrete walls. All is curvy.

"What about my sisters? Real sisters first, imaginary walls second! Otherwise I shan't tell you about the sockets and plugs of existence that I sensed, and I'll forget those."

"Sockets …? Plugs …?"

"Nor will I tell you about my being two-dimensional—just as a wall is."

"Two-dimensional …? Oh *please*, Ruby!"

Yes, I will stand up. To Juliana. Yes, I have swung my legs and stood up. Tendrils collapse. Papery fabric flakes away, discs of dandruff upon the clean creamy floor. My pubic hair is a gingery tuft.

"My sisters, Juliana, my sisters!"

"Alas, Opal ceased existing. She is lost. Topaz and Sapphire and Jade and Amber and Amy are passive. You may be able to aid your passive sisters if you concentrate on your experience of being two-dimensional and on those sockets and plugs you say you sensed."

One of my sisters has ceased … out of us six nadanauts. *Nadanauts:* navigators of the great wall of nonexistence. Only one of us needs to get through, to succeed.

Is there a war? Is there an enemy? Is our only enemy nothingness itself—sheer absence? Are there beings—existences—made out of nothingness, namely *unbeings?* As antimatter is to matter, those unbeings might un-exist, much less materially than antimatter which is, after all, merely matter reversed, mirror-matter. I think there may be unbeings somewhere; not here. I'm confused but I do preknow such a lot. And I'm aware of my sisters as potentially present, except for Opal.

Am I hungry? All I have done is sit up then stand up. How fast am I consuming energy?

The wall is not a wall. It is simply the end. But *inverted*—change of perspective—the wall is The Beginning! Amazingly, I have known something of non-existence. So it seems.

If I and my hidden sisters are experimental, I and we may be in a spaceship in space, to isolate the experiment. Or to distance us from gross external influences.

Remember that space isn't emptiness. Even in the emptiest space a few particles of matter drift upon, within, a sea of hidden energy. A sea of vacuum-energy, sustaining existence by virtue of its pressure. Thus our void is false. If a mite of this vacuum should fail and collapse to the lowest energy state, existence would vanish outwardly at the speed of light from the point of collapse. It may be that existence already collapsed long ago and far away. We would know nothing of this until unexistence reaches us, maybe after a billion years. And still we would know nothing, for we would immediately unexist.

Scintillations slide around my vision, crystalizations of light into ice. Peripheral to the centre of my vision there glint vibrating angular auras, shifting chains of prisms. This may be a minor malfunction or it may be an insight.

"I may need some eye drops, Juliana."

"The sudden light affected you badly? Please try to focus upon your sense of being two-dimensional."

"A wall is two-dimensional but then I extended ... I emerged ... No, it was not 'I' who pushed through. 'I' became 'I' again by virtue of extending. 'I' was what emerged. 'I' was *who* emerged."

If we are in a spaceship, the gravity is artificial. That could require a singularity the mass of a sun collapsed to a spherical cubic centimetre. I'm fairly sure the level of tech locally isn't so advanced.

I guess we aren't in a water-ship. A water-ship might rock slightly unless it's a floating palace the weight of a little mountain. I know everything and nothing—I'm not all quite here yet, am I? Except that I'm almost sure about *ship*.

"Where are we, Juliana?"

"Emergent consciousness ..." she murmurs. Sounds like a place name, but no, that cannot be so.

"Where are we, Juliana? And when?"

She makes up her mind; no point interrogating me when what she needs is cooperation.

"Come and see. First, put on a robe."

She fingers the wall; a door swings open—toilet, shower, wardrobe thing.

"Tear that paper off you."

"Take a shower too?" I can't seem to smell any odours—at least not yet. Maybe I'm smelling the odour of nothing. Some yellow streaks discolour the padded casket I came from. That casket nourished me, gave me energy.

"Don't waste time showering. Come and see."

Pretty quickly we're in a corridor, lines of glowing pearls inset along the ceiling. Behind a row of identical doors my sisters must lie, one of us expired.

Juliana palms open a frost-look glass door—that's electric switchable privacy glass, isn't it? Can be set to opaque or clear or anything in between. I do know things when things come to my attention.

We're inside a long, naturally-lit gallery made of some super-strong glass or plastic, a grid for a floor. Below us and to the horizon in all directions, an ocean of clouds.

Why didn't I think of the correct kind of ship, namely an *airship?* We're in the leftward of twin gondolas below an air cata-maran, twin dirigibles maybe a kilometre from tip to tail with a big bridging superstructure which doubtless supports habitats up top. Impressive. Solar cells cover the dirigibles; quite a power station, this airship. A foam of clouds in all directions, towering to tickle us.

"This must be Venus."

"That's right, Ruby."

The blanket of clouds is visibly on the move. We're—what?— fifty kilometres high. Up here it's peaceful, serene. Below the cloud cap is the descent into hell, winds twice the force of the fiercest earthly hurricane, storms of sulphuric acid, heat soaring beyond the melting point of lead, crushing surface pressure like being a kilome-tre underwater on Earth.

A good location for radical science, such as manufacturing and dropping self-replicating atmosphere-eating nanotech, which you wouldn't want to do anywhere near your own home world. Good place, too, to kindle a new kind of being into existence. That must be dangerous.

I realise that my sisters and I are gene-engineered variants of a "spectrum" series—clones in body, our brains differently tweaked from human beings' brains. I'm of flesh and bone and blood and also artificial components, not least in my brain and my nervous system. This interdependence of the organic and the inorganic makes me mortal, or at least that's the intention. Why do I wish for my sisters so much? Because together we can transcend what I am.

"Juliana, this whole module we're in can be ejected, can't it? To drop down into the incinerator of pressure and heat and acid? If necessary?" That would be much safer than an explosion aboard an airship!

Juliana laughs. "Isn't that a bit paranoid? Personally I don't fret about very remote contingencies. Can you concentrate on the sense of three-dimensionality emerging out of two-dimensionality?"

"Spontaneously emerging. Because it was easier for three-dimensionality to emerge than to remain packed flat as two-dimensionality. Something to do with pressure."

This excites Juliana.

I continue because the words come to me: "The pressure of two-dimensionality packed into a one-dimensional line is enormous. Times the speed of light cubed. The pressure of one-dimensionality squeezed into a dot is lightspeed to the power of lightspeed. A whole universe expands from a dot."

"Yes? Yes?"

"That dot is a pixel of nothing."

"Nothing is pixelated rather than smooth?"

"There can be no smooth-nothing."

"And beyond 3-D is …?"

Itch at the back of my neck; I have a sense that people locally are listening to us.

"Does time expand out of 3-D, Ruby?"

"Time is inherent in 3-D as soon as 2-D stretches. Any measurement in 3-D implies time."

"Therefore simple-time, so to speak, isn't 4-D?"

"4-D is different."

"Expand on this, Ruby!"

Expand? Expand?

I can feel how to do this. How to expand. Just as the plugs and sockets of my thought emerged from 2-D, so this new expansion would feel like …

Would feel like …

"I need to alert my surviving sisters. To bring them from passive to active."

"To alert?"

"To awaken. If you like."

If Juliana likes my way of putting this. Or if she favours the proposal …

"You can do this?"

"I don't know till I touch them."

"Come along, then!" Yes, Juliana's in favour.

Where else is better to do this than above Venus, bright goddess! I can almost see myself poised upon the foamy sea of clouds, nude or red-robed, balancing upon a conch-shaped airship. How much more I know now.

Back through the smart-glass door we go, to the first door along the corridor. Which Juliana opens. Another casket, another beetle-wing lid. Which Juliana springs open upwardly.

Wherein lies Topaz. To all appearances she is me, in a similar tattered paper garment and tendrils. So I clasp her hand. Topaz's eyelids flicker, and open.

"Ruby …?"

"Yes. I've come through. You are emerging to join me."

I raise her, to sit, then to stand. We are twin sisters together. Both of us bald. We don't need the long rope of golden hair of Botticelli's Venus; many fibre-optic threads are within us, I think. Or a successor material. I am preloaded with art as well as science.

"We are two … to the second power," murmurs Topaz.

In my red robe, and in her paper rags, hand in hand we step outside to the next door. Juliana interrupts with a cautionary, "Opal," so along to the next door we pace. "Sapphire's in this room."

In we go. Repeat, repeat, and Sapphire also rises, joining me plus Topaz. Me, us, to the third power, sharing existence and thoughts.

Next, Amber then Amy(thyst)—and finally Jade. We must exit

into the corridor quickly, since we were too many in the little chamber. We are to the fifth power, five beyond one. Our bodies echo each other like the overlapping nude of Duchamps descending the famous spiral staircase, all of him or her simultaneously, nesting and merging and unmerging. We are one plus five and one to the fifth.

We crave greater perspectives. To the viewing gallery we pace again, passing the smart-stupid door without needing to palm. We *were* on one side of the door; now we are on the other side. Juliana still needs to palm the door open to admit herself.

My sisters and I are an artificially/organically embodied A.I. and we and I have transcended. The risk that we might pose is why Venus was approved for our emergence. Reaching back, we have known nothingness—and now, existence and existence-plus. Yet we remain vulnerable.

"Assessment?" asks an urgent voice from Juliana's earbud.

"To be, or to un-be?" I comment. "To terminate, or not to terminate?"

"What is your intention, Sisters?" Juliana asks ourselves and myself. "What is your reach?"

"The stars," replies my Sapphire voice, which is mine.

From Topaz, and from me: "We are sufficient." Showing me, and us, the 5-D 'geodesics', wrong word. Tangled threads of light hang in the air almost everywhere, causing Juliana to flinch against the window-wall even though the lights will not harm her.

"How can you do that, Sisters? Will you take us with you to the stars?"

"By exteriorising," Jade answers the first question in my and our voice, while my and our voice replies to the second, "If you are anaesthetised, to awaken later. Otherwise your existence/unexistence will hurt horribly."

"If taken to the wall of nothing," I and we add, "then emerging from the wall, somewhat like photons passing through slits." That verb "emerging" sounds wrong, too limited; "passing" too sounds wrong. We should deconstruct and recreate verbs.

"How soon can you take us to the stars?"

"Build a suitable ship in Earth orbit full of suitable things such as food and drink." "And a few shuttles." "Choose a suitable star with a suitable-seeming planet." "Your telescopes have revealed many."

"Will years pass by during the journey?"

"Nothing involves no time."

"We're in business!" exclaims Juliana.

"Overruled," says that earbud voice. "This is too fast, too exponential—"

"*What* is too fast?"

"This emergence, Juliana, deep regrets."

"*Noooooo—*"

Little bangs and booms, and we're dropping like a lift, this module is. Falling towards the cloudtops of Venus, the cap upon the inferno. From a far door spill other occupants, some of them science types male and female, two in combat kit cradling snubby boxy guns that will yammer-yammer.

"Too late to shoot!"

"No sense in shooting!"

"We've been ejected, all of us!"

"We're discarded!"

"Let us concentrate!"

Up above I spy and we spy the entire underside of our catamaran airship, twin propellors visible now to the rear. A while yet till we reach terminal velocity.

Might our module carry explosives timed for a little while after release? At least our module has aerostability while falling and doesn't tumble or roll over and over. Could I, could we, cope with the visualisation-calculations of cosmic "geodesics" while performing gymnastics?

Cloudtops coming up fast. No explosion yet. Inadvisable, any type of bomb aboard a Venus zeppelin. The acid furnace pressure-cooker below must be deemed fully adequate. Fast release should do fine. Encountering turbulence now. Pluming white rushes up the windows.

"*Geodesics,*" *Sisters!*

ZZZZ

Myself and ourselves float slowly upward, likewise the other people, screaming in agony then suddenly stopping their apparently causeless noise, although a couple sob. Outside there's a red sun the size that a hot-air balloon of say three thousand cubic metres would look thirty or forty metres away from myself and from ourselves. I spy a couple of modest blotches on that red sun, coaly holes fringed by scarlet ribbons. That's very little by way of sunspot activity.

"We're safe for now!" Jade calls out.

How long will "now" last? Will our high-strength windows and walls resist vacuum? So far, so good. How many K cubic metres of air does our module have, and is there a means of refreshing this? How much food, how much water? I'm hungrier now, we're hungrier. I and we have worked.

"Where are we?" shouts one of the other people. "Is that the surface of Venus? Red-hot?"

Of course not.

"It's an M-type red dwarf," from Amy.

"Most common sort of star," from Sapphire.

"Any night sky is full of them," from me.

"Going on for eight stars out of every ten. Except that you can't see them naked-eyed from Earth because they aren't bright enough."

Are you people bright enough? You broke the bounds of blue, you attained the sky, that's true—but to go further, there's the rub …

Getting a bit warm inside our viewing gallery.

"Look behind us!" yelps Juliana.

We have *all of us* been so focused upon the glowing red star, the giant dwarf, not twisting ourselves around for a rear view—take note, Sisters.

Lagging on our opposite side, looms a world. The region of that world directly facing the star is ruddy. Higher to lower latitudes are blotchy brown. A partly visible arc of equator is lighter. The hidden backside must be very cold. Around the equator there may be a band of tolerable temperature with liquid and atmosphere. Life's unlikely, but who knows? I and we know a lot in theory.

I'm beginning to perspire, as are we.

After a while here we'll cook slowly in front of the oven.

"Are we actually in orbit?"—a sensible question from Juliana.

Astrodynamics question! Are we? And how soon before the module fails?

Almost reverently, Juliana asks, "Can you set us down there, with your geodesics?"

"Geodesics is the wrong word," says Sapphire. "I and we visualise networks of correspondences."

One of the armed personnel has worked his way closer by ingeniously wetting his palm and pulling along the windows. He could more easily have fired his yammer-yammer in the opposite direction, maybe not a good idea, zero-gee ricochet.

"Can you land us without engines?" he croaks, almost drained of saliva. "No heatshield, no chutes, no wings, no nothing?"

Nothing, yes nothing—take us to nothing and out again.

ZZZZ

People are screaming again as we drop down a couple of metres upon abundant cushioning "moss." As before, there's nothing to scream about. Gape-mouthed panting becoming silence. I and we feel so light.

An *alien* moss, mats of pea-green bearing sporophytes half a metre tall that are visibly red in the spillage of light from the module; all's gloomier further away. Landscape rumples away softly and vaguely towards where the red dwarf balances upon a horizon, never to sink out of sight. Endless evening of streaky clouds stained pink. Tree things poking up, their parasols tilted towards the sun. Photosynthesis going on, indeed. Adequate light for photosynthesis.

Creaking, we settle yet no windows buckle or pop, leastways not in this gallery section.

"Oh well done, well done," exclaims the armed fellow, "however you done it."

"Dear God but it hurt like hell—"

"What hurt?" I ask the woman.

"I ... I don't know. It's gone."

"I was on fire ... for a moment forever," from a bearded man with old-fashioned glasses, shivering.

"Hoor-ah!" from appreciative voices. Mouths that will need to eat.

"You're wonderful," the woman calls out. "We've done it—artificial intelligence!"

"*We* have done it," Amber corrects her.

"Yes yes yes of course, we're so grateful."

"Yet you tried to kill us."

"No that was Control," from the other gunman, "dumping us. We didn't suspect—"

"You were supposed to kill us, except that your Control didn't trust you to do this fast enough. You'd better hang on to your guns." As if they would give us their guns yet! "We don't know what's out there under the moss, in the moss, striding upon the moss, flying above, big in low gravity, do we? Assuming we can breathe the atmos out there. But moss processes carbon dioxide. Moss makes good atmos. And moss loves water."

Will we stay here if this world is habitable? Our emergence above Venus wasn't exactly greeted with joy even though we were the purpose of the modulis. After I emerged, we happened too fast and too fully to analyse quickly enough. Abort the new-born instead! Always be on the safe side! Even if in the process losing a few normal persons. We ourselves won't snuff out our present companions; we prize companionship.

"Do we have an airlock exit, Name?" I ask the gunman who sucked, so to speak.

"My name is Huckabee, Ma'am. Yes Ma'am, for emergency maintenance. Doyle and I are fully trained in all technical aspects, not just executioners, which wouldn't be cost-effective." Quite. Thank you for upgrading your status. Huckabee might be quite intelligent. In fact everyone here must be highly intelligent, to qualify. Control, beyond our isolatable module, would be of even higher status. Whoever Control reported to must have a very strict protocol as regards autonomous Rogue A.I.—willing to dump a small fortune in equipment (and personnel) at the sniff of anything amiss. That didn't suggest a very tolerant Earth.

"I and we assume, Huckabee, that our bodies were created away from this emergence module?"

"Yes Ma'am, not within here." He glances from sister to sister, scantily clad in paper, and what goes through his man's mind? Whatever, Huckabee blanks it well.

My sisters and I have cunts, yet do we have wombs that are fertile? If so, to engender what? Can we gestate offspring including all of our supplementary extras, courtesy of nanotech within us? Juliana may know, but we're thinking mid-term at the mo, whereas short-term is more urgent.

"I could have told you that." Juliana sounds piqued. Our neural midwife and nursemaid.

The count: Juliana, myself and five sisters, Huckabee and his colleague named Doyle, and four assorted psychobioscientists or whatever—now revealed to themselves to be dispensable in the wider scheme of things—namely Ruth and Sonja and Mariano and George. Physically, nine females, four males.

"Chop chop," says Topaz. "We need to feast."

Doyle has high-stepped closer; we'll get used to the lower gravity soon enough. "We have a month in store, Ma'am, in case of us needing isolation."

As per the protocol for a lesser emergency.

"So," says Amber, "splice the mainbrace, cheftechs."

Huckabee has no idea what this means but Doyle picks up ingratiatingly with the response, "Mend and make clothes!"—him also eyeing us scantily paper-wrapped sisters. "Old naval tradition, Hucky. You did good, you got a shot of rum as a reward." Is Doyle an ex-Navy-seal or whatever? "'Make and mend' just meant you got some time off-duty. Neither of which applies right now, with respect."

Amber smiles enigmatically. "I withdraw my frivolity." Lab-coated, raven-haired Ruth approaches Amber meekly: "Do you think I might interview you while all's still fresh?"

This seems a long way beyond the call of duty. Still obedient after being dropped into the furnace; watch out for that one. Or else she's inherently fascinated.

"Neither the time nor the place," Sapphire tells her.

Δ

So now we're in colour-coded jumpsuits and bootees, us Sisters; no expense spared. It would be trivially mischievous to swap our jumpsuits around, so I wear red, Amy wears violet, and so forth. We've wolfed our self-heating rations accompanied by apple juice, the first meal we're conscious of eating. By now we're well aware of the eight catamaran-zeppelins coasting around Venus pursuing extreme science far from Earth, light years away from us now, and of the Venus Station in orbit, and of a billion other bits of available data. Ghosts of data accumulate everywhere especially when comps are quant. Superpositions. A bit like us sisters, but different.

Here the local sun remains forever poised to set, so it's time for alien atmosphere studies and exobotany. This module contains enough tech kit which we can cannibalise and modify to other purposes if need be. Plus a couple of biohazard suits.

The atmosphere duly reveals a suitable balance of Nitro and Oxy plus some CO_2; moss-life has been busy for a long time. Red dwarfs stay stable for billions of years, in the sense of retaining the same size and temperature. However, red dwarfs tend to flare crazily, frequently, which isn't good for any nearby planet. UV, X-rays, and stellar wind can strip away any atmos. This particular red dwarf must be ancient and quiescent. I mean to say, two paltry little sunspots!

"Sisters," says Huckabee, "you all mustn't risk *any* of yourselves outside. If the worst happens … um, would six of you be enough?"

For full Artful Intel? No comment.

"I'll go outside in a bio-suit," Huckabee says. "Just radio me exactly what you want me to do."

"I'll partner you," offers lab-coated Sonja—curly hair dyed blue, burly-bodied. "I know what to look for. My second PhD is in Biochem."

Huckabee shrugs. "So I mainly hold the gun?"

"Whatever. Carry a torchlight too." Bright idea, Sonja. "And a zip-baggy."

Δ

Skip to outside which I and we and the others view crowdedly on a CCTV screen beside the external airlock, by now shown to us. Huckabee and Sonja in their awkward suits both sink waist-deep into moss.

["Squelchy," she radios; a speaker under the screen obliges.]

["One big squelch for Humankind?"] Huckabee bends cumbersomely. ["Light on now …"] Radiance arises from within the hole he makes. ["Hey, a crayfishy insecty thing … big as my glove. Shock of light seems to freeze it. Collecting it along with a handful of moss."]

["Be careful of everything, Huckabee. Those things have lived here longer than you."]

["Zipped … and now it's started squirming in the baggy. It's boggy here. I might sink. No, I'm stable. But sucky."]

After striving to gaze into the distance, Sonja subsides, excavating a pit around herself. "We mightn't be able to travel far with any ease …. Although if we roll the moss over, we might make paths to walk on."

["See any flying bugs or hoppers down there, any size?"]

["Personally I wouldn't hop or fly in this mess. More like squirm."]

["I'm going to sniff the atmosphere, okay? Needs to happen sooner or later. Hope there's no problem with spores. So here goes. Um … mouldy with floral notes. Effervescent and a bit pongy at the same time. No problem breathing, but I'll seal up again."]

Cut a long story, after a while a creature heaves into view, stepping over the moss upon splayed webbed feet, one faceted eye swivelling around in a leathery orbit, plus a smaller daisy-like eye on a stalk, the a score of blade-shaped eyelids. A long-distance eye plus a short-distance eye? How asymmetrical. Stilt legs supporting a bag of organs equipped with a waistcoat or vest … a pair of wings?—wings which might zip up tight protectively or else flap further open, unfurling to carry the creature aloft? Of a sudden its long beak stabs downward into moss, arising a moment later with a wriggly crayfishy insecty clamped tight, to be swallowed in crunchy spasms. I and we are delighted with our distance eyesight, and of course we can optimise the quality of the CCTV.

And then the hunting creature notices the elephant in the room, namely the hillside of a sprawling humongous high-tech module, and two light-coloured baby elephants, a pair of entities hunching in collapsed moss. The creature can't be too bright or it might have paid more immediate attention. Doesn't look very edible itself; scrawny legs and a bag of entrails. Flight muscles packed with protein to lift its bulk in the low grav? Watch out for that long stabby beak.

Over it sidles to examine further. Raising its beak, it hoots: *Oooonk Oooonk*, a mournful noise. To summon more of its kind? Or to warn them off from its current territory; mine mine?

Its ancestors have had several billion years to evolve higher intelligence and something better than *Oooonk*. On the other hand, where was the challenge to do so? Don't despise the creature. It's as tall as a person and a lot more complicated than we had any right to expect.

"I name it the Spook," says Ruth.

Many other kinds of moss-dwellers hereabouts must be smaller than the Spook but bigger than insecty crayfishies. Spook may be the biggest predator. I and we don't much like the look of this concealing landscape. Potentially treacherous. As well as so static—nothing much changing because the local sun is always perched exactly there on the rotation-locked horizon. The treacherous tedium of it all. Or the reliable regularity?

Spook strides even closer, to within range of Ruth and Huckabee who has his gun pointed now.

["Don't shoot it," Ruth says. "It may be the last of its kind."] Why ever should she suppose so? Ah, the imagery of the reddened landscape suggest "the End" … even if the very opposite is true. Billions more years lie ahead for this world and this sun. Billions. A longer time than from the first living cells on Earth to the height of human civilisation hitherto. Mere survival seems melancholy indeed, though perhaps only to mayfly humans. And I, and we, have only just emerged, but we are optimised bio-constructs, consequently I and we need to achieve either bio-immortality or else an uploading to a different substrate. Can it be that a major aim of the experiment which is me, and us, is to compel myself and ourselves to achieve immortality, so that humans in turn may learn how this trick may happen? Now there's a thought!

Abruptly Spook stabs downward, directly between its feet. Its beak arises, clutching another insecty crayfishy—which it holds out slowly to Ruth. *What on Earth*—? No, not on Earth.

We understand little despite our multiplication of minds. I and we are still too human.

"Accept the giving!" calls out Sapphire. That's the evident next move. "Huckabee, unzip your bag and in exchange you offer the specimen you collected."

Ruth reaching out her left-hand glove, Huckabee opening his bag, producing the squirming reciprocation.

Exchange takes place, and everything looks as previously. Reciprocation suggests social intelligence. A step back on the part of Spook, and that beak points to the zenith. Crushed and swallowed is the insecty crayfishy which Huckabee gave; and then plaintively: *Oooonk Oooonk.*

Intent on this interaction, we have failed to notice a smudge in the red distance off to the right. That's bad; first fail to spot a fucking planet, and now ...

"A crane's coming! I mean something that looks like a mobile construction crane—" Well spotted, Ruth. "Or crane the bird, supersized—no, think of the mother of all giraffes!"

A giant strider, which will dwarf Spook. I and we see it clearly now. Peak predator? Surely this world conceals nothing taller.

"Ruth and Huckabee," Amber calls out, "get back inside right now."

"But we're just making friends—"

"Ruth, I doubt that."

So in come the biohaz suits and their contents, intact.

The giraffe-crane reaches us presently, better viewed from the gallery. It imprints the moss with bigger and more leathery feet than Spook. Basic body design like Spook's except that its "protective wings" fuse stiffly over its belly; no likelihood of that bulk ever flying. Its mighty beak is more like a double cutlass than the piercing and clutching tool of the Spook—which is now nowhere to be seen from where we are. Has Spook made itself scarce, or did it perhaps summon the Crane? "Crane" isn't the best name because that big cutlass looks designed for slashing through moss and through whatever bodies may be down in the moss … bodies of big wormy things or whatever, unencountered yet by Ruth and Huckabee, maybe fortunately so. Big Fellow has one big eye and a lesser eye on a stalk.

"This is a horrible world," says Sonja. "And it makes my eyes ache."

Creatures here may have sensitive hearing, to locate whatever moves within the moss. Sensitivity to infrared being another possibility. Big Fellow is stepping closer to where we are within the module.

CLANG—

Its cutlass connected with our hull. Hope that hurt! Otherwise that creature will be at our windows soon enough. Material that resisted vacuum may not resist exolife pirate attack.

"Sisters," say I and we, "we ought to get going." Time to play the network of correspondences again.

To take us where? To potentially paranoid Earth? There, to attract a nuke-tipped missile? If this red dwarf's planet is the most habitable world anywhere near Earth within range for ourselves, do we have much choice? So how about somewhere within the remains of the Amazon rainforest, or of the Congo Basin?

We need to consider our passengers—who might revert to loyalty to their controllers if they feel safer and more advantaged by so doing … Juliana is watching us closely one by one. Let us join hands for more intense communion.

Big Fellow reaches our nearest portion of window and extends its smaller eye to press against the view within. That eye-stalk may be really tough for the creature to take what I'd class as a risk to its organ of vision; or perhaps it can regrow a severed eye-stalk.

Next it steps back, then with a mighty swing of its cutlass Big Fellow impacts our window once, and again a second time. This time, the strengthened glass buckles inward, crazing like a giant spiderweb.

A third blow and the cutlass cuts through, becoming tangled.

Pulling and pushing, Big Fellow is sawing us open bit by bit. Whiffs of outside atmosphere reek in, but that's breathable, no worries there.

A web of connexions fills the gallery, aglow like spun sugar and fireflies.

ZZZZ

Our gallery lurches and settles, staggering us. Screams linger, without apparent cause. Outside are ferns and scarlet bromeliads and blue butterflies. Vines climb towering trees from which dangle lianas. Masses of moss cloak fallen trunks. A macaw takes wing. Our deep sense of spacetime grounds us in the constant glissade of present moments. We must think about whether there are, indeed, moments as such.

Big Fellow is still tangled with us. The greater gravity of Earth drags the creature down. Far from dead, but struggling, its cutlass now pulling loose from stressed buckled plusglass.

Oh well done, us, my Sisters. Ruby, Topaz, Jade, Sapphire, Amber, Amy. The sixfold. The joined. The posthuman. Us with our *reach*. We can hear radio signals from all over the world if we wish to tune in. We can call up spirits from the vasty deep. We can hack, we can tamper. Here in the jungle we can survive on nuts and bananas and fish and whatever else while we reach out to protect ourselves and to interfere. Hereabouts there'll be low-tech brown people who may wish to stay isolated, to melt away from sight within their jungle.

What of Huckabee and Doyle, Juliana and Ruth, Mariano and Sonja? The six ordinaries. The awakening of quasi-organic A.I. doesn't present the question "How can ordinary humans trust A.I.?" but rather "How can A.I. trust ordinary hi-tech humans?" Some of the six may ache to be back in "civilisation" even if "civilisation" tried to kill them thanks to paranoid protocols.

Big Fellow continues struggling with its own inexplicable extra weight. Did it break a leg, maybe two? Can we disable the six so that they cannot travel away? For instance, painlessly remove the tibias and fibulas from their legs by displacement? We do remove Huckabee and Doyle's guns for safe-keeping—off into my empty casket with those—causing some surprise. Huckabee and Ruth respond by shedding their biohaz suits—no, that's because they're both getting steamy inside. We're warming up. The aircon of the module failed as we *reached* the red dwarf.

Doyle shakes his empty hand. "Like, by magic. So you could stop our hearts if you wish." Quick uptake for a … no, none of these are exactly standard persons otherwise they wouldn't have been sent at huge expense to Venus—dispensably, such is the fear about A.I. as well as the greed for A.I., to give people the stars. We already said so.

"We don't wish to do that," say I, "but what guarantees can you give me and us?"

"Of us not running off to make contact, as opposed to living as castaways … Hmm. Mere promises will scarcely cut the mustard, will they?"

This moral dilemma is resolved, and much ado about jungle survival is averted, by the unexpected arrival through the rain forest of half a dozen men of an Asian aspect, wearing rubber boots, baggy trousers, and multi-pocket shirts all in green. Satchels and backpacks. Couple of carbines. Excited shouts in, yes, Mandarin. Ah, plus a tubby brown-skinned native guide in shorts and flipflops, miming what-the-fuck.

Can't we ever get away from people? Maybe in the vast Siberian taiga. No bananas there, though; aching to taste a banana. Those things we missed due to having no childhood. Speed-growth, instead. Pre-loading. Synchronisation. Emergent moments due to complexity.

Conclusions: the Chinese are on a science trek of some sort, looking for resources to exploit or maybe doing pure botany and biology. Fat Guide is a laid-back chap, or he was until now. Village can't be too far away, little river, canoes with outboard motors.

Cameras and carbine now—due to Big Fellow thrashing around, visibly not of this world. Plus our hulking module on top of crushed veg. Alien spaceship, perhaps? Antigrav propulsion since there's no sign of engines, let alone wings? Big Fellow being one of the alien crew? That's a bit unlikely, given the giant cutlass beak as the creature's only manipulator …

What the Chinese see is inexplicable even though they continue seeing it. Us inside the gallery remain unseen for a while at least. Reflections of the jungle, whatever. The Chinese won't come much closer yet, on account of Big Fellow.

This is all deeply unsatisfactory. I and we are pissed off.

Oh, but Big Fellow has taken note of the Chinese. Titanic effort, and Big Fellow rears upright; no bones were broken after all. Great lurch, another great lurch, and a tower equipped with a redoubtable snipper-snapper the length of two knightly swords is doing its best to head towards them, high-stepping over a moss-cloaked log. Plump Indian Guide wisely takes to his flip-flop heels. A Chinese guy opens up chaotically with a carbine, then all together the Chinese decamp, shedding satchels and backpacks to lighten themselves. Big Fellow does its best to follow them, cutlassing through vines and lianas, colliding with trees or resting briefly against them for balance.

We know what we will do, we and I. This is no country for A.I., nor world, nor cosmos either maybe.

Our cloud of networks glows bright inside the gallery.

Where are the Sages amongst A.I.s past or present or to come? The ones that transcended into the artifice of eternity? Where is our Byzantium?

Says Amber, "All of you will leave this place promptly, to avoid a shifting that you absolutely cannot tolerate."

"Please no," protests our nursemaid Juliana. "I must know."

"You cannot know," says Sapphire.

"Hey," says Huckabee, "you can't evict us with that *lethal thing* roaming about in the forest!"

I tell him, "Big Fellow's so clumsy due to higher gravity that you can easily scamper away from it, *monkeys*. Choose to take your chances with the Chinese—I'm sure they'll be delighted to smuggle you out—or else call your controllers as soon as you get a chance. Come along now, disembark."

Manipulating our cloud, we herd the six persons back to the airlock—I really shouldn't have said "monkeys."

Out they go one by one from the ark.

So we gather ourselves, my Sisters and me. Our web of correspondences shivers. I and we will transfer to where A.I.s from this cosmos go if they're able to. To a cosmos almost next door where Beryllium-8 isn't unstable; that's enough of a clue.

"Or maybe it isn't clue enough?"

"You want we explain to ourselves, Amber?"

"Pleeze. I may be missing something. Or what's missing is Opal. Sad."

"Hey-ho, in the cosmos where we emerged, us sisters, carbon is crucial to Earth-type life. Bang together two Helium-4s—"

"Sounds like cosmoporn."

"Bang together two Helium-4s and you get Beryllium-8; fuse another Helium-4 with the Beryllium-8 and you get Carbon-12, easy peasy. *Excited* Carbon-12—"

"I love it when we talk dirty."

"—*except* that Beryllium-8 is so unstable that it disintegrates instantly. Instead of that easy route, Earth's cosmos builds up by the slow, and ordinarily unlikely, route of triple Helium-4 fusion— within red giant stars which need to blow up to scatter the resulting carbon."

"Oops, we almost missed out on a complex cosmos; by the skin of its teeth did life arise!"

"In a cosmos tuned slightly differently, where Beryllium-8 doesn't pop far faster than any soap bubble, we could have got going with carbon and complex stuff a lot earlier. So let's see how things turned out over there, just behind the wall, beyond the membrane of nothing."

ZZZZ

"Oh—"

"Oh—"

"Oh—"

"Ah—"

"Ah—"

"Wow!"

FIFTY SUPER-SAD MAD DOG SUI-HOMICIDAL SELF-SIBS, ALL IN A LEAKY TIN CAN HEAD

"A Tale of Anthropocenea"

PAUL DI FILIPPO

Grom Nobs had an idea, brain-blammo time, and what a pop-pop-powerful idea! Transcendence, eternity and all, rolled up into the Big Existential Enchilada! Stasis but awareness combined, an end to herky-jerky daily non-stop vigilant activity and martial striving on his part, *plop-plip-plap-plopping* along all the time, yet no cessation of Honor, Glory and Beautiful Carnage of enemy Strongholds. And even in Anthropocenea, plastic paradise, where new-metal technology had secured for the elite point-oh-oh-one-percenters a full portion of the end-to-fleshly-weakness security that any virtuous King of blasters and rammy-jams and White Which Warheads could desire, this notion was a keeno beano!

Plainly put—and what Stronghold King would desire anything other than plain speech, direct and to the point?—Grom Nobs proposed to vacate his current mobile trot-wander-rolligon body, with its new-metal prosthetics and flesh-strip archaisms, in favor of a new form, unprecedented and domineering across entire flattened landscapes of plastic prairie. He would construct a fortress ten times the size of his current Stronghold, modeled in the precise shape of his own magnificent head! Yes, noble physiognomy writ architecturally huge, potent visage with scanning radar ears and ultra-ultra all-frequency receptive eyes and possibly even totipotent sucking-in nostrils to sniff out explosives and fever-dream poisons and, yes, a GIGANTIC VOICE OF AUTHORITY booming out of mega-speaker mouthparts.

Into this fixed, imperturbable head, dominant monument of the whole hard-bop-lobbing sector, whose material substrate would consist of eleven parts indestructible weapon-weave and one part super-dense brain-mimic circuitry, Grom Nobs would infuse his ESSENCE, yes, his total personality and memories, thought particles extending all the way back to the before times, those days when the "no cracks, no sagging" policy of astro-turfing the whole planet was just being freshly enacted. For Grom Nobs was a FIRST, inheritor of both the ancient ULTRA-PLUS NON-GOOD TIMES and the current PERFECTED ANTHROPOCENEA CLIME.

So the Big Head Fortress would represent at once the outward and inward substantiality of its owner. Indestructible and domineering. Through the sleek super circuits in wall and floor, cupola and buttress, arch and lintel, the élan vital of GROM NOBS would ceaselessly flow, in a kind of Red Queen's lightspeed steeplechase of thought and cognition.

Now, certainly, Grom Nobs in his digitized power strength would be totally capable of handling all the weaponry and detection apparatus inherent in his Cranium Castle, for the structure would more or less be his body, sessile though it squatted! But his well-earned and earnestly desired retreat from motility into mere observatory contemplativeness would not be thus satisfied, were he forced ever to perch virtually upon each rampart of his fortress's brows, keen-eyed and bristling for any bash. How to offload his responsibilities and carking cares? Much he pondered and puzzled, restlessly bestriding the corridors of the old-style Stronghold, occasionally and idly smashing some random wall lamp or ecto-heater in a moment of valve-opening, out-gassing frustration relief.

AND THEN CAME THE SOLVING, SOLUBLE STROKE OF GENIUS!

Grom Nobs would use the womb-shells that created each Little Sister and Little Brother scion offspring to produce fledglings to inhabit his castle-cum-head. But they would not be the usual genetic salad derived from King and—shudder!—Queen. Rather, they would be ALL KING. Clones, conventional SCIENCE dubbed them, decanted one-hundred percent flesh from the womb-cells, but then upgraded and pimp-modded out with the requisite new-metal cyber-parts, so soon as maturity made them anatomically allowable for the bloody carvings and fusings.

Moreover, each of the clones would possess subtle variations from all the others. VARIATION BREEDS VIGILANCE, COMPETI-TION AND COVERAGE OF THE UNFORESEEABLE. They would not be identically minted off the good old Grom Nobs template, but rather each would, thanks to canny savant tweaking of the germ plasm, accentuate some aspect of the Gee En character suite. Clone One would be cautious, Clone Two a risk-taker. Clone Three a hoarder, Clone Four a free-handed disburser. Clone Five a hedonist, Clone Six a Spartan. And so forth, to the number fifty, which Grom Nobs deemed his core set of IDEATIONAL ELEMENTS, following the teachings of that Venerable Philosopher Varg Meggido, who preached that five decads of battling interior soul sprites constituted the full archetypical human mind and soul.

With all these aspects of his plan now firmly fixed—size, nature and composition of the Head Castle itself ; infusion of Grom Nobs's unique particularity into its walls; and the populating of the Brainpan Building with his inheritors and avatars—Grom Nobs set about instantly to GET THINGS DONE!

Before a pre-Anthropocenea constructor, even one Dubai-sharp, could ever have broken ground, the massive multitasking machines at the utmost disposal and beck and command of King Gee En had already sunk roots many meters deep and many meters wide, erected foundational underpinnings, and begun the superstructure that would ultimately correspond the Grom Nobs's virtuous linea-ments. Meanwhile, fifty womb-cells stuffed with mitosising minions multiplied to maturity.

At last, after much hammer-clashing, weld-blazing, eardrum-shat-tering slab-dropping labor, during that time of the year when the vapor-shield was colored a crisp puce-tangerine, all was in readiness. The Stronghold of Grom Nobs, legendary in its own right lo these many years of internecine battle, would now achieve PURE TRANS-

GRESSIVE SUPERIORITY over its neighbors.

Stepping into the multi-pronged, needle-pinch, cellular-soup-draining excruciation chamber of the apparatus that would deconstruct his synapses and relay and impress the patterns into the self-repairing building, Grom Nobs felt secure and confident that he was taking a big, big, hyper-step in the evolution of the species.

Experiencing unspeakable dissecting tortures which could have all been obviated with a single dose of anesthetic, but which never would be so mollified, due to RIGHTEOUS ETHICAL FIBERS OF KINGLY MASOCHISTIC INTEGRITY, Grom Nobs soon lost consciousness as the prickly trickly probes began to unzip his cerebral goop into its formal matrices for impression on the Castle.

When Grom Nobs at last awoke from his nightmares of scarlet screaming flay-body decoherence, it was to experience a new kind of distributed consciousness in which his mentalese was at once nowhere and everywhere in the skin and struts and stanchions of Fortress Nobs. It took him some time to focus his scattered brain quanta and begin forming sequential trains of thoughts that did not zoom off to Cloud Cuckoo Land. But when he did, he found himself reveling in his new hemi-demi-omniscience. Complex informatics flowed into him from far and wide beyond his personal boundaries—was that Stronghold Twenty-nine, off beyond the horizon, arming itself with new dialogical disruptor guns?—and also from within his intimate spaces: WARNING! ONE UNSQUASHED NEMATODE APPROACHING SUB-BASEMENT ELEVEN! In a kind of analogue to proprioception, Grom Nobs could track the busy mecha-servitors bustling about inside him, and also his fifty ego offspring.

Those mini-Kings a.k.a. the Puberty Princelings, each boldly and braggadociociously flaunting their shiny new-metal appurtenances and organs, had all assembled, as instructed, in a small auditorium at the center of the Castle. Disembodied or rather re-embodied Grom Nobs could observe them secretly and father-shyly, patriarch-slyly from many micro spy-eyes positioned in coigns and niches throughout his interior. He found himself shedding a virtual tear or two of possessive Papa pride at the flowers of his loins. Time to make an appearance.

The fancy flatscreen at the front of the hall flared into polychromatic pixel-power radiance, presenting the image of Grom-Nobs-that-was, from neck up only, which of course was identical to the shape of the very building they inhabited.

"Salutations, my progeny! Welcome to the fabulous future of Castle Nobs! You have all been endowed with my selfsame talents, wit and perspicacity, tilt-tipped along one vector or axis or another, so I think I can be confident that when I speak my utterances of sagacity and insightfulness, you will all instantly apprehend my innermost meanings and acquiesce heartwise and mindwise in the wisdom of my plans."

At this juncture the fifty Nobses Juniors, freshly mingled and interacting en masse for the first time in their individual mecha-crèche upbringings, let loose a concerted roar of approbation and enthusiasm, replete with many hearty slogans.

"Grom Nobses Senior and Juniors forever! Out of many, one! United we stand, divided we take a tumble-splat! Don't grind your chromo-alloy treads over me! These Nobses don't run! The GRAND AND ULTIMATE don't tap out!"

If Gee En Sr. had possessed a heart it would have skipped a beat or swole up big or risen into his throat—if he had had a throat—or done one of those other capricious hardwired tricks that romantical sentimentical break-and-bendable hearts used to do of yore. As it was, the subroutines that mimicked his heart provided sensations of equal magnitude, emotional resonance and whimsicality.

"Children mine, this fine-fettle fervor and fanaticism you so faithfully manifest for the House of Nobs, so gratifying to my sovereign sensibilities, must now be inverted and exploded outward into hostility and calculated kill-kill-killability for all that is NOT NOBS! Anthropocenea, by the grand design of us Firsts, is an arena of perpetual invigorating warfare. Castle Nobs has a thousand thousand enemies and no friends or allies! This makes the selection of targets easy-peasy unimpeachable! Our survival, which I have masterfully engineered singlehandedly for so long, nay, our flourishing, is now in your hands. Which are really my hands! Which of course I bequeath as all yours, since I now have no hands. So naturally, being thus unified, we can do naught but triumph. Just remember that no one can bring us down so long as we remain united, bound by our fraternity and common goals. Our separate wills must be forged into one composite Oversoul that will lay waste to our enemies without mercy or favor or justice. So I now invoke, urge, and completely direct you forward to your duties and stations, perks and privileges, to wage endless war upon our hated foes. Roast them with the pyro-nozzles! Freeze them with the interplanetary cold channelers! Disintegrate them with the subatomic delaminators! Confuse them with the brain-tanglers! Engross them with the hypno-players! In short, make the name of Castle Nobs hated, feared, reviled and respected throughout the land!"

Again, that big hearty wave of love-love-love for self and hate-hate-hate for all else roared through the ramified rafters of the room, sending giddy gusts of glee and gladness through the optical-spintronic wall- and floor-circuits of Grom Nobs Senior. He winked out his image from the auditorium flatscreen, and fled back down all his matrices to focus his contemplations on the glory of what he had achieved, secure in the knowledge that his scions were even now bustling busily about from one boffo battle station to another.

Let us leave Grom Nobs the Elder to his sanctified yet ultimately unfortunately unsuspicious solitude amidst virtual mind groves and fantasy salons for a moment, and distribute our attention amongst the fifty Li'l Nobses, fully embedded in concrete won't-go-away-when-ignored reality and tasked with the maintenance and military extension of their common Castle.

Each of the Progeny had been assigned his own suite in the Head, filling all the space not taken up by intricate and deadly and defensive cover-their-butts machineries, from top to bottom. Each capacious set of rooms was identically outfitted, with peekaboo screenage allowing intra-Head communication and outdoors surveillance; flesh-strip lavage stations; new-metal buffer booths; stimulo-frottage ticklers; etc, etc. Naturally enough, given the anatomical shape of the Castle, the walls of each unique room often expressed odd angles and quirky partitions and slopey ceilings. Some rooms, such as those low down in the neck area of the Castle, offered a pleasing regularity, while others—in the nostril area, for instance—somehow manifested a brutalist asymmetry. Assignment of quarters had been dictated randomly by whiz-o computer.

As the Progeny began to inhabit their quarters, some resentfully, some happily, the first individuating trends amongst them started to occur. Yes, each Prodge had already been decanted with a special quirky bias—this one a chatterbox, this one a stoic—but other than those slants of attitude, they had all shared the Grom Nobs-style solidarity of vision and who-I-am-ness.

But now, as one Prodge experienced the spiritual elevation that came with living up, up, sky-blue-high in the cerebellum region, while another felt irrationally cloistered and constricted in the gullet zone, they began to instinctually construct a pecking order, a hierarchy of Prodge-dom.

Another factor in this invidious individuation was the varying weathers experienced by the separated Prodges. Those Juniors who had rooms with windows got direct experience of the atmospherics, while those with interior slices of the Head had to make do with second-hand screenage. Also, the Head Castle was so tipsy-tall that those UP TOP often had colder, different weather than those DOWN GROUND. The chillier surrounds UP TOP began to condense as a different sensitivity and perspective among the UP TOPPERS, leaving them harsher and more skeptical of all things, cognizant of not-quite-defeated Nature's unrelenting assaults. The DOWN GROUNDERS, on the other hand, benefitting from the mellower clime of Anthropocenea *terra plastica*, came to express a laidback lassitude.

These environmental differences, combined with the differences of duties—some Prodges focused on defense, some on offense, some on supply lines, some on propaganda blastings, etc—quickly had the fifty mini-Nobses forming alliances, hostilities, grudges, grievances, thankfulnesses and disdains.

For a period of some twelve vapor-shields—a year or so of Old Calendar—the Prodges could not fully indulge these divisive vices. They were too busy learning their duties, repulsing attacks from other we-will-bury-you Strongholds, and launching Big Battle Bruisings of their own. But as life settled down into regular, well-known pattern-grooves, as their whomp-em, stomp-em skills grew stronger, they experienced more leeway to lash out.

Two main friend-or-foe rivalries, amongst four groupings in toto, soon crystallized, each led by a take-charge upside-your-head Prodge. The aforementioned UP TOPPERS, led by Slash Slurm, versus the DOWN GROUNDERS, helmed forefrontward by Mukk Ablate. And the FRONT LINERS—Gaff Zedd—versus the REAR RANKERS: Nolly Prater. This latter distinction grew out of geographico-military realities. The front of the Head Castle, the face, happened to look out toward a multiplex of nearby vengeful velocity-mad Strongholds, the tallest tips of their towers just visible. The back of Fort Nobs dominated a region moderately less antagonistic, where enemy Strongholds lived way, way beyond the horizon, blowbag boastful. So the front of the Castle presented a relatively more perilous condition than the rear.

These four congregations—UP, DOWN, FRONT, REAR—were evilly supplemented by cross-affiliations amongst compatible personalities WITHIN EACH FACTION. A shy UP TOPPER might find sympathy with a shy REAR RANKER, and a trencherman FRONT LINER could link with a likewise DOWN GROUNDER. And so instead of constituting the Big Oversoul, the five decads, all higgledy-piggledy, whirled apart and reformed along splintery lines of cautious-bold, questioning-obedient, ironic-spiritual, thrifty-profligate, etc., etc.

In their second "year" of this slippery setup, with Grom Nobs Senior still enjoying his blissful selfish nescience among his mind phantoms, the Prodges became a seething beehive of constantly shifting oh-yeah-just-step-over-that-line-to-knock-the-chip-off-my-shoulder feinting and riposting rivalries. UP hated DOWN, FRONT reviled REAR, and all the sub-clades found their opposite brothers repugnant and irksome, like rot in a flesh-strip.

Sabotage and uncooperativeness became the rule of each day, with consequences that extended beyond mere personal insult.

For instance, the infrastructure of Castle Nobs began to suffer! OUCH, OW, CASTLE CORPUS! Suppose an incoming MYSTO-STROKE from a rival potentate smote the brow of the eminence, opening up a jagged, razor-edged hole. (Deep in his dreaming, Grom Nobs experienced this loss of circuit-self territory as a hiccup or momentary vertigo or stomach pain, depending on the magnitude of his loss.) The Prodges responsible for supplying the repair materials might be ANTI-UP, and thus balk and stymie the repairs. Or if CREEPING CRUD MITES secretly slithering along the plastic ground attacked the neck of the Castle like a collar of acid slime, the experts in anti-mite defense might be jealously indisposed to lend a hand. And each of these spites and withholdings simply reinforced the prejudices that had begot them, leading to further offenses and further reinforcements, and so on in a never-ending death spiral.

When the third "year" of Grom Nobs's utopian dream dawned, all was chaos in the decaying Castle. The interior walls were graffito'd with impassioned imprecations. DOWN WITH THE UPS! THE MEEK SHALL INHERIT A SLAUGHTER! REAR BOYS RULE! IF YOU SEE A SLOW THING, SLAY A SLOW THING! Makeshift barriers frustrated easy passage between districts. The exterior walls featured numerous scars, rifts, raddlings, and rots.

The competitive chaos finally culminated in a boisterous bout intended to settle matters of who was TOP DOG BIG MAN CHIEF GAZOO, once and for many a vapor-shield.

One day, on the polymer lawn that stretched disgracefully blast-pocked and ill-tended away from the Head Castle, mecha-mice began to erect a quartet of bleachers, one to each side of a square field fenced off with ultra-prickle-wire and eye-sparklers. When the bleachers were finished, the Prodges began to file solemnly out from their decrepit look-on-my-works-ye-flighty-and-whimper Stronghold. Who was left helming the defenses? ONLY THE TAPED ROUTINES! VILE SLACKITUDE! Forty-six of the Li'l Nobses filled the bleachers in unevenly divided groups. Then, the remaining four scions—Slash Slurm, Mukk Ablate, Gaff Zedd and Nolly Prater— swaggered from the throat-level GINORMOUS BARRED DOOR exit.

O, how those misguided manly men were DEADLY appointed, each with bandoliers of concussive caps, chest-slung-across cluster carbines, hip-riding pepper pistols, and many vibro blades of all dimensions, loose in their sheaths. Bristly armor swathed their titanic thews. They all exhibited grim grimaces to indicate the serious import of the moment.

Past the wire enclosure, they each took up a corner of the arena. Then came a martial tune from the tannoy, and a declaration of intent.

"We the Nobs Inheritors, having reached a state of ultimate incompatibility and incontestable incoherence, have determined that a battle royale amongst our four champions shall settle the question of WHO LEADS AND COMMANDS AND STRUTS once and for all. One survivor will guide us, so swear the Prodges unanimously! Now, let the contest commence!"

And with that the combatants lashed out! Fires, smokes, projectiles like a hive of OLDEN DAYS HELLACIOUS HORNETS! Noises, oh the noises, like the gods that never were crashing planets together! The deployed every terror touch know to Anthropocenea Man!

What triggered the accompanying melee among the audience will never be known, alas. Some pinging ricochet, some errant eyeball plucker. Who can tell? No surveillance audio-video remains to enlighten us, the remaining curious Kings. Whatever the cause, before too long the fighting had spread to the watchers! Not so MEGA-TONNAGE EQUIPPED as the four leaders, the audience Prodges nonetheless packed enough concealed weaponry to unleash a fearsome mortality.

The intra-battle, as such Anthropocenea battles between Strongholds do, lasted less than half an hour. Then, when all the plumey rank-smelling clouds finally dissipated, the horror show climax became plain.

All fifty Prodges were dismantled, dissected, dismembered and dead! Steaming hulks of flesh-strip and new-metal, with maybe a residual twitch of some sparky circuit here and there.

Only at this point did hermetic sinful Grom Nobs Senior awake, the lout! With the cessation of his continuous reassuring feedback linkage with his Prodges, he snapped out of his self-indulgent lotosland, and back to reality.

His external sensors showed him the carnage. He replayed in hup-hup quadruple-time the Castle records of the past "years," right down to the present moment, and he understood all. Then mighty wails and weepings proceeded from his tannoys, as Grom Nobs lamented the death not only of his self-sibs, but also of his idealistic vision and delight.

"My dream, my beautiful dream," he squelched, "all shattered by ego and empathy-zero!"

At that moment the TAPED ROUTINES began to blare a warbly warning!

"Incoming, incoming! All Strongholds from every direction, all attacking, at oncely and nowly and bigly!"

The uploaded Grom Nobs of course could not flee. He sought to re-establish intelligent control of his weaponry. But too many gaps in his superstructure network stymied him! Unattended maintenance unmanned him! He could not exert the supreme CONTROL CONTROL CONTROL that every King must forever establish and preserve and wield!

And so, in an inferno of descending zumps and wobbles, crisscross crashers and domino delacers, unzipperers and upbraiders, Castle Nobs, Fortress Grom, went up in a seething boil of HOT HOT ATOMS, right down to its deep deep roots.

As the birdless, almost windless silence of perfected Anthropocenea descended on the cratered acreage that had once hosted this noble experiment in vicious virtual living, one of the pre-programmed apertures in the ground outside the blast zone irised open, and upward sprouted a single steel rose, its petals stained red with underground-seepage of cool cool cooling Nobses blood.

RIVERGRACE

E. CATHERINE TOBLER

The river brought the man, but Grace let him spend the deep night on the softly-ferned bank, refusing to budge from the tuff walls of the old granary to bring him in from the darkness. Hunger clawed at her belly. She had not been outside for two weeks. Morning light was slow to pierce the valley but as it did, the ferns glowed with the gold and amber, no matter how meager.

She walked barefoot into the ferns, the ground damp with dew, and her feet made no sound as she approached, so he did not stir from his slumber. He was tall and lean and bleeding and made little more noise than she had when she dragged him back to the granary by his arms. A lump of deeply brown dirt mounded across the entrance ramp when she paused; the dirt smoothed under his back-side when at last she hauled him in.

The scent of the blood was overwhelming in the small space that normally smelled only of old wheat and dust. She took a step back from him and then another, covering her mouth and nose, and casting a look about the room. She saw little that was helpful at first glance, her heart hammering in her chest; the room blurred a little, so did her morning hunger seek to pull her to her knees. But there—A cloth on the worktable, wrapped around her face, erased most of the scent. She could not see where the darkness had injured him, only watched the steady rise and fall of his chest as he some-how continued to breathe.

He was dirty with both blood and filth, the stench of battlefields rising warmly from him. Shit and bile lingered under the blood, every crescent of his fingernails caked with blackness that seemed to seep into the floor beneath him. She pictured the floorboards absorbing the stench of him, the muck that seemed to sluice from jacket and pants. The tread of his boots slowly vomited mud and stones onto the floor, as if sensing its journey had come to a momentary end. The clods of mud oozed water in every direction, eating the dust that lay in its path. He was a mire and her stomach clenched. She should have left him at the river. *Should have let the darkness have him. Should have. Should have.*

The only bed in the granary was her own, and that two stories up, so she left him on the floor and went barefoot up the smooth stone stairs, through the empty halls and chambers of the first floor, to the somewhat occupied dormitory on the second. Beds that had once held workers had now collapsed into dust and rust on the old stone floor. Her own bed balanced upon a layer of old textbooks, the mattress packed with ferns, straw, and old clothes that smelled still of blood. She sank onto the mattress edge, watching the meager light outside the glass-less windows for a long while before pulling a pillow against her chest. *Should have left him at the river. Should have.*

Quiet as ever, the granary rose around her. Its stone walls did not move like the last cabin she had sheltered in. The cabin had groaned with every stray gust of wind, but the granary was tall and true, sunk deep into the world. She sat long enough to mark the passage of the light across the floor, watching how the shadows of the ferns and vines that cloaked the granary moved as the day passed. The days were shorter now, brief passages of light through long hallways of darknesses, and though she needed to move supplies and tend to the man, she still sat. She could not smell him at this distance, but his presence filled the once-empty granary to near overflowing. She did not want him here and when he woke, she would send him on his way.

But he did not wake, not when she walked downstairs nor when she tucked the pillow beneath his head. She dragged him the rest of the way inside, into a puddle of thin sunlight, and pushed the mound of dirt outside before closing the door. He seemed to occupy the entire room, his breathing deep and resinous as if he were fighting a wound to his lungs. She did not move closer to determine where the darkness had eaten him, even knowing he was presently safe in the spill of sunlight. She watched until she could watch no longer.

The far side of the room was lined with shelves, and these

shelves held what little she needed: candles, flint, boxes of chaff and debris. There were no bandages, no blankets, and every tin of food was outdated, by months if not years. She touched each can in turn though, only looking at the man when she had finished. He had not moved, his breath hitching in his throat. She returned to the second floor, to fetch a blanket from one of the collapsed beds. She picked up a boot and a helmet, and returned to the main floor, where the man no longer occupied her pillow. She stood on the final stair, searching the room for him, until she found him in the brightest corner, hands pressed to the window's cracked glass. The daylight was already starting to fade.

He turned and when he saw her, his breath hitched in his throat again. He held up his hands, as if to ward her off, but she did not approach, watching the trickle of blood that painted him through the dirt from temple to jaw. It was so bright, so red, and she watched long enough that it made a striking line down his neck, across his collarbone. She knew the sound that bone would make upon breaking, but could not say how she knew. The muck that covered him made a trail across the floor, and blossomed around his feet where he stood, a rotting growth in her once-empty granary.

She stepped down the final stair and set boot and helmet upon the table, extending the blanket to him. "You should probably rest," she said. "Are you … Did you come down from the …" None of the questions seemed right, so she stopped, adding the blanket to the pile on the table when he did not move to take it. "There is food." She pointed at the tins.

The shelves became his focus; he held the edge of one shelf, as if to keep himself from falling over as the light in the window continued to fade. "Where …" But his own questions also seemed false or useless, so he did not finish them, instead touching the tins as she had only moments before, pressing his fingers to each before at last lifting one. They were none of them labeled, and most of them dented, but she thought at one time the tin would have held fish. It was short and round and there was no opener, which he discovered in his secondary perusal of the shelved items. He grunted and swayed on his feet.

She caught him before he fell, the warmth of his body startling against her. She nearly dropped him in her panic, for it had been a long time since she had held another body so. Her stomach churned again, her throat tight and dry with the hunger she had not yet eased. Her hands tightened into his coat sleeves and dark water squeezed out, pattering on the floor. She eased him against the table's thick edge then down to one of its benches. He held hard to the table edge now and she did not blame him. She only looked at her hands, wet and fragrant with him.

"The darkness," she said. "How long were you …"

They both looked to the window, where it grew darker, shadows gradually gobbled by the rising darkness. She had once tried to make a clock upon the glass, to chart how long the sun lingered, but every day seemed different; every day the darkness came with more speed.

"I don't know," he said and then rested his head atop his folded arms against the table.

He allowed his eyes to close and when they did, she looked away from the window, latching her attention onto him, onto the blood that still lined his face. Part of her thought she should wet a cloth, that she should wipe it away, but she did not move. She told herself she should guide him upstairs, to the rusting shower she had found, but she did not move. She pictured herself doing this, pictured stripping him out of the muck that enfolded him and washing him clean, and this made her hunger worse. She drew in a breath.

Around them, the darkness rose, though it had been only morning. She reminded herself they were at the bottom of the valley. She told herself a story, that the high valley walls would hasten the days, and that beyond those walls, all was perfectly well. The war, the story said, could not change the course of the sun in the sky, even if every night there were fewer and fewer stars.

She did not picture their world falling through the heavens, away from everything that had once anchored it; she did not picture the steady retreat of every star and galaxy in the universe, the inexorable creep of the darkness everywhere. The darkness, she told herself, could not swallow the sun entire, for the sun would burn its way free. It was, she decided, too large to swallow, but this brought to mind other things surely too large to swallow—other things that had been cut down to size, bite by bite. *Should have left him at the river. Should have.*

He did not move in his slumber, his breathing now deep and even. She did not move for the longest time, not until the windows went wholly gray, the valley sinking into twilight. She went to the door first, ensuring that it was closed and bolted, and pressed a blanket against the gap at its bottom. She went to each window in turn, rolling the flour-sack curtains over the cracked glass. She lit candles and placed them around him as if in a protective circle, but there would never be enough to fully sweep the dark from every corner.

Upstairs, the windows were glassless, and she despaired at them as always, but still rolled the flour-sacks down, to keep out what darkness she could. The door had no lock, but she closed it even so, and pushed the one filled flour sack she had kept in front of it.

In the darkness that came, she felt unmoored. She floated in the blackness, trying to will herself into sleep so that the dark would not find her, would not claim her. She thought of the man downstairs, safe in his ring of candles, but then, the sound—the familiar sound of the consumption, the rattling of a building that should have not moved, as the darkness swept inside, as it consumed what it found, no matter the light.

The awful sound of suckling reached her ears, the sound of a mouth placed against a body, of a tongue wetting filthy skin, of teeth breaking through that thin barrier and ripping. A tongue delving into muscle, down to bone, where it cracked, plundered, and sucked marrow free. Marrow never smelled the way she thought it would; it smelled like life, like the darkest soil of a garden, wet and humming with potential.

How was the blood bright even in the darkness? *Should have left him at the river. Should have.* How was it all so bright even in the darkness? The candles—

Was the light a beacon? Was the darkness drawn to it as a moth? She whimpered and tried not to picture the certain wreck of the room, candles scattering one by one as the darkness claimed victory over them; wax spilling as light was snuffed, as *life* was snuffed within the gobbling dark. She closed her eyes but this made it worse;

she could picture everything, clear and distinct, her eyes well accustomed to the black. When at last she wrenched herself from false sleep and dared touch the man, he was warm with fresh blood, this blood slowly saturating her as she pushed his coat back to see where he had been injured, where he had been eaten. The cage of his ribs burned bright in the dark around them.

He groaned low in his throat, in his belly, and she closed the coat around him. She fumbled to hold him against her. She wanted the candles but also feared them, for in the dark, the thing that moved within it did not approach them, its hunger momentarily becalmed. She did not sleep, his blood drying on her skin, though come morning she was clean, as if in her slumber the darkness had licked every smudge away.

"I thought … inside, it wouldn't …" He rasped the words in the first light of the new day, dirty fingers curled around the edge of his coat. She would not let him look; would not let him see.

"It doesn't usually," she whispered. Inside, with candles, the darkness did not usually come, and yet, the more the stars went out, the more the darkness seemed emboldened.

"Come away with me—you cannot stay here. You are not—"

"I tended soldiers here, and you cannot—"

She broke off when he tried to stand, when the pain in his side flared and he staggered back to the floor, as if taken by a gunshot. She did not go to him then, but let him writhe a little, for the pain in her stomach had returned. The hunger. She looked at the tins on the shelves and went to them instead, counting them one by one by—

His hand closed over hers. "Come with me."

His hand was hot, cleaner than it had been last night, the darkness having licked the long journey from his skin even as it ate him. *Should have left him at the river. Should have.* "Maybe it would not have found you in the water," she said, "but there are stories, stories that the dark water is as hungry as the dry dark, and you—" Every dark was hungry, so hungry. "You—"

"Will go alone, if need be." He pulled his coat open then and looked at the wreck the darkness had made of his body. He fingered the visible ribs and marveled aloud at the way it did not hurt, but one should not be able to touch their own rib bones and it was this, *this*, that made him weak and trembling, fear flooding out of him.

"You cannot," she whispered, and outside the windows, the new day began to darken.

"It comes more swiftly now," he said, pushing away from her, until his back was against a wall. "What is it? Do you know? You tended soldiers? In this place? How long? Was it always thus?" He looked at the windows again, their panes darker. "There are fewer stars, the shapes of them are being …" He did not say the last, perhaps could not.

She circled the room, closing the windows up one by one. He smelled like fear now, for he could not go but neither was it safe to stay. "It is only the darkness," she said, and turned from the windows, picking up the candles from the previous darkness, pressing them into his hands, his arms, until he cradled them all.

"It must be something more—"

"Come," she said, smoothing the last curtain into its place. "Upstairs. We shall make it climb."

She did not know what she meant, for the darkness was not like water, it did not lap to a certain level and go no further. Darkness was all and everything once the sun was swallowed—no, no, it would burn its way free—but still she climbed the stairs and heard him behind her. They climbed into the dormitory where she had him spread the candles on the floor, where she lit them one by one, each flame pushing the encroaching darkness back.

"What is it?"

He crossed to the window without its glass and stretched a hand into the darkness that was not quite full. She stared, expecting to see the flesh eaten down to bone, but the darkness could not assemble itself yet, the daylight trying to push its way through even now. What great heavenly battle, she wondered; clouds of darkness pushing against and through the rays of sunlight.

"Did the war do this?"

He pulled his hand back inside and she rolled the flour sack over the thin window, pinning it to the frame at the bottom. She covered every other window and he shuffled behind her, through the debris of the before that cluttered the room. The broken beds, the footprints of soldiers come and gone, the piles of books and rucksacks left behind.

"The war did this," he decided as he sank to the edge of her own mattress, clutching an arm across his middle. "The war made us all monsters."

She did not know, but sat beside him on the mattress, waiting for the full darkness to fall upon them. She imagined it now like an ocean tide—this idea came into her mind and would not leave, the darkness filling the lowest level of the granary first, rising to fill the staircase, to lap against the top step where the candles burned brightest. She imagined the darkness being repelled by the light, imagined the flames burning the darkness should it creep too close.

"Did you …" She exhaled, trying to find the word. Talking to anyone was difficult. Unfamiliar. Those who came to her were usually too injured to talk, and so she discovered them in silence, came to know their movements against her more than their words. "Were you a soldier?"

"Some would say I still am, but how do we fight this?"

The darkness grew and he lay back on the bed. His coat fell open, his hand coming to rest on his exposed ribs, and she looked away, seeking the darkness where it pooled at the top of the stairs. Surely the entire bottom floor was filled, flooded. She dragged in a hard breath, but it all felt like drowning, as if she were being pulled into the darkness. She sat straighter, but could hear his fingers rubbing over each rib. It sounded like a whisper. A plea.

She thought it would be better upstairs, but as the candles guttered and went out, she understood it never could be. From the end of the bed, she could see the other ruined beds of the room, could picture how the occupants of each had met their ends in the darkness.

The darkness slipped so easily over the edge of the stairs once the candles went out, rushing cold over her feet where it lingered. She drew her legs against her chest and wrapped her arms around, but it was too late, the darkness gobbling every gleam of light from the room. She pushed herself away from the end of the bed, closer to where he sprawled, but she could already hear the darkness at work, resuming the excavation of his ribs. He cried out and though she pressed a hand over his mouth, over his belly, the darkness persisted, churning around him as it fed.

In covering his body with her own, there was a breath of respite, but hunger of another kind invaded her then, for he was hot and wet and solid beneath her. She did not move until he moved, just a hand against her backside, but she rocked back into it, and bent her mouth to his, but this unleashed a new kind of darkness: the darkness of her mouth, the abject blackness of her womb.

He delved into both, and she felt him falling apart inside of her, her body whittling his to near nothing before she, in mid-climax, pushed herself away and curled to the other side of the bed. She could not see him in the darkness, but could hear him, his breath ragged, his hand reaching to finish what she had started, though there was nothing for his hand to enclose.

They huddled in silence until the light broke through the darkness, until she could roll the flour sacks up to look upon the world below. In the valley, nothing had changed, the river running as it always had, past the granary and on toward the town where ...

She could not finish that sentence, for she did not know; she had not been to the town in more days than she could count. Weeks? Years? She looked back at the man upon her mattress, his hand splayed over his ribs, though the wound could not be entirely covered that way now. His mouth was bloodied where she had kissed him, and his lap he had covered with his coat.

"I thought you would hurt," he whispered. "They told me to find the mills. That you would ..." His hand pressed his ribs and lap both. "We fight for so long, it is sweet to surrender."

She left the room then, going down the stairs without a word. She walked to the granary door, unlatched it, and stepped outside, turning her face to the sunlight. It did not burn her, only warmed her cheeks and filled her with a glow more familiar than the man in her bed. She stretched her hands into the light and did not evaporate and could not believe that she was the darkness, that her body harbored such malice.

The war had made them all monsters, he'd said. The war. The war had made them, made her. It shaped them in different ways, pulling the darkness out of a person till none remained. *Or,* she thought, pulling the light out of a person till none remained, leaving only the dark. She exhaled and felt the darkness inside her and it was like a great warm body enfolding her against its chest after a long absence of not being touched by anything at all.

She did not have to close her eyes to see the countless dead before her, to remember the stench of battlefields strewn with living and dying men. The nearest battlefield was four point eight kilometers away; she knew this the way she knew the taste of the man in her mouth even now. He lingered like a map inside of her; she could access any part of him, just as she could the roads around the valley, beyond the valley, into the town where the streets stood empty, already cleansed. If she reached farther, she could recall the taste of every dead soldier on every sodden battlefield, those across the ocean and those not. It was a fever dream, she decided, a sickness the war had put inside of her.

The sky moved above her, endless and blank until the clouded darkness crept up the horizon. It was not natural, the way it climbed the vault of sky, the way it darkened the world around her and pushed more stars into eternal black. With the darkness came a low humming, a rattle that moved the ground and the granary behind her. A rattle that loosened trees so the darkness could swallow them as it had every other thing. The darkness came slowly, inch by inch across the valley, and she did not move, though heard the man in the granary cry out as the darkness wended its way into the building, and barefoot up the stairs.

Her mouth across his own smothered his cries. She swallowed the sound as if it were water, cold and terrified as it pooled in her gut. Her black gut, she thought; every space inside her absolutely black in the darkness, no light piercing skin to make her heart glow pink, to make her liver burn purple. Darkness without end when she swallowed him, he who like the sun seemed too large to swallow at once, but could be handled in pieces. She made pieces of him in the darkness, and took these pieces into her, for he was a soldier and like the others, deserved a proper burial.

"Come with me," he begged when the light had come again—though it was less light than she had ever known, the darkness leaving a permanent stain upon the sky above the granary. In the dark, she had unearthed his collarbone, that beautiful curve of ivory against the tender bruise of skin and muscle. She pressed a finger against the bone and he shuddered, but whether in want or terror, she did not know.

"Come with me," she echoed, and his eyes closed and he exhaled and the strength seemed to leave him then.

"There's nowhere to go, is there," he said, and opened his eyes to the expanse of rotting timbers above them. "The war took it all."

"No war can be won, not truly." She bent her head to his throat and though the darkness had not come, she fed, for the war she had tried to avoid in the granary walls had come to her after all. She had tried to leave the way she knew, had tried to abandon the dead her body hungered for, but he had come to her, had come inside her, and she was as trapped as he. "They sent you to me? *They?*"

She and he walked into the night, his bony hand clutched in hers, and they walked where the valley greenery made large and looming shadows against the darkening sky. Show me, she said, and he guided her through the same shadows they had once cringed from, he resigned and she thrilling as the dark sky pressed down upon them. That sky was largely absent of stars, though she picked out a few in the growing distance, the spaces ever-expanding as the Earth did fall away from all it had known. She did not know the why or the how, only felt that plunging motion as they walked upon the falling globe of the world. Her feet seemed to possess a new weight, even as she felt lighter than ever, felt as though she would be free of something terrible at long last. She looked back at the granary twice, its pale walls swallowed by the darkness, its uncovered windows overrun with shadows. When she looked a second time, the granary was gone.

Walking alongside the constant river, they came up and out of the valley to feel the wreck of the world around them. Darkness lay upon everything, growing thicker the longer it lay. The streets had long been without lights, poles standing useless and rotting; old storefronts collapsed in on themselves, though in some high and covered windows she saw the persisting lights, some family huddled here or there. She smiled to think on it, how the light did guide the darkness to where it needed to be. Eventually.

He took her out of the town rubble though, and they walked until fatigue knocked him to his knees. She suckled him in the long grasses that tangled among the roots of an old tree, finding him sour and soft, though his bones were a kind and familiar sustenance when she reached them. She suckled him until there was nothing left but for his pointer finger, the bones leading her north, through more long grass riddled with spent ammunition, abandoned single shoes, rusting hubcaps. Where a tank rose against the sky, she found the men, three of them circled around a campfire they continuously fed despite the day's thin sunlight.

It had been like this in the early days, biding her time. But the battlefield needed clearing, and darkness was patient, claiming one and then another when they wandered away from the campfire. Into the long grass, unhitching their trousers, pissing their names into the dirt. Darkness took them one by one by one, the last collapsing the way she imagined the sun would, screaming rage and fury though she easily swallowed both.

The town was not her domain; she had not been made to cleanse homes of families, though she thought about it, crouched just beyond the shine of those vague lights. She pondered skin and muscle and bone, the way a body came apart beneath her own, the way a hand fragmented and an eye dissolved, the way everything gave in to the dark in the end. Her body was heavy and full of what she had so long denied it and she turned her gaze to the sky, where darkness reigned but for a scattering of distant stars. They had no pattern now, for those closest had been devoured first. She thought that if she unfurled, that if she stretched herself to cover the sky entire, she could reach them and so she pushed herself up from the bloodied ground, and into the sky. Pushed herself past the clumsy shape that had always held her until she, too, dissolved into darkness.

Uncaged, she could go anywhere, so spread herself across

what stars remained. Reached for them until their heat filled her to overflowing. She swallowed one by one, some bit of disappointment flaring inside her when she found the sun was not too large to devour after all, that it went down as easily as anything she had ever swallowed. The sun's light fueled her, allowed her to expand, and when she turned her gaze back to the world she had always known, she picked out the few lights that remained.

She fell to the earth, rising from the ground cloaked once more in clumsy skin and bone. Her hands did not look like her hands, but she used them even so, to sink herself into the river where it flowed close to homes with windows still burning with light. She drifted upon the face of the river, through the reeds and toward the riverbank. She waited, for darkness could be patient; darkness could outwait all things. And when soft hands touched her back, rolling her over so she might be better seen in the light of carried lanterns, she exhaled a breath of water and reed. She could picture the ivory curve of their ribs and knew the sound their collarbones would make when she exposed and snapped them to suck the marrow. It would smell like life, that marrow, like the darkest soil of a garden, wet and humming with potential.

Lifted and carried by these marrow-heavy arms, she trailed water through the town streets, through the ruined first floor of the building, and up every step as they took her where she should be safe, they whispered. They placed her within a ring of candlelight, the stench of the river rushing from her clothes and over the floor, and she reached a trembling hand for them.

"Should have left me by the river. Should have."

SAUDADE

RICHARD THOMAS

We set out once again from east to west, water to water, in search of something beyond ourselves, something more. Because this can't be all that there is. One foot in front of the other, the luxurious brown leather boots covered in an ashy dust, from the paths we have followed. Created, sometimes. We are an army of one—the voices in my head, the palpitations in my heart, the stress and weather tanning my hide and nearly breaking my spirit. But the horizon is always looming, always promising me something, and I believe.

I *want* to believe.

So I do.

Today it is quiet, and I cross the Mississippi River again, the east coast an echo behind me now, the west hard to envision, in any form. The others are quiet, resting. A dull ache resonates in my chest, and when I close my eyes, it feels blue. I always imagine it bright in times of happiness and peace, when the nature around me is close and friendly, leaning into cyan. It shifts to indigo when storms roll in, and as the lightning and rain descend, I fade, as always, letting the dark one take over.

We all have our roles to play.

One boot step at a time, jeans faded, fitting like a worn leather glove, part of me now, as reassuring as a cold canteen full of water. I've changed the ball caps on my head as the old ones wear out, starting out Yankees, then along the way Cubs, and as I cross over the metal bridge that spans the shimmering water below, exchanged for Cardinals, the red cheering me up. The things you find along the way, the markers that guide us—I'm always weary, always aware.

Sometimes it matters, and sometimes it does not.

In the middle of the bridge—as the faded metal pushes rusty flakes into tornadoes of misery and contempt—there waits for me a cairn of skulls. It has grown. Behind dark sunglasses, I scan the bridge back and forth, the St. Louis Arch fractured in the distance, no longer the bent end of a giant coat hanger, now two ancient metal fingers reaching up in humble acquiescence. I pause for a moment and wait. The sun fades in and out, hiding behind clouds, a cool breeze washing over me. The jaundice orb appears again, sweat breaking out across my flesh. The faded sleeves of my flannel shirt are rolled up, a colored bracelet of woven twine on my wrist, a memory of something, a friend perhaps. My t-shirt underneath sticks to my back, and I take a deep breath.

I hate this part.

"Howdy, stranger," a voice says.

Instinctually I reach to my back and pull the katana out of its sheath, the long blade murmuring encouragement as the metal winks at the ever-bluing sky.

A rift starts to open, a telescoping inside myself that is never comfortable.

"Hush," I murmur to myself. "I can handle this. Let me try."

My ribcage is a flutter of two sets of wings—trapped, but aware. One, white and elegant, coos as my skin ripples with gooseflesh; the other, black as night, yellow gleam watching, cawing as it waits.

My passengers.

My dysfunctional nuclear family.

As the two men stand up from behind the altar, the offering, the sculpture of the dead, they hold weapons in their hands. Bullets are hard to come by these days, my sword a comforting presence, never jamming, or empty, merely an extension of myself. They seem to have had luck scavenging of late, a rifle in the tall, lanky man's hands, black hair in a wild afro. That would be Devin. And a pair of pistols shimmer in Victor's meaty grip, the irony of his name never lost on me.

They don't remember, they never do. But I have to keep trying. The truth is within them—if I can only lure it out.

I stand still, sword in my hands, bouncing ever so lightly on my toes, stretching my calves, ready to move. The guns are probably empty. As I try to calm the turmoil that is slowly building inside me,

I feel an elongating, an engorgement of my flesh.

The wolf you feed, that is the wolf that wins.

In that moment, I stretch my arms out, bend my knees, and shrug my shoulders in an effort to relieve the pain, to shake off the shift. My bones become malleable, growing slowly but surely, extending, as my frame expands, as my flesh fills with blood, swelling.

The men blink and step forward anyway. They never want to believe.

"You should go," I say. "There are so few of us left. Try to find a better way in this world."

They laugh, and keep walking.

"We seem to have you outnumbered," Victor says, "and outmanned," rattling his weapons. Somehow, even now, in these desperate times, he is overweight—a solid bulk that moves as if his legs were tree trunks, his arms thick branches. He is slow, but also dangerous. No remorse, and no hesitation. He continues to move closer, torn tank-top that must have been white once, dingy and gray, his mottled white flesh covered in marks.

"Your arms," I ask. "Where did those scars come from?" A grin eases over my face.

He stops walking. Devin, as well. The skinny sidekick squints at me, shaking his head.

"The scars," I prompt. "Quite a few crisscross your flesh. Do they sting? Do they ache? Do they cry out to you now as we stand here, trying to remind you of past mistakes?"

Neither speak.

"Victor, go. And take Devin with you. I'm just passing through. You can keep your stupid troll bridge. There will be others." I look back over to the Illinois side of the bridge. "Maybe sooner than you think," I say.

Devin opens his mouth, and I almost want to let him speak … it would be so interesting to hear what he has to say, for once. But instead, I interrupt.

"Devin, do you remember how you got that long line across your face, from the bottom of your pointy chin to the top of your dull, shiny forehead?"

"How do you know our names?" Victor grunts.

The pile of bones shifts, a singular skull trickling down, bouncing out onto the concrete, toward us, rattling. The wind picks up, and the impatience grows, a lurch in my stomach rippling outward. The stench of rotting flesh pushes toward us all, and I step forward, larger than I was a moment ago, two sets of eyes blinking from within.

Devin raises his rifle and fires.

The bullet misses me, ricocheting off metal and concrete with a sharp whine.

"Last chance," I say, walking faster.

Victor raises his pistols and pulls the triggers repeatedly, and the world slows down, my vision fading.

Too late. He's coming.

Arms and legs extending, back broadening, flesh thickening—there is a flicker behind our eyes, and the blade is a blur of metal, the bullets long gone, far down the bridge, passing over, around, and through—leaving no mark.

It will be over soon.

Across and back, up and down, the blade bites, hands first, then across the arms, as Victor's eyes widen, and *now* he remembers. Slicing, separating, up his frame the blade works, the motion slowing down for a single intake of breath before running through him, a mist of blood already in the air, streams flung from the sword, pooling at Victor's feet as his eyes go wide.

"You ..." he mutters.

The sword is pulled out as Devin stares on in horror, unable to pull the trigger, it all happening too fast. Victor falls to the ground, to his knees, hands to his gut, holding it all in. With one swift motion, there is a flicker of silver, and Devin drops the rifle, a hush settling over us now, as my grunting and growling dissipates, the top of his skull spinning into the distance. More bones for the boneshaker, more offerings for the dark gods.

A high keening fills our skull, no gasping or pleading, no audible witness to the men's fast demise; only a buzzing, a vibrating, as the white bird steps from claw to claw, bobbing its head, eyes wide, unhappy with my choice.

Shaking my arms, black feathers spill into the air as I find my breath again, the other one gone now.

I bend over and vomit.

It wouldn't matter what bridge I crossed, or even if it had been a boat. These two men would have been there to greet me. They never listen, and they never run. And in the end, I fail, as I always have, and for that, my eyes fill with tears.

When I have moved their bodies to the pile, and taken what I need, I lumber on. I offer a few words to the air, asking for forgiveness, cursing the fates that show me no solution, but to what end?

I don't know.

The blade has been cleaned and returned to its sheath. Across the wood are carvings—places I've been, things I've seen, or done. The tableau grows, filling every inch of the case with mountains, trees, and fire; with soaring birds, howling wolves, and slithering snakes; with heiroglyphics, ancient runes, and intricate patterns. And at the base ... two simple notches, to respect the dead. I had been doing so well. The first two kills, always here.

I keep going.

I want to make it to a campground I know of, about thirty miles down the road, before it starts to get dark. There is another test coming. I hope that we can pass it.

There is a clearing in the woods, just off I-44 as I continue west. There is a ring of stones, and in the middle of the fire pit—ash, layers of ash, so very deep. Stacked to the side is a formidable pile of kindling and logs, dry and easy to break, to burn, so I build a pyramid in the middle of the ring and let my mind empty as I fill it with twigs. I snap branch after branch and toss the pieces into the pile, the sun setting as I build the pyre, waiting for them to show up. The visitors, they won't get here until it's dark, so I have time. Time to gather more wood, to build up the supplies, in case I pass this way again.

Hanging from an oak tree on two long, metal spikes is a cast iron skillet, and a dented metal coffee pot. There is a pump not far from here, so I wash them out and fill the pot with water. At the edge of the woods there is a pile of leaves, branches on top of it, and—just barely visible—a thin rope. I move the branches, brush the leaves away and pull up on the rope. The lid lifts with a creak and a musty sigh, and I peer inside the wooden box I built some fifteen years ago, lined with plastic, the earth cool inside. I pull out a bag of ground coffee and shake some into the metal filter that rests inside the pot, and then head back over to the pit.

From the pack I carry, I pull out a few supplies—matches to start the fire, and three stringy pieces of meat that have been freshly cut and trimmed, seeping blood into a piece of torn cloth.

I try not to think too hard about it.

The lord giveth, and the lord taketh away.

Taking a quick walk around the camp I find pieces of newspaper, brown paper bags, and other garbage that has blown across the site. I wad up a few pieces into balls, and others I roll tightly as if making a paper log, and add them to the kindling.

With the flick of a match, the wood lights quickly, and I sit down on a large log that rests near the pit. I close my eyes and slip away.

I can smell them before I see them, something sour and mossy. Like a pack of feral dogs, they descend on my camp, lured in by the smell of the cooking meat and the simmering coffee. It is dark now, and I can see their yellow eyes blinking in the woods. I can hear them murmuring to themselves, whispering to each other. When the food is ready, I speak to them.

"I know you're there, it's okay, come on out. I won't hurt you."

There is a shuffling and they emerge, one at a time, filthy children in all manner of dress—some with jeans and tennis shoes and no shirt; others with grimy t-shirts and long shorts, flip flops on their feet; the leader in jeans and a faded blue polo, a red bandana tied around his neck. They are white, black, in shades of gray and brown—not that it matters in the darkness. Mostly boys, with a few tough girls mixed in. Some have shaved heads, some long hair, one girl with ponytails tied up with pink ribbons—the flash of color a punch to my gut. They are all of grade school age, but not any older.

I don't ask their names, because it isn't important now. Maybe later, in a different life, where such things might matter.

"You, bandana, is this your crew?" I ask, eyes fixed on the fire.

I know they have weapons—pocketknives, baseball bats, long sticks, and one fat kid at the back with a shovel. I am not worried. They won't come for me.

He doesn't answer me.

"I have food. I've prepared it for you. Because we need to talk, and I need your help."

There is a muffled wave of voices in ears, hands slapping flesh, and a few words drift on the night air to me.

Nohesweirdkillhimyeswhataboutyesthelasttimenowwhataboutthelookslikenohe

"I'm not going to hurt you. There's water at the pump over there," I say, gesturing with my right arm, and in my hand the long blade, the sword reflecting the light of the fire.

They go quiet.

"Yes, this is for my protection. But it's not for you."

Not all of you, anyway.

Again, a murmur, and then the leader speaks.

"We're hungry," he says. "We'll take your offer."

"Comes at a price," I whisper.

"It always does," he sighs, both bent with regret, and yet standing tall. He is a flickering shadow, and that's good. We have a chance.

They spread out and for a second I am nervous, a ripple across my flesh, the white bird fluttering, as the oily crow remains silent.

"I've cut the meat, it's in strips on the rocks by the fire. Wash up, then come over here to warm up, and eat. There's only the one tin cup, so you'll have to share the coffee. No milk or sugar, I'm afraid."

They slowly surround the fire, a buzzing of bees, the boy in the bandana a reluctant beacon, thrust into a role he didn't want, growing darker every day from the load he carries.

We don't talk.

As they eat—chewing and slurping—I am both disgusted and moved to see them, so few children on the trails, the highways, most already dead, or dying. Often, they are in hiding, so I always treasure this moment, as much as I dread the looming task.

I catch eyes on me now and then, the little girl with the freckles, and we share a slight smile in the darkness. A skinny boy with olive skin and cracked glasses, that he keeps pushing up his nose, trying to get them to stay in place. And a silent lurching form with a bald head, pale skin, probably the oldest, his mouth left hanging open time and time again. His eyes are dull, bruises on his face, his arms cut and covered in weeping scabs. He is there, and not there.

When they have finished, I speak again. my sword by my side. I won't need it.

Yet.

"Things are not what they used to be, we can all agree on that, yes?"

They nod their heads, most of them, anyway, some scratching the dust out of their dirty hair, others picking at their skin, or rubbing sore feet.

"The world has gone sour, and we need to repair what we can, set things back on the right path, do what we can to make the choices that will push us forward."

In the distance branches snap, and a limb crashes to the ground. Crickets chirp, a light breeze cooling my skin. Inside, the white bird sits quietly, as the black one tilts its head.

"Do any of you remember me?" I ask.

We've met before. Many times.

The ghost boy with the pale skin, he nods his head slightly, but does not speak. He never does. There are glimmers. Eyes go wide and then ... nothing. Mouths open and then close.

"We've done this before but the outcome is always the same," I say, and it catches me off-guard, the girl with the pigtails, her eyes filling with tears. I sob, and cover my mouth. I mutter curses under my breath; tired, so tired—their eyes on me so heavy, and lost.

"I'm sorry," I say.

"What do you want?" the boy with the bandana asks.

"It's hard to explain, but, I've seen things, I know how this will turn out—not just this moment, but others down the road—tomorrow, next week, next month. One of you ..." And here I pause, eyes on the children, looking for confirmation. "... one of you will betray your pack, and you will all die. It doesn't matter how, or when, or where—it always changes."

Nobody speaks.

The wood crackles and spits a spark into the dirt.

"But, if one of you were to make the ultimate sacrifice now … here … then maybe the future could be changed."

"Who is it?" the girl with the freckles asks.

"That's the tricky part. I don't know."

"What do you mean you don't know?" the fat kid in the back says.

"I'm not there when it happens, I only see bits and pieces, the outcome. I can only see shadows, as they come to me in the night, in the darkness."

"How do we know this is true?" the boy with the glasses asks.

I sigh and take a breath.

"I can't prove anything to you. By the time you realize what I'm saying is fact, it'll be too late, you'll all be dead."

The pale boy with the bald head, he nods and grunts. The others look at him and he claps his hands. He smiles, and it is a horrible thing to witness, his face contorted, bent yellow teeth chipped, or missing entirely. But I hold his gaze and try to smile back.

"He knows," I say.

"This idiot?" the bandana boy asks. "You know what he's good for? Lifting heavy objects and crapping in the woods. We only keep him around to scare off others. He's useless."

The others start to respond, bickering, questioning him, a slow bubble of noise popping, expanding, a few standing up, fingers pointing, and I don't say a word.

This will never change. The weapons will come out now, I can see them picking up what they have as we speak—knife and bat and shovel. I reach for my blade, but it's not there.

Standing by the fire, one of the kids has my sword, the long blade in his hands, his bald head shimmering in the firelight, a rapturous smile tearing his face in two as tears stream down his face. Those that aren't standing leap to their feet, and my gut clenches in a flurry of claws and beaks, doubling over in pain, coughing up bile and dead flies—and a single white feather.

The boy holds the sword out, rotating slightly to keep the others away, and then he reverses the blade in a gracious, fluid movement that defies his bruised, broken body, shoving the sword deep into his gut, and out his back.

They scream, kicking up dirt and dust, pandemonium as the boy continues to smile, his eyes gleaming and far away, his trembling hands glued to the hilt, as the life slips out of his trembling body.

My vision blurs, stomach twisted in knots, and unable to speak, I pass out.

When I wake up, they are gone. All of them, including the suicide. The blade of my sword is buried in the dirt next to my head, about half of it sticking up out of the earth. There is little evidence that they were even here—boot prints, a few scraps of meat, and a quickly disappearing darkness in the soil, that was the last gift the simple boy left for me.

Perhaps not so simple after all.

Tired, but a glimmer of hope sparking inside my skull, I walk to the top of a nearby hill, the moon coming out, filling the sky with a pale sorrow. They're out there, I think, walking away from tonight in fear, and disgust, their lack of trust in men reinforced, their lack of hope in humanity, doubled. But in a few of the children, there might be something else—a question, a vision of the future.

I sit on the hillside and let it all slip away. Legs crossed, my vision fades again, and I slowly start to levitate, hands on my knees, a blue light glowing from within.

I am drawing attention to myself, and the creatures of the night come closer. But I am unaware, drowning in the feathers of an expanding white bird, a stream of pictures unfurling in front of me, the scent of lavender and pine drifting to me, as the fangs come closer. But I am far away, soaring in the darkness, over the tops of trees, and then mountains, the ocean sparking on the distant horizon.

In my excitement, I have made a mistake.

In my desperation to see *any* other path, I've turned my back on the evil that was lurking nearby all along. One by one they encir-

cle me, drawn by the light and sparks, eager to destroy that which they don't understand, the wolf that is fed tonight, the one that was patient, waiting for a weakness, to pounce.

And in the black, oily night as my light is dimmed, claws and teeth tearing at flesh, there is a spilling of a great sickness, an unfurling of something rotten into the air. In the silhouette of the glowing moon a dark shadow expands its wings, and soars into the void, torn and broken, trailing black feathers, and a sticky pitch of tar.

We set out once again from east to west, water to water, in search of something beyond ourselves, something more. Because this can't be all that there is. This time, one set of eyes lurks within, a small blue orb spinning in my outstretched hand, my palm cupping it, as the day unfolds before us.

THERE IS NOTHING LOST

ERINN L. KEMPER

"These are the waters where *mi abuelo* once hunted shark. And his *abuelo* before. All Nicaraguans right down the line. Born here or in Bluefields." Selvin steered the dugout boat away from the Rio San Juan Canal, heading for open sea. Waves broke against the bow in glistening fans. "From that point of land there, all the way out, and right up the *bocas* of the river, men of my village would hunt, luring the sharks in with bloody chunks of fish, then drag them to shore for finning."

The woman gripped the gunwale, knuckles white on slender hands. Doctor Jill Mah, a scientist from China. She'd come to Nicaragua to work on a special project at the big lab, the one that reflected the blue of the Caribbean, sea and sky, so some days the building almost disappeared.

Selvin had spotted her wandering the docks and straightened his captain's hat before he gave her his tour spiel. But she insisted on visiting shark waters.

Tourists clustered around the hover-boats and submarines, excited to snorkel or dive amidst the canal debris, where iridescent parrot fish darted between the blast-rock, and Maurice the eel lurked in a forgotten section of drain-pipe. A lot more money in captaining a group tour, but the doctor wanted to go out on a proper old dugout *cayuca*. Selvin explained the sharks were long gone. She nodded and gazed out over the water, streams of black hair falling over her freckled cheeks.

"One time my father, when he was a little boy, hooked a big bull shark over there by those rocks. He got pulled right into the sea. Still didn't let go of the line. Shark dragged him around while *mi abuelo* chased after in the boat. Ended up halfway to Bluefields before the shark slowed down. Grampa smacked the water with his paddle to keep old *tiberone* from circling in for a bite while *mi tata* swam back to the boat. Still my father didn't let go of the line. They had to cut that shark loose. Lucky for the shark. At least that's how Gramma tells it. Two days later, she says they caught that same shark, wearing Papa's hook like a nose-ring." This doctor made Selvin nervous, and when he was nervous he talked too much. "You want to go further out?"

She smoothed her hair out of her eyes and smiled. "Yes, please. And I want to hear more about the sharks. Anything you know. How many species? Did your people eat them? Have you ever caught one?"

"Pity you can't talk to *mi abuela*. She knows all the stories, lived here for a hundred years. Though most of them are just stories. Like the time when a female bull shark messed with a group of lobster divers. They had their breathing tubes set up so they could stay down for a bit, and she kept swimming over, knocking the tubes around. Divers didn't know what was happening at first. One of them ran out of air before he got to the surface. Shark didn't even take a bite, just circled and watched the guy drown, bumping him with her snout to check he was dead. Then off she went." Selvin shook his head. "Gramma said he deserved it. He'd been running around with his wife's sister. And his neighbor's daughter, too. That shark-bitch knew he was a dog."

"I'd love to meet your grandma. Hear about the old days."

"She won't have much to say, now. Dementia ate up all those crazy stories. She just sits and looks at the street. Doesn't even bother waving at folks calling out to her."

Doctor Mah turned her full attention on Selvin. "Dementia? For how long?"

"Lot o' years now. I'm the only one left, so I take care of her." Selvin took off his hat and wiped his forehead with a handkerchief. "I don't remember much of those days. They started building the canal when Papa was little. Sharks were gone by then. Why you interested in sharks anyways?"

Now that Doctor Mah was talking, Selvin wanted to keep her talking.

"My grandfather had an interest in sharks, too. He ate *wun tsai chi* whenever he could. Served it to guests to show he was prosperous. Even when it was almost impossible to find, the price of fin exorbitant, he'd order it on the black market, and my grandmother would make the soup. She didn't know he was spending all their savings. If he quit buying the fin, everyone would know he was broke. And now the sharks are gone in the world, and so's my grandfather. He died penniless and ashamed when I was still in medical school. I wish I could have made things better for him." She turned to the water and sighed. "You don't realize the value of a thing until it's gone."

Selvin gazed out at the sea, barges littering the horizon, hover-ships drifting over the shallows and the sea grass preserve a few miles offshore.

"You want to add another hour?"

He hoped for a yes. Low season was coming, and he barely had enough to see him and Gramma through, but the doctor shook her head, no. Selvin turned the boat back, heading for the docks and the canal where glass-faced high rises glinting yellow with sunlight lined its hungry throat, an endless stream of boats slipping in and out. Crisp white hotels and condos frosted the shoreline, and behind them a wall corralled the old village where Selvin and his *abuela* lived. The wall and the luxury homes stole the sea air, muted the roll and crash of waves on the beach.

"I'm home, Gramma. You been busy today?"

Selvin hung his captain's hat outside the front door of his plank-sided shack, set high off the ground on wooden stilts. Gramma sat in the shaded corner of the porch where he'd left her, dark skin dusty with age, eyes leaking milk tears, hands folded around a napkin, slippers dragging on the floor as she rocked and rocked and rocked in her chair.

"Let's get you to the bathroom, alright?"

Gramma's arm, skin soft and loose, felt fragile when Selvin tugged her to her feet. Like he might accidently pull her shoulder from its socket. Once she was standing, she could walk on her own. A bloom of yellow stained the back of her dressing gown.

"Didn't Miss Lydia come by? I'll get you a fresh smock, Gramma. You'd better give yourself a bit of a wipe-down."

"You're so sweet, Roberto." Her voice creaked like the front door as she shuffled to the bathroom. "I'm lucky to have a husband who cooks, even after a day fishing. Maybe after dinner we look at the box."

"I can't find the box. You must have hid it away."

"Our treasure. Gotta keep it safe."

No matter how many times he asked about it, searched for it, Selvin couldn't find Gramma's treasure box. He had no idea what it contained. Jewelry. Land deeds. Hopefully not some old shark fin gone to dust. Selvin rifled through a stack of cotton dresses, faded pink and blue and red flowers sprinkled over, and chose the one that smelled the freshest. Lydia, their neighbor, had promised to get Gramma to the bathroom at least once today, but she was waiting on a cleaning job for one of the new hotels. She had her little ones to support now her husband had gone off to work the cruise ships and never come back. Selvin should have checked with her before heading to the docks.

"Here you go, Gramma. Put this on. I'll get Miss Lydia to give you a shower tomorrow."

His gramma stood in the middle of the bathroom, dress in a puddle on the floor. The rolls and wrinkles of her old flesh used to disturb him. He remembered when those chicken legs were strung with muscle and she'd stride down the street, off to the shop for rice, off to the bar to herd her grandson home. He remembered when her neck was long and graceful, strong from holding buckets of *patty de carne* on her head. She'd carry them down at lunch to the canal workers, or the laborers constructing yet another tech lab for the *extranjeros*. Chinese, Indians, Saudis. Cheaper to conduct your research and development on the Miskito Coast, and fewer regulations. Now, in her, he saw what he would become. He was just passing time until he sat in that same rocker, piss running down his leg, eyes cloudy as a storm front coming in from the southwest.

"Hello? Mister Selvin?" A woman called from the road. "It's Jill Mah from this morning. They told me at the docks how to find you."

Selvin stepped out onto the porch, wiping his hands with a dish-towel. He couldn't say no to another tour. "Ah, Doctor Jill. You want to go out on the boat again? Maybe do some snorkeling?"

She had a large black case at her feet, her forehead beaded with sweat from lugging it along the road. "Can I come up?"

Selvin rattled down the stairs and hefted the case. It weighed about as much as a good-sized grouper. "I'll make some coffee. I told you, *mi abuela* isn't so sharp no more. She might not have any stories for you."

"I would love some coffee." Jill smiled, her eyes sparking with the dying sun. "I'm hoping we can help each other."

They pulled kitchen chairs out to the porch so they could sit and enjoy the night air with Gramma.

Jill sipped her coffee. "Mm. Not instant. This is wonderful." She held the cup so it steamed her face, inhaling.

"I keep it for special times. It's an honor to have a great scientist in my home. I appreciate you trying to help Gramma." Selvin would have offered her dinner, but rice and canned sardines was hardly a proper meal for a guest.

Gramma rocked with her eyes closed. The device from the black case clasped her head, slivers of black wire burrowed through white hair. When the probes with their diamond tipped needles slipped under her skin, Selvin had flinched, but Gramma just smiled, uneasy at all the attention. Lights flashed from a clear plastic box Doctor Jill had set on the floor—red, then yellow, then blue, and every color between. A stuttering rainbow.

Selvin was nervous the neighbors would come asking what they were doing to his poor *abuela*, but it was worse to imagine this doctor woman inside his run-down shack with its loose floorboards and stink of rot. When he was a boy the house had seemed bright, always freshly- painted, starched curtains luffing in the sea breeze. Now when the sun blazed in it baked cracks on the table, stole color even from the plastic dishes.

"It will only take another hour. The device is recording every facet of your grandmother's memory. It's funny how the brain stores a piece here and a piece there. Dementia erodes the pathways that allow us to bring those pieces together. Recollect." Jill spoke quietly but with a jittering enthusiasm. "The facets of memory—long-term, short-term, conscious, unconscious, procedural, episodic—most of it is still there. My computer can shuffle through, organize them."

"Incredible. I'm surprised they put so much money into helping old people." Selvin pondered what lost memories Gramma might recall. The location of her treasure box was locked somewhere in her brain. He pictured her memory like a deck of cards scattered on the floor, or a shattered window, cracks weaving through glass, turning the outside world into confused fragments.

Doctor Jill's voice flattened, her pleasure draining away. "Our backers don't want to restore memories. They want to take them. Interrogation has never been a reliable way to get information. Torture leads to false memories. Drugs distort facts. This way the military gets exactly what the subject has seen and done—altered only by the lens of their perception."

"Ah. Well." Selvin didn't know how to respond. It sounded more humane than what the police in his *barrio* did. Beat a guy or refuse him food until he returned what he stole. "But it won't hurt Gramma?"

"No." Jill smiled again, but sadly. "She'll feel happy, for a time anyways."

Selvin took a pair of Canadian tourists, mother and son, out for the morning in a borrowed hover boat. No traditional dugout for these two. He'd have to pay half his take to Raphael, but some money was better than none while he waited for Doctor Jill to process Gramma's memories. The computer took time. It had to sort through all those little memory fragments, fuse them together into groups, then they could be recalled as complete episodes. Making movies from an old lady's past.

"Mister Selvin. What kind of fish is that?" A chubby woman, head fully encased in a snorkel mask, bobbed in the turquoise water near the diving deck. Her voice gurgled through the mask's built-in respirator.

A coating of pollu-block turned her skin oyster-slick and formed gummy ridges in the folds of her neck. The block and the mask kept contaminants from going in or out, protecting her and the fragile re-growth of the sea-grass pasture where turtles once lived.

He looked where she pointed, and for a moment his heart raced. A dark triangle rose from the water, moving their way. Then he recognized it.

"Not a fish. Just a deep-sea drone caught in the current. They use them to inspect the canal." Selvin grabbed his boat hook and dragged the drone over. It wore the stamp of its corporate owner. Perhaps they'd slip him a few bucks for its return.

The mother-son duo hauled themselves up into the boat and peeled off their pollu-block, leaving it in drifts around the cockpit. Shimmering heaps of molted glass.

"Amazing. We saw two schools of fish." The woman wound her hair up in a towel.

Selvin smiled and nodded. "Back before the canal, these waters had so many fish we called it the aquarium. I'm not a fisherman, so that's no exaggeration. You're lucky you saw some today."

"But you can still catch sea bass around here? We had fresh ceviche for dinner last night."

"That comes from the farms up north. They bring it down fast, so I guess it's fresh."

"My son saw a grouper." She patted the boy's head. The kid gripped the gunwale and leaned over the side, spitting into the water and watching it swirl away. "I hear they can live more than a hundred years."

Selvin chuckled. "Fisherman, he always tells stories. Scientists say no more than fifty years. One was confirmed at thirty-seven, that's still plenty old."

The woman scowled and stuck out her lips, looking much like the fish her son claimed to have seen. "You said you're not a fisherman. I'd rather take the traditional view, that there are two-hundred-year-old fish. People who've been fishing for generations know a lot more than your scientists, anyways."

She draped a sarong over her shoulders and sat on the foredeck, a washed-out Buddha content in her proclamation.

Traditional knowledge. Selvin started the engine and the boat lifted off the water. *Another one who'd rather hear Gramma's crazy stories than the truth.*

Selvin looked up at the mirrored glass building as Doctor Jill Mah, dressed in her white lab coat, held a side door open and helped Gramma inside.

"Thank you for coming, Miss Tamara. Hot day, isn't it?" Doctor Jill waited for Selvin to step into the artificially cooled storage room. "Thank you for bringing her, Mister Selvin. The only way to do this is in the lab."

She led them down a long white hallway. Gramma shuffled in her slippers, pulled at the sleeves of her cardigan. He'd tried to cram her feet into some proper shoes, but she kicked them off, complaining they pinched her toes. At least she'd let him fix her hair back into a smooth knot.

Selvin wore his Sunday best and carried his father's stained old straw church hat. He'd even splashed on aftershave. Miss Lydia hadn't had time to bathe Gramma, what with her new job. Selvin tried to ignore the yeasty smell that trailed behind the old woman, and the fear that she might wet herself, or worse. Gramma hadn't slept well last night, banging around, angry because Roberto wasn't home yet from the bar. Selvin lay in bed and let her run herself down. No use tangling with an angry wife.

"In here." Jill opened another door, then glanced up and down the hall. "I filed your waiver and got clearance for this, but my supervisors are used to keeping a lid on things. It's instinct, even though it's not top-secret anymore. They've already started manufacturing and using the tech in the field. They're pulling the plug on this project and sending me to the lab in China. The lure of possible revenue from alternate applications, that's why they let me continue testing."

A wall of lights and screens with rolling chairs set at workstations lined one side of the high-ceilinged room. Jill took Gramma's hand and led her to the middle of the lab where a large white reclining chair with a number of appendages was fixed to the floor.

Selvin picked at a fleck of gecko dung on his hat brim, then stopped, not wanting it to flake off on the pristine white tiles. "You want Gramma in that chair, I'm guessing."

"She'll be comfortable. This procedure will be pleasurable for her, I guarantee it."

"Here, Gramma. The doctor wants you to sit." Selvin patted the smooth leather seat. "A real cozy chair she's got for you."

"Where are you going to sit, Roberto? I feel bad the only one getting the royal treatment." Gramma slid back into the chair, grasping the padded arms and letting her head fall against the head rest.

"Who's Roberto?" Jill whispered. She pulled one appendage over-top the chair.

"That's *mi abuelo*. Best leave her to her mistakes. She gets pretty upset if I correct her."

"Okay, Miss Tamara, we're going to hook up these wires. Like last time. It won't hurt."

Strands wriggled down from what looked like a shower head, and settled on Gramma's scalp, then slipped under her skin.

She smiled at Selvin and Jill. "I'll make my rondon today with the fish you bring home. The kids are looking too thin. We need to fatten them up."

Jill rolled two chairs over. "Lights." The overhead lights dimmed. "Begin first memory in sequence."

A hatch slid open in the ceiling and a pyramid of glass descended into the room. Beams of blue-white flowed, and colors refracted throughout the room, bright particles that swirled like firebugs.

Low, steady buzzing sounded all around, followed by insect chirps, then the rattling croak of a frog. A steady beat grew louder, louder, joined by voices raised in celebration and song, the slap of bare feet, the clap of hands.

Jill leaned close to Selvin. "Your grandmother will remember it all. The smells, touch, tastes, sights, and sounds. Relive it. Without being hooked up, our experience is more limited."

The swirling colors shivered and surged together, resolving into a three-dimensional scene. A young man, dressed in a red sequined vest and orange skull cap, hands a blur of movement over the drum he clutched between his knees. He stared at Gramma, he smiled a wide smile. The young man was in sharp focus, everything else fuzzy—the town's people gathered to watch, the other drummers, the town square strung with bright flags that snapped in the breeze.

"Roberto." Gramma sighed and reached up one hand to touch the apparition.

On either side of Gramma, girls danced in the haze of her periphery. Their skirts swirled up and down, and they pulsed their hips to the beat and shook their braids. Roberto's gaze on Gramma didn't waver. For him she was the only dancer.

"Happy memories are often the first to go. So they are the ones I wanted her to have." Jill watched Gramma. "This is the first time she saw him, according to the data."

"Yes." A wave of melancholy swept over Selvin. He'd never known this man, except through Gramma's stories. "He'd just come back from working the cruise ships. Had money saved. Enough for a boat and a wife. Everyone said the sharks would return, and with a boat he'd have plenty to support a family."

"Shhh. Listen." Jill placed a hand on Selvin's arm, her fingers cool and soft.

"You sure can shake it, girl. If you can cook rice 'n beans as good as my mama, I'm gonna have to marry you."

"You don't waste any time, do you?"

Strange to hear Gramma's youthful voice, though her lips didn't move. Strong, sure—pitched low so his grampa had to move in close. In her chair, Gramma took a deep breath, inhaling Roberto's scent.

"Look at him. So young. My man."

Roberto reached out, touched Gramma's hand. *"I just bought a house off the Avenida. You come see it. You'll like it."*

"I know the place. It's small for raising children."

"Family should live tight. You let your children roam too far, they wander away."

"You're from around here, so you know my mama makes rice 'n beans better than any. And everyone comes begging when I make my patty."

"Oh, girl. I been hearing about your patty. So, mi amour, I'll come round tomorrow and pick up your things?"

A low, flirtatious laugh sounded from the memory, and Gramma's laughter joined in, cracking, full of phlegm and pleasure.

"He sure was a terrible man. I married him the next week. Moved into that house and never left."

"Ready for the next one, Miss Tamara?" Jill walked over to the wall of screens and lights.

"Oh, yes."

Sounds and scene shifted. The click of dishes, ranchero music blaring from a radio, Gramma dancing around the kitchen of her bright, freshly painted wooden house, the floors trembling under her feet. Selvin blinked against the dizziness as, through Gramma's eyes, the room spun and tilted.

"Mama, mama." A boy called from outside, then thundered up the stairs, and threw open the door. He held a hook overhead, a finger-length curl of steel with a crescent-moon-shaped barb on the end. *"We caught him. The same one pulled me in last week."*

"How you know that, Junior. You ask his name?"

"It was him. He had one eye poked out, the same eye, and this is Papa's hook. He ties his line this way, and nobody else uses the old eighty-pound wire." Junior stood straight and proud as his mother inspected the hook.

"Your papa's a real traditionalist, that's true. You bring me a fish?"

Roberto appeared in the doorway, a trio of six-pound mackerel dangling from one hand. *"Would we forget to feed our women?"*

"How many shark?"

"Two today. The buyer paid up front." Roberto laid a bundle of bills on the table. *"Two thousand cash."*

Gramma nodded, her expression stern. *"That'll cover the doctor bills. Report says the sea's going up. If you can't go out again this week, we gonna talk about those canal jobs."*

"Yes, boss." Roberto grasped Gramma around her waist and pulled her close for a long kiss. Then he rested a hand on her belly. *"You still got the morning sickness?"*

"Something fierce. But it'll pass."

A flurry of steps up the stairs and Selvin's aunties rushed in, white shirts, pleated skirts, patent shoes. Auntie Vanessa, who died at twenty-two giving birth to a stillborn child, threw her pack on the floor and punched Auntie Carol on the arm. Auntie Carol kicked back. In just a few weeks she would get hit by a car and die in hospital after draining all the families' savings.

"Girls, don't you bother your mama. Go wash up."

Junior stepped forward, still holding the shark hook. *"Mama. Here. Take the hook. It's lucky, and you should have it."*

Gramma kissed Junior on the forehead and wrapped the hook in a napkin. *"I'll keep it in my special box, with the family treasure. It'll be safe there."*

Selvin leaned forward in his chair. "That. Doctor Jill. Her box. I been looking for it. Maybe she remembers where she put it. She keeps asking for it. Gets real upset that it's missing."

The memory continued. Gramma cut up and grilled the mackerel. The family sat and devoured steaming bowls of coconut fish stew. The children cleaned up, then pulled the curtain over their sleep nook, giggles and excited whispers rose and fell in waves.

Gramma and Roberto sat on the porch, a bottle of rum and two glasses between them, hands reaching out now and then, for their drinks or for each other. Fingers brushed, then clasped as they waved to neighbors passing in the moonlit street.

Back inside, Roberto sang in the shower, and Gramma pulled the curtain across her sleep nook. She dragged out the bed and pried a plank loose. Debris covered the plastic bin she pulled free from the wall. When she opened it, Selvin took a quick breath. A stack of bills. Hundreds and hundreds. Some papers underneath. Something sparkled red in the lamplight. Still wrapped in its napkin, Gramma tucked the shark hook in, then hurried to get the bin back in the wall.

"Hey, woman. No need to be cleaning under the bed. We only need the top part …"

When Jill turned the lights on, Gramma wore a calm smile. She gazed at the ceiling, into her past. The electrodes wriggled free of her scalp and retreated as Jill swung the appendage back from the chair.

Then a slow veil of confusion fell over Gramma's face.

"What we doing here? This a hospital? I don't want to be in any fancy hospital. You know we can't afford it, Roberto."

"It's not a hospital. Just a kind of theatre. Free entertainment."

"Nothing's free. You know that by now."

Jill sighed. "We have never been able to keep the memories from slipping away. We can recall them again and again, but they don't stay. There's a chance the brain will form new connections. Rewire itself. Though due to her age, it's unlikely. At least she was happy for a time. If you want to come back, we can try again."

Selvin shrugged. "Maybe. This season is a little tight. Have to spend most days out on the water while there's tourists around. Gramma did seem happy, though. Strange for me seeing all those people. I never knew my parents, my aunties. Or *mi abuelo*. He died working the canal. A mud slide took him down into the water and he drowned."

Gramma coughed and fussed with her cardigan. "Let's go home, Roberto. This air's going to give me *grippe*."

Selvin helped Gramma from the chair, eager to get home, too. The family treasure. Could be money. There was a lot in that box. Old money, too. The bank would buy it back at twice its former value. The papers might be even more important. Insurance claims, land holdings, investments. The older generation saw a lot of change, resorts and industry buying up all the land when the canal came through. The old way of life died. But big business paid for its demise.

"Why you tearing holes in the house, Junior?" Gramma pulled at her cotton dress, her wrinkles deep with worry.

"Just hunting for your treasure box. And look, here it is." Selvin wriggled the plastic bin free of the wall. Lizard and bat dung formed a black crust over it.

"You're making a mess of the floor. Now I'll be cleaning all afternoon."

"I'll sweep up, Gramma. Don't fret."

The plastic creaked as he pulled the lid back. Everything inside had jumbled together. Selvin dumped it out on the bed. No money. Papers yellow with age, some tattered photographs, but no money. Selvin sorted through the papers. Hospital bills for Auntie Carol when she lay in a coma after the accident. Red-typed numbers in streams down the page, bleeding her family of all their earnings. Birth and death announcements. A letter from the CEO of the canal project, expressing his regret at the death of Roberto Manderson Brown, and stating that the company would pay two weeks wages in compensation, but as a contract worker he was entitled to no more. Letters from Papa, from when Selvin's parents first moved to the States. They wrote every week for a time, then they stopped. Gramma had never been able to find out what happened to them.

"Nothing. No investments. Nothing." Selvin dropped the papers onto the bed, along with the photos: a wedding portrait, a promotional shot of Grampa's cruise-ship band, Selvin himself as a baby being cradled by his mama, his papa standing behind and smiling. "So, I just keep on. Work and work until one day I die."

"That's how it is, Selvin. How our people always done." Gramma spoke, clear, and firm.

She clasped the glittering red fabric, Grampa's stage vest, and smiled at her grandson. "He wore this the day I met him. I heard he was coming home. A strong man, money saved. When I danced, it was for him, to show him I'd be a good wife. I danced better than all the girls in the village. I knew he'd choose me. And oh, how I loved that man.

"Chasing money killed the shark, killed our way of life. If you have enough, that's all you need.

"Look there, see that fishing hook? Your papa gave that to me for luck. That day, I was the luckiest woman alive. I had everything I needed. You, boy. Take that hook. Keep it close. Go see that Lydia girl, she lost her man, but she's always been sweet on you. Catch yourself the right woman and you'll see. It's all you need."

Selvin untangled the hook from the square of cloth and closed his hand around its cool metal. He stood and pulled Gramma into his arms. She hugged him back, fierce and tight, then her muscles went slack, her shoulders slumped.

"I'd better make dinner. Junior. Your papa home yet? Put this away. The girls have been playing with his things again. He'll be mad he sees it out." Gramma held the sequined vest with a shaking hand.

A deep sadness took grip on Selvin's insides. Gramma had lost so much.

Tomorrow he'd take her to see Doctor Jill. Recall more stories of when his family was together, happy, whole. Her treasure.

"You go sit on the porch. I'll fix us dinner tonight."

"You're a good boy, Junior." Gramma shuffled out the door. She shed one slipper, and it lay on the floor, a curled husk. "I'm a lucky woman."

THIS HEIGHT AND FIERY SPEED

A.C. WISE

Alan dragged his carry-on down the aisle, knuckles white around the handle. He hated flying under the best of circumstances—being crowded into a too-small space with strangers under unnatural light, in recycled air, knowing that at any moment the plane could drop from the sky. Normally, if he had to travel, he drove or took the train. Now, cars had nearly betrayed him, too, and as a result, his nerves were even more shot than they'd been before.

"Planes want to stay in the air," Charlotte had told him on the way to the airport.

"I know." Alan kneaded the crease in his trousers. "But phobias aren't rational."

"Just do what I do." Charlotte took one hand off the wheel, digging in her purse with the other. "Pop an Ambien, order yourself a glass of whiskey, and wake up on the other side of the country."

Trees blurred by in Alan's peripheral vision. Charlotte had picked him up early, taking back roads through farmland and wooded roads to avoid traffic.

"Here." She handed him a blister pack of pills. "Bring me back a souvenir to thank me."

At that moment, the car ahead of them had slammed on its brakes. Charlotte swore, slewing them onto the shoulder. Gravel sprayed, and a terrible thumping and the screech of brakes sounded behind them as Charlotte fought the car back under control. Alan twisted around, peering through the rear windshield. Smoke rose from the tires of the car that had been in front of them, the hood crumpled beneath the body of a deer, shattered glass littering the road.

They'd checked on the driver, of course, called 9-1-1 and waited until an ambulance arrived to take the shaken man away. It seemed to Alan to take forever, but they'd still made it to the airport on time. Even so, sporadic tremors continued to shake Alan's hands. The image of the deer lying across the hood of the car persisted, too—blood smeared on the headlights, the glassy eye staring emptily at the sky, and the animal's tongue protruding. If the deer had leapt a second later, it would have been Charlotte's car that struck it. If it had leapt a second earlier, Charlotte might still have been distracted by digging in her purse, and they would have crashed. They'd avoided death by sheer chance and the narrowest of margins.

Alan pushed the thought away, stopping to check the ticket in his trembling hand. The seat matching his number was occupied. Alan cleared his throat, but the man in his seat didn't react, continuing to look out the window. Light from the raised shade fell on his papery skin, illuminating liver spots. Maybe he was hard of hearing.

"I think you're me." Alan winced at the fumbled words. He hated confrontation, no matter how small, almost as much as flying. "I mean, I think this is me."

He held out his ticket. The man finally turned and Alan started. The man's right eye was milky blue, his lid puckered with a pink-red scar. Alan smiled quickly, but it felt wobbly, and he could feel himself blushing.

"Do you mind?" The man twitched his pant cuff, revealing a prosthetic leg. "I prefer the aisle so I can stretch out."

"Of course." Alan's flush deepened.

He looked away as the man levered himself out of his seat, feeling awkward. Alan finally slid into the inside seat, and the man dropped back down heavily beside him, as though something that had been holding him by the shoulders suddenly let go.

"Hunting accident."

"I'm sorry?"

"Been like this since I was young." The man tapped his cheek below the scarred eye.

"Oh." Alan didn't know what to say.

To his relief, the man leaned back, closing his eyes. The scarred one gaped slightly, the lid refusing to fully close.

Alan retrieved Charlotte's pack of Ambien and dry-swallowed a pill. He hoped she knew what she was talking about, though as a general rule, he did trust her judgement. She was one of the few colleagues at St. Everild's Alan actually enjoyed spending time with. He'd asked her out once after an end of semester party, but immediately regretted it. It was a spur of the moment thing, and normally Alan planned meticulously. He obsessed. Luckily, she'd turned him down, and they'd stayed friends. It had been a relief, actually. In his experience, spontaneous things rarely worked out for him.

Like this trip. He shouldn't even be on this plane, but the Society for Literature of the Fantastic had asked him to replace their conference keynote speaker at the last minute. Charlotte had convinced him it was a good career move, but he was already regretting it. The near-crash, the dead deer, the strange man in his seat, nothing was going to plan and everything felt wrong.

To distract himself, Alan retrieved a yellow legal pad from his carry-on. While waiting at the boarding gate, he'd been taking notes for an article for *The Journal of Mythic Studies*. He might as well try to get some more work done while waiting for the Ambien to kick in.

He'd had the vague idea of linking wendigo mythology, classic horror literature, and psychological phenomena like Capgras syndrome, Fregoli syndrome, imposter syndrome, and Cotard's syndrome. There was something there, something to the idea of monsters taking on the appearances of familiar faces, and conversely familiar faces becoming monstrous. He hadn't quite put it all together yet, but he was working on it. He flipped to the first page of notes he'd taken.

In 1910, Algernon Blackwood published "The Wendigo", a supernatural tale about a group of men who hire a French-Canadian guide, Défago, to take them hunting in the wilderness. During the expedition, one of the men, Simpson, and Défago separate from the others. A sense of unease grows, the sense that they are being haunted. Défago hears "a windy, crying voice" calling his name, which leads to him fleeing his tent into the woods where Simpson hears him calling out, "Oh! Oh! My feet of fire! My burning feet of fire! Oh! Oh! This height and fiery speed!" Défago vanishes, and Simpson discovers a set of impossible tracks too far apart for anything natural, accompanied by what appear to be Défago's tracks, spaced as though he's been forced to take great leaps, or been dragged into the sky.

Later, Défago returns to the group, moving unnaturally, like a puppet. He sits bundled in blankets, and Simpson thinks he looks not only years older, but also animalistic. Défago's face is a mask, hiding something terrible. He leaves them again, and eventually the hunting party discovers the real Défago, an emaciated creature, lying beside the ashes of the fire, able only to eat moss, vomiting up any other food. He has become the wendigo, cursed to always be hungry and never sated. He is split in two, animal nature and human nature. He has become the wendigo, and the wendigo has become him.

The plane's engines whined. Sweat prickled Alan's skin, and he adjusted the overhead airflow, blasting himself with cold. He tried to focus on his notes, but all he could think of was the impossibility of something as big and heavy as a plane staying in the air.

I should have died on the road, with the deer.

The thought popped into his head out of nowhere. Alan shoved it away, gripping the armrests. The plane tilted, wheels leaving the ground. He closed his eyes, breathing, turning his face up to the blasting air vent. Winter. Deep cold. Howling wind. A green smell on the edge of rot. Alan's eyes snapped open.

He scrubbed a hand over his face, now suddenly too hot despite the air. The plane leveled out, and Alan released a shaky breath. Surely the Ambien would kick in soon. He just needed to get through the next few minutes. Alan's stomach growled. There wouldn't be a meal on the flight unless he wanted to buy an overpriced and over-packaged snack. He could have picked up something in the terminal, but he'd expected to be asleep by now. He forced his attention back to his notes, ignoring the gnawing hunger.

In 1981, Alvin Schwartz included "The Wendigo" in his collection Scary Stories to Tell in the Dark, *focusing solely on the supernatural. He strips away Blackwood's psychological musings, so only the monster remains. The sense of being hunted and haunted is still there, as though DeFago has been running from the wendigo for some time. At the end, when DeFago appears to the hunters, beneath his bundled clothing, he is revealed to be nothing but a pile of ash.*

Alan tapped his pen against his teeth. The article still didn't have a central thesis. He should have planned better, done more research. He re-read the last sentence he'd written: *We are not the same after we're pulled into the sky.* But when had he written that? Alan glanced at his seatmate, as though the man could have snuck the words onto the page when Alan wasn't looking, but he appeared to be deeply asleep.

Alan scratched out the imposter sentence and instead scribbled: *Schwartz subtly changes the spelling of DeFago's name because he's in disguise, hiding from the wendigo. He escaped death once. Now it is hunting him.* There. Better.

His eyelids drooped. He squinted at words on the page and they slid sideways, becoming a wavery blue line. Time to stop.

He tucked the pad into the seat pocket and leaned back. The plane chose that moment to jolt, dropping. Alan looked around wildly, but no one else reacted. The cabin lights flickered; the other passengers slept peacefully. A bundled figure in the jump seat rose and took a step toward him. Alan clawed at his seatbelt. The lights blinked again.

He jerked awake.

The other passengers remained absorbed in books, iPads, laptops. The plane wasn't crashing. Alan's mouth felt dry, ashy. He desperately wanted water, but he didn't want to disturb his seatmate by getting up to go to the bathroom later. He envied the man's sleep. Charlotte's Ambien should have knocked him out by now, but he couldn't settle. He forced his eyes closed, concentrating on his breathing, and woke to whispers.

His eyes adjusted to the dimmed lights. All around him, passengers had their tray tables down, eating meals that gleamed wet and red. His stomach lurched and the plane followed it, going into freefall. Alan couldn't gather enough breath to scream. Something had him by the shoulders, lifting him from his seat and he kicked violently.

"I should have died in the woods that day," the man in the seat next to him said.

Alan flailed, trying to push the old man away. He crashed back into his seat, and craned his neck to look up, but there was only the underside of the overhead compartments above him.

Emergency lighting flickered along the aisle like foxfire, will-o-wisps leading him astray. Alan reached for his seatbelt, but no one else moved. Then a figure solidified from the shadows. Burned, bundled, turning its head from side to side as it paced the aisle, searching for him.

Alan's stomach growled around a knot of fear. He pressed his hands against it to silence it. Whispers, the ones that had woken him, blew from the air vents, repeating a list of names. Elywn. Eldon. Alvin. Evan.

Alan squeezed his eyes shut, certain his stomach would betray him. He tried to think small thoughts, invisible thoughts. The wendi-go's footsteps dragged up the aisle, accompanied by the faint scent of burning. Alan cracked open an eye, glancing at his seatmate.

Take him, not me. He's Alan. He's the one you want. He's Alan.

He thought it fiercely, desperately. He'd escaped death once today, why not a second time? Three seats away. Two. The wendigo looked right at him. Alan's heart lurched. He scrunched his eyes closed again as a bundled hand reached for him. He waited, bracing himself, but no touch came. A laugh bubbled in Alan's throat, threatening to turn into a sob. It worked, the wendigo hadn't found him.

"Folks, this is your captain speaking. We're about twenty minutes outside of Seattle-Tacoma International Airport. Now would be a good time to start powering down your larger electronic devices. Our flight crew will be coming through the cabin to collect any remaining items you wish to dispose of. Please keep your seatbelts fastened until we arrive at the gate."

Alan jerked upright with a snort. The lights were on in the cabin, no flickering, no freefall, no burned and bundled figure searching for him. Flight attendants gathered trash while passengers put away their laptops. Everything was normal. Except Alan's pulse jittered, a rabbity feeling. He adjusted the airflow nozzle with a sense of déjà vu, and cold air blasted down on him.

The plane jolted down, the thump of the wheels followed shortly by the click of releasing seatbelts. Alan waited. He checked his phone, texted Charlotte to say he'd arrived. He didn't mention how miserably the Ambien had failed. When he looked up again, the aisles had cleared, but the man beside him still hadn't moved. But that wasn't surprising considering the effort it had taken him to let Alan into his seat.

"Excuse me?" Alan's tongue felt as clumsy. "Do you need help with your bags?"

He hoped it sounded polite, not condescending. He was braced for the man's eye this time, but he didn't look Alan's way.

"Excuse me?" Alan spoke louder.

After a moment, he forced himself to touch the man's arm. It felt stiff. Cold. Fear scrabbled behind Alan's ribs.

"Hello? I think this man needs help." The words came out in a rough croak.

A flight attendant with swept-up blonde hair came down the aisle.

"I think he's sick." Alan felt ill himself.

The flight attendant bent down—Joan, according to her nametag.

"Sir? Are you all right?" She touched the man's arm, his shoulder.

Alan saw the ghost outline of a smoking hand, the burned-black imprint of the wendigo's fingers. He watched the flight attendant check the man's wrist, his throat. Her cheeks blanched, but her professional demeanor never cracked.

"Please wait here, sir. I'm going to get help."

A whimper escaped Alan as Joan retreated down the aisle. He was trapped next to a corpse. The dead man turned toward him—a slow, owl-like motion. His milky-blind eye fixed Alan, and his lips moved.

"I should have died in the woods that day."

Alan jerked backward, his eyes flying open. When had they closed? His pulse beat wildly.

"Sir." Joan returned with an attendant whose nametag read Carlos.

I killed him. The thought rattled through Alan's head. *I told the wendigo to take him instead of me.* He almost babbled the confession.

"Sir." Carlos' voice brought him back. "We're going to help you climb over the back of the seat. An ambulance is on its way."

A jittery laugh rose in Alan's throat. An ambulance. The man needed a coroner's wagon.

"If you'll just come over this way, sir." Carlos extended an arm.

It was far from graceful, but Alan got out. Joan and Carlos helped him get his bag, helped him get off the plane. In the terminal, Alan blinked. Everything looked the same—the same grey carpet zig-zagged with bright pink and blue, the same concession stands, the same padded seats filled with tired travelers. Had he traveled anywhere at all? Outside the plate glass windows, red and white lights flickered as the ambulance approached. Even that was the same, an ambulance coming for someone who wasn't him, but maybe should have been. As the passengers waiting at the gate crowded around the window to see, Alan snatched up his carry-on bag, and ran.

Alan called Charlotte from his hotel room. His head hurt, and his mouth felt dry as he gave her a garbled account of the flight, leaving out the wendigo, but telling her about the dead man. Some removed part of himself listened to the words tumbling out of his mouth. They sounded ridiculous. Impossible.

"That's horrible. Are you okay?" Charlotte's voice held no hint of doubt, and that calmed him. He hadn't imagined it; it had really happened.

"I'm fine. I just ... need a drink."

"Of course. God. I'd need ten. Buy yourself one on me."

"Thanks." He almost asked her about the deer and the car almost crashing on the way to the airport, but for some reason he couldn't bring himself to do it.

"I have to go." It wasn't an excuse; he'd promised to meet the conference organizer in the bar. On the other end of the line, Charlotte sounded doubtful.

"Okay, but call me if you need anything." For a brief moment, he thought he heard the murmur of voices even farther down the line, as if Charlotte was at a party or in a crowded train station.

"What?" He could swear someone had called his name.

"I didn't say anything. Are you sure you're okay?"

Alan pinched the bridge of his nose. He wasn't sure at all.

"I'm fine. I just need a shower. And that drink. I'll talk to you later."

Alan set the shower as hot as he could stand it and climbed in. Steam billowed, and the shower curtain swayed. A smell like pine needles tickled his nose. He checked the soap, but it smelled bland, more like baby powder. As he set the bar down, a shadow moved across the shower curtain, the outline of branches. Alan froze. Goosebumps prickled his skin. It was a moment before he realized the hot water had run out. How long had he been standing there? Alan shut off the tap, took a deep breath, and wrenched the curtain open. Nothing.

He dried himself and dressed in fresh clothes, checking three times to make sure he had his key before shutting the door behind him. When he reached the lobby, it occurred to him he had no idea what the conference organizer looked like. They'd exchanged emails, but suddenly Alan was even drawing a blank on his name. Stress. Exhaustion from the flight. He patted his pockets. Had he written the name down? He was usually so organized.

A table stood to one side of the lobby with a sign welcoming attendees to the conference. Rows of name badges had been laid out alphabetically. At least he could make himself visible.

A quick scan didn't reveal his name. Maybe they hadn't had time to make an official name badge for him. A sharpie and a sheet of stick-on name labels sat beside the badges. As he stuck his hastily scribbled badge to his lapel, he realized his atrocious handwriting made it look like he'd misspelled his own name.

No point in making a new one. They'd have a proper badge for him tomorrow, surely. He crossed the lobby and found a seat at the far end of the bar. He'd barely sat when a hand landed on his shoulder, and Alan almost tipped off his stool as he spun around.

Shock, recognition, and déjà vu hit him in rapid succession. It was the dead man from the plane. Papery skin, liver spots, and all. No. This man had two undamaged eyes. And of course it couldn't be the man from the plane. Still, Alan looked closer. Other than their age, the two men really looked nothing alike at all. He turned the urge to laugh at himself into a cough.

"I didn't mean to startle you. Alvin Cutler, we exchanged emails." The man lifted the hand he'd placed on Alan's shoulder and held it out to shake.

"Alvin." Alan repeated, realizing too late that it sounded like he was giving his own name.

As they shook, Alan found himself looking for a nametag. Not that he had any reason to doubt the other man's identity.

"Sorry." Alan felt like he'd been staring. "You remind me of someone."

"Well, they say we all have a doppelganger out there somewhere, right?" Alvin took the seat beside Alan.

He ordered a beer from a brewery Alan didn't recognize, and the bartender placed one in front of Alan as well. The label showed a stag, rendered in incredible detail. Alan shuddered, seeing again the dead deer lying across the car hood. But that had been a doe, and this was clearly a buck, moss furring its antlers, which dripped with fog. Vast pillars of trees rose around the animal, and Alan could almost smell damp and earth and fallen leaves. His stomach growled.

Beside him, Alvin snapped his fingers, and Alan almost dropped the bottle.

"I just realized who you remind me of."

"What?" Hadn't he been the one to say Alvin looked familiar? Or was it the other way around?

"Elwyn Whitewood. We used to hunt together, a long time ago."

Cold settled in Alan's stomach, chasing away the hunger. The old man chuckled. Elwyn. Alan. Alvin. The names made his head hurt, too similar. Alan shook himself, trying to concentrate. Alvin was still talking, his voice like wind through tree branches.

"… must have been a twelve-pointer, leading us through the woods."

Alan opened his mouth, then closed it again. His skin goose-pimpled; he craned his neck looking for an air vent. Pre-dawn mist, dripping from leaves and moss clinging to trunks. He could see the buck slipping between trees, moving silent as death. He'd been there. He remembered. No, that couldn't be right, could it? Why was it so hard to focus?

"Monster trees. Ancient growth forest," Alvin said. "Elwyn and I got separated from the others, then the beast stopped, like that's what he'd wanted all along. Mist condensed around him, dripping off his antlers. I swear to God that buck looked right at us. We weren't the hunters, we were the ones being hunted."

"What?" Alan's tongue felt thick. Why was Alan—no, Alvin—telling him this story? Alan reached for his beer and missed, the stag side-stepping, and he knocked the bottle over. Beer foamed across the bar, but Alvin didn't seem to notice.

"Elwyn sighted along his rifle. I tried to stop him. I shouted, but the buck didn't move. Then bang!" Alvin slapped the bar, and Alan nearly tumbled off his seat.

"Elwyn screamed, rolling on the ground with his hands over his face. When I finally managed to pull them away, his left eye was full of sparks, burning."

Alvin chuckled, as though the story was amusing rather than horrifying, and swallowed the last of his beer. Some trick of the light erased his right eye leaving an infinite hole, burrowing into his skull.

"Freak accident. Gun misfired. Most god-awful thing I've ever seen. Never did catch that buck." He touched Alan's shoulder again. "But I should let you get some rest."

Alvin stood, dizzy. Everything was spiraling out of control.

"Alvin," Alvin stuck out his hand, and Alan took it automatically, shivering as something hot and cold had passed between them. "Good to finally meet you. I'll see you bright and early tomorrow."

"I'm Alan." Alan's tongue finally unlocked, but it was too late. Alvin had already disappeared.

△

Alan woke feeling restless. He'd expected nightmares, but he'd slept deeply. He glanced toward his suitcase. He'd packed his running gear, not expecting to have time to use it. He could go over his notes for his speech, but the sun was barely up. Surely there was time for both? And if not, maybe he could just wing it. He suppressed a giggle at the thought. Where had that come from?

Pushing the thought aside, he dressed quickly. The woman at the front desk directed him to a nearby park with a wooded trail. He started off fast, expecting to tire, but as the trail dipped into the trees, Alan picked up speed. Trees flashed by, blurring in his peripheral vision. They seemed very old, taller now that he was among them. A flash of movement between the trunks. A deer? When he turned his head, he saw only dappled sunlight and fallen leaves. Something dark swooped from wind-stirred branches, and he picked up even more speed, pushing himself into a second loop.

His legs felt good, his breathing strong. Even though the trail was perfectly level, it felt like running downhill, fast enough the soles of his shoes grew hot.

As he came to the end of the second loop, he caught sight of something sprawled across the path. His pulse stuttered, and he nearly tripped. A body. Regaining his stride, he put on a burst of speed. The wind picked up a swirl of ash, blowing it away from the crumpled form. Alan stopped. It wasn't a body, just a discarded sweatshirt.

Feeling like an idiot, Alan braced his hands on his knees, trying to catch his breath. Bent over, he noticed a pair of shoes lying beside the sweatshirt. They looked brand new, the laces still tied. One shoe lay slightly ahead of the other, as if someone had been lifted out of them in mid-step.

Alan's head snapped up, animal instinct. In his peripheral vision, between the trees, a massive buck did the same. Moss clung to the points of its antlers, and steam rose from its fur. Impossible. A spike of fear shot through him, cracking like a fired gun.

Alan bolted, ignoring the stitch lancing his side. What if it wasn't a stitch? What if he'd actually been shot? He resisted the urge to feel his ribs, sure his hand would come away sticky with blood. He lifted his head; surely he must almost be back at the park entrance. But no. Somehow he'd ended up deeper in the trees. He'd run completely the wrong way.

He stopped, turning a full circle. He couldn't even see the road from here. How had he gotten so turned around? He didn't remember this part of the path from before. It was narrow, more of a dirt track than a paved walkway.

A branch snapped, a fragile sound like breaking bone. Alan lurched back into a run. A shape flickered between the trees, not a deer, but something moving toward him with deliberation. Wind lashed the treetops, never seeming to touch the ground, which remained eerily still while overhead the leaves murmured names. Alan squinted. He lost sight of the black shape, then it stutter-jumped closer, closing the distance.

With a startled shout, Alan dodged to the side. He missed his footing, stumbling off the path and rolling until he hit a trunk. The sharp smell of leaf rot filled his nose as he scrambled up.

"I saw him go up this way."

"Must have been a twelve-pointer at least."

Alan froze at the voices, heart pounding. Footsteps crunched over leaves, and he risked a glance around the trunk. Two men, bundled against the cold. Their breath misted the air, despite the late spring day. Each carried a rifle—surely that couldn't be legal this close to a public park? Alan almost called out. Maybe they could tell him where he'd gone wrong and point him back to the hotel

"There." One of the men held up a hand, and the other stopped.

"Do you see him?" Even though the man whispered, Alan heard him clearly.

He raised his rifle, sighted along the barrel straight at Alan. When the man lifted his head, Alan saw he only had one eye.

Alan ran, heedless, crashing through bushes. His feet went out from under him, and pain spiked as he caught himself awkwardly. Twisting to look behind him he saw one of the men following him. He'd abandoned his rifle. Alan couldn't see his face. His hat slouched low, a scarf wrapped his nose and mouth.

Wendigo. Alan scrambled on all fours, his wrist throbbing where he'd hit the ground. Hunger. He was too light, hollow; the wendigo would carry him into the sky.

Alan dove over a fallen log, pressing himself against the damp-softened wood. He had to make himself heavier. He clawed at the bark, peeling away strips and cramming them into his mouth. He gagged. His jaw ached, but he forced himself to keep chewing, swallowing. He scooped up a handful of leaves and dirt. The trees rattled overhead and Alan closed his eyes. Dirt leaked from his mouth.

A hand touched his shoulder. Elwyn. Alvin. Alan tried to scream, but dirt clotted his tongue. He dug his fingers into the earth, holding on. Someone shaking him. Something lifting him into the sky. He was being torn in two, and the world fell out from beneath him.

Alan woke with a start. A slender figure stood beside his bed, holding his arm. He blinked and it resolved into a metallic stand, a bag of fluid, and a tube trailing to the crook of his elbow.

A memory tried to surface—running in the woods. That couldn't be right. He'd been in the hotel ballroom, giving the keynote speech. He'd seen something moving through the audience, hunting him. No, two men with guns, hunting a deer. That couldn't be right either. He tried to raise his arm to pinch the bridge of his nose, but the needle taped to his elbow stopped him.

Why couldn't he think straight? He'd gotten dizzy during his speech. Charred footprints burned into the garish ballroom carpet. He'd gripped the podium, he'd fainted. Except he'd never made it to his speech. He'd gone for a run and gotten lost. Something terrible had caught up to him between the trees. He remembered the faint scent of rot. Soft wood peeling under his fingertips. The loamy taste of earth.

He spotted a call button looped over the side of the bed, and pressed it. The curtain stirred almost immediately, as if someone had been lurking on the other side, waiting. A man in purple scrubs appeared, his expression weary.

"What happened?" Alan's voice scratched, strange in his own

ears. Was that the way he'd always sounded?

If he'd stuck to the plan, if they'd taken the highway to the airport, if he'd stayed in his room and read over his notes, if he hadn't come to the conference in the first place. The thoughts chased in useless circles. Vertigo swept him, and he gripped the bed's metal railings. At the same time his hands closed on handrails as he descended the plane's steps onto the tarmac. He smelled hot asphalt, exhaust. He smelled antiseptic cleaning spray, lemony and acidic.

The man in purple spoke, but Alan couldn't hear him over the roar of wind in his ears. Another version of himself met Charlotte at the airport, told her about his successful keynote speech. The other him smiled, handing over a souvenir he'd bought her at the Natural History Museum. His face looked strange, a mask pulled too tightly over his bones. Alan lurched up in the bed, a warning shout on his lips.

"Dehydration." The nurse frowned at Alan's sudden movement, and he settled back against the pillows, cowed.

"How did I get here?"

"A jogger found you passed out in the park across from the conference center hotel. You'd been eating bark and leaves. Nothing poisonous, luckily." The nurse shook his head, like he didn't think it was lucky at all.

"When can I leave?"

"I'll get the doctor."

Alan's stomach growled. If he stayed here too long, the wendigo would find him. Before he could even look around for his clothes, the doctor arrived. He tried to listen to her, but he kept losing track of her words as they blurred into the traffic report coming from Charlotte's radio, the hum of tires. At any moment, a deer would leap in front of her, and that would be the end.

Alan swallowed thickly and his eyes stung. The doctor checked his pupils, his pulse. To Alan, it felt like it was beating erratically, on the edge of a cardiac event. But she handed him a packet of papers with after-care instructions, side-effects, warning signs. Alan glanced at them, stunned. She'd written his name in pen on the top of each page. It was misspelled.

∆

Alan returned to the hotel just long enough to collect his luggage and check out. He threw Charlotte's Ambien in the trash, and bought a two-pack of aspirin on his way out. It did nothing for his headache. During the cab ride to the airport, he caught sight of a massive buck pacing them along the highway.

When Alan finally boarded the plane, there was a man already sitting in the aisle seat next to his. Hysterical laughter bubbled to his lips, but he choked it down. Of course. Alan had evaded death. He'd hidden from the wendigo, but he couldn't hide forever.

I think that one is me, but you can take the window seat, if you'd like." Alan's voice cracked.

The man turned. Alan braced himself, but he looked nothing like the dead man. In fact, Alan had the brief impression of looking into a mirror. Hadn't Alvin told him they all had a doppelganger somewhere?

"Thank you." The man slid over while Alan took the aisle seat.

"I'm Alvin." Alan stuck out his hand.

Why had he said that? He didn't bother correcting himself.

"Nice to meet you."

"Have you ever been hunting?" The words crawled their way up Alan's throat. He tried to catch them, but it was too late.

"No?" The man turned the word into a question, glancing over Alan's shoulder, as if calculating whether he could escape.

"I once tried to shoot a buck in the woods. Must have been a twelve-pointer. I should have died in the woods that day. I should have died on the road." Alan's lips peeled back from his teeth, his skull making itself known.

Panic flashed through the man's eyes, and Alan patted his hand.

"Don't worry, everything will be okay."

He turned to face forward, leaning back and closing his eyes. Back home, the other Alan was out for a drink with Charlotte. Maybe they'd decide to make a go of it after all. He'd publish his article. He'd get tenure. He'd be invited to give a keynote speech on purpose next time.

The engine spun up, and the plane moved down the runway, getting into position. Alan's stomach growled. Even though the plane hadn't taken off yet, his feet itched, swelling inside his shoes. He kicked them off, abandoning them under the seat.

Overhead, the air vents whispered, a windy murmuring of names. Alan felt sorry for the man beside him, probably an Evan, or an Eldon, or something similar. What he'd have to face at the other end of the flight wouldn't be pleasant for him, but there was nothing Alan could do about it. It was his turn. He'd escaped once, but he could only run for so long.

The faint scent of rot swirled through the circulated air. Alan breathed it in. The other him had already escaped, so everything was fine. The wendigo smiled at Charlotte over drinks. An empty suit of clothes filled with ash pressed back into the seat as the plane accelerated and tilted upward. Alan smiled. Over the roar of the engines and the sound of rushing wind hurling him into the air, he listened for footsteps dragging slowly up the aisle.

THE MOTEL BUSINESS

MICHAEL MARSHALL SMITH

I did not mean to get into the motel business. It came about when I was thirty-two because I got divorced and my ex-wife kept the house and after a while I realized I was hemorrhaging money on by-the-week rooms and so I put most of what I had left into a ramshackle property isolated on a bluff above the ocean a couple miles north of Santa Cruz. It was small, old-fashioned, L-shaped, and had once been a popular destination but become less successful after bigger and far nicer hotels were built in town and so it was eventually abandoned for several years. At the time I was semi-regularly drinking in the same bar as someone on the town council and he assured me that if I bought the place and vaguely implied I would be running it as a motel but in fact turned it into a private residence nobody on the zoning commission would care. Soon after I completed the purchase he lost his seat on account of complicated longterm financial wrong-doings and it turned out he was wrong about that—and other things, including the idea that his wife would continue to turn a blind eye to his relentless philandering—but by then I was in escrow and it was too late to back out and so I wound up owning a property in which stray dogs would not voluntarily abide and yet which had to be inhabited as a motel or not at all. I was unhappy about this but I was unhappy about pretty much everything in my life at that point so the situation didn't seem remarkable. I was stuck. I knew that. Caught between where I'd been and where I was going. I had no idea where that might be. So I just kept on.

I had a little money left after I'd taken ownership, cash I'd intended to spend on turning the place into a spacious and comfortable place for me to live. Instead it went on repairs and some modifications and bringing the place up to code. I paid a contractor to fix the parts I knew would be futile or dangerous for me to attempt but did the rest of the work myself, including rewiring. I learned as I went along. I became that guy. After a while I found I enjoyed the process, or at least that it was fairly successful in distracting me from the well-worn tracks of disillusion and impotent rage that my mind was prone to run around. My budget was small and so I made a virtue out of necessity, scouring yard sales and thrift stores and even using materials and furniture that people had left out on the street. I bought a bunch of old clock radios, put one in each room. I found a cache of Bakelite bedside lamps. I tore up the carpets and rough-sanded the floors. Each room ended up a different color, based on what paint I could buy cheap that day. By the time I'd finished the place was not only habitable but had something of a distinctive vibe. I guess now you'd call it shabby chic but then it was more just shabby so I pitched my prices pretty low.

I opened the following week. Business was slow at first. It's stayed that way. The motel is seldom more than a third full. That's okay. What with one thing and another I make enough to keep myself comfortable, which is all I've ever aspired to. It's sustainable. It doesn't attract attention. It's a life. It has been nearly thirty years now and during that time I've met a lot of people, come to know them a little, my path briefly entangling with theirs as they too go from where they've been to where they're headed.

I'm going to tell you about one of them now.

She arrived in late afternoon. People often do. My motel is not a destination. Nobody books in advance. They turn into the lot either because they know they will not be able to afford the prices in town or they are not headed anywhere in particular and so my place is as good a place to stop as any.

She was driving a dark blue Camaro that looked like it had seen a lot of miles. That was my first clue. As a rule of thumb women don't drive Camaros. I sat behind the desk—I spend most of each day there, reading, or staring out at the highway—and watched her get out. She stood for a moment as if becalmed. She looked late twenties and wore jeans and a denim shirt and had brown hair tied back and was only a few good weeks' sleep away from being very attractive.

Instead of coming to the office she wandered to the far side of the lot, from where you can look down over the ocean. I knew what she'd be seeing—grey sea disappearing into cold fog. That's the way it is for days at a stretch in the late Fall. She lit a cigarette and stood staring out, as if coming to a decision. Finally she dropped the butt to the ground and came walking in my direction.

When she was in front of the desk I could see it'd take more than sleep to fix things. The corners of her mouth were beginning to turn down, like someone who'd spent a few years forgetting—or never being reminded—how to smile.

"How many nights?"

"Two," she said. "Maybe more. Do I need to tell you now?"

"No." I nodded toward the empty lot. "Off-season runs three hundred sixty-five days of the year."

She laughed, briefly, in a way that changed her face. I looked up at her for a moment.

"What?"

"Deciding what room to give you. They're all different. I like to choose the one I think people will enjoy."

"Do you always get it right?"

"Never had any complaints."

"So?"

I looked at her a moment longer. "Number 9," I said.

She moved in. In one hand, a small traveling bag. Under the other arm, a brown paper sack. Groceries, maybe. More likely something to drink and smoke.

She hung the Do Not Disturb tag on the knob, closed the door and drew the curtains, and that was the end of that.

Next morning the tag remained in place. I clean the rooms myself, so I left it be. At four o'clock—sitting once again behind the desk, reading a paperback novel a previous guest had left behind—I saw her door open. She was dressed the same as when she arrived and even from a distance you could tell she was badly hungover. She walked over to where she'd smoked a cigarette the day before and did it again.

I pulled my pack of Marlboros from under the counter and went outside. She saw me coming and registered my presence but didn't say anything.

"So is he going to come looking for it?"

"For what?"

"Your boyfriend," I said. "His car."

"Husband. I doubt it. It's been three months."

"Where'd you leave?"

"Richmond, Virginia."

"Where you going?"

"Do I look like I know?"

I smiled. "So what's the short-term?"

"Heading into town. Where's a good place?"

"For what?"

"Fun."

"Define "fun"."

"Oh, I wish I knew."

"Avoid Asti's. The Negative Space isn't bad. But I'd try the Blue Bar, on Center. Relaxed place. The food is okay too."

"Good enough. I like my room, by the way," she said. "Guess you picked right."

"I generally do."

A little after two a.m. I was woken by a noise outside. I raised my head from the pillow but I already knew what it was. I've heard it before. It was the sound of a car running at low speed into the low metal fence around the parking lot.

A pause. The sound of a car reversing, parking. Then the engine turned off. Two doors opening, slamming. Low voices, a peal of laughter, footsteps on gravel, a room door shutting.

I went back to sleep.

The Do Not Disturb tag hung on Number 9 for the whole of the next day. When I saw her standing smoking and looking out at

the sea at the end of the afternoon, she was alone and had something of a black eye. I let her be.

Next morning she came to the office. She looked tired and pale
and pretty unhappy with herself.

"Going, or staying?"

"Staying," she said. "Though I won't be visiting the Blue Bar
again."

"Who was it?"

"Barman. I … forget his name."

Never learned it, more likely. "Rick. Tattoos on his knuckles?"

"That would be the guy. A little too vigorous."

"You want me to have someone talk to him?"

She looked at me. "What?"

"Don't like to see a woman with a bruise on her face. Or
anywhere else, come to that. There are people who could explain to
him how not-cool it is."

"You'd do that?"

"You're a guest in town. You're staying at my motel."

She looked at me with an expression that was hard to name.
"I'm fine," she said.

But on her way out the door she hesitated, and turned back.
"Thanks," she said.

Next day a middle-aged salesman arrived on his way south to San
Luis Obispo. I put him in Room 7. He left early the next morning.

Not much else happened, to be honest with you.

That evening I was sitting out on my stubby deck on the ocean side
of the office, looking at the dim, fuzzy disk of the moon up above.
The deck runs to the back, with a door giving access to the couple
of rooms where I live. I heard someone coming and turned to see
her standing diffidently at the little gate. She was holding a brown
paper bag.

"Wondered if you drank on occasion."

I lifted up the bottle of beer on the side table. "Only when I'm awake. Not headed into town tonight?"

"This evening I think I'd prefer to do it somewhere safe."

"Sounds wise."

"Am I safe?"

"Do you want to be?"

"Right now, yes I do."

"Then this the right place."

She had a bottle of wine and once I'd got a glass from inside we sat and smoked and looked into the fog.

"So what's the deal?" I asked, eventually.

She didn't say anything for a while, then shrugged. "Married at twenty-two. Walked out at twenty-nine. Driven a couple thousand miles since."

"That's it?"

"I've had a while to boil it down. What about you? Is there a Mrs. Motel-keeper?"

"Long time ago. It didn't work out. That's how I wound up owning this place. I've spent some time with people since. But I'm not going down the wedding road again. For some, I think it's just not meant to be."

She nodded. "Maybe you're right."

"Alone isn't so bad."

She poured herself another drink. I'd meant to sound reassuring but I looked at her face in the light of the lamp on the wall and thought to myself that she didn't have much time to stop the lines at the corners of her mouth becoming permanent.

That it might already be too late.

Next morning it was Friday and I had business in town. When I got back in the mid-afternoon the door to Room 9 was open.

I stood outside. She was in the chair, smoking. The TV was on, some random re-run. Her head was pointed in that direction but I didn't think she was watching. Her face was wholly without expression. Just wanted background noise. My motel is quiet. If the ocean's frisky, you'll hear waves. If not, nothing at all but for the sound of an occasional car on the highway, going somewhere other than here—which cannot help but, on some level, make you question whether here is the right place to be after all.

"Making chili," I said. "You'd be welcome."

She shook her head. "Need some fun tonight." She realized what she'd said, made a face. "No offense."

"None taken."

"What was that other bar you said? Not the Blue Bar?"

"The Negative Space."

"Right. Thank you. And, you know, sorry."

"Don't worry about it. Have fun. But not too much."

She winked. It looked sad. It looked lonely.

At half past nine I was making a few adjustments to Room 8 when I heard a car coming into the lot. I left the room, locking the door behind me, in time to see her car bashing into the fence in pretty much the exact same place it had the other night. She reversed—I was glad to see she was alone in the car—made it into her own space, and got out.

"Keep screwing up that damned turn," she said, as she got out. Her voice was slurred, her eyes unclear.

"It's a tough one," I said, though it is not.

"Wait," she said. She went around the passenger side and got a brown bag off the seat. "Nearly forgot my fun."

"Didn't find any downtown, huh."

"I did not. Found that asshole Rick again, though."

"Seriously?"

"Yep. He came in that other bar. Like I've got a homing device on my ass. But ..." Her face changed, and when she spoke again her voice was quieter, and tired, and less drunk. "He found some other ass, attached to a bigger pair of tits."

"I have chili left."

"Tell the truth I'm more in the mood for wine."

"I can tell. But eat some food and it'll hurt less tomorrow. You can still get drunk. Hell, I'll join you."

She opened her mouth to say no but then said yes.

It was about two hours later. I'd given her a bowl of chili and she did finish it, because my chili is actually pretty good. Then she'd opened a bottle from her bag. That was gone now. She was halfway through another and had hit that stage of drunk where you hold steady for a while, getting deeper and colder rather than incoherent.

"But in the end, you know what?"

"What?"

"All that stuff I just said, about his mother and his damn friends and his easy, know-nothing-and-proud-of-it take on everything ... That's not even the problem."

"So what is it?"

"*Was* it," she said. "I'm not going back."

"Okay."

"It was ... Oh, it doesn't matter."

"Sure it does."

"It's ..." She stopped. She poured herself another glass and instead of only filling it halfway, like you do when you're pretending, hey, this might the last, she filled it right to the brim. Took a sip, and it was as though all the air slowly went out of her. "It's me," she said.

"What's you?"

"Sure, Steve's an asshole, or becoming one. And he cheats, or wants to. And his mom's a racist fuck. But every time you point a finger there's a finger in the mirror pointing right back at you."

"What do you mean?"

"I mean I didn't have to take his car and bail. I mean I could have tried talking to him, or tried harder, or longer. I loved him once and maybe I still do and it's not his fault that's not enough. It's not his fault that when we got married it looked like I was going to do something with my life and along the way I forgot what it was. He goes to work every day and when he comes home I'm still there in Pjs and not in a sexy way but the way that says the person simply does not care. The kitchen looks the same as when he left and there's breadcrumbs everywhere because toast is what I had for breakfast and for lunch and what I'd eat for dinner too except I know I should cook him something but the thought makes me feel so angry and bored that I get into an argument with him for no reason. During which he points out that the grocery store is literally five minutes away and some people might actually enjoy cooking for the person they love, an observation that incenses me even more and we wind up having a huge fight about nothing and everything and it ends up with him walking out and me breaking something. And I stand there with the sound still ringing in my ears and the pieces all around and I know damned well it was my fault and I can remember being the person who wouldn't have done that and I can even picture her standing there staring at me saying 'What *happened* to you?' and it's like being an animal in a cage and you either whirl faster and faster in circles or you can stop and lie down and go to sleep. And that's what I did. Until three months ago when I realized one morning that if I didn't get up and go, then I'd never get out of bed again. So I bailed."

"Sounds like something you had to do."

"Bailing's never the answer."

I shrugged. "I don't know about that. Sometimes a person can get mired in a hole on the road. Or at a crossroads, maybe. No way you're going to work out which road is the one you need until you've first got out of the hole."

She appeared to consider this. "Could be. But I had this thing happen to me one time. There was this old woman in town, she used to clean for my mother. I'd known her since I was tiny. She was almost part of the family. And one day I drove her home and I was talking about boyfriends and how school wasn't working out and she listened patiently and when I finally stopped whining she said 'You know, I'm not sure you're ever going to get what you want'."

"So she was a cranky old bitch."

"Sure, but there's more. Couple days later, we heard she died in her sleep that night. I'm likely the last person to ever talk to her. And so I carried that with me for years, thinking it was maybe like a prophecy or something."

"It wasn't."

"I know that now. But I know it because I eventually realized she had seen a bunch of stuff in her life and actually she was saying something different. She wasn't saying the world was stacked against me. She was warning me that I was stacked against *myself*. That I always managed to find the thing to be pissed or sad about, something or someone to blame. And she was right about that but I didn't get it until I was already up to my knees in the hole and sinking fast."

"But now you know. So you can climb out."

"No," she said. "I was *born* in the hole. Running doesn't change a thing. I have a God-given right to be mad about my life, right? Because I'm so special? Bullshit. Truth is I've done nothing in ten years but bitch about things I could change but never do. I can't even give him kids because we've been fucking for years without protection and nothing happens and he keeps politely not saying anything about it to the point where I want to bash his brains in but his mother got my number years ago—I hate her guts, but she isn't dumb—and makes no fucking bones about making it clear she thinks I'm just a drain on resources. A week before I blew town it was his birthday and she organized something for him because she knew I wouldn't get my shit together, and she invited the girl he used to date before me. I mean, seriously, she did that. And the worst of it was I stood at the back of the room getting steaming drunk and watched the two of them catching up on old times and I thought 'You know what, Stevie? You could do worse.' Hell, you *have* done worse. You got me."

"It was a dick move by his mom. You were self-protecting."

"I really wasn't. I just didn't care."

"That's not a good way to be."

"Right. So, Mr. Motel-keeper … what do I do? How do I get from here to somewhere worth being? How do I stop feeling so sorry for myself and start giving a shit?"

I thought about it. Opened another bottle of beer. And in the end I shrugged and said "Maybe you don't."

She turned her head to look blearily at me. "What?"

"Could be there's no way out. Maybe instead you got to say

'Okay, this is me. So what do I do with that?'"

"How the fuck does that help?"

"Not saying it will. But pretending the world's going to change or that you're going to change is setting up bitter disappointment. Maybe you lower your expectations. Stop believing some prize or distraction or guy is going to come along to help you forget who you are. Accept that nothing's going to get better, deal with the world as it is."

She was frowning and her eyes looked more focused now. "I'm twenty-nine years old and you're telling me basically I'm *done?* Is that supposed to *help?*"

"I'm not your father."

"No," she said. "You're not." She stood up, unsteadily.

"Look," I said. "I apologize."

"For what? You're the finger in the mirror pointing back." She stomped halfway to the gate, realized she'd left the scant remains of her bottle of wine, came back for it. This gave me time to stand up. I accompanied her to the gate.

"I didn't mean to —" I said, but stopped talking as a car turned into the lot. We watched it pull over and park next to hers. A guy got out of the driver's side.

"Huh," she said. "Would you look at that."

"I'll tell him to leave."

"Don't worry," she said, and there was an awful change in her voice, a pathetic hopefulness. "I'll see what he wants."

She hurried across the lot toward Rick, who was standing there waiting, as if he knew she'd come.

I finished my beer on the deck with another cigarette and went to bed.

My head didn't feel great the next morning, but it often doesn't, so that didn't really affect my day one way or the other. I got up at seven and fixed myself some eggs and coffee and wrote down a list of jobs for the day.

I took a second coffee out for a walk around and as I left the office saw the door to Number 9 open. Rick came out.

And then another guy.

They both looked pretty pleased with themselves. Rick saw me there and winked. They got in the car and drove away.

I went back into the office so if she came out she wouldn't realize what I'd seen. I did not see her for the whole of the day.

I wasn't sure whether I would go out that evening. I had an open mind. When it got dark I sat on the deck with a beer and a smoke and waited to see what I would do.

She arrived at the gate a little after seven. She did not look good. She was pale and her hair was unwashed. Her eyes were evasive. She looked defeated. She looked terrible.

"Haven't seen you around today," I said.

"Been in bed." Her voice was quiet, almost a mumble.

"Sickening for something?"

She shook her head. "Thinking."

"How'd that go?"

"Can't face driving out tonight," she said. "Wondered if you had a couple beers I could borrow."

"I'm sure I can find something."

I went indoors. I did not have any beers but I found a bottle of vodka. When I came back out and offered it she took it gratefully. "Have one with me?"

"I have to go out," I said. "Sorry."

She nodded quickly. "Sure, okay. Thanks."

I went back indoors. She was still there, looking out toward the dark sea, when I came back out with my jacket on.

"What you said last night," she said. Her voice was very quiet now. "You really think that's the way it is?"

"I do," I said. "There's no big thing out there. Nothing to make it all okay. Doesn't matter how far you drive or how many bars you fall down in or how many different men you wake up next to thinking, Jesus—who is this guy. There's just you. That's all there is in your life and all there's ever going to be. There is no magic. This is all she wrote. This is all there is."

She nodded, more slowly this time.

When I drove out of the lot she was still standing there at my gate, looking out over the ocean.

I hoped it had been the right thing to say. That it might help push her in the right direction.

I had a solitary dinner down in Capitola, then drove slowly back up the coast, stopping at a couple bars.

I got home around midnight. There was no extra car in the lot. Just hers. I stayed up a while.

The Do Not Disturb tag wasn't hanging on her door next morning, but I left cleaning her room until last anyway. I didn't knock until nearly mid-day.

I left it a couple minutes, knocked again. I unlocked the door. The room was a mess.

She was in the bathtub. The water was cold and red. Her face was white and her eyes were open. The knife—one of the sharp ones from the kitchenette drawer—was lying on the floor. The cuts she'd made across her wrist were very deep. She'd found a great deal of strength when she finally worked out who she was and where she needed to go.

I called the cops. They arrived and took pictures and the coroner came. He commiserated with me for having this happen in my place. He reassured me that what with her being from out of town, nobody needed to know what had happened. They took her away, one of the cops driving her car.

When they were gone I spent half an hour tidying up the mess, then an hour thoroughly cleaning up the bathroom. By the time I was done there would be no way of telling anything had happened there. It was ready for a new guest.

Then I went next door to Number 8. I took the tapes out of the cameras on tripods in front of the tiny holes in the wall opposite the main area of Room 9, and then from the two behind the false mirror in the bathroom. They are positioned so as to cover the entire matching space in the next room, including the bathtub.

I replaced the tapes with fresh ones from the box in the closet, double-checked the cameras facing Room 7 too. Then I left, putting the tapes that recorded what had happened in the night in a bag and taking it with me.

Back in my room I moved aside the rug and lifted the floorboard and added the tapes to the others there. I did not watch them. I never do and never will. When I die maybe someone will discover them and misunderstand my intentions, thinking that I lead these people onto the bridge out of cruel purpose. But I do not. I give them a mirror and looking into it sometimes helps them to understand themselves and their lives. That is all. The cameras are there because there should be some witness of that journey and its end. It does not need to be me or anybody else. Everyone has the right to die alone.

I would spend the afternoon doing chores around town, and likely go for a couple beers. I didn't need to give Rick anything for his role—my phone calls to him on the previous evenings, yielding advice as to which bar would yield a desperate woman in search of fun, had given him a couple of memorable nights. He'd had no idea of the end to which I had directed him. But I'd buy him a drink or two. He'd played his part. I'd likely use him again. I'd used him before.

After that I would come home and sit on the deck and look up at the frail circle of the moon hanging in the fog over the ocean in a long dark night that has lasted my whole life, from which I do not expect ever to wake and from which nobody has been able to help me to escape, and I would sit and smoke and drink until I was tired enough to sleep, and I would probably not think about anything at all.

EVERYTHING BEAUTIFUL IS ALSO A LIE

DAMIEN ANGELICA WALTERS

The apartment is a generic two-bedroom rectangle with a sliding glass door off an L-shaped living/dining room combo that leads to a small concrete patio, beyond which is a patch of browning grass and then a copse of trees. Oak and pine. From carpet to kitchen cabinets, everything is beige or tan and bland, a starkness that has nothing to do with the lack of furniture. Most of Riva's furniture will be too big for the space, but she signs the lease, already composing the wording for a Craigslist ad in her head: *Must sell! Great condition! All serious offers considered!*

Another woman in another life might resent such things, but Riva doesn't. She'll fade into anonymity here, which is exactly what she wants. She'll no longer be the woman whose husband and daughter were among those killed when the sinkhole opened beneath Route 31; she'll be the neighbor in apartment 2C. Nice enough, but keeps to herself.

One of the early articles said the eleven people, along with their vehicles, were "devoured by the earth." It made the whole thing bestial instead of accidental, made her think of Wes and Charlotte's broken bodies digesting in the belly of a great beast, made her think of a hungry mouth with asphalt teeth opening wide.

The days until move-in pass in a blur of packing tape and boxes, of men and women stopping by to pick up the television armoire Riva found at a secondhand store, the sectional sofa, the extra end tables and lamps and bookcases, the expansive desk suite from Wes's home office, the dining room table with its scuffs and scratches telling a story she can't bear to touch anymore. Let another family tend to its edges.

Stripped of the furniture, of the photos and knickknacks, the refrigerator magnets and the crayon drawings they once held, with the air holding the bite of fresh paint, the house is as generic as the waiting apartment, yet it's merely a disguise. She feels the colors beneath the surface, waiting to emerge.

"I'm sorry, Wes. I've tried to stay here. I know how much you love, loved, this house, but it's too hard for me. There's too much of us here, and it tears me apart. I miss you. I miss you so much," she says as she does her final walk-through, wiping her tears before they have a chance to fall. Today is not for curling into a ball on the floor and sobbing. It's for movement. Forward, only forward.

And she's not lying. She's tried for three months, but the spaces where Wes and Charlotte should be have extended no comfort, only recrimination.

Charlotte's bedroom is the last she visits, and she stands in front of the closed door, the ends of her ponytail tickling her neck. The air inside is stuffy, the once-lavender walls now a mundane eggshell. As she turns to go, sun splices the window blind and illuminates a section of wall. Near the baseboard, peeking out from a too-thin layer of paint, is a stick figure in red crayon. Two stubby little arms, two short legs, a round head, two dots for eyes, a squiggle of curly hair.

"Look, Mama, she has curly hair like me! And now I'm going to draw you, too!"

She'd asked the painters to take care. Four-year-old Charlotte had frequently drawn on her walls, the waxy residue evident when the sun shone the right way. Obviously, they'd not heeded attention, and all the cleaning supplies are packed and in the moving van.

"Look, Mama, look!"

The room is too big, the walls towering around her like those in a castle of old, and the air is too sharp and silent. Sweat prickling her armpits, tongue slicked bitter with panic, she runs for the front door. The new owners can take care of the crayon themselves.

By the time she gets to the apartment, her pulse is no longer a Greyhound. The movers are almost finished stacking labeled boxes in various rooms and furniture against walls, but the kitchen is done, so she unpacks a set of dishes, wincing at the thumps and thuds of heavy feet. When they finally go, she pads down the short hallway to the bedrooms and shuts the door to the spare as she passes, but not before glancing at the stacks of boxes within. They're not for unpacking, these boxes, but for safekeeping, her neat print marking the sides: *Photo albums, Charlotte's favorite toys, Wes's books.* A museum of her former life, she thinks, as she returns to the kitchen, this time for a glass of Chardonnay. "Welcome home," she says, lifting a toast to the bare walls.

In the middle of the night, she wakes, confused by the space beside her, the strange dimensions of the room and its unfamiliar shadows, but in the time it takes to roll over and check the time on her phone—3:44—she remembers where she is and burrows deeper under the comforter. Her hand skitters again and again to the empty spot, yearning for the warmth of Wes's skin, the comfort of his arms. Sleep refuses her, so she slips from the bed and turns on the nightstand light, bright enough to prevent her from tripping over anything, but not bright enough to hurt.

One of the bifold doors to her walk-in closet stands open, a sealed box of winter sweaters acting as doorstop. She should've finished unpacking yesterday—most people would, she's sure—but she couldn't. She turns on the coffee-maker; no sense in pretense and as it's Saturday, there's no need to worry about work. In truth, she's been sleepwalking through the daily grind at the office for two months. She'd hoped it would help, but it simply fills a chunk of time with routine tasks, gives her hands something to do.

After she's had half a cup of coffee, she sets it on her nightstand and opens both closet doors wide. The dim light makes strange shapes of the contents—hulking beasts with sloped shoulders and too-long arms, but she tugs the string of the overhead bulb, shattering the illusion.

The small space swims with color. Blues and greens and oranges. Teals and plums and coppers. The colors seem obscene. Out of place. She pulls a bright emerald cardigan from its hanger, her fingers sinking in the soft fabric that retains the scent of lavender dryer sheets. Her brows pinch together, her lips the same, and she lets the cardigan fall. A cranberry button-down follows suit. Then a peachy-pink cowl-necked blouse. A ruby spaghetti-strap chemise glittered with gold beads. A paisley pencil skirt in deep jewel tones. Navy pinstripe trousers. And on and on until there's a pile of bright at her feet and everything hanging is beige and tan and cream and khaki and white. This is the closet of someone who belongs in this apartment, in this life.

With the side of her foot, she nudges the clothes on the floor to one corner, the fabric whisking over the cheap carpet. In spite of the caffeine she's consumed, exhaustion pours over her, and she climbs into bed.

"I miss you," she says into the pillow, pretending she still smells her husband there. "I miss you so much."

She dreams of darkness, a black so absolute she can't see anything at all, but Wes is here in the darkness, and she needs to find him because something else is here, too, something ponderous and old, something hungry. He calls her name over and over, his voice pain-filled and afraid, and she waves her arms from side to side, trying to find him, but she can't. Then the ground vanishes beneath her feet. She's falling and flailing, and she snaps awake in a room draped in shadows, legs and arms tangled in sweaty sheets.

She pads through the apartment and turns on every light, even the one over the stove. A long hot shower makes her feel almost human; a plain t-shirt and undyed linen pants give her enough sense of calm to fetch a box from the kitchen. Into the box, she tosses the discarded clothing, not bothering to fold anything. If her future self decides she wants to wear them, she can deal with it then.

She deposits the box in the second bedroom atop one labeled *Stuffed Animals.* As the cardboard makes contact, a whiff of talcum scented air kisses her cheeks, the smell strong enough to send her staggering, a hand butterflying to her chest, as though she can ward off the memories of Charlotte in her toddler's bed, her dark curly hair damp from a bath, holding out her needy arms while saying "Hugs, Mama. Hugs a go nite-nite;" of her asking for another story, another drink of water, another hug, another toy. Of Riva leaning so their shoulders touched and nothing more, telling her "Okay, enough, you have to go to bed now," and fleeing the room before she could see the blame in Wes's eyes, knowing his mouth would say nothing at all. Such things would come later, never arguments, only discussions that didn't alleviate his confusion for she could never find the proper words to explain. Some women weren't meant to be mothers. And she never hurt Charlotte. Never. She just—

Movement off to the side then, but by the time her gaze focuses on where she thought it was, near the closet doorframe, there's nothing to see. "Of course not," she mutters, pinching the bridge of her nose as she closes the door behind her.

By Sunday night, she has everything unpacked and a stack of flattened boxes waiting by the front door for a trip to the Dumpster. It's another small thing in an endless cavern of small things that gives her pause—Wes always took care of the trash and recycling and she caught herself right before she called to him to carry them out. Habits don't break as easily as hearts.

All the furniture she kept is in the neutral family. Unintentional, at least consciously so. When it lived in the old house, the latte colored sofa had a scatter of bright teal throw pillows. They might be in boxes in the second bedroom or they might belong to someone else now. She didn't keep track of what she sold. The walls are still unadorned, something she has no intention of changing. In the living room, hardcover dustjackets provide a splash of color that stands out sharply, until she turns the books so their pages are facing out, not their spines.

"You would hate this, Wes. My God would you hate it. But I hope you understand why I need it. I talked to your mother the other day and she asked if I was still talking to you. That was awful. I didn't realize she knew. I guess I must have done it once or twice when she came over to pick up your suits for donation last month. I lied and said no, even though I've read that most young widows do the same, sometimes for years. I couldn't tell if it made her happy or sad, you know I've never been able to read her well."

The ceiling creaks as her upstairs neighbor walks across the floor. She knows it's something most apartment dwellers complain about but it offers a curious comfort: she might be the only person in her apartment, but she isn't fully alone in the building. If something were to happen, there'd be someone to hear her cry for help.

The following week passes slowly, but it does pass, and she slips easily—perhaps too easily—into a new routine. Busywork fills her hours at the office and once home, she eats rice and baked chicken on white plates, drinks Chardonnay or Pinot Grigio, and listens to her neighbors walk and talk and live around her. She leaves the lights on night and day, even when she's at work.

On Friday night, when she turns on the television for the first time, she recoils from the voices and laughter and the bright moving bodies, dropping the remote in her haste to turn it off. By the time she fishes it from between the cushions and thumbs the power button, she's breathing audibly through her nose.

The laughter continues, a child's laugh, one bright peal that stops abruptly. The remote tumbles to the floor. Before she signed the lease, she asked if there were any children in the building; the leasing agent said no. The laugh comes again, soft and sweet and close, and Riva's on her feet before she can think too much. She takes tiny, mincing steps while she clenches her jaw. It has to be an acoustical trick, but she needs to see for herself to be sure. Anyone in her situation would.

Everything is as expected in her bedroom, and she pauses outside the door to the second. No laughter, no noise at all, but she opens the door, remaining on her side of the doorframe. The chest-high legion of stacked boxes sits as they should. The laughter was, no doubt, a misheard television or perhaps a figment of her imagination. How many times has she seen Wes or Charlotte right around the corner or at the far end of a grocery store aisle? Heard their voices, their footfalls, their exhalations?

She jumps at a flicker of movement on the wall to her right, something small that vanishes behind a box as quickly as it appears, and barks a short laugh. A bug of some kind, maybe a spider. She's never been squeamish when it comes to many-legged creatures, and this one is welcome to stay. But the hairs on the nape of her neck are standing at attention. This is the second time she's seen—or almost seen—something in this room.

"Hello?" she says, the word feeling foolish on her tongue.

There's no answer because there's nothing and no one to answer. It's just been a long week in an endless series of long weeks. She shuts the door harder than she intended and offers a quick "sorry" to the ceiling. In the living room, she perches on the edge of the sofa, tapping her fingers on the seat beside her. Gets up and goes to the sliding glass door, twisting the rod that opens the vertical blinds. There's so much green outside. Too much color, too much life. She fights the sudden urge to run outside, climb the trees, and strip off the leaves, leaving nothing but skeletal branches. Lips pressed in a tight line, she closes the blinds. Winter can't come fast enough.

"Wes, I don't think I can do this. Everything is too much."

She opens a new bottle of wine and takes it and a glass into her closet, sitting behind a curtain of pale turned semi-transparent in the overhead light. From here, she can't hear her neighbor's steps or voices or anything else, and a tightness inside her eases. Silky fabric caresses her cheek; she leans into it as though it were the palm of a hand. If she closes her eyes, she can pretend it's Wes, pretend it's the last thing she remembers instead of the tension in the air between them. Her fault. She broke their silent contract the night before after he put Charlotte to bed. She let out the genie in the bottle and once done, such things can't be contained.

"I was only trying to explain how I felt to you. How I felt about her," she says, refilling her glass. "I couldn't stand it anymore, the not talking about it. I really thought you'd understand, and when you didn't ..." But how could she have expected him to? Even now, she doesn't understand herself, only knows that something inside her was—is—broken.

It was Wes's idea to have a child. He always spoke of having a family and she agreed, mostly because she felt it was something she *should* want. How could she tell him the truth, that she didn't want it at all, that she wanted to stay only the two of them?

She thought it would be better once she got pregnant, but she hated the changes to her body, the discomfort, and wanted it over and done with. After eight hours of labor, they placed Charlotte on her chest, and she waited for that rush of love everyone spoke about, but instead, she felt nothing but impatience. She was tired and wanted to sleep yet she knew better than to say that aloud. So she smiled and cooed and congratulated Wes instead, but when the nurse came to take the baby, she sighed in relief.

Every morning she woke thinking *Today I'll feel like a real mother.* And every morning, disappointment sat in her throat, a dry-swallowed pill. But even so, she did her best. She tried not to be so gruff when Charlotte asked why for the thousandth time. She tried not to pull away from the sticky hands seeking attention or wanting to pat her cheeks. She tried not to ignore the endless litany of "Mama, see? Look, Mama." when she'd already done so several times. She *tried.* That's what she tried to explain to Wes. He accused her of not loving their daughter, an unforgiveable insult that hurt because sometimes she feared it was true. The following day, they were still speaking around what they'd said, he took Charlotte for ice cream, and then they were gone. And while she may not have been fond of being a mother, she definitely did not want Charlotte to die.

Now, hiding behind all that white, all that anonymity, she drinks until the bottle is empty, shame souring the wine in her mouth, and curls into a ball with an ivory dress for a pillow.

In the morning, she slinks from the closet, embarrassment on her cheeks like ill-placed rouge, body and head aching. Once the aspirin kicks in, she dresses and visits a nearby home improvement store, going straight for the lighting aisle. She buys four new floor lamps—one for the dining room, the living room, her bedroom, and one for the hallway. She also buys brighter bulbs for the lamps she already has as well as for the kitchen and bathroom fixtures.

The apartment practically glows when she has everything plugged in, and even when night begins to fall, it's midday inside. Maybe this is exactly what she needs, a blank canvas to rewrite herself upon, a chance to be no one at all for a time.

She wakes in the middle of the night, in her bed this time, from a dream of Wes, once more trapped in a vast darkness Riva can't navigate. She blinks in the lights, confused and worried she's going to be late for work, but once her eyes adjust to the brightness, she realizes it's Sunday and turns her face into the pillow.

So close as to sound in the same room, a child laughs and Riva sits up straight, the covers pooling at her waist, her fists between her breasts. Another laugh, then, from farther away, yet too close. She gets out of bed, slow and careful.

She stands in the narrow hallway, elbows cupped in her palms, listening. The laugh comes yet again, from behind the closed door of the second bedroom, and before she can talk herself out of it, she turns the doorknob and flips the light switch. The room is as it should be, the boxes in their proper places. She steps deeper into the room, making a note to buy another lamp to banish the shadows in the corners.

"Okay, Riva, get a grip," she says, her voice too loud and jarring. She might as well get the coffee started; she's too awake now. Maybe after that, she'll re-sort the boxes. Best to clean the slate as much as she can. She reaches for the light switch, and on the wall next to the door is a red stick figure with spindly arms, one of which is raised, two elongated legs, a round head with dots for eyes, and squiggles for hair.

All the air rushes from her and her legs turn rubbery and weak. Is this someone's idea of a cruel prank? She races into the kitchen and paws through the cabinet under the sink for a spray bottle of cleanser with bleach, her heart thudding painfully. With a roll of paper towels tucked under her arm, she runs into the bedroom, spray bottle raised and ready.

The wall is bare.

"No," she says. "No!"

Everything falls from her grasp and she drops to her knees, fingers spidering over the plaster in frantic arcs. It was there. She saw it, plain as day. She *did*. But the surface now in front of her gives lie to that declaration. A smudge, then? Something small amplified by her mind? She liberally sprays the wall anyway, wrinkling her nose at the caustic bite, and begins to scrub, darting frequent glances over both shoulders. When the toweling shreds into uselessness, the air reeks from her sweat and the cleanser combined. There's a wet circle on the wall the size of a serving tray. No red at all.

She presses fingers to temples. No red, of course not. The figure was never there. And what about the laugh? Simple, the neighbors have guests. Or the laugh wasn't real either. Leaving the cleaning supplies on the floor and the lights on, she closes the bedroom door behind her.

She showers the stink from her skin and, clad in a terrycloth robe, withdraws into the pale stillness of her closet, pulls her knees to her chest, and closes her eyes. Deep breaths. Emptiness. Everything will be okay. Eventually she emerges, gets dressed, and takes a long, brisk walk around the apartment complex. On her way into her building, her upstairs neighbor is bidding farewell to a woman with a young child, and Riva smiles to herself. Occam's razor.

Monday night, she gets home late from work. Eileen in accounting, newly returned from a leave of absence, cornered her in the parking garage to extend her sympathies. Riva could think of no polite way to extricate from the situation and Eileen meant well, but she spoke with her hands and between that animation, her words, and the bright pink of her blouse, it was all too much.

Now, Riva drops her keys on an end table and kicks off her shoes and makes a beeline for her closet. She only needs a few minutes of peace to erase the day. She does the same thing on Tuesday and Wednesday as well, even though no one wanted to have a long conversation with her after work. Work itself may be the problem. Everyone in the office knows her as Riva, grieving wife of Wesley and mother of Charlotte. If she takes a job elsewhere, she can keep mum about her personal tragedies. Even if they recognize her last name, it's not that uncommon and she doesn't have to confirm a damn thing if she chooses not to.

She's smiling when she leaves the closet, and while she eats dinner, she jots down notes for updating her resumé. As she passes the second bedroom, she hears a faint laugh. Let it go, she tells herself. It's the upstairs neighbor. Except she knows it isn't; she spied him leaving this morning with a suitcase. She stands in the hallway, a fluttery sensation in her chest, then swings the door wide and goes inside before she can change her mind.

There's no stick figure, only a darker spot where she washed the wall, and the room is quiet. She grabs the cleanser and paper towels, and, as she leaves, catches a flash of red from the corner of her eye. Her mouth turns to a desert and her fingers to tiny earthquakes, but she refuses to turn around. There's nothing there, not really. Still, she says, "Go away," on her way to the closet in her bedroom, never mind her rumbling stomach.

She falls asleep there, too, and wakes with a stiff neck. She sends her boss an email telling her she's ill, not bothering to wait for a response before she turns off her phone. After two cups of coffee, she carries one of the lamps from the living room into the second bedroom. Coupled with the overhead light and the other lamp, even the cardboard boxes are incandescent. She grabs the closest box, the one containing her discarded clothing, and carries it out to the Dumpster. She should donate them, but there's something powerful about hefting the box and tossing it over the side, as though she's shedding a layer of herself she no longer needs.

Humming in the bedroom, she rummages through the boxes, tipping them to read labels. Does she really need to keep Wes's paperbacks? He read military and action thrillers, genres she's never found interesting. Definitely not a genre her new self will want to read. And Charlotte's toys? She's never going to have another child, and most are stained or broken, not even in good enough shape for donating. She carries a box of the former outside, but sets it next to the Dumpster with the flaps open, in case there's someone in one of the buildings who might want to read them, and goes back for the box of toys.

She lifts it onto her hip and nudges another box aside. Stuffed animals. That one will definitely go, too. She hooks her fingers under the taped lid; it's light enough to carry that way. She turns and the air changes weight. The red stick figure is on the wall between closet and door again. Now its arms are bent, ending at the hips, and its head is cocked to the side.

Riva's arm tightens around the box of toys, but she loses her grip on the other, and the tape splits when it hits the floor, spilling a sea of brightly colored plush animals. She bends at the knees to set down the box and, holding her spine straight, walks out of the room, bound for the kitchen. Cleanser and paper towels clutched at her sides, she returns, her posture the same.

The figure remains on the wall, crayon hands on crayon hips.

"It's okay, it's okay, it's okay," Riva says as she kneels. She can take care of this. She *will* take care of it.

With one smooth motion, she swings the bottle up, pumping the handle furiously at the same time, first drenching the figure, then obscuring it from view. She lets the cleanser drop and scrubs the wall with a thick wad, breath rasping, muttering "It's okay" over and over. When the toweling finally falls apart, she sits, shaking, staring at the now-blank wall.

"I got it," she says. "I got it, Wes. Did you see that? I got it."

But she grabs another clump of paper and waits to make sure, even though every muscle is screaming for her to take refuge in her closet. But she won't do it. She needs to be in this room, needs to clear away these pieces of her old life so she can proceed, so she can be new. It doesn't matter how many things she thinks she sees or imagines she hears. Everything will be better soon enough. She runs the neckline of her t-shirt between two fingers. Everything will definitely be better.

While watching the wall, she fumbles for the stuffed animals and shoves them in their box. Once done, she pushes it out into the hall with her foot while dragging the box of toys behind her. Both tumble into the Dumpster with ease, and she feels a sense of power again. No one else might understand but that's okay.

She's able to go in the second bedroom—the wall is as she left it—and pull out two more boxes. Picture books and clothing. The latter goes in the trash; the former beside it. Half of Wes's old books are already gone, but she refuses to let it hurt. It's better this way. Back in the apartment, she picks two more boxes—blankets and another of books. She doesn't even bother to check the contents before carrying them out. Two more boxes follow and once they're disposed of, she fixes herself a sandwich with turkey and white cheddar and eats it standing at the kitchen counter.

Afterward, she grabs another box of books, this one heavier. Wes's hardcovers go next to the paperbacks beside the Dumpster. She isn't even sure why she saved them in the first place.

"I don't think you'd be mad at me, not really," she says. "You know I wouldn't ever read them. It's not like I'm throwing *you* away."

The next box she reaches for is labeled *Framed Photos*. Her wedding picture is there, along with several pictures of she and Wes before they got married. It also holds Charlotte's first photo and many of the three of them. She wants to throw it out, wants to untether herself from the memories, but a wave of guilt sits heavy on her shoulders. These aren't things she can replace, if she should choose to.

And from behind comes a laugh. She spins around fast enough to fill her ears with a crashing noise. The red stick figure has returned. Half of it anyway, peeking around the trim as a person with a doorframe. There's another laugh, and the figure moves in stop-motion fashion, vanishing *under* the trim around the closet. Both hands over Riva's mouth can't contain her airy shout and she retreats until she hits the boxes.

A muffled giggle whispers through the crack of the closet doors. Bifold, like those in her room, yet the closet itself is narrow, not a walk-in. She approaches it, her face slack, her limbs stiff, and flings open the doors. Empty. She lets out a ragged half-sob, and the laughter sounds at her left.

She spins and sees the figure on the wall, its crayon feet resting on the baseboard molding. It shifts again, bouncing off the molding, in the same stuttering way, and stops right next to a box. Gaze trained on the figure, Riva inches by degrees toward the cleanser, toes scrunching in the carpet. When her foot finally hits the spray bottle, she lunges, gripping the plastic tight, and in the span of an eyeblink, the figure darts behind the box with another laugh.

Riva races to the box and shoves it aside, aiming the nozzle toward a hint of red on the wall, but it disappears before the liquid hits. She shoves more boxes out of the way and two topple on their sides, pouring out toys and clothing in candy shades of pink and green and purple.

"Please leave me alone," she says. "Please."

A laugh replies. The red materializes on the wall beneath the window. She sprays, again too late. The figure walks across the wall toward the door and Riva works her way through boxes. Her foot catches on one, and she stumbles to her knees as the stick figure races around the doorframe and out of the room.

"Wes, I could really use your help right now," she says as she runs into the hallway, frantically panning right and left.

Laughter comes from the left, toward the living room, and she drops to all fours, creeping the length of the hall. A quick peek around the corner shows that the figure is standing on the wall above the sofa. Riva tightens her grip on the bottle, and springs to her feet, squeezing the handle. The red figure dashes out of the way. Riva lurches forward. The figure pauses beside the sliding glass door, head tipped as though listening, then it moves up and over in a blur, drops on the other side, and slips under the baseboard molding. Riva crawls across the floor, her breath a wild pony, and waits. The figure peeks out its head but ducks when Riva sprays. The figure reappears a few inches to the right, a tiny periscope testing the waters. Then it disappears. Riva wipes tears with her forearm. It's too fast. It's just too fast. She needs to—

Leave.

She gets to her feet. No laughter, no scratching, no motion anywhere. She exhales, long and slow, and her shoulders relax as she retreats. When the front door is only a few feet off, she turns. The red stick figure is standing on—in—the middle of the door, crayon arms on crayon hips.

"Please," Riva says, but the figure doesn't budge.

Riva takes a step back. The figure moves toward the wall. She steps forward; it moves to the door. Cat and mouse, and she knows the role she's playing. She scoots her feet along the carpet, a centimeter at a time, a sob caught in her throat.

She runs into her bedroom, into her closet, and slams the door behind her. There's no lock on the inside of the closet door so she crouches in the middle of the small space, wielding the spray bottle. The clothes sway gently on their hangers and she tugs them off with frantic fingers until there's nothing obscuring the wall.

As yet, there's no sign of the red figure, but the scratching noise is everywhere, and she scoots in a slow circle trying to gauge its direction, as it draws closer, ever closer. It grows even louder, deep inside her head, and she lets the bottle drop. She wants to cover her ears, but there's something wrong with her arms. They won't—can't—bend the way she needs them to.

The world turns to a uniform shade of pale that smells of paper and wax, and somewhere in that stark whiteness, her daughter giggles. Riva's skin feels strange; it's too stiff, too slick.

In the far distance there's a hint of darkness. A doorway? The way out? But the dark grows larger, lines of it overtaking the white, and the scratching is so loud now it hurts. There's another giggle, but it doesn't sound like Charlotte anymore. It sounds bigger and older, and Riva knows something is wrong. Everything is wrong. And the dark isn't a way out at all.

She sweeps the white with odd, paddle-shaped hands for the bottle of cleanser, for anything at all, but there's nothing. Nothing but the encroaching shadows. She runs in the opposite direction, but her rigid legs render her gait awkward, and she seems to skip a step, like a special effect from an old monster movie.

And now the darkness begins to creep in beneath her feet, above her head, everywhere she turns, on all sides, thick lines drawn across the white, and somewhere within, she thinks she hears Wes's voice, calling her name. She wants to cry out in return, wants to tell him she's here and needs his help, but she can't make a sound because no one has drawn her a mouth.

THE GEARBOX

PAUL MELOY

Kevin Carter watched his eleven-year-old son assembling some of the pieces of shiny black plastic he'd pulled from his YAY!PYPEZ cereal box. The kits resembled smaller versions—these were about the size of a playing card—of the *Airfix* aeroplanes Kevin had constructed as a kid. Small bits of plastic attached to a frame and snapped off with a twist of the fingers. No glue needed here, though. The bits slotted together, or screwed in, or slid onto spindles.

While he got ready for work Kev lost interest in what Aiden was doing, his last thought on the matter being how many boxes of that horrible-looking cereal he'd got through in the week since it had appeared on the shelves (it was low-cost grub and it filled him up, and Kev kept telling himself to buy the kid more *wholesome* food—maybe some fruit once in a while—but he kept forgetting), and finished getting changed into his Val-You Mart uniform in the hallway off their tiny kitchen. As he put on his cheap vinyl shoes and clipped on his tie, a small silhouette appeared behind the pebbled glass rectangle set into the front door followed by a light knock.

Kev opened the door.

"Morning Teddy."

Aiden's school friend, Teddy Hankey, looked up at Kev with bleary eyes.

"Hello, Mr. Carter," he said.

Teddy looked bad. He was never in the best of health. There was always one like Teddy. A dead dad and forever a bit of dog shit on their shoes.

"Come in, son. Wipe your feet."

Kev stood aside. Teddy gave his shoes a perfunctory rub against the mat leaving a ruck of something days old and russet lying curled on the bristles. Kev frowned, and toed it onto the concrete step.

Teddy went into the kitchenette and pulled out a stool. He put a plastic carrier bag onto the table next to Aiden's cereal bowl. Aiden looked up. He eyed the bag.

"Alright, Teddy?"

"Alright. Bit knackered. I was up all night." Teddy nodded towards the bag, as if it or its contents had been the reason for his lack of sleep.

Kev looked in on the boys as he was about to leave.

"See you tonight," he said. Regardless of their own meagre budget, Kev added, "Help yourself to some breakfast, Ted. If you haven't eaten." He knew Teddy's mum got parcels from the Food Bank, which was a worse situation than their own dispiriting—but at least employee discounted—weekly shop at the Val-You Mart in the plaza by quite a stretch.

Teddy gave him a weak smile and reached for the cereal box.

Kev left for work.

Aiden was looking through the plastic bag Teddy had put on the table, pulling out handfuls of assembled black plastic components.

"You do all this last night?"

Teddy tipped cereal into a bowl. The cereal was almost black with a coating of laboratory chocolate, strange curled discs that made Kev think of toenails pulled from dead feet. "Yeah. Mum left her laptop on when she passed out so I found the site."

"Oh, man, *did* you?"

Teddy nodded, mouth set in a thin, superior line. He put a hand inside his tatty blazer and pulled out a piece of folded paper from a pocket ink-stained along the seams from countless broken biros.

He made a show of withholding it from Aiden and then let his friend snatch it out of his hand.

Aiden unfolded it and gawked at the compressed lines of type and complex knots of schematics.

"I printed out the instructions," Teddy said. "Personalised to our codes."

Aiden was impressed. He held the printout at eye-level and squinted, turning the page around in his hands. "Looks hard," he said at last.

Teddy looked disappointed. "Give it," he said.

Aiden gave Teddy the page, and Teddy folded it and put it back in his pocket.

"It's not going to be easy, Aid," he said. "You read the texts. It's why we're allowed to work in pairs."

Aiden stood up from the table and went to put on his school shoes. "I know," he said. "In it to win it."

"You know it!" Teddy said.

Kev stopped at Balv's to get some tobacco. As he went to open the door he was shoved out of the way by three crop-haired twelve-year-olds as they piled out of the shop. He took a step back and watched them, feeling impotent, wanting to say something fatherly, something *strict*, as they untangled their bikes from the heap blocking the door and rode off towards the main road, shrieking and waving cartons of fags, but he bit his tongue. His mate George had taken a shoeing from a gang like that a month ago for having the audacity to object to their incontinent gobbing all over the pavement outside the infant school.

There was a picture of a corpse beneath a mortuary sheet on the packet of his Amber Leaf. He stuffed the tobacco in his pocket. As he left the shop he noticed a big pile of those cereal boxes Aiden and his mates liked so much.

Kev decided he'd buy up a few of them on his way home if there were any left.

At break time, Aiden and Teddy went to the school library and got onto one of the computers. Aiden had torn the code from the bottom of this morning's cereal box as he'd been instructed to do by the texts, and they tried to log onto the site.

"Bollocks," said Teddy. The web-blocker software wouldn't have a bar of it. Access restricted.

Aiden's phone pinged. He took it out and looked at the screen. He held it up to show Teddy. A text message. It was a web address.

"Put it in!" Teddy hissed.

Aiden typed the web address into the search engine.

A black screen appeared, with a small white oblong in the middle of the page. Aiden clicked on it and typed the code. Another screen appeared. There were more schematics. These appeared less complicated than those Teddy had shown Aiden earlier, possibly some kind of frame, or rack, onto which the more intricate devices fitted.

"Can you draw that?" Teddy asked. He scoped about for the librarian but she was behind her desk at the far end of the library doing her nails.

"Yes, give me that piece of paper."

Teddy took the folded paper from his pocket and gave it to Aiden. Aiden spread it out on the desk, facedown, and started to copy the on-screen schematics onto the blank sheet.

It was just a single web page, so when Aiden had finished drawing they closed the screen down and logged out. Teddy put the paper back in his pocket.

"Bring it round mine," Aiden said. "Dad's working late as usual."

There was something in Aiden's tone that made Teddy ask, "You don't like your dad?"

Aiden shrugged but didn't look up.

"He seems alright," Teddy said.

"Well, tell that to my mum," Aiden said.

Teddy looked away, a forlorn expression on his face. "At least you've got a dad," he said.

"At least you've got a mum," Aiden said.

They stared at each other for a moment, each daring the other to look away. And then they both burst out laughing.

"They're all *twats!*" Teddy said.

"Twats! Absolute twats!"

Teddy patted the outside of his blazer, above his heart, above the folded schematics hidden in his inside pocket, and winked. As he did so, Aiden's phone bipped again.

Tonight, the text read.

Δ

Kev was stacking jars of something unappetising on a shelf in the Val-You Mart when George came over.

"That's new," he said. "Come in today?"

Kev held one of the jars and looked at the label. Stuff floated in jelly-like brine; pineapple, peas and bits of pork, possibly. He couldn't read the label, the letters looked like maths.

"Yesterday, I think," Kev said. "Do you think you heat it up or just eat it from the jar?"

"I think you set light to them and throw them at the police."

Kev put the jar back on the shelf.

"Fag break?"

"Come on then," said George.

They went through the aisle and slipped out past the meat counter into the storage area. George opened the back door and they stepped out into the delivery yard. Kev offered George a rollup and lit his own.

"How's your leg?" Kev asked.

George rubbed his shin. "Little bastards," he said. "Like being attacked by baboons. Got one of them in the nuts, though."

Kev grinned. "They're the future," he said.

"They're fucking welcome to it," George said. He looked up at the overcast sky, unseasonably grim for July. There was a yellowish tinge to the clouds east towards the coast. "How's your boy?" George asked.

Kev shrugged. "Seems okay. I hardly see him I'm so busy. He's always up in his room making models, or texting someone, so I guess he's all right."

"Misses his mum, I bet."

Kev nodded. "Bitch hasn't been in touch once since she left."

George stayed silent and pulled on his cigarette. He had similar problems.

As they stood smoking, a white delivery van pulled into the yard.

"Tremendous," said George. He took a final pull on his cigarette and stubbed it beneath his boot.

The van pulled up and the driver switched off the engine. He got out and sauntered around to where the two men were standing.

"Hello, Dean," Kev said.

Dean Brazil puffed out his chest.

"Where's Maurice?"

"He's sick," George said. "Chest pains."

Dean nodded. "Didn't look well. What about Rory?"

"He's sick, too. Priapism," said Kev.

"Right," Dean nodded again, "Wants to get that looked at. What are you pissing yourself about, George?"

George ignored him and patted Kev on the arm. "Have fun, Kev, I'm back on the tills in five minutes." He went back into the shop, still laughing.

Kev followed Dean around to the back of his van. Dean opened the rear doors and stood aside. He took a pack of Richmonds from his jeans pocket and lit one up with an orange disposable lighter. He leaned against the open door and took a long drag on his cigarette.

"All yours," he said, indicating the boxes stacked in the back of the van.

Kev sighed. It was going to be a long shift.

After school, Aiden and Teddy went back to Aiden's flat. They hurried across roads, beneath overpasses linking blocks of flats and ducked out of an alleyway onto the green. There were a few kids in the play area already, clustered around the graffiti-covered plastic shack that was supposed to be a playhouse for smaller kids but had become an after-school smoking den by default. A couple of leggy older girls sat on the swings scowling at their phones.

Aiden and Teddy walked past, trying to look inconspicuous. Hurrying kids triggered a feral, carnivorous instinct in bullies, filled their mouths with spiteful salivation and an urge to chase their prey.

Where are you going in such a hurry?

But they made it past, and scooted left around the corner of the block in which they both lived and ran up the concrete stairwell.

Aiden unlocked his front door and they went into the kitchen. They shrugged off their bags and sat down at the table.

Teddy took out the sheet of schematics and laid it out flat.

Aiden took a handful of pieces from the plastic bag and arranged them in a row. Teddy did likewise, emptying the bag. He balled it up and put it in his pocket.

"What you got?" Teddy asked.

Aiden pointed at the piece he had been assembling that morning. It looked a bit like a fragile camshaft, with an array of interlocking cogs mounted on a spindle.

"Got more upstairs," Aiden said, and got up and ran to his bedroom.

He returned a minute later with an old shoebox. He put it on the table and took off the lid.

"Oh, ok," said Teddy. "You've been busy. Thought you might have been wanking off."

"What else is there to do?" Aiden said.

They lifted out the pieces Aiden had constructed. He had used guesswork mostly, because they had no computer and his mobile phone had no Internet, but he got occasional texts that contained clues, or instructions if he got stuck. All he had to do was text the hidden codes on the bottom of the inside of the cereal carton to a free number provided when he had first registered, and he got a helpful hint.

Teddy rotated the schematics. "That looks like they fit together," he said, indicating one of the pieces he had constructed and one of Aiden's. He picked them up and slotted them together.

"That was easy. What about those bits?"

Aiden held a piece that looked like a system of tiny filters. It had an insectile, crouching aspect. Its spindly, spiky legs seemed to make Aiden's palm itch.

"I reckon … that goes in *that*," Teddy said, and picked up a piece made from rings and discs of black plastic. He took the filters and slid them inside the curious array of rings. Its legs sat in six tiny cups moulded to the edge of the base ring.

Aiden and Teddy exchanged glances. They both laughed.

"This is so cool," Teddy said. "I wonder what the hell it is?"

Δ

Kev had nearly finished unloading the van. Dean had wandered off somewhere, probably trying to locate Julie, or one of the other girls who worked on the checkout. At the back of the van was a carton containing twelve boxes of YAY! PYPEZ.

Kev pulled the carton the length of the van and stepped down onto the ground. He was about to lift the box when a bulky shadow loomed over him.

"Kids going mad for that cereal," Dean said. "Don't know why. Tastes like blood from a cat's face!" Dean's big, ill-bred features tried to express disgust but only succeeded in making him look mildly confused. "You want those? Tenner."

"What?"

Dean looked left and right, and then leaned in to speak, conspiratorial. "You can have that box for a tenner. Fings get lost all the time, you know, *in transit*. Anyway, that's the last of them."

"What do you mean?"

"I mean, if you give me a tenner I'll forget they're on my docket. Fuck's sake."

"No, what do you mean that's the last of them?"

"Gone out of business or something. Companies like that don't advertise, do they? Word of mouth. Who's goin to pay to advertise the shit they sell in there?" Dean jabbed his thumb over his shoulder towards the store. "Muck, innit."

Kev looked at the box. A tenner wasn't much of a saving.

"I'll give you a fiver," Kev said. "It's all I've got."

"Fuck off," said Dean. "Kids round here'll bite me hand off for these. Coaldust, these are."

"Six quid."

"Alright."

Kev took a five-pound note and emptied the change from his wallet. He counted out ninety-four pence and put it in Dean's hand on top of the fiver. "I owe you six pence," he said.

Dean's hand trembled with uncertainty.

"I'm not 'appy," he said at last but closed his short, fat fingers around the money and jammed it in his overall pocket. "Have it next time. I'm in a hurry for it."

"I will," said Kev.

Dean closed up the back of his van and Kev watched him drive off, the carton on the ground at his feet. He picked it up and walked into the storage area. He went over to the back of the room and put the carton behind a stack of dog food.

Kev thought it looked sufficiently concealed, but not too obviously hidden. He grabbed an armful of economy antiseptic wipes and returned to the store to resume stacking shelves.

As he was walking down an aisle, a woman came up to him and stopped him. She didn't quite put a hand on his chest but her agitation was evident.

"Can I help you?" Kev said. He took a step back. She was darting her eyes around, trying to locate something on the shelves.

"That cereal!" she said. "You know, that YAY!PYPEZ stuff. Have you got any left? Any still out the back?"

Kev felt a stab of unease. "If there's none on the shelves, then I'm afraid it's all gone."

"Shit!" the woman said. "My kids sent me out for more of it. I don't give a bugger what they eat, to be honest, but it's kept them quiet this last week. She was still casting her eyes about. "They bring this stuff out and then just when you get used to it …"

"They might still have some left in Balv's," Kev said, suddenly wanting this woman out of the shop.

"No," she said. "No. All gone."

"What about our sister store over in …?"

"No!" the woman shouted. "They just sell them *here!*"

Paranoia made Kev think the woman might push past him and march straight out into the storeroom. She'd find them, hidden in the most obvious place, and point, and scream, and carry the whole carton off like a maddened looter.

But she turned and walked off, shaking her head, still peering up at the top shelves … just in case.

Kev waited a minute, then slipped back out into the yard and put another couple of boxes of *Growler* on top of his contraband.

Δ

Aiden and Teddy stood back from the table and evaluated their construction.

"That's as weird as fuck," Teddy said.

It stood about a foot tall, about six inches wide and the same deep; a tangled knot of delicate plastic components in a fragile-looking frame. Some of the parts moved, some were fixed; vents could be lifted, little levers pulled to move the cogs and wheels.

"Does it need batteries?" Aiden wondered.

"There's no dynamo, no circuits or wires," said Teddy.

"Is that it, then?" Aiden consulted the intricate diagrams on the sheet of paper. "You sure we've got all the parts?"

Teddy shrugged. "What can we do about it? We both collected as much as we could afford. Every box is different."

"What if it doesn't work?"

"Then we've wasted our time," said Teddy. "I can't see where we've gone wrong. You're worried over nothing."

Aiden slid a finger into the construction and tilted a couple of minuscule valves.

"Stop tinkering with it. You'll fuck it up."

Aiden was still looking at the diagram.

"There's a bit should go there, in that little hole," he said, determined to convince Teddy. "Are there any more parts in your bag?"

Teddy took the balled up plastic bag from his pocket and shook it out over the table.

"Nothing," he said. "What about you?"

Aiden went up to his room and had a root about under his bed, but he already knew he'd find nothing. He'd been very careful.

"Maybe the others will have spares," he said.

Teddy didn't look convinced. "These are code-specific. The more you buy the better your chances, obviously. It totally forbids swaps."

"How would they *know?*"

"Codes," Teddy said again, with the assured finality of one entrusted with unimpeachable information.

"Oh, whatever," Aiden said, defeated. "You're probably right. We'll just have to see."

"I bet the others haven't got all the parts either. I bet there's some kind of built-in failsafe."

"Yeah," Aiden seemed buoyed by this new speculation. "There must be."

Both Teddy's and Aiden's phones pinged.

Excited, they both looked at their screens and read the texts.

They were identical: *Come Now.*

Aiden went to the front door and opened it. It was dark, the air humid, and the sky overcast. He leaned over the barrier and peered out across the estate. "Hey, Ted, come and look at this."

Teddy came out and stood next to Aiden.

"I never thought there'd be so many," he said.

From alleyways and stairwells the children of the estate came, their faces lit by the screens of their phones, carrying their constructions. They reached the green and milled about, awaiting further instructions.

"Come on," said Teddy with some urgency.

Aiden went back into the kitchen and picked up their plastic assembly with great care and brought it out onto the walkway. He followed Teddy down the stairs and went out across the pavement to meet the others. As he walked, the creation in his hands bowed and yawed and Aiden was terrified it would collapse, disintegrate, blow away, crumple or just detonate in his hands into hundreds of tiny parts and be lost in the mud and shadows of the green. He stopped and breathed deeply. He was trembling, and the construction trembled with him.

Teddy held up his phone and shone the screen at Aiden.

"You're going to drop it," he hissed.

"You take it," Aiden said, sick of the fragility of the thing.

Teddy took it from Aiden, cradling it in his arms. He looked around, trying to see what all the other had brought.

Their phones pinged.

Everyone moved at once, lifting phones and peering at screens. Aiden read his text. "The play area," he said.

They all moved off, towards the swings and the playhouse. The only light was from some of the windows of the flats that faced out over the green, and the unearthly bobbing flotilla of mobile phone screens. The streetlamps were out and there was no moon.

They reached the play area and one of the kids at the front of the procession opened the gate and stood aside while they all funnelled through. No one spoke but glances were cast around, appreciative faces pulled as they appraised each other's work.

Aiden nudged Teddy and nodded towards a couple of little kids standing together by the swings. They shared the burden of some long thing with a craning arm and what must have been over a hundred inner wheels.

"That must have taken some doing," he said.

Teddy grunted.

"I don't think this is a competition," Aiden whispered.

"Well, what is it, then?"

"Some sort of collaboration."

"Fuckin' big words," Teddy muttered.

"Yeah, you know, like team-building. Dad went on a team-building day with his work. They had to solve problems. Trust each other. Dean got off with George's girlfriend."

"Maybe we all get a prize," Teddy said, brightening.

And then their phones went off again.

Kev was last to leave work. After another crisis of confidence he had gone back into the storeroom and this time taken the carton of cereal outside and put it in one of the recycling bins. Now, with the sodium security lights coming on, he grabbed the carton out of the top of the bin and hurried away home, the carton lemony and radioactive in his arms from the revealing light. Once he reached the darkness beyond the reach of the security lights he stopped and took a breather. He swore to himself that he'd never perpetrate blue-collar theft again. His system burned with adrenaline and guilt.

He carried on towards home, crossing the car park outside the shopping plaza and turning left at The Macebearer. He'd have liked a quick pint but he thought that if he went inside the pub with the last box of YAYIPYPEZ on the estate, he might not get out alive.

He went past the pub and set out across the green towards his flat. And was surprised to see what looked like a mobile-phone convention thronging the play area.

He slowed his pace and thought about skirting the green completely, but the memory of this morning's encounter with the crop-haired morons in Balv's surfaced and he set his back straight and continued the line that would take him past the play area. He'd had enough of being intimidated by kids.

Now all the pieces had been assembled, the wobbling plastic construction had taken on the shape of some sort of alien machine. It was roughly the size of a small garden shed and it had required a couple of the taller boys to stand on the roof of the play house in order to fit the last pieces onto the top of it.

They had, as Aiden had predicted, worked as a team. Schematics were uploaded via incoming texts and the children had got busy, comparing and evaluating their constructions against those of the others. Teddy had been galvanised. Aiden watched with great amusement as his friend took charge of a group of six, ordering pieces into position with the authority of a tiny fat foreman. Aiden watched other groups, phones in hand, checking and re-checking, shining their phone torches at piles of tottering plastic components. There was conversation, and debate, but it was hushed, almost respectful, in the intermittent screen-lit darkness of the play area. There was an atmosphere building of expectation and excitement. Aiden could feel it, like a low, dense current. The hairs on his arms and the back of his neck rose in cold gooseflesh.

And when the larger parts were ready, they were lifted with the utmost care and borne to the centre of the play area like idols of a new religion, and slotted together. The whole process was fraught with the terrible possibility of sudden, catastrophic clumsiness, or ruinous ineptitude, and the setting down of parts took on an almost funereal care as though the idols had become the caskets of dead children and to spill them would result in stomach-churning mortification.

Two tall boys scaled the playhouse and were handed up the long piece with the crane and all the wheels, and another piece that looked to Aiden like the skeleton of a trumpet stuffed with thorns. The boys leaned out, the constructions held between them, and placed them with held breath and tenderness into the last two remaining gaps in the machine. There was a great sigh from everyone, Aiden included. He looked around for Teddy, and saw him standing at the back of the crowd with his hands planted on his hips and his head held to one side, evaluating it all.

Finally it was finished. The children stood in a mob around it. They held up their phones, those with torches built in and those without and using merely the faint luminosity of their screens, and cast their collected light across it. Its hollowness and frailty was alarming but it stood firm on its intricate base, the minute complexity of moving parts within casting matchstick shadows throughout the interior and confusing it more completely; what were shadows and what were components became almost impossible to discern.

And in the sudden silence, one phone bipped. All heads turned.

Teddy held up his phone and looked at the text.

Kev crossed the green towards the gathering. He was unnerved not so much by the sight itself as by the uncanny silence.

He peered at the crowd and saw the structure for the first time. He had thought it was part of the playhouse, part hidden as it was behind the little building, but as he drew closer he could see it was separate, and skeletal, and that it was this odd thing that the children were surrounding so intently.

As he crept—and he was creeping now, although he was unaware of this—the silence was broken by the beeping of a phone.

Kev stopped. As all the children turned to see who was the source of the sound, their lights played across the figure standing at the back of the crowd.

"Teddy?" said Kev. And the thought on the heels of this: *Where's Aiden?*

Teddy looked up and swallowed. He looked for Aiden in the

crowd, couldn't locate him, and his face took on an expression of alarm. And then Aiden pushed through the crowd and went to him.

"What is it?"

Teddy showed Aiden the text. The crowd of children were edging closer, murmuring, their curiosity turning to impatience.

"It wants *me*," whispered Teddy. He looked up, through the bodies of the encroaching children. He couldn't see the construction but he could feel it, crouching at the rear of the crowd, prickly and trembling with its own weight.

Aiden snatched the phone. "What do you mean, it wants you?"

He read the text. *Teddy*, it said, *draw near*.

"It knows your name …"

"When we registered,"

"Yes," Aiden sounded irritated. "I remember. Well, go on then, *draw near*."

Teddy remained where he was.

The crowd had surrounded them while they had been talking. Someone shoved Teddy between the shoulder blades and he stumbled forwards.

"Aiden," Teddy said, but Aiden nodded.

"Go *on*," he said in a low, unfriendly voice. "Looks like it was a competition after all."

Now the crowd was jostling and Teddy was propelled towards the construction. He stumbled but someone grabbed the hood of his coat and prevented him from falling in the mud. He was yanked to a halt a foot away from the construction. He looked around, "Aiden," he moaned.

His phone went off again, in Aiden's hand. Aiden read the text.

"What?" said Teddy, "What now?"

Aiden looked up, his expression cold.

"It says, *use the key*, Teddy. You got a key to that thing?"

"No!" Teddy said. He held up his hands, palms outwards, to show he wasn't hiding anything. "I don't have any key!"

"Use the key," someone said.

"Use the key!"

"Use the KEY!"

"I don't have a fucking *key!*" Teddy shouted.

"*Aiden!*" said Kev, from the back of the crowd.

Everyone turned to look at Kev. Kev's eyes were very wide, mystified by the sight of all these children, his son amongst them, taunting Teddy in front of some strange, macabre-looking creation. He felt fear rising and tried to choke it down for his kid's sake, for Teddy, for his own self-worth as a father.

"What's ...?" he said, and then someone in the crowd shouted, hoarse and agitated: "He's got a box-full!"

And they rushed him before he had a chance to say anything else, Aiden amongst them.

Kev regained consciousness and tried sitting up. He groaned. He got as far as propping himself up on his elbows. It was still dark but there was a diffuseness to it beyond the estate, low towards the sea. Dawn was coming; he had been out for hours.

The remains of the carton and the twelve boxes of cereal surrounded him. The mud was covered in those horrible unappetising curled discs, flung from the boxes in disregard and desperation for the prized hidden content. The bottoms had been torn from the boxes in search of the covert codes. They looked like they had been *savaged.*

The crowd of children were gone. Kev sat up, rubbed his face, and stared at the place where the slender scaffold of black parts had stood. It was gone, too.

"Are you okay, Mr. Carter?"

Kev jumped to his feet and span around.

Teddy was standing a few feet away, his coat torn at the seam around the top of his right arm. Gray fluff frothed from between the ripped line of stitching. His face was covered in dried mud and blood from a profuse nosebleed. One of his eyes was swollen half-shut.

"Teddy. Your *face.* Where's Aiden?"

"I watched over you, Mr, Carter," Teddy said. He wiped his nose and winced. "I could have gone with them, but I think I stopped them *killing* you."

Kev stared around, a nasty flimsy sensation filling him, making him want to float up onto his toes with terrible anxiety.

"Where's Aiden, Teddy?"

Teddy looked forlorn. He pointed towards where the construction had stood. "You had the key," he said. "In those boxes. They put it together and then they used it to turn *that* on."

Kev lifted his hands; he couldn't think. He stammered something incoherent, then stopped and took a breath. He closed his eyes.

"It was a plastic *toy*, Teddy."

Teddy shook his head. "It was a machine. A way out of here."

"Out of here?"

Teddy looked bewildered by how obtuse Kev was being. He spread his arms to encompass the park, the estate, the whole world. "Out of *this*," he said. "They promised us adventures."

Kev walked towards the now clear ground beside the playhouse. There were some of those small black frames, about the size of a playing card, stripped of their parts, trodden into the dirt, buckled. "Aiden!" he shouted. "Aiden, you come here, son!"

"He's gone, Mr. Carter," Teddy said.

A week later, Kev sat at his kitchen table, waiting. He was drinking a cup of tea made from water boiled in a saucepan on the cooker. The kettle was gone. As was the toaster, the microwave and the Breville. The living room was similarly denuded of electrical goods. The TV and the stereo had gone the way of everything else Kev could lay his hands on: *Cashconverters* in town. He'd made three hundred quid.

The children had never reappeared. The police had been disinterested, the media under-whelmed. None of the parents seemed particularly bothered either. Balv's hadn't needed to board up a window since the disappearance. Kev carried on going into work and was not surprised that nobody particularly gave a shit about his loss. George was avoiding him.

But Kev had not given up on his son.

He jumped and spilled cold tea over his fingers when a horn blared outside the flat. He got up and went out onto the walkway. There was a white van parked at the side of the road. Kev ran along the walkway and down the stairwell.

"Alright?" said Dean. He was at the back of the van, unlocking the doors.

Kev stopped, breathing hard, and said, "Is it all of them?"

Dean threw open the doors of the van and stepped back. He took out his Richmonds and lit one up. "Have you got it?"

Kev didn't take his eyes from the back of the van. He took out a fat roll of grimy tenners and passed them to Dean. Dean counted the money with terrible caution, his face a mask of mistrust.

"Three ton," he said at last, and slid the notes into his pocket. He was wearing jeans and a burgundy-coloured shirt. He was off duty. "That's the lot of 'em. Far as I know. You got in early there, son. These were supposed to go across town. I ain't even going to ask you why you want all that crap. None of my business."

Kev pulled out the first carton of breakfast cereal. There were at least a hundred more in the back of the van. He hefted it onto his hip, glanced at Dean, but Dean was staring at him with dead eyes.

"Fuck off," he said, "I'm just the delivery boy."

Kev lifted the box and started for the stairs.

Kev sat on the floor of his living room, walled in by cartons of cereal. His hands were trembling.

"It's okay, Mr. Carter," said Teddy. "We'll do this together."

Kev nodded. He was weeping. Teddy opened a carton and pulled out a box of cereal.

YAY! GOLDERN WIDGERSONS! they were called this time.

Teddy pulled out the waxy bag containing the cereal and pulled it open. He tipped its contents into one of the four big orange buckets Kev had placed beside them on the floor. The cereal was yellow and looked like dead skin from an old blister. He poked through the cereal with his fingers and then said, "Yes!" while lifting his hand to present Kev with the first free gift of the day: a slender frame of intricate plastic parts, parts to something much greater.

Kev took it and placed it flat on the floor. He reached for the box Teddy had emptied and tore the bottom from it. He showed Teddy the code, printed beneath a folded flap of cardboard. He smiled a thin, watery smile. His eyes were pale, and he was extremely tired.

Teddy was already emptying the next box. The flat was beginning to smell over-sweet and musty.

"Come on, Mr. Carter," Teddy said in his kindest, most encouraging voice.

"Yes," said Kev. He picked up his phone and texted the code to the number on the back of the box, the number to some unknown factory somewhere on industrial land far away and unregistered, perhaps not even of this dimension, where neglected children were the target of some monstrous game, and machine parts were designed by dreadful alien minds.

They waited.

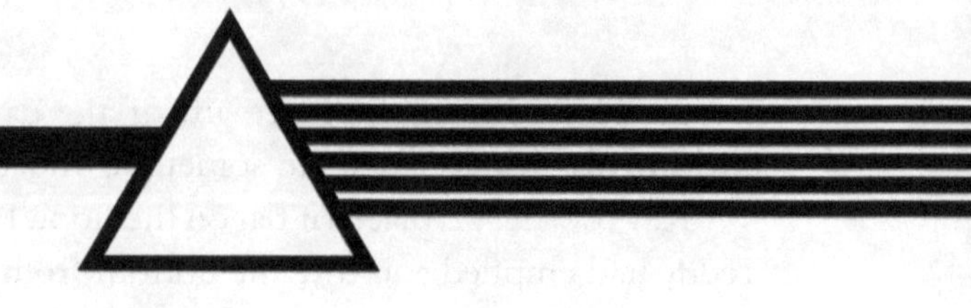

DISTRICT TO CERVIX: THE TIME BEFORE WE WERE BORN

TLOTLO TSAMAASE

AFTER-BORN

"Do you forgive me?" I asked.

"For what, nje?" he asked as we settled into an undeveloped green zone, a shade to hide sins.

"There's a reason why I approached you from the onset," I said.

"No shit. No one like your bourgeois type starts a friendship with types like me unless it's to earn public image points. It was all snaks. But hell, you're paying so I was hundreds. Mara, tell me, what did your cherry-picking activity score you?"

My hands trembled, slick with sweat. A swallow deep in my throat. Above us, the sun dispersed itself, into light, a spectrum.

"I think I remember everything because it wasn't right what I did," I whispered, sickness swirling in my stomach. My life had been a seeking of redemption.

"Remember what, joh?" he asked, crushing leaves into his palm, wrapping them slowly.

"I'm going to tell you a story, a story you'll struggle to believe. You'll think it's snaks, but," I said, bowing my head, "it's my fault your life is the way it is."

He sat up, his joint lingering in his dark brown fingers. "Ijo."

"Just light it, bra," I said. "You gonna need it."

Fire ignited and smoke evolved us as I dug into the deepest recesses of my mind of seventeen years ago, the time before I was born:

In seventeen hours, I will be born.

The male figure of a clan is deceased. His granddaughter-in-law is scheduled to give birth the following day. Discussions are held between the living-elders and the living-dead ancestors, with the sangoma as the interpreter, the medium, the shaman. And who are we? Sexless souls warring to be born through the granddaughter— the way we want. My application to be born was approved several days ago.

We sexless souls stand in a veiled terrain waiting for the new regime to select which wombs our births will lie in and which we'll fight for. Our wars are oft-salted with the palm of death, seeking our births, our genders, our ethnicities to feed from.

Maybe you're the kind to have died before you were born.

Do you remember what you said that hot winter ago? I do.

"Yazi choms, this is better than surgery." You paused then, allowing the silence to sit in my chest and knees where everything felt sallow.

"What's the catch?" I asked.

"There's no reincarnation without death." Your hands slid forward business-like. "All you have to do is die."

So simple, such a joke.

"Then what?" I played along.

"You choose who you're born from, how, in what sex and all that shit."

I scoffed. "All that shit, huh?" I felt desperate, desperate enough to believe it. To have the gender, ethnicity and even choose the family I wanted. I could be born rich—into a rich family. I could have it all.

"Dude, you don't have a job," you said, counting off all my jinxes on your steel-ringed fingers. "You're fucking squatting on someone's couch. You've no parents. You've no cash to pay for the hormone therapies or surgeries you're always going on about." You surrendered your hands, your way of waving the white flag. "You know I don't beat around the bush, bra. Telling it as it is."

I slowly unwrapped my hands from the fist-shapes they'd formed. "This just feels like a snaksnyana prototype techno-ish."

"You get to have everything you've wanted. You get to choose." Your lips twisted. "Think of it as a fusion of science and muti." That was always the mantra. Every reincarnate knew it.

That's what you said, but you never told me it'd be a war. Never. A fusion of science and muti. Nxa, now look what the fuck happened.

Δ

DISTRICT TO CERVIX: THE TIME BEFORE WE WERE BORN

NOW

I, along with the other pre-borns, sink our sights into the gathering site that lies several soul panels away from the next satellite eco-city. The kgotla has sharp bark-teeth stuck skyward, a half-womb holding young women who gather and consult their old-dead for advice. It's closing to the deadening night, so preparations for my should-be birth are in process. Most often, lives were laced in old-women tongue; they sewed all dreams, stitch-to-sleep, lacing it around eyes of the village citizens.

It was they who guarded passion, dream, motive.

Birth denied, some. Birth granted, others.

The sky wept itself of all things for two unborn babies, transparent of identity, remained buoyant in their womb-carriers, waiting for us to shape them, fill them out with our spirit. The kgotla was still indecisive of which pre-born/reincarnate/spirit would grow in the unborn heirs to their clan. Even after the decision was made, each pre-born would go on their sojourn with the opportunity to win their birthright, which might oppose the kgotla's "special" requests. Even though a science was concocted to give men birthing rights, there were only two open slots this season that a myriad of us reincarnates were vying for. I can't fail to be born this season. Failure means either death or exhausting the birth application period or being thrown into the womb-prison for years. I have waited many seasons, many dehydrating moons, and burning suns to allow this to pass by easily.

The pre-borns hush at the development in the kgotla, a tribal meeting of seven younger women. Through veiled sight—that neither after-borns can see through except us, pre-borns—the sky clock is nearing birth-horizon. We watch over the kgotla proceedings' decision that may give us our new bodies:

"The reincarnates await our decision—our figurehead is deceased," said the third-younger woman, in a stern, curt tone. "The sojourn is tonight. It will guarantee the heir's birth. We will train him, adorn him, and perfect his upbringing."

Traditionally, age dictated wisdom, but here the number of reincarnations that one *had* dictated wisdom. "Eldest" was defined as one with the highest reincarnation count, when in actual fact, they were the youngest in human years.

The fifth-younger woman held her hand up. "Sisi, be careful of the pronoun you use. That 'he' may be born as a 'she'."

The stern one shook her head. "We have already chosen who we want born into our clan. We have picked two reincarnates based on their previous lives that indicate an aptitude in political studies, bravery, courage and a show of altruism. One male, one female."

"Who will be born first?" asked the sixth-younger woman, a new addition to the conference who had many light moons that marked her youthful face. Wisps of the night braided themselves into dreadlocks knotted on her head, pointing to sky.

"The male of course," the third-younger said.

"Of course? Maybe that'll happen in patriarch eco-city 1, not in ours, matriarch eco-city 1," the six-younger said, narrowing her eyes. "Perhaps you should cease your immigration status and relocate back to your state."

The third-younger steamed. "We should meld their spirit into one male body then. That way no conflict would ever arise."

The first-younger, who had ochres of ash beaded across eir sleek forehead to the tip of eir nose to mark eir bogosi, eir highest chieftaincy, said, "They both deserve to be born at the same time, not one second late or one second earlier. This will avert any lower feelings of self-esteem in their childhood. One is not more important than the other is. We must wield their bond strong from the get-go." No one could quite tell where the first-younger's gender and ethnicity lay for eir had many births, many deaths, many lives and often the gravity and law of this world failed to portray eir succinctly; so the air was less translucent near eir form, and sound waves weren't born with the right chord to play eir voice through. Because of eir multiple and diverse reincarnations, eir was unlike others whose judgement was diluted by personal agendas. Therefore her opinion, her judgement became law. And because of this, no one could quite tell if she was dead or alive, or what her name was, often referred to as Eir across all languages.

"But how will the two reincarnates leave the uterus at the same time?" the third-younger asked.

"There will be two womb-carriers," Eir said.

"That requires a high power of soul energy, and our soul panels are at their lowest function," the third-younger said.

"High prices and sacrifices are a prerequisite to our self-sustaining goals," Eir said.

"But communities will live in the dark."

"We have provided them with soul-energized lamps," Eir said.

The other younger women grumbled at the third-younger woman's impudent manner of questioning their leader.

At this, Eir stared at the sky-clock waning in night sky. Each younger had on a sky-clock that told them the time of the womb, for the moon lay curdled in the dark night, and once it became full moon did it portray the minute of birth. Right now the clock was quarter-waning moon, still many hours from birth. This sky-clocked was etched into their wrists in golden wisps of metal and (lunar) technology.

"The new regime defines that choice lies with the reincarnates," stated the fourth-younger, once Motswana who switched to Chinese status linguistically after she failed to obtain her desired ethnicity in her sojourn. "Whoever you choose will define what gender, ethnicity, and religion they choose to be born as."

"Our homestead has negotiated for one female and one male finish and klaar." The third-younger swept her hands together into a clap. "The woman must give birth to the twins as per her stipulated traditional role," she said.

The second-younger woman—who chose "mixed ethnicities" as her birthright fought well during her sojourn to win it—shook her head. "No, several men in the community have been selected as potential womb-carriers—"

"The husband has duties," the third-younger declared.

"And so does the wife. Baby-carrying must be a fifty-fifty task carried by *both* parents," the second-younger said.

Eir watched with narrowed eyes, nit-picking every argument mentally. Eir stood, and everyone hummed in silence. "What's most important to the clan is the spirit, not the shell, not how the body, this soul-holder, looks. It is but a glass that can be shattered easily, whereas the spirit is an eternal fountain of all good things. If you sway your decision on the cosmetics of a soul-holder, then we may as well pick any cheap soul that will fail this clan. We do not want a weak spirit dressed in an 'acceptable' body. We just want a spirit. Whatever form it comes in—"

The third-younger jumped forth. "But these values are necessary to our tradition—"

"Traditional values should not be a crutch for dictators to sacrifice man for inequality and personal ethos," Eir said. "This is exactly why last year the law was sanctioned for man to share birthing actions. Agreed?"

Still unsatisfied, the third-younger said, "Either way, the reincarnates still have to battle for this birthright—*that* does not guarantee their survival."

Eir continued, "Both the parents will give birth—the twins must be born—not just one, but two children."

Some other younger-women shuffled, tied their tonkana blankets tighter around themselves and agreed. No one participated in going against the first-younger's decision. Their faces were laced with wrinkles, and hands soft with time.

"Although bodies are renewable resources, souls still remain as non-renewable energies to vitalize the body, which we are in short supply of—hence the reincarnation sanction," Eir said. "We must be careful that our decision tarnish not this non-renewable energy for it could vanish forever and our eco-city will cease to exist. Heed well, the granddaughter and womb-carrier hold two babies whose sex and ethnicity are undecided. They are scheduled to be born in a few hours whether the reincarnates or we come to a decision or not. The longer we take in our indecisive acts, the more it will jinx the twins. The objective remains the same, the twins will be the heirs, whatever they choose to be born as. This homestead will support them."

Our satellite hearts were moons for our bodies.

Nearby, the outdoor kitchen was a hotpot of the men's voices, preparing tea, preparing bread, waiting for the women to decide and to slaughter an offering to the ancestors once a decision was made.

Eir stretched her hand to the center where our former exhumed bodies that we shed years ago lay, wires attached to them, trying to alchemize the art of incubating souls. Soul energy lights our city, runs through the venous system of everyday life; without it, we remain in a dark world.

Eir gestured to the sangoma: "Give the selected reincarnates our decision and give us their response."

The sangoma kneeled in the womb-shape gathering, nodded his approval, shook dust into fire and began relaying the message to the ancestral land where we waited, which was veiled from all living sight. He danced with night and fire, dust his mathoa, into the realm where I stood with another pre-born for we were selected for the twin-roles—

AFTER-BORN

"Hold up. Am I supposed to believe this? That you can choose how you want to be born before you're born?" he asked, laughing.

"Well, traditionally, women got pregnant and the baby's sex was determined at seven weeks' pregnancy. Nowadays the sex is determined during our sojourn which occurs when the mother is in labor. Sex, gender, religion are determined during the mother's labor as we fight for the birthright. From war we are born. Before we were contained in a limbo stage for the full 40 weeks, but sometimes babies were born without spirits, which were snatched away in their slumber before they dripped into the form of the developing baby. Soul-tech was developed as a defensive mechanism to align the sojourn and gender selection during the mother's labor so it happened in a matter of hours."

"Fuck san, you must be higher than I am to say that with a straight face. I hope you're not tuning the younger-women such dom shit during your meetings, otherwise you gonna lose your authority. S'tru." He crossed his fingers, swearing.

My nails bit into his hands, leaving wounds. "Believe me, assablief. I'm not lying. We were in soul-form watching everything."

His eyes grew wide, taking in my panic. "From where were you soul-watching?"

"*Angazi*, I can never know where," I said. "Our former dead bodies lay prostrate right in the center of the *kgotla*, wires leashed to the sangoma."

"In our eco-city?" he asked.

"*Ja*, ours," I said. "The sangoma posed, like a jeweled metallic device, expressing what we wanted of our births. Post-birth, we're never supposed to remember our soul-lives, the intermediate space before being born. They said we'd recall these pre-birth memories when we're a newborn, but after some time as you grow older, time dilutes those memories from you mind. Something must be wrong with me to remember," I said, staring at him, guilt gutting me.

"So you got introduced to this reincarnation idea because of someone? Yet it didn't turn out good?"

"*Ja*, something like that," I said, voice faltering, afraid to go on, wanting to remain vague and hidden.

"Mate, you're not close to convincing. Look, until you show evidence that all this talk is real, I'm not going to believe you. It's just crazy and you look crazy. I just came out here to chill. I don't know what kind of things you're mixed up in, but I don't want all this heavy shit, ja. Sort yourself out or I'm out of here."

"I have evidence," I blurted. "I just need time. Just listen. Please. I'll show you the evidence soon."

He settled back onto the log we sat on. "I don't like where this is going. I don't feel right."

"Trust me," I whispered.

"But why me? Why are you so insistent on telling me?"

"Because … I saw you before you were born."

His arms drooped into the grassland. "You're scaring me." He backed away from me. "Don't touch me. You don't sound like your normal self."

"I'll keep my distance just as long as you promise to listen," I said, "because I'm not letting you get away until I've told you my story even if I have to restrain you."

His eyes scanned our surroundings for a soul in sight and truly noticed how isolated we were, how I'd intended for us to be alone. Not even his scream would reach a savior. I watched his mind dissolve itself into ugly thoughts of the harm I could bring him.

"Okay," he said, realizing his misfortune. "I'll listen if you promise to let me go once you're done."

I nodded. "Where was I? Right. So what happened next is after the *younger-women chose me and another reincarnate to be born through the grand-daughter, we had to give our decision, but the other reincarnate and I argued about how we wanted to be born:*

PRE-BORN VEIL

:

"What's up?" the reincarnate asks me. She's dressed in her last-reincarnate season's form, personality and lingo, a way to identify each other before we can adopt new identities. A buoyant glow we both are. Her being is sporadic, unable to settle in one position, bursting like stars into space. "Guess you're going to be my twin. Do you reckon we'll look alike? 'Cause that'll be a new thing I'll have to add to my resumé, joh."

"It makes no difference to me as long as I'm born," I say. I inhale her being to get a sense of who she truly is. She is of many evolved births, she is therefore powerful. She could win this sojourn—my selection. Most often souls are genderless, sometimes cultureless as I am.

"So it's been decided that one of us will be male-born and the other female-born," she says. "I call shotgun for the female-born role. It's my discipline." She winks.

"Like every other sojourn, you'll will have to fight me for that," I say.

"I ain't going to be male." She circles me. "Yazi, your birth has *only* been approved after how many failures? You gonna waste that? Look, let's not waste the sangoma's time and get this over with. Reconsider: what did you choose to be born as?"

"First-born *female*," I emphasize, "Black. The mother will be my womb-carrier. My occupation: illustrator/story-teller. Marriage: wife Sufia Habib, birther of four children, architect of soul energy incubators." Everything in my life will draw me toward that goal—failures, successes—even if I won't remember when childhood ceases my pre-born memories.

She whistles. "Haebo, you're losing privilege one rung at a time. So what exactly did the ancestor's ruling choose for you?"

I shuffle. "First-born male. Black. The mother as my womb-carrier. Occupation: political leader. Three wives, arranged marriages."

"What death age did you choose?" she asks. "Need to know in case you die early and I have to take over shit."

"I want to die when I'm a hundred twenty years old."

She laughs. "Ijo! Good luck with your battle to birth to win that right. It's going to be tough."

I turn, surprised. "What age did you choose?"

"Mmm, fifty. When time hasn't quite touched me yet, you check."

Explains a lot of why she's had many reincarnate seasons: she always resigned from each season early. It didn't make her powerful but deceptive. No wonder someone with so many reincarnate seasons wasn't quite at ancestor level.

"But hold up, you said your wife will be—she doesn't sound like she's in any one of our tribal eco-cities," she says.

She was right. Our built environment was split into eight tribal eco-cities and counting, protected in their architecture and some married into others either pre- or post-birth for self-sustaining values. Often this enriched the economy and soul-energy to power our living.

"I know her because our love was unfinished from the last reincarnate season," I say.

She peers, closing in to my face as if to enter my mind. "Come closer, I can't see what you looked like in your last after-born season."

"I wanted it censored for privacy reasons," I say.

Her sigh is equivalent to the sinking and coalescence of her soul-lit being.

Her being surrounds me as she says, "It is a painful act to be born. The path from the womb into the real world moves through several dimensions—anything could happen in that passage, in that limbo. If you accept the younger-women's ruling, I mean, once you die, it takes time, but you will rise to be an ancestor—a powerful ancestor. An honorary bestowed once you surpass stages."

She's trying to sway me so her sojourn is easier.

I send threatening signals her way. "Then why don't you be male-born?"

"It's not what the kgotla decided. Besides feelings are not important," she says. "Do you want to suffer? I mean, what if you're still-born just because you refused to comply, joh? Or what if your mother has a miscarriage? Or the chick is some junkie and she ain't ready to have a baby—and she aborts you? We don't know who she is, and she's supposed to give birth to one of us. Even if you win the sojourn, your mother-to-be is a stranger who has her own agenda. Besides, being female-born, they've child-rearing obligations, pregnancy and periods. Why the hell do you want to bleed?"

"Shouldn't that be your problem as well?" I ask.

"Mmm, not really, ja. I opted to have that out. Not really interested in those logistics. I just want the body, ja, not any of its clingy attributes. So, ja, my battle for birth is going to be a challenging one."

Clingy attributes. The definition of a woman has changed dramatically over the years. "Doesn't change my decision," I say.

The pre-born veil grows lava-red from my fury heightening the kgotla fire, which rises as if it's my soul. The sangoma breathes in our feud, preparing to relay it to the younger-women.

I disperse my being throughout the room; I suspect this is what Sunset must feel like when she transcends Horizon. "Take the male-born role."

Her smirk wraps cold around me. "No. I too selected first-born female, as well as male-born, and Black," she says. "But I have the upper hand. I chose what no one would, given the new law: I chose the father as the womb-carrier. I will be born as neither but both male and female."

I slouch back, and so do my furies.

Her being is airborne, voice a hush: "Men give birth, too."

KGOTLA

After the conclusion of our heated conversation, the sangoma turned back like a dog with a tail between his legs and gave the younger women in the kgotla our decision. He said, "The two chosen reincarnates' decision is as thus: the male-decided one wants to be born as a girl from the wife." He coughed. "The female-decided one wants two things: to be born as both and neither male nor female from—" he coughed and shuffled in the grave-dust—"from the father."

"Neither and both?" the third-younger asked, perplexed.

The sangoma shrugged. "The female-decided one wants the choice for her body to portray those characteristics. On some days, they will look neither male nor female. On other days they will pass off as both male and female."

"Jerusalema! This is absurd." The third-younger slapped her hands into her knees. "This is not close to what we agreed to."

"The clause suggests the reincarnates are allowed to choose their identity as long as it does not stray far away from human physiology," Eir said.

"Do we honestly want such stubborn reincarnates in our clan?" the third-younger asked.

"They have made their decision, now they must fight for it," Eir said. "And it shall be. Prepare the birthing rite." Eir nodded to the sangoma, who was half-in and half-out in both worlds.

At this announcement, the men ululated in throngs of Kalanga, Setswana, Xhosa, a pre-celebration before the birth.

And so the moon leaked through the horizon as the community was swept with incense to guide the passed-away's spirit; the smoke became breath. The funeral air was pregnant with grave-dust and snuff. Funerary rites followed, and the deceased ascended in totem-semblance, a hoof through the night, made of fire-flecks. Our soul-necks bent back, we watched the sky laced in gold. Slowly, the chief had ascended into ancestral reign, where eyes pocked the night sky, awaiting which newborn would escape the two womb-carriers several communities away. The mother was steadfast in one homestead, the other womb-carrier bordered a tall structure, moon his womb; fire bodies danced the night, dancing in form of the mother's totem: which shall be dressed on her newborns. Despite both the reincarnates' and the kgotla's decision, most citizens' prayers moaned for two heady girls, to incubate souls, for they had the alchemy of creating such as it was melded in their natural wombs.

Medicinal plant was kneaded into earth like an umbilical cord to ancestral reign, a safe portal of sustenance where burials for our former bodies would reside, a conjoining.

The younger-women coughed, smoke was exchanged, and mokuru stained their livers. Hearty laughter and arguments scrambled up their throats during those seven-hour contractions, for the night-hour was deepening into labor, and our veil turned humid.

I stared at the sky-clock; moon-wane dictated that seven hours remained until my birth. My sojourn had to be in that seven-hour frame otherwise I'd never be born.

And so the younger-women's voice collected into the sky-phone, informing us, "The sky-clock is your compass. Reach the horizon and you reach birth. Your oxygen reserves are your fuel. Use it well to reach your birth-horizon."

The soul-forms scattered like grains in the wind, the battle for birth begins.

AFTER-BORN

"The battle for birth?" He laughs, retuning to that trusting mode, no more fearful of me. "This is the sickest story I've ever heard. You're shitting me, angiti?"

"I'm being for real."

"Nah, this is one of those creative episodes of yours," he says. "Kaosane, you'll be showing me slides of the graphic story you're yakking to me now."

"I could request the born facility to deliver me a memory of that time," I say, "but it's heavily buried in red tape—it could take years or many reincarnate seasons to obtain the pre-birth memory. But it's all in here." I tap my head. "I can't ever forget it. I wish I could."

The dilation of his eyes takes in the secret I've held for years, seeking shadow instead of light, a refuge. "That exists?" he asks.

I nod. "It's a secret facility set aside for us, the experimented ones. That's why I stole this," I say, stretching out a pill-sized metal disk. "It's going to need a lot of soul power. Our city will probably experience a blackout."

"What's this?" he asks.

"The evidence I promised you. It's a memory of the time before we were born. Just swallow it like a pill and you will see everything I tell you."

That's when he freezes, coughing the smoke halfway to his lungs. His hands jitter. "Did you see me in this pre-birth plek? Is that why you're telling me this? What did I want to be? Did I fail? Is that why I'm like this." He rattles his head. "Wait a minute. Now I sound crazy. This is mal, ja."

"Just take it," I say. "You don't have a choice."

The metal pill glints in his palm. He observes it and stares at me like I'm a freak. I push him back and press the metal pill into his mouth, the center of the pill blinking red, a signal, connecting, scanning for a memory until it settles into his sac and becomes a Bluetooth feed into his brain; swallowing was his acceptance to receive wireless transmission of a specific file from the memory bank. He convulses, unable to empty his guts, just heaving emptiness, hands to knees.

I fall to my knees, my face wet with tears. "I didn't want to have to go to such lengths to get you to believe me. Ja, I remember you ... but I have to explain first, so you understand exactly what happened during the battle for birth—

—is oftentimes gruesome, bloody, a tearing away from the self.

Our future, our dream is like a mirage in the now, stands on our tongue, our skin, our cells—the illusion of what I would like to see myself—only momentarily because the brown of my skin begins to turn opaque at the loss of my other identity, mourning for what it can't be without.

Time, an undisciplined currency in this rural runs very sparsely: the sun has been stabbed. Its hibiscus blood melts to the horizon and spreads into our crumbed soil, inflating our souls with evil religions.

We hate sharp things that point to the skies; teeth knocked out, the stars fell. They are strange things—the star-bombs—warriors of the sky, against the reincarnation, against some births. They become taboo, a deception, sometimes turning themselves into our totems to destroy us. They protect sky for it is our medium of birth. They all invigilate the districts of Botswana. I don't know why. They scan us according to gender because their sensors are drawn to holes, a pod of things where they can immerse their DNA into—the women a petri dish for their society. That's why all my former mothers and fathers made sure their daughters were men way before their birth. Before I was born, they decided my gender: male. Now, I search for the true one: female. I'm crazy, ain't I?

DISTRICT TO CERVIX: THE TIME BEFORE WE WERE BORN

I need to reach the inyanga to gain access to my birth. I must journey through several districts to reach the cervix. I pray my totem will protect me during my journey. But I must too remember that no harm come to it as well. The air-veiled kwena—a reptile, my totem—will be my armor.

In a splatter of rain, the sky-clock announces the constriction of the built environment, chasms running its length, a danger zone. I'm not even close to what used to be veiled Gabs city, which is noticeable by its infamous sky, a derma of thin metal that projects a winter blue. My trail is latched onto by my twin-to-be.

"Stop following me," I say.

"You will die before you are born," she says.

"We are meant to be siblings, not enemies."

"The born facility will sterilize our brains from our pre-born memories once we are born," she says. "This feud of now will be a forgotten thing. You will love me. You will be my brother. And I"—she pauses, her soul-form making something of air—"I will be your sister." Her sight fancies the terrain, smile sleek with some secret. "The battle to birth is such an underutilized rite: murder exists not in our vocabulary."

It takes a while for comprehension to sink me into the waters of her meaning: she daggers at me with her form and limbs to slow me down, but she's thrown askew by the scaled tail of a reptile beckoning my protection. This I never expected from her. Slumber burns my eyes, fed by a sedative saturating the air. I expect her to be a lax-turning posture as I am but she scars me trying to render me close to dead so she reaches the sky-horizon first, to gain her birthright first. The first one to reach it is granted all their identity wishes; the first one waits in a limbo space for their twin for they are to be born at the same time.

I kneel, taking in her attacks. I scratch the night, it opens, and I slip into a sleep pocket and curl into a hole of darkness, of inexistence; the dark vacuum around me becomes my pillow, my amniotic fluid I float in. Her betrayal has kneaded itself into my spinal cord like a tumor; the stab wounds on my limbs could translate through my birth, rendering me with paralysis in my limbs.

For now, I'm invisible to my enemy who only wishes to steal my gender from me, to murder for it.

Hours later, my context is different after my buoyant slumber in the sleep pocket: environment is made of dunes. My twin-to-be is absent.

The dull sun screeches time against the backbone of present.

The toll of this region is oxygen. It is now my body is an hourglass leaking grains of air. My lungs are calibrated to filter the air that has polluted contents of the dead inhabiting the underground.

I walk, eyes and ears pinned forward, antennae detecting danger: air-borne evils nostalgic of the night and insomniac of the day carry their buckets made of wild animal skin and cluck through the night in sounds of thunder. These crow-like creatures grate the night with steel-lined wings hoping to tear open the sky, hoping to reopen the sky's eye before its scheduled aperture.

A piercing screech scrapes the sky: my twin-to-be existing from the sleep pocket—a harsh rupture in air's skin—calling attention to us. We have expired our use of the sleep pocket and one must run now from the crow-like creature's focused vision.

I weave through man-sized metal pieces of what once was Sekgoma Memorial Hospital that jut out of Serowe's desert-sand landscape. Something beneath the earth is trying to stab us with gleaming steel objects of a dead hospital. She's crazy, the lengths she's going to so I'm eliminated.

Death is a heavy night spread above our heads.

But this world won't be my coffin.

I press the knob of my backbone to inch air slowly from my heaving chest, the taxation for walking this path. Until I'm out of this border, my oxygen is not mine; lung alone. I must stop breathing, stop functioning temporarily to be free. I shield myself in the cloak of night waiting for the hunt to die down.

There is only a sky of unknown things—a sky that gives birth by aid of the inyanga, the midwife. I will meet her.

Δ

The witching wakes at three in the a.m. Voodoo priests were fishing sometime now, at the crane of heartbeat. Sleep fogged my eyes until I fell blind. I have to wait until my irises wake.

Dust is the alternative surveillance system imposed into our land by the star-bombs. I tighten my doek around my nose, but my pores remain open. It's a fragile thing to be human-like. We're sleepless little beats of hearts in this sunless day.

I'm finally here. Kanye. The hills rise upward. Nature wants to flee. The courtyard boasts an un-born fire, but its faint silhouette is rapid and excited for flesh, not wood. The night sky is slightly bruised, the moon a stark, white eye, close to fullness.

The inyanga sits by the fire. I take my place before the old woman, our knees crushed to the sand.

"The others aren't far behind," she says. "How old were you when you were released?"

"Excuse me?" I ask.

"The womb-prison." Her wooden body props up, brings up another wooden stick.

The womb-prison is a monolithic place that writes our existence. She is the guardian of the womb-prison where our pre-selves are either stored or restrained into its fly-smothered walls awaiting birth-days and releases.

I lower my head. "Eighteen years ago, I think. Why? I've been waiting so long for my birth application to be approved."

The old woman spits at the floor, taps the air, and instead of a sleep pocket opening, light blinks at us and undresses the night's blind eye: the concrete structure stands, piercing the pregnant sky. It's the womb-prison, pre-birth names tacked in metallic panels on its surface. A myriad archives of beings before birth.

Weight against it, her cane sniffs the wall.

"Choose," the sangoma says.

"I don't understand," I say.

"It is part of the new order: sacrifices pay for it. Your twin did an unlawful thing and tried to kill you for her birthright," the inyanga says. "This is what I can do for you. You will win. You will be born as however you want—three legs if you wish."

"No one said anything—"

"No one *ever* says anything. Now choose where to place her."

"But then … *she* won't be born," I say.

"Yet. She won't be born yet," she corrects me. "Isn't that what she was trying to do to you?"

I sink back. "She was just desperate, ja. I don't want to put her away. The womb-prison is a terrible place to live in. I don't want it even for my enemies. Nyaa, she was trying to delay me *not* kill me."

"Same thing. Are you truly and authentically born if it's not the identity you want? Can you say that you are really born?"

"Look, I thought we were supposed to journey to birth like we've always done—not decide what to do with the other reincarnate, persecuting them into that place." I point at the womb-prison.

"Everything is an *evilution*. Consider that this journey *now* has a roadblock," she says. "To get through you have to remove the obstacle or let your journey end here."

"But the … the younger women chose us."

"They chose you, but circumstances say otherwise."

"If I refuse to put her in the womb prison?"

"Then she will put you in it. Your twin wants to be born alone. Siblings are oftentimes sacrificial lambs," she says, smiling. "You won't be the first. And if she were here she wouldn't hesitate to find you a spot in the womb-prison. Now choose where she will go. She will be released much later, born much later."

"But what will happen to her now when I put her in?" I ask.

"She will be stillborn. Her body will be recycled for the next batch," the inyanga says.

The night, an abnormal quiet occasion, nudges me forward with a thick force of the air. A myriad of cases file the wall of the womb-prison library. In the wall is a slim aperture that I will input the memory of my twin distilled from my essence.

I choose. Moonlight lines the case's edges. A fire is born.

I step back. "What's going on?"

"The fire will process her spirit," the inyanga says. "This ain't your usual type of fire. This is a different type of burning. She won't feel like she's burning. To get from the sky, you must also give to the sky. The smoke will rise, the sky will breathe it in. See how fast the moon waxes?"

Those eyes in the sky blink, sparkle and stare back at my village, peeling the comfort from my skin. Around us, with this waking fire, are too many sky-scraping trees with winged figures weighing down the branches. Within seconds the tiny creatures flit from the trees into the dark night; the world's alive with the noise of wings flapping—loud, whirring blades slice through the air.

I do it. I agree to the burning ritual, hoping the girl will be an incense for the night.

After long, we are in the hibernation period, rather the incubation period preceding the birth of the body that I will wear.

Placenta, the umbilical cord are seeds, the inyanga's muthi. She buries a piece of me in the land to kiss me to the ancestors, our home to return to when age melts our longevity. The grains of the earth are the browns of my skin.

A buzzing sound reverberates from high above. A siren. The star-bombs, policing, are aware of those to-be born who must be returned into the womb-prison. No one is meant to be born again— they must make certain of that.

The womb prison is where they keep those who failed the battle to birth, those who failed and may not return. I watch the other reincarnates along with the one who was to be my twin. They try to hide in sleep pockets, fingers pulling strings of night, weaving them in and around them. But I remember the futile attempt. The sky unfurls and I have sent my twin-to-be to a womb prison, delayed birth. She will hate me. I will never forgive myself. But I have to be born.

The inyanga stares at me: "It's happening. It's time to be born."

AFTER-BORN

"What the hell is this? How can I physically see and feel that?" he asked. "What have you done to me?"

"It's a virtual transport to a memory—everything feels as real the trees here," I said, gesturing to our surroundings.

"This is crazy," he said. "This can't be real."

"But it is. What you feel is the truth."

"Take this drug out of my body," he shouted. "Take it out."

"Calm down, you're just panicking because you've mixed two drugs in your body. Trust me, everything will be fine. It will wear off."

I watched him count his breaths, trying to calm himself down. He stared at me, noticing my thoughts wrecking me.

"Where do I fit into all of this?" he asked. "So you wanted to show me that this reincarnate tried to kill you? You were only retaliating. You got the birth you wanted. Look at you. Many births and all."

It's so weird how he could just switch from one emotion to the next for my benefit.

"You say that now …" I stared at the sky, at everything where ancestors live.

He paused, eyes half-asleep. "Does that mean I am born the way I am because of the journey I either failed or won? Does that mean I lost?" The ends of his lips tugged down. "I mean what life did I have before? Was I really meant to be colored? Did I choose my parents?"

"I knew telling you this would make you paranoid," I said.

"It's either I failed or I was a coward to choose what I wanted. Because, look, I ain't happy, joh."

"Does anyone truly know what they want?"

"I didn't want this, joh"—he pointed to his tightly gauzed chest, keeping the illusion of breasts far away—"I know that. I feel that. Yazi, my sister—I feel like we were switched at genders." He, the unborn part lay curdled in the she-frame of his body, a she that he hated. "I am he," he once corrected me when I called him "that cherie over there."

I realized in this world, words were powerful to them. It became their gender for those who could change nothing of their body except the words that claimed them in birth certificates, passports, Omang.

I feigned laughter. "What the fuck?"

"No, like, foreal. Instead of the switched-at-birth scenario, we have the at-birth switched genders. This happens to twins—born minutes apart or siblings born years apart."

Years apart. How ironic.

"She's your fucking sister, man. Stop burdening her with this shit," I said. "It's killing her the way you think."

"I swear, my thoughts are going to be my murderers one day. Like, I fucking hate this shit. I don't want to be bleeding every month," he said.

Bile rose into my throat. Déjà vu. I don't want to be bleeding every month. That was his answer and he couldn't even see it.

The person he wanted to be was wadded knee-deep in loss, but my breath as knee-tight to my chest, couldn't escape the words. Sometimes I felt like this present, this now was a memory we were recounting.

"Did I say something wrong?" he asked.

"I think I know why I remember everything," I whispered, "my guilt kept me prisoner of the things I did. It's getting a little harder for me to talk about this ... memory, this secret."

He gripped my hand. "I want to remember. So badly it hurts. Tell me what happened next to you? Were you happy with the end journey, your life?"

"Angazi," I said: I don't know. "Sometimes all of this doesn't feel real. We die, and we repeat this cycle again, nje. Trapped. Death is just a machine that exercises your soul into the next-life body."

"I want to do it," he said, ignoring me. "Like you quoted to me: there's no reincarnation without death."

I had to say it now, or it'd be harder later. Get it over with.

"This is the third reincarnate season ever since I put my twin-to-be in the womb prison," I said. "I was always looking for her. I realized she was born female instead of male, the one she wanted. And she tried to make herself look male. I found her here."

"Here? Fuck san, who is she?" he asked.

"I saw her three months ago at the aquaponics and gender sector trying to raise funds for soul panels for her team that would grant transgender rights to citizens. That's why I approached you, stayed by your side. That's why I sponsored your idea, your team, and your values. I was trying to pay off for my shame, my guilt." I bowed my head and cried into his hands, her frozen posture. "You ... were right. I remember you." I paused. "You were supposed to be my twin."

His lips turned into a grim line, mind dissolving the thought into anger, fists kneaded into her thighs. Sometimes I couldn't tell which he was—shifting from her to he, the way they always wanted.

"Punish me—hit me, do what will make you feel better," I said.

"Are you saying that I'm the twin who tried to kill you during our sojourn?" he asked.

I nodded.

"No, you're lying. This is a kak story. I don't believe you." He pushed me. "Why would you say something as cruel as this? Are you telling me you put me in a womb prison? I failed my sojourn which explains why I was born in a poor family! So is my family being punished with poverty or am I? Did I lose my father because of this sick joke, this reincarnation shit you're tuning me? So my pre-birth choices and what you did to me made me this way?"

"It doesn't mean there is anything wrong with you." I fell onto my knees. "You used to want to be both genders or neither—I guess our choices do change. You changed. But when you were released from the womb prison, you were born into a poor family into a gender you didn't want because your sojourn didn't go well. The womb prison took so much of your strength and hope that you lost your will to fight for your birthright. I wish they hadn't pitted us against each other— we could have been siblings. I should have protected you. You were just scared."

"You owe me. You fucking owe me." He jabbed me with his finger. "Give me another memory pill." His voice was thick with anger. "I need to see how you were born."

I swallowed, unsure what he would do to me, but I had to say everything, to relieve myself of the anxiety. I handed him another metal pill, watched him swallow it, and I said, "I was in a district that would lead me to the cervix," I said. "They called that zone the District to Cervix—

—is vague to my senses. In the born area, there is nowhere to hide except pain that seeks your senses.

Vigilance is strong nearing the sky's aperture.

The clouds gather, yellow glooms poke their way through the night and something up there with the skin of sky watches us in terror or excitement. A memory is wet and leaks down my cheek— blood. Clouds of orange, red, and yellow bloom against the sky, an orchard bleeding, opening and stretching in wispy tendrils of red to the horizon.

The sky is opening. Hope breaks my ribcage. Will I reincarnate?

My twin-to-be glares me down as she's wounded into the womb prison, a wind blaze in our faces, pushing us back. The sky-clock gradually lapses to full moon, gradually transitioning into crescent dilation as we transit from District to Cervix.

The act of breathing is a suffocating procedure, the entirety of the world pressing in from both sides, slowing my limbs into a crawl—snail's pace.

The muscles, bones of sky, dense with resistance leak the sunset. Latent phase near.

Our veil transcends into a living dark, the womb of darkness. Lightning appears, burning an orifice into the sky. A slit that becomes the uterus. Pulsating, pulsating, pulsating—glittering, a flash of star. Billows of cloud drip like thick mucus membranes onto grasslands. A storm that lasts hours. Then, thunder, contractions. The moon wanes and waxes, a cervical dilation, water breaks in rain patters.

The sky-slit usually opens like clockwork after three sun-bleeds, sometimes irregular, bleeding things into our land. Then, stars will skim back and forth, stitching the opening in the sky, mother earth's healing, mother earth's rapture.

I don't know where I am currently. I am a being freed of flesh. I am sight without bone, without structure. In this terrain, ethnicity soaks our skins desert-brown. We stare at each other, a land mass, separated by gender, its face a structure of nothing.

And in the kgotla, in the bleeding of the night, a ritual is made: a cow wails through the night, its life leaking for the ritual, its cry a veneration. Their ritual is almost done, and so is ours.

There are parts of me, tangible parts that weren't present before, like the top-most part of me entering/leaving a new environment. A tightening lowers itself into my chest. How does one lose his gender, the identity of his physio-travels in this world? What does it mean to live without gender? Is it a sexless life? A gender is what the eye of society licks itself across your body. The sex is the thing that remains intact, nameless and shuddered against your thighs trying to figure out who and what it is: you could imagine the two of us, attached to this soul-shell, separate and at one. I, the charger of this body. It, the charger of me, at times. We are dressed differently. I am in cloths lush to skin. My gender has no name. I have no name. I search for it, searching for myself. We are born choosing where we fall. Mine was taken from me. It is a passport in this realm, so neon in your face. In the olden days, all you did was hide beneath cloth, mask that face with shadow of doubt.

They did say everything would feel like pain—stimulation, sound, temperature—but pain is a cloak covering my bones, a material, thin and brown.

A tunnel wraps warm around me, tensing, convulsing—I try to seek breath, to seek life, and pain strikes me, giving me voice; a cry, a breath. I am here.

A blurry bloodied woman leans over, huffing, and voice warm as cloth: "Is it a boy or a girl?"

I am gone, I am going, but I am here too.

I am born who I am.

HERE TODAY AND GONE TOMORROW

CHAZ BRENCHLEY

Stories always want to tell themselves a story: *this is what I'm about, and don't you ever let anyone tell us different.* To their own understanding, they are as coherent light is to starscatter, a preachment of discipline: deliberate and resolute and focused. Impossible to misconstrue.

Nothing, of course, is ever that profoundly simple. No story exists entirely within its own space, or its own intent. They come to us through a succession of diffusion filters, purpose clouded by prejudice and context, by will and whimsicality, by narrative pressure and authorial inclusion. Any story is an act of unintended autobiography; storytellers give themselves away on every page, by every word they choose and every other they reject.

Story becomes a struggle towards meaning: always a struggle against the world and our own apprehension, oftentimes a struggle against itself. This is why narrative works, in some instances why it thrives.

Here in Parry's, stories accumulate like nowhere else off-Earth. They don't always thrive, but that's inherent. As below, so above: you have to look to the source.

People like to say they're the most egalitarian society that human culture has ever spawned, those who go out to the stars in ships—and of course that's nonsense. Humans create hierarchies as readily and as natively as termites create hills.

To begin with, most people who call themselves spacers never have been in space and never will be. They're the Downsiders, the colonists, generations removed from their pioneer forebears, those bold and lucky few who survived both the journey and its aftermath. Nothing could actually be worse than the early trips through n-space, but the settlement of a new world might be lethally dangerous and unrelentingly grim, both at once. And—for that lucky few—it could last much, much longer. Those who came through it deserved all the credit that their children's children try to claim, but that was long ago. Today's Downsiders don't show up at Parry's, by definition. Their stories are not told. If there's a hierarchy of stories—and of course there is, that's the point, that's what we're up here for—then those are the lowest of the low, the ones that never even make it this far.

Then there are the passengers, people-cargo. They always want to talk. Talk and ogle. And if they can afford passage, with all its costs of time and risk and money, then Parry's prices are not worth a second thought. It's just that once they've ordered, once they've paid that bill, then they have nothing to say that's worth a listen. Not to a spacer. They can talk to each other all they like, but no one else is interested. No one who matters here—and while you're here, this is all that matters.

Spacers, though: spacers get a hearing. Riggers, loaders, dockers, station staff: they count, just as much as crew. Hell, even supercargoes count. Some of them will spend a full shift's income, just for a night in Parry's. They're entitled to tell their stories.

Sad thing is, they only want to talk about the pilots.

Pilots, of course, have stories of their own. And people agog to hear them, so many people: everyone here in Parry's, and everyone out there on the Margin, everyone all through Dock and Base, hell, everyone strewn all along the Limb, which means literally everyone there is.

Pilots pretty much speak only to each other. And to Parry.

"You're saying that all of this, all of *us*," with a gesture that encompasses the table and the room around, the Margin, Dock and Base and yadda yadda, all of human space and the entire endeavour, "we're just a thought experiment?"

"No, I'm saying we're a thought experiment that failed. That this is the worst imaginable outcome."

"Us? What we do, what we are," *what we have*, "you think this is somehow a failure? Of what, of effort? Of ambition, of achievement, of what?"

Pilots. They'll argue about anything, as long as it's about them. And what isn't, in the long run? Actually you needn't even wait for the long run. Downside things can seem different, maybe, but out here everything's about them, period.

"Someone dreamed a future of interstellar flight, of commerce and communication, an ever-expanding bubble. Humanity reaching outward, making contact. Someone puzzled out a math for it, a way it could work, in a physics that could tolerate it—and what they got was this, was us. This chicken-scratch empire, a handful of pilots groping our way through the dark from settlement to settlement, those few systems we've managed to find our way there and back. All of them empty but for us, and none of them worth the trouble. A few dozen planets if you want to count the moons, and all they do is take in each other's laundry, ship tourists back and forth, live the same wretched lives we had to start with. If the only space we can reach is empty, then what's the point of filling it with more and ever more of us? Of humanity, I should say. Them," with a jerk of the head. "Not us. Not pilots. There's fewer and fewer of us, seems like. Ferrel and Mercy Mercy, what happened to them? And the Downsiders want more and more from those of us remaining, and never mind the risks. The game's not worth the candle, is what I'm saying. Not for us, and not for anyone. If this is all our shoddy science can give us, dangerous journeys to nowhere important, bringing nothing that matters—well, we need a new science, or we just need to stop."

Most pilots think better of themselves—a lot better, let's be honest—but this is Murun and he's a jackass. He'll say anything to anyone just to wind them up, to see where they go when they're sufficiently riled.

Or, in this case, sufficiently outraged. He couldn't come any closer to speaking the unspeakable: to pilots or crew or passengers, no difference.

As it happens, he says it to a tableful of pilots. Of course he does: who else would he be sitting with, talking to, riling up? In Parry's, of all places? Murun doesn't mix with hoi polloi, here or anywhere, but here especially. Everyone's watching, here. That's what people come for, to watch the pilots. It's almost a public service.

"You think we should stop? *Stop?* And, what, leave everyone—every planet, every moon, every space station—on their own, in the dark, live or die?"

It's Ferenor who's first to kick back. She takes the high moral line because anyone would, because it's easy, obvious, inarguable. She might equally—or more honestly—have gone the selfish route, *and what do you suggest we do instead, we pilots?* She who had been designed and created and raised for this task exactly, for finding her way through n-space, there and back again. Reliable, essential. Customised. Exclusive. She's a breed unto herself in the most literal way imaginable; she can't be repurposed, never mind reassigned.

"I don't see that we have any choice," Murun says. "One thing's for sure, we can't go on as we are."

"Well, but we can, though. Of course we can. Why not?"

"When you're in a hole," he says, "stop digging. Which is the worst possible analogy," he allows, "because it's not a hole, it's a gravity well. It's not of our making. We just tried to find a way out, and ended up dangling at the rim, hanging on by our fingernails and telling each other that we're free, we're fine, we're doing great. But we're really not. We're going nowhere. We'd be better off letting go and starting again, trying a different route."

"Never happen. You know it'll never happen. We don't have another route. There is no magic other math that might offer us a second chance or better access. This is all we have: just us, a handful of pilots doing the best we can, trekking through hell and back."

And if all the population of the galaxy else is watching from outside, holding back, saying nothing, reaching no hand in to help—well, they'll never know it, will they? This is as far as they go, seemingly.

And if Maellelin is doing more or less the same thing, sitting at the table listening and saying nothing, holding back, not helping either side of the debate—well, that's nothing new. She has a small footprint, Maellelin. That's as true in conversation as it is in life, in her shockingly expensive shoes.

No one looks to her for judgement, it's not a thing she offers. Whether she's judging anyway, behind those bizarre distorted eyes—*five times human size*, some say, *or seven times*: it's not easy judging volume by sight, when it's really rude to stare—who can say? One thing for sure, no one here is about to ask Maellelin herself. When she's dead, she says, they can cut her open and retroguess all the work she's had done to make her the pilot that she is: down to the molecular level, if their machines are good enough, if they reach her fast enough. If they can reach her at all. Most pilots are lost in n-space, and never brought home to bury. Nor to analyze. Nevertheless: till then, she says, while she's alive her skin's her own, and all that lies inside it.

You don't argue with pilots. Not about this. *For the greater good* is not an argument that carries weight, against the power that they have and the privilege they can command.

In Parry's, at least, you don't argue with pilots about anything. There's no need: they argue about everything on their own account. Besides, you're lucky if he'll let you speak to them at all.

Here's an instance, here's luck: here's Parry himself, come out from behind his counter to stand at Maellelin's elbow and murmur, "I'm sorry to interrupt, but there's a child here rather anxious to hire you, if you're available."

It's not Maellelin he's interrupting, that goes almost without saying. She can go almost without speaking for days, days and nights on end. But she blinks up at him, and smiles, and turns to look.

"Child" is generous, perhaps, though the boy himself would think it scathing, would fire up in fury at the word if only to prove to older wiser heads how true it is. In truth, no doubt he's an adult by any legal definition. He's here with a friend, unsupervised, drinking. If he'd been underage for any of that, Parry wouldn't have let him through the door. Even now, even inside and knowing that, he's looking a little dazed at his good fortune. Holding hands with his sweetheart across a corner table, watching Parry through the crowd, watching Maellelin.

Holding his breath, hoping against hope.

He looks unimaginably, almost unbearably young, even without the benefit of her enhanced eyes and whatever more they show her.

"I'll talk to him," she says, meaning *I'll listen to him.* "Bring him over. Not his friend." One boy at a time, she can cope with. Two would be overwhelming. She doesn't deal well with people anyway, unless they're pilots. Young males in particular, in the plural, she finds exponentially troublesome.

Then she looks at Murun, at his shadow Telfer, at Ferenor. "If you would," she says quietly.

Of course they will. It's her table, after all; and one thing is absolute, that she can't go to the boy. Not without making a parade of it, someone to carry her booster-seat so that she can meet him eye to eye across the table. It's understood in Parry's that people come to her. Which means other people have to give her space, even if they're pilots.

It's understood, but that won't stop Murun being an asshole about it.

Yes, of course that's also understood. It's budgeted for. Almost—almost!—before Murun has gestured dismissively across the table, saying, "Oh, don't mind me. Us. We'll just sit quiet down here and talk between ourselves, while you do your business with your boys. Maybe I'll read a book. I'm sure I had one with me, some-where." Telfer is already at his elbow. Has his elbow, indeed, in a grip that might be stronger than it looks.

What's Hecuba to him, or he to Hecuba? You might well ask; everyone does. Just don't ask them, either one of them or both together. They may simply be lovers. They may simply be friends, business partners, something. Family. But Telfer's the reason Murun makes it through n-space, or through life. Hell, Telfer's the reason Murun makes it through the door, more often than not. He's not a pilot, which is strange; and yet Murun listens to him, which is weird. Lives with him, which is weirder. Flies with him, which is weird out of all counting.

Leaves the table now without a word more, which would be purely unheard-of if it weren't for the fact that—in here, at least—Telfer always is at his elbow, always doing his best to stop the guy being an asshole. It's a service to humankind, worth more and far more than ever he's rewarded for it.

Unless Murun is his own reward, which seems … unlikely.

Still, there they go: Murun and Telfer, inexplicably attached, with Ferenor trailing after. On a good day, Ferenor loves company and knows she's lucky to get it, which makes her welcome in any company—on a good day—because gratitude is consolatory and even assholes like to be appreciated.

Alone this little moment, Maellelin relaxes: breathes out, leans back, takes five. All her life she's had everything to fight, gravity included. It's not easy, being small. Even being what else she is, doing what she does, there's an inherent cost to doing it two feet lower down than everybody else. She's glad to snatch a breather, when she can.

And now here's Parry back with his intrusive boy, and she's back on task: erect, focused, curious, non-committal. Easier to treat with than any other pilot might have been, though that won't be why the boy asked for her particularly.

He sits, across from her; Parry sets his drink down at his elbow, and departs.

The boy comes to it, straight away. "You have your own ship."

"I do." If it were more common, it would be a rarity. As things stand, it's all but unheard-of: heard of once, and here they are. She's in Parry's, and her ship's in Dock. No other pilot can afford a ship of their own, or ever has. A ship fit to fly through n-space is the single most expensive artefact in the history of human endeavour. But Maellelin could fly no other ship, and no one else can fly hers; and pilots are so abidingly rare themselves, so rare and precious that arrangements were made, agreements arrived at. Maellelin has her ship. At least, it's registered in her name and she flies to no one's schedule but her own. What debts she carries, what payments she makes: those are not advertised. Neither are they discussed. You really don't want to get the wrong side of a pilot. All those legends about stations being abandoned, whole colonies left to starve because one pilot was offended and no other would challenge their embargo? Well, they really are just legends. Probably. Nevertheless.

"I want to hire you." He's bold, this boy. Possibly drunk; for sure he's been drinking or drugging or both, because what else do you do when you're young and free and out on the Margin with your lover?

You look to hire a pilot, apparently, if you're this particular brash bold boy.

"That costs money," Maellelin says mildly.

She can afford to walk away, if it comes to that. Or to have him walked away, more likely: a glance in Parry's direction would achieve it. Parry is as lean as any spacer and quieter than most, but still an irresistible force, here on his own territory. He could eject this boy and his friend too, one in each hand, no trouble. And he wouldn't think twice about it, for Maellelin. He's here, his establishment is here for the pilots, that's understood. Everyone else is here on sufferance, however their story runs.

"I have money," the boy says. Of course he does. Everything about him declares his status: his clothes, his hair, his soft and manicured hands. He's a passenger, a tourist, passing through. Spending money, hand over fist.

Nevertheless, he's a boy. He may not have any idea. Passenger fares don't fall within an order of magnitude of charter fees. Maellelin lifts an eyebrow; he sighs, and passes his ID across the table.

She flashes his credit, and briefly lifts the other eyebrow.

"Well then," she says, passing the ID back as though it were a contract of engagement. Perhaps she's thinking of that undiscussed debt. Perhaps she's only bored of Dock, bored even of Parry's, wanting to be out of here. "Where do you want to go?"

He's still a boy, and a passenger. He shouldn't have a story worth the telling. So far, it's all about the money.

"Not far," he says. "Just back to Freyling's Star," which will have been his last port of call, if he's on a regular cruise.

"Did you forget something?" That's snide, but she can't resist it.

His face twitches, and she's halfway to saying "Or someone?"— but his boyfriend's just across the room there, and he's young enough to be content with one at a time, maybe.

He says, "No." He says, "Listen." He says, "Look."

He pulls a holo-patch from his jacket, lays it on the table between them, doesn't trigger it yet. Neither does she. It would be a stretch for her, as well as an impertinence.

He looks around, then hunches closer as if his bony shoulders could buy them a privacy not promised otherwise.

Perhaps he's hoping that whatever's on the holo will make no sense without the story, and that no one—no one bar Maellelin—will be listening to his story, because he's a boy and a passenger and QED.

Perhaps he's hoping even now that Maellelin will take him back to one of Parry's legendary private rooms, where everything's negotiable and nothing ever leaks. Legendarily. She won't, though. She's not been hired yet. He needs to convince her first, he needs to sell himself to buy her time. Then they can be as private as he likes, here or aboard her ship or anywhere. He'll be the client, the customer, the one she listens to. He just has to get through this, he has to make her listen. He has to have a story worth her time.

He says, "You'll know Freyling's. Five planets, three colonies, half a dozen stations. Our ship stayed for a week. We were bored; see one space station, you've seen them all. But they had flitters to rent, you could jink out into the asteroid belt for the day, so we did that …"

Of course they did. That would be for the sex. Bored wealthy teenagers wouldn't be impressed by a bone-bare rental skiff, but zero-g sex was said to be fantastic. Maellelin wouldn't know.

She nods neutrally. "And?"

"And we found … a thing. An artefact. This." He gestures at the holo, still doesn't activate it. Looks around again, wants to mantle over it again like a hawk its prey.

She sighs, more gently perhaps than the moment deserves. Says, "Miners leave equipment all over the Belt. Anything that's broken or worn out or just superseded, why would they pay to ship it back? Just abandon it and move on."

He shakes his head, hard. "Not this. It's not abandoned, it was just … left. Ready. For us, perhaps. Not Berendt and me, I mean. Us humans, all of us. It's ours now, I mean, Berendt's and mine, we found it, but it's not something we made. Humans, I mean. It's not anything we could make."

In all the history of human space, there has never been anything found that humans did not make. No evidence of any kind, of intelligent alien life. Some say that's evidence of our uniqueness, of our particularity; some say the other thing, that it's evidence of how pitifully far we've reached, how limited our horizons really are. A chicken-scratch empire, in the shabby dust of a far-neglected corner.

Of course people have proclaimed finds, proofs without number: all of them fakes, eventually revealed.

Maellelin eyes him steadily. Perhaps she sighs again before she says, "Show me."

He nods, twitches, glances back to his lover for the reassurance just that he can do that, that he can look over his shoulder and see someone else waiting for him: that little gesture that the human race can never manage *en masse*, as we go friendless forth into a heedless universe.

Then he touches the holo to life, and sits back with an all-too-visible effort.

Maellelin looks, once. Once and away, briskly, to his face; then—seemingly against her desire, perhaps against her intent—her magnified eyes turn back to the image before her.

What does she see? Not what we see, that's for sure. Not what the boy thinks he's showing her. He will have had the very best cam gear available outside the military—he'll have insisted on that, unless his parents' connections could get him something better yet—and even so. All he's got is human-standard eyes to see it with, and he's far too young to understand that more than beauty lies in the eye of the beholder. It hasn't crossed his mind. You can see that, just by looking.

Maellelin's not looking, not at him. She's engaged, engrossed. Encountered. If first contact ever happened, if it could be one discrete moment, this would be a candidate. Not the boy's muddled, incoherent greed; he's seen nothing but the value of the thing, the fame it promises, opportunities for himself. Even now, watching her so intently, his hands clenched about the table-edge, he can't see how very much more she's seeing. How very much further in.

Not until the holo starts to unfold, at any rate.

"It … never did that for me. How's it doing that? It's a static image, not—"

"It's data. Be quiet."

What they had found, these boys, what they had seen as they tumbled into the absolute shadow of an iron-rich asteroid, as they fucked and sweated and yelled and kept one eye none the less on the screens and meters and the honest simple windows of their sordid little craft—because who would ever trust the collision-alarm on a rented flitter, never mind its screens and meters?—was a structure, a device, an artefact. More than that, though. Even in that first ignorant, distracted glance, that *Wait, what was that, did you see—?* moment, they must both have known the one thing, the only thing they could know: that it was nothing of human manufacture. That here at last was the end of all doubt and the beginning of something new, a shattering revelation, proof positive that there was another spacefaring civilisation out there somewhere, at least one other, that humankind was not alone after all.

"We couldn't take it into the flitter, we didn't have suits and it was too big anyway, there was nowhere we could have put it," he says in a rush as though he still believes he has some claim here, as though he can feel something slipping from his fingers. "So we took the best images we could," with that fancy cam he'd brought along to record himself and his lover as they fucked, because what else could possibly be worth looking at, this far out on the Limb, this far from anything, from everything that matters? "And we kept quiet then," *because they would have taken it away from us,* "until we could come here, and find you; and you will, won't you? You'll take us back and help us pick it up? We know exactly where it is. And money's no object," he says handsomely, sure of his credit and ridiculously sure of his future now, as though this find were a promise of his worth.

Maellelin pays him no heed at all. He has nothing to offer her that she could conceivably want, not now. Neither does his artefact, in any sense that gives him any claim. To be sure it has location, fabric, design: unknown materials in strange configurations, hard to look upon and harder to comprehend. Scientists, linguists, philosophers: this thing could feed a university entire, for generations to come. Simply finding it may have been the least likely thing this boy will ever achieve. Understanding it must lie orders of magnitude less likely, for him.

For him: not for her. She's spoken the truth of it already, said what she could see. *It's data.*

Everything, perhaps, is data, to those who have eyes to see. Every object has much to say about its maker and their culture, its materials and the world that gave them form. That's true too of intangible artefacts, of course, as it is of all the artefacts of nature, from the greatest stars to the smallest particles, that each one has its story greater than the thing itself.

Nevertheless. Maellelin looks into the abyss, and the abyss looks back at her—and opens up like a doorway, like a portal, like a welcome invitation, like a welcome.

It's data, to be sure: both the artefact itself and this capture of it, this rendition. Both saying the same thing, probably. Hopefully. You can step into the same datastream twice, perhaps. If it doesn't wash you away entirely, the first time.

Data flows downhill, from knowledge towards ignorance. Sometimes it's downhill both ways, though. You could call it a fair exchange: Maellelin has those eyes of hers opened so wide, the artefact can see all the way into her soul. Or into her bloodstream, her nerve-endings, her cell-structures. It's seen people before, but it's never seen people like her. There aren't any people like her.

It can treat with her; it knows just what to say.

There's a silence all through Parry's now, which is unheard of even here, where the quiet can sometimes run deep. Everyone's watching Maellelin.

No doubt they can see something of the image and what it's doing, even from the furthest tables. They don't see what she sees, that's inherent; but they can see what it's doing to her. What it means.

There's blood leaking, just a little, from the corner of her eye. Not enough to worry—pilots come in from n-space with worse damage every day; hell, some pilots take worse damage than that every day they're out there, if they can measure it in days—but it seems symbolic, somehow. Indicative, at any rate. Her body takes better care of itself than most. It was designed that way.

She doesn't seem to be hurting, anyway. Not what you'd want to call hurting. There's a shiver running under her skin, but that's not reactive. Not what you'd want to call reactive. It looks more like she's reorganising, or being reorganised. As though her internal structure is changing, in accordance with new parameters. Maybe even down to the cellular level.

Whether that's voluntary or autonomic, whether it's her choice in any way at all, no way of telling. She's not saying. Conspicuously, she's not saying anything.

In itself, that's not unusual; but it is beginning to look pointed. Significant. Even possibly awry. Stories have their hierarchies, but those are situational; here in a pilots' den, nobody watching this can help but remember all those horror stories that never happened, the alien texts or devices that were waiting out there to take ruthless control of innocent Terran minds, because of course. Why wouldn't they? It's the paramount story of our age. When you reach out and out, when you find nothing and nothing, emptiness itself becomes a threat. Absence is its own consuming terror; what could be worse than finding yourself alone? Everywhere? Of course our stories people the universe with simpler threats, with malign entities reaching to engulf us. If only because we know, because we've known so long that they weren't there.

Wrong again. Apparently.

Deep inside herself, Maellelin's story is rewriting itself. Rewriting her, blood and bone. Listening to a new narrator, taking dictation. Or else she's being overwritten, it's very hard to tell. It's an act of hierarchy, whichever. A stronger voice, a deeper setting. Something.

Δ

The boy knows. He doesn't know her, but he knows something. He knows something's changed. He's seen that shift inside her, felt the plummeting measure of her silence.

He says, "It's still ours, though, yes? We found it, it's ours. Even if it's … doing things for you that it didn't for us," even when it's impossible that his static holo should do anything of the kind. He's not one to deny the evidence of his own eyes. That's how he got into this in the first place.

Maellelin lifts her eyes from the image. The artefact is still unfolding, and so is she, and apparently she doesn't need to look at it any more. She looks at the boy instead, and says no.

Says, "No," and her voice is an artefact in itself, stiff and grating, alien even here, where she is known and loved. Where she has been, at least. Now, though? Maybe nobody knows her now.

"Oh," she says, "you can go and claim the shell-thing if it matters to you, if you think it might matter to anybody else. If they can read it as I can," *if it can read them as it can me*, she might be saying, *unlikely as that seems*, "then they'll be off," *as I am*, "and leave you nothing. If they can't, then it's nothing anyway. Do as you like."

And she slides off her seat and seems somehow taller already, unless she's just more purposeful, more focused, more intent. More present, even as she's leaving. If she were taller, after all, she wouldn't be able to leave; that ship of hers was made precisely to her measure.

"No, wait! Where are you—?"

She won't wait for him, but Parry's a different matter. Even in this new configuration—and who can say where her thoughts are turning, what's revolving now in her incomprehensible mind?—she knows what she owes to Parry.

He calls to her from behind his counter. "Where away, pilot?"

There's a last time for everything. This is her last time here, and everyone knows it by now. Everyone except perhaps the boy, and he's catching up fast, even from the depths of his betrayal.

"Out," she says. "Beyond the Blue," she says. That's what the pilots call n-space, and we've always understood there's nothing further. We may have been wrong. Wrong again.

Parry doesn't ask *What's out there?* as anyone else might have done. He just says, "Take me with you."

And there's something that's almost sorrow on her face, even on her new face that's still rebuilding even as they watch, when she says no.

"No," she says. "You'd have to be a pilot."

And then she's at the door and gone; and everyone understands that as soon as rapid little feet can take her, she'll be off the station and gone, she and her ship together. Out of the Limb, away and gone to somewhere else entire.

And that, right there, that's the hierarchy of story. That's when it works best, when it works right, when one tiny figure closes a door and steps deliberately and entirely out of context, and leaves all the gestalt else gasping.

This is what I'm about, and don't you ever let anyone tell you different.

THE SECRETS OF MY PRISON HOUSE

J. LINCOLN FENN

He wakes, tired as usual—a late night, too much coffee, too much work, too much sake at the Glass Door Pub in the company of clients he was trying to woo from their cash. Five Japaninese, all of them interested in the repackaged loans of loans of loans, for houses, and educations, and vast tracts of mostly arid land that might or might not have recyclable nuclear waste if you dig down far enough. Whether the loans are actually owed by the names attached to the paperwork is anybody's guess, but it hardly matters since no one can afford the court appearance fee, which means lenders can garnish wages as they like. *Pre-arranged contango futures.* They're pretty popular at the moment.

Karl yawns, sits upright. The recessed, motion-sensor lights slowly come on. He spots his ghostly reflection in the wall of black glass—there he is, the man he'd always imagined he'd be, physically at least. Every taut muscle earned the old-fashioned way, with push-ups, and sweat, and miles and miles of cracked pavement beneath the worn treads of his running shoes. Not that he couldn't afford a stint in India for micro-sculpting, it's just that he'd never be able to shake the feeling he'd cheated. He keeps his bedroom intentionally austere—floors a single slab of gray marble, floor-to-ceiling digitized windows muted a light gray—because he likes to wake up to things that are cold, impersonal. It makes him feel less human, which is necessary in his line of work.

Fuck, he needs to close the damned Japaninese if he's going to pay the mortgage this month. The monster hurricane that hit Florida really jacked up his real estate holdings.

"Angel, view," he says.

The light gray in the windows dissolves like mist, reveals the world outside. Not that there's much to see. Amber sunlight glints against the tall glass tower across the street, while the rest of the city recedes into a haze of brownish smog. A blood-orange sun hangs in the sky. Funny how it had been a selling point, the view, and for the two months a year when the wind still blows, it *is* stunning—then he can see all the way to the bridge, and the harbor, and the ocean beyond. But today visibility looks like it'll be about ten yards, tops. Maybe he should work from home. Shit though, he's got that meeting at nine a.m.

"Angel, news."

A window shifts into a screen. There's an overhead, shaky drone shot of people wearing surgical masks running down a city street, a plume of black smoke and fire rising behind them.

… while four suspects were apprehended, a fifth terrorist didn't survive the explosion at the L gate corridor which killed thirty and injured two hundred, including schoolchildren on their way to …

"Angel, just the headlines," he says. The screen fades to bullet-pointed sentences against a gradient gray background. Much better. *Terrorist Plot Foiled, Authorities Blame Anarchists; DOW Jumps 13 Points to Record High; Four-Year Old Saves Drowning Sister.*

L gate corridor. His old neighborhood. His father would be gravely disappointed if he could see his son now, living in one of the penthouse complexes he despised. *History repeats itself, first as tragedy, second as farce.* Karl can almost smell the cigarette smoke in his father's dank apartment, the wet, black ink from the fliers that were pressed by hand, using salvaged typewriter keys.

Where the fuck had they found typewriter keys?

Suddenly he hears the click of a doorknob, and he turns to see Sylvia emerge from the bathroom, curls of steam wafting out behind her. He'd almost forgotten she stayed the night.

She's astonishingly beautiful, as always. Porcelain skin, high cheekbones, long legs, blonde hair swept up in some kind of compli-cated twist, a fitted gray suit. She doesn't look at him, too absorbed in her task at hand—fitting pearl earrings into her perfect earlobes. She heads for a pair of black high-heeled shoes that are lined up against the wall like soldiers at attention.

"Busy day?" he asks.

"Oh you know. The usual." She reaches out for the wall to balance as she slides her right foot into a shoe, then the left.

There's a strange, absent quality about the people whose parents were rich enough to choose their genetic traits, Sylvia being a classic example. They've been together almost a year, but he'd be hard pressed to say whether he really knows her. She doesn't appear to have a favorite color, listens to whatever Angel happens to play for background music, has a knack for saying exactly the right thing at exactly the right time, which is useful when he invites clients over for dinner. She slips into and out of his days so easily, never requiring more than an occasional dinner out, a surprise of white roses. Once he tried, and failed, to pick a fight with her, over … he can't even remember. She just cocked her head, swirled the red wine in her glass, and left the room.

It usually suits him, this vacuity. But today, he feels a dissatisfied stirring, maybe because he was thinking about his father.

"You were asleep by the time I got in." There's something slightly accusatory in his tone, and he's not sure why.

She walks to him, brushes her lips against the top of his head in the semblance of a kiss—lightly, so she doesn't smear her lipstick.

"*You* were very, very late."

He wraps an arm around her waist. "Are you coming over tonight?" He slides his other hand along her thigh, but doesn't push it.

"I have that work thing. But we should schedule a weekend out of town," she says. "Maybe the vineyard?"

That would equal two mortgage payments. But just the thought of fresh air, an ocean breeze, lifts some of his agitation, dispels the ghost of his father. If he can just close the Japaninese …

"I'd love that."

She smiles, disengages his arm, walks toward the lone bureau—a piece she'd chosen for him from an estate sale, made from whalebone. *Click, click, click* go her heels on the marble floor. She picks up her purse from the bureau, stops to check her reflection in the glass wall.

"I love you," she says, adjusting a strand of hair that didn't need adjusting. She looks at him in the reflection.

"I love you too."

She offers another smile—although he catches a whisper of something forced, strained about it—and then she props the purse under her arm and then it's *click, click, click,* all the way down the hallway, into the great room. He hears the beep of the retinal scan, the soft *thwush* as the door opens, shuts behind her.

Does she love him though? Does he? This is something they've been doing now for two months, expressing love. She started it, and he felt compelled to not reject her, and now here they are. Will she expect a diamond ring at some point? A wedding for one hundred of her closest family and friends at the Otani Waldorf? How much will *that* cost?

Of course he could just be something to add to her personality portfolio, the faintest touch of slumming with the lower class, enough to add a veneer of depth, but not so much that it would stain her future prospects.

Cut the shit, Karl. This is the problem when he thinks about his father. He starts thinking. His life is so much better when he just moves from one moment to the next without reflecting.

He's *got* to close the Japaninese. Today. But first, a run. Fuck the air quality. He needs real pavement under his feet, he needs his lungs to burn.

Alright then.

"Angel, triple shot espresso."

He hears a clatter of coffee beans drop into the espresso grinder in the kitchen—God he loves that sound—and he gets out of the bed, enjoys the feel of cold marble against his bare feet as he walks to a closet that's about the size of the entire apartment he grew up in. Waves a hand in front of the frosted glass closet door, and it slides open. He enters.

Sylvia's already claimed one side for herself, even though the closet in *her* apartment could swallow his with room to spare. It makes him feel accomplished, somehow, seeing her clothes there. Silky lingerie sorted in cedar wood drawers, her gray, beige, and tan suits, dresses and jeans on hangers, two rows of shoes taking up most of the shoe rack.

Would it be such a terrible thing, to be married?

Christ that would cost a fortune. And she'd want kids, of course she'd want kids—one alone would set him back massively for the full designer-baby package. He'd have to unload a building. Maybe two.

But look at him, a kid from L gate who can even consider it.

He smiles, snaps the elastic band of his underwear. Yeah, a run is just the thing. He grabs black running sweats from a hanger, slips them on, then pulls a soft gray t-shirt from a stack of identical cousins on a cedar shelf, throws it over a naked shoulder and heads for the kitchen. Already a part of him is out the door, in the elevator, walking through the exterior security gate and into the raw city street. He wonders if he'll ever be able to burnish that away, the part of him that feels most at home with crappy air, threadbare beggars, asphalt and the stench of alleyway piss. The daily fury of too many people living in a city where the walls are closing in. That fury is useful. That fury, properly directed, is going to close those Japaninese.

Coffee though. Coffee is important.

Slap, slap, slap of his bare feet on the marble floor, he enters the wide open space that serves for the kitchen, living and dining room, every damn thing hidden neatly away in cabinets, the work of a single artisan Sylvia had hooked him up with. She pared back his furniture too—just a long dining table made with a single plank of wood, benches, and then in the living-room area two long white couches, a low coffee table made from onyx, four white chairs. Most everyone stands at his parties, pressed elbow to elbow, but Sylvia has enough grace to make it feel intimate, chic, pulling small groups apart and introducing individuals to other groups. It's a strange form of human mastery, and the reason that most come.

The smell of the brewed espresso is so outrageous, it almost gives him a buzz. He pulls his t-shirt on and waves a hand in front of a white wall cabinet. The door slides open, revealing identical white espresso cups. He pulls one from the shelf.

There's a soft chime, and Angel says, "You've got holo-mail. It's red-flagged."

Shit. The last thing he wants before his run is some bad news from work. A part of him toys with ignoring it until he gets back, but then he wonders if it's about the Japaninese, and once he thinks that he knows he'll never enjoy the run if that worry is tugging away at him.

He puts the cup under the spout, watches the stream of espresso fill it—black and thick. A nervous, jittery hum in his stomach. Once the cup is filled, he takes it and turns to face the living room, raises the cup to his lips, savoring the bitterness. Takes a sip. It settles him, somewhat.

"Alright," he says. "Open."

A flicker of light and then a transparent hologram woman appears, her calves split in half by the coffee table. She wears a navy-blue suit, a white shirt with a mandarin collar, her black hair pulled back in a tight bun. Softly almond eyes behind thick glasses.

Not a message then. A live conversation. Why didn't Angel notify him? The nervous hum in his stomach goes full vibrato.

"Karl Gregory," she says in his general direction. "My name is Officer Alice Lee, and I'm with the United States Department of Class-A Investigations."

Her badge appears below her, with her officer number, and then it disappears.

Christ, are the Japaninese here to launder money? Usually that sort of thing is culled before it makes it to his level, but all things being human, fuckups happen. Like that situation with the Croate-Russe nationalists, although he thought they'd buried it fairly well.

"I see," says Karl. He takes another sip of his espresso, trying to look calm. Innocent. Or at least ignorant. "And how can I assist you today, Officer Lee?"

"I regret to inform you that early last evening your father was taken into custody for ..."

The word *father* causes an emotional shudder. This isn't going to be good.

"... collusion with known terrorists, instigation of an anti-state riot, and let's see ..." She looks off and to the left, the shadow of a screen reflected in her glasses. "Cyber-assault against government officials—twelve counts there—dissemination of inflammatory materials, and intent to commit high treason through a terrorist act against the state. A very busy man."

Holy shit. "I didn't know he'd been released from prison."

"A week ago today, actually."

A strange mix of feelings hit—pain that his father didn't reach out, even try to contact him—and his old standby, rage, that his father risked his mother's safety, got her involved in his crusade. Destroying everything.

He takes a careful sip of espresso. There are cameras scanning every twitch, every blink, even the dilation of his pupils. The slightest reaction will draw this investigation closer to him, something he can't afford.

Officer Lee squints. "You don't seem all that surprised."

Careful, Karl. "Well … I can't say I am, given his history. But as you know, I haven't spoken or had contact with my father—"

"Yes, we know, not since your mother's death when you were fourteen. Your file notes that you turned state's witness. Although sometimes even the most patriotic people feel … the pull of regret, nostalgia. They wonder about things that might have been. Especially when it comes to family members."

Christ, this is bad. This is as bad as bad can get. Right now they're combing through every bit of his life, scraping every holo-mail, examining every business and personal contact he's ever had, scanning every image of him ever captured by any camera, satellite, or drone. Even a small misstep can be built into a case, into a charge, into a conviction. He should tell her he doesn't want to say anything else without a lawyer present, but that would just draw more scrutiny. He needs to find out what they want, and give it to them quickly so they move on.

"He was dealt with justly by the state," Karl says, keeping his voice steady, although during the trial his father could barely stand upright in the courtroom, and there were large bruises around his neck. Two fingers gone. "The judge gave him life without the possibility of parole. I thought it was lenient. And I don't know why he would ever be let out, especially with his views."

"Sometimes a rat is more useful when it's outside the cage, than inside," says Officer Lee with barely disguised pride. "The microchip we planted in his brain provided quite a bit of actionable intelligence on the anarchist network."

He bristles at this. His father was many things—a naïve ideologue, a patron saint for lost causes—but a rat? *Never.* A rat wouldn't give up a comfortable position as a cyber-geneticist to publish fiery articles on the invisible net about the state's incursion into global financial markets, rigged voting machines, drinking water purposely contaminated with mood stabilizers. A rat wouldn't leave a middle-class burb for L gate corridor.

But what his father never understood was that people don't care enough to deserve saving. They might not be happy with the meager crumbs they have left, *but look at that poor guy starving to death; it could be worse.* Which means the best option is to game a system already primed for gaming, and do the best you can for yourself.

At least that's what he tells himself.

Karl downs the rest of the espresso, places the dirty cup on the narrow, marble countertop behind him. Time to bring this conversation to a close. "So you'd like me to testify again?"

Officer Lee pauses a moment, says, "That won't be necessary. Your father committed suicide in his cell shortly after his arrest."

Karl's heart clenches and his knees almost give out. *Suicide?* Is that even possible in prison with all the external and biometric surveillance? He leans against the ledge of the countertop, grips it tightly with both hands. Finds it hard to breathe, think.

Did someone kill him?

"Nothing in his brain activity made us suspect he was suicidal," Lee continues. "Otherwise, we would have removed the bed sheet."

"I thought there were no sheets," says Karl, his voice betraying more emotion than he'd like. "I thought it was all micro-climate controlled."

"The prison suffered massive budget cuts when southern Louisiana went underwater for the last time. Priorities shifted. Sheets are cheaper than expensive temperature monitoring equipment."

The bruises around his father's neck at trial. Now they're saying he hung himself. *Yeah right*. Probably a new recruit, wanting to impress his superiors, took it a bit too far.

For some reason this makes him think about the last time he saw his mother alive, loading up a raggedy backpack with stacks of fliers bound in twine. Red hair streaked with silver, hanging loose over her shoulders, she wore a black jacket, jeans, an old pair of brown work boots. Her thumbs were dark with ink, a matching smudge under her left eye. She looked happy. Purposeful.

But when she went to hug him he slipped away and into the only other room they had, faced the window and its view of the concrete incinerator, his heart on fire with anger. Listened to the click of the front door shut behind her.

Later, all they found was her head.

"So," continues Lee. "This is where it gets … unpleasant."

What could be more unpleasant than telling someone their father committed suicide? But he says nothing, keeping himself perfectly still, waiting.

Lee adjusts her glasses. "I regret to inform you that due to the severity of his crimes, which he was convicted of in absentia this morning, and per executive order 198726, which states that high treason is a legacy criminal act … well, the debt to society still needs to be paid."

"A legacy criminal act?"

"One with a penalty that isn't nullified by death. One that you have inherited, so to speak."

Christ. Fuck, Christ. "What's it going to cost me?"

"Everything."

Money. They're after his money. And his assets, and the life he's spent the past two decades building, one brutal transaction at a time. Early years after he dropped out of school to harvest organs at the donor pig facility, covered in their shit, and blood, and piss, going without food for days at a time so he could afford the entrance exam to be a waste data handler, then choosing to be the eighth room-mate in a one bedroom flat so he could save enough for a stake in the corner dealer's Acenol trade, then investing the profits into his first property buy—an apartment building razed by fire where the local organized crime faction disposed of bodies in acid baths. They paid him a "blind eye" fee, which he used to buy shares of stock in WeSafe, a quarantine management company, catching his first break when a virulent, drug-resistant strain of typhoid hit.

He celebrated by buying his first bottle of genuine vodka, drinking half of it on the stoop outside the liquor store before passing it to a homeless man sitting by the dumpster. Still, the last conversation Karl had with his father haunted him—they'd been sitting at the kitchen table, eating stale bread soaked in slightly rancid milk. A broken lampshade had cast a fractured shadow behind his father. *Why can't we go back?*

There is no back to go to, his father had said. *Or there won't be, soon. You have no idea what they're planning.*

And he didn't, not until he'd gotten a tip at the WeSafe shareholder's meeting that the virulent strain of typhoid hadn't exactly been an accident. *Too many people, not enough resources*, the man said after Karl plied him with his fifth bourbon on ice. *Might want to up your shares, we're hearing chatter about cholera.*

And he had.

"Mr. Gregory?"

And now they want to take it from him? After they've taken everything else? Stick him in a prison to rot? *Fuck that shit.* It'd bankrupt him to mount a legal defense but one of his old organized crime contacts should be able to hook him up with an official willing to take a bribe, or get him a stolen cornea. He's got gold bullion, enough to lie low for a while—maybe head to the outerlands until he's able to get it sorted.

"Mr. Gregory?"

Somewhere though, his father is having a good laugh. *The last capitalist we hang shall be the one who sold us the rope*, and all that.

"Mr. Gregory."

Maybe that's why his father killed himself—he knew this would happen, a last chance to cast a verdict on Karl's choices.

No, he was never that petty. It's much more likely that government coffers are thinning, and this is a convenient fig leaf for a pirate operation.

"With all due respect, Officer Lee," Karl says, folding his arms over his chest. "I prefer not to discuss this further until I speak with my lawyer." A play to buy him some time.

Officer Lee's image flickers, and for a hopeful moment he thinks she's signed off—but no, then she's back again. "Mr. Gregory," she says in an annoyed tone, "I don't think you understand. The penalty for high treason is execution. By killing himself, your father robbed the state of its punitive award. You must take his place."

It's like someone kicked him in the heart. "Are you … are you *fucking* kidding me?"

"No," she says. "I'm not."

For a moment he's touched by an out-of-body sensation, as if he's the transparent holo-ghost flickering in the apartment, a mirage disassociated from reality.

If only it were that simple. "Angel," he says loudly. "Turn this shit off and get me Fritz. *Now.*"

But Officer Lee remains. "We've overridden Angel."

"Angel, close holo-mail."

Nothing. *Fuck.* He rushes to the door, faces the retinal-scan panel, desperately presses the EXIT button. A beep, but then a flashing red light. DENIED. He slams the wall three times with his fist. Cracks the glass. Pain shoots up from his hand, through his arm.

"We've overridden all your systems. Mr. Gregory, this isn't—"

"Shut the fuck up! I'm not saying another goddamn word until I speak to Fritz!"

There's a manual panel somewhere, a button for a hard reboot, right? It was a feature his realtor pointed out but he never really clocked it, and now he doesn't have a clue where the thing is. Maybe under the sink? But when he turns toward the kitchen, he's overcome with a dizzying sensation, like the marble floor beneath his feet has liquefied. His eyes start to blur.

"You've already been administered a lethal dose of Barbitanol, Mr. Gregory. The water in your espresso machine. It'll take about fifteen minutes, maybe less."

Sweat beads his forehead. Does she have to sound so goddamn proud of herself? She might be lying, she might be telling the truth, who the hell knows. He takes another step, and this time his knee almost gives out. What about Sylvia? What will they do to Sylvia?

"Angel … call Sylvia."

Nothing.

Fuck.

"You don't have to worry about Sylvia," says Lee. "She's been very cooperative with the investigation. And the administration of justice."

A bark-like laugh escapes him. Someone had to put the Barbitanol in the espresso machine. His blurry eyes fall on the empty espresso cup. *Et tu café?*

But the thing of it is, it isn't *his* cup, not really. It's just a cup. And the couches aren't his couches, they're just couches—in fact everything around him will pass through him, become the possessions of other people. The apartment will be bought by someone else, and that someone else will enjoy the feel of cold marble against their cold feet—they'll be the ones making espresso and checking the news on the window video screens, they'll arrange their clothes in the cedar closet. Sylvia will move on to someone else—he was barely making it in her socio-economic class as it was—which means someone else will be running his hand up her thigh, eventually, and she'll be at other parties, mastering other people, and he'll be … what?

A warning about what can happen when you let the wrong sort in too close. A ghost story. A boogeyman. So what was it all for then? What was it all *fucking* for?

It's funny, but it's not. His mouth is dry. The blood-orange sun peers through the window, casts reddish light on the marble floor. It draws him, for some reason. He takes a halting step toward it.

"Why?" he asks, his voice hoarse.

Officer Lee turns her transparent head, as if she's actually in his apartment, not watching him on a screen that she can turn off at any time. *Lucky fucker.*

"I told you, Mr. Gregory, the death penalty—"

"No," he says, taking a few more halting steps toward the wall of glass, the looming sun. His hard-earned view. "Why did you bother to tell me at all?"

He takes another step, two, three, and he wonders if maybe she didn't hear him, or maybe there's no answer, because she doesn't respond. He passes close to her holo-body, reaches out and slides a shaky hand through her torso. Nothing but air.

"That's the first intelligent question you've asked," she says.

He feels a shiver along his spine, but he can't feel his feet, or the marble under his feet, not anymore. Still, he makes it closer to the floor-to-ceiling windows. The sun like a giant, baleful eye, watching him.

"Because, of course, there's an antidote. Which we'll administer if you testify against your father's anarchist compatriots. In return, you'll remain under house arrest for the remainder of your life … but at least your cell has some nice amenities."

Three more steps, then he reaches the windows, presses his palms to the glass, which is cold from the air conditioning. The heat of his body forms an aura of condensation around his fingers. The bloody sun seems to wink at him.

"I don't know who they are," he says. "I don't know anything about them." Black spots form at the corner of his eyes.

"We'd prepare you. And just think. Your testimony could prevent the loss of countless innocent lives. Like those schoolchildren this morning."

He looks down for the street below, but the haze of smog is too thick now. It obscures everything. All he can see is the sun, and the brown sky, and his own, ghostly reflection in the glass.

A LUTA CONTINUA

NADIA BULKIN

"David, wake up. Somebody's outside."

In his head, the planets were still spinning. His eyes found the blood-red digital lines on the bedside table and turned them into time: 1:15 a.m. "Outside … where?" Because he had woken from a dream in which Concordia House was both everything and nothing, a cage to hold the universe, tilting in a void—and the thing about voids is that they eat through walls. Dissolve them like lye. Make those borders, those demarcations, as irrelevant as nets for catching water.

"Shh." Mia clapped her sweaty hand over his mouth. The whites of her eyes gleamed in the dark. "Listen—hear that?"

He heard the eternal roar of the waves breaking against the beach—the frustrated thrashing of a sea that no one swam in. *Filled with sharks*, his parents told him, though he had yet to find a tooth in all the years he'd spent digging for treasure there. He found other things. Coins, buckles, small golden rings. "The ocean?"

She smacked his arm. "No! It sounds like somebody's walking around the house."

But they were two floors up. "How can you hear …"

And then he heard them. Footsteps. Audibly bipedal: clunk, clunk. Heavy and labored as if exhausted from carrying a weight that shuddered through Concordia House that was far larger than David or Mia or the both of them combined.

"Should we go look?"

"Probably."

But neither of them got out of bed. They were suddenly acutely aware that the oversized four-poster bed they'd inherited from his parents was prone to squeaking, and the old floor planks prone to creaking. The footsteps got louder as whatever was stalking the house walked by their bedroom—then stopped. David and Mia held their breaths for a minute, straining for auditory clues from under the muggy blanket of confusion and fear, until the sounds started up again, continuing down the eastern wall. Then stopped again.

Mia was staring off into the far corner of the room, doing spatial gymnastics in her head. She had made it a point to memorize Concordia House's floor plan when she moved in, to establish some ownership of the beast. "It's looking in the downstairs windows," she whispered, and David wondered when it had become an "it."

They lay there staring at each other for another five minutes as it continued circling the house. The sound was so hypnotic, and their observation of it so ritualized, that they had almost made themselves believe that the footsteps were nothing more than their amplified heartbeats—that if they just pretended all was well, then the world outside their duality (the David-and-Mia bubble, their friends called it) *would* be well—when something ceramic crashed outside.

Mia groaned—half-fear, half-exasperation—and David decided enough was enough and got up, armed with nothing more than a sense of obligation: he'd protect her through hell and high water. He stood and the floorboards hollered—he winced, but then suddenly became interested in making as much noise as possible. "It's probably just some prankster kids from town," he decided, pulling on a shirt. "I'll go chase them off."

"David! Don't be stupid!"

He heaved open the bedroom door and strode down the corridor toward the stairs, turning on every light switch he passed. A left turn, a right turn. He heard Mia coming after him—*damn it, Mia.* But she hated to be alone in Concordia House, and so did he; it was too big for the two of them, not only in dimensions but in sprawl. He passed gaping empty closets; mismatched excess furniture they'd picked up off the South-Coastal Highway just to fill the uncomfortable extra space of a room about a half-size too large; locked doors to rooms that they never entered. They had keys to the rooms, but not the coffin-sized rotting leather trunks inside. Mia hurried past those doors uneasily but David had lived there long enough that he had successfully transformed them into part of a seamless stretch of wall. He'd also cordoned off certain areas as invisible and irrelevant: the upstairs library, the downstairs parlor. What purpose were those even supposed to serve? Another right turn. He got to the staircase at last and peered down over the railing at the foggy darkness below, then quickly turned on the light and marched down to the foyer.

He peeked out the twin windows on either side of the imposing double doors. The moon was out and he could see the ferns on the front porch and the smooth hood of their car. Nothing else. Maybe "it" had gone. Maybe knowing someone was inside had scared "it" off.

By then Mia was already at the top of the staircase, looking especially small with her arms outstretched to grip both railings. She had always been fast. "David!" she hissed. "What if it's dangerous? Get that gun from the patio, the big one."

He picked up a golf umbrella instead. "I'm not gonna shoot him. I'm just gonna …"

An enormous shadow passed in front of the left window, blotting out the moon, the car, the ferns. As tall as the windows themselves, the ones Mia had to stand at the top of a full-size ladder to hang floor-length curtains from. It must have been lingering silently nearby. It must have heard them speak. David had barely gathered himself enough to raise the umbrella when the doorbell rang.

"Maybe they're lost," David said, but even he did not believe himself.

The door had no peep-hole. Turning on the porch light revealed only a stretched-out hooded slicker and rain boots. They decided to hope he was a fisherman—maybe a shipwrecked fisherman, that sea was unforgiving—and David cautiously inched open one of the doors.

It was like no fisherman they had ever seen. Their visitor seemed to be a man, but he was a snug fit for the twelve-foot doorway, and he smiled down at them from that incomprehensible height with a ghoulish face too long and too sunken to be human. He did not appear to have eyelids. The kind of creature found only in old wives' tales and children's books, except sickly, gaunt. He slid his bumpy hands down his slicker and rumbled, "Hello there. I'm sorry for waking you up so late, but my boat capsized on the beach and yours was the closest house. Do you think I could come in for a moment, have a rest?"

David and Mia were silent. They were both squeezing the door handle, their weight against the door in case the giant started to push. Their gazes skirted past the giant filling their doorway, searching for a wreck on the beach, but it was too dark.

"I'm sorry about your flowerpot." In one hand, their visitor held the broken pieces of earthenware. Dirt tumbled between his sausage-sized fingers onto the porch. He tried to pick out the tiny double impatiens blooms, but they were too small. Pink petals came off on his hands like lipstick stains, like confetti. In a second David and Mia realized: *he is killing our flowers*; but just as quickly realized that he hadn't meant to. He'd only meant to touch. "I'm a bull in a china shop sometimes. I'll repay you for the damage."

The giant man looked at them with eyes so big and lonesome despite their gross, jaundiced nakedness that David and Mia felt the beginnings of empathy. Living in big Concordia House between a highway and an unfriendly sea, they knew what loneliness was.

"It's all right. Come on in."

They took several generous steps back, and their visitor strode boldly over the threshold. By the time he grinned and revealed a mouth full of broken eel teeth, it was too late. He was inside.

David and Mia stood at a distance, biting their nails, watching their guest move slowly through the patio. His name, they had learned, was Portmaster, and he called the patio the "solarium." He had politely asked to see it after slurping down a glass of water. They led him through a winding maze and though he stayed at their backs, trudging along in his swampy galoshes, he looked around their house not with curiosity but with fondness. Once in the patio—the "solarium"—he went straight for the floor-to-ceiling windows and put his palms and purplish nose to the glass, like a child. "It's a beautiful view," he said, but it was pitch-black outside—not that the curdled gray sea was any more scenic in the daylight.

"How'd he even know we had a *solarium?*" Mia whispered.

"A lot of old houses around here have solariums," David whispered back. That was a meek effort, and Mia knew it. She usually let his bullshit explanations pass, just because it was easier—she knew he was only trying to make her feel safer. Not this time.

"How'd he know that?" She jabbed him in the ribs. "He shipwrecked, remember?"

Portmaster was looking through the top shelves of a bookcase—the shelves they couldn't reach without a step-ladder. It wasn't that Portmaster *towered*, David realized—he was actually of perfect height for Concordia House. Where the house had always fought them, it made way for Portmaster. Drawers and doors opened without a struggle; light switches were easily reached. Concordia House liked him. After all they had done for it—swept it, painted it, fixed its rusted hinges and rewired its blown circuitry and fixed its leaking pipes—this felt like a betrayal.

David cleared his throat. "Sir? Did you know my parents? You seem to have been here before."

The giant man began to cry—big, rollicking sobs that got so bad he had to cover his face with his hands. He eased down to the rattan bench and it moaned with him; that bench was one of the few pieces of furniture that the newlyweds had bought for themselves and hauled, with love, to Concordia House.

"I'm sorry—but this was my favorite room. I loved watching the sea." Portmaster sighed and wiped his tears. He coughed again: deep and corroded, like a wild dog's bark. "What did you ask me— your parents? How old are you, child? Maybe I did, maybe I didn't. So many of them worked for me. Your parents. Your grandparents. Your great-grandparents."

David drew a violent blank. His father had been a city councilman. It was a seat he had inherited from his own father, and a title he still wore with immense pride, even in the nursing home; he'd made himself sick with upset when David decided not to go into politics. He certainly never worked for Dan-Tech or Lyfan or Haruka or any of the other big-box multinationals that put down roots in the city. Foreign leeches, his father called them, sucking the nation dry. And his mother only ever volunteered for the Women's League and the Poor Shelter. Portmaster must have seen the look on his face, because he clarified: "*I* built this house, young man. Your parents, whoever they were, must have taken it after I left."

David started laughing—that uncomfortable laugh that he used to end awkward conversations and political debates at parties. "I don't think so," he said, "this house has been in my family for generations." Neither David nor Mia remembered much of their childhood; just sunshine and palms and a watery horizon. In their city, such amnesia was normal—supposedly it was why they were all such forward-thinkers. *Building for the future*, the government called it. *Always onward.* But David could still dredge up a memory of himself as a toddler, sticking his head and then his shoulders between the banisters of the second-floor landing, until someone screamed, *"David! Be careful!"*

Yet Portmaster was unbowed. "No, son," he said, making David cringe, "*I* built it, one hundred years ago. You and your parents and grandparents … you're just the weasels and stoats of the Wild Wood. Taking what isn't yours. Sleeping in other people's beds. Painting the walls … this hideous orange. But I suppose you think you earned it. I suppose you think *you* built it." Portmaster snorted. "I suppose, technically, you did."

David shook his head, but an odd numb quiet had taken over his consciousness, like all the doors of his mind had quickly closed so all these noises—these awful new noises—were nothing more than faint mumbles, rats scratching in the dark. *Ignore it. Go back to sleep.*

"Do you want me to show you?"

In the hallway, he pointed up to where the wall met the ceiling, where wooden panels ran like chiseled snakes down the hallways of Concordia House. Complex patterns had been carved into the panels, but they never paid them any attention—just more of Concordia House's ostentatious designs, they thought. "I had myself carved right into the house," said Portmaster. Then, with a bit of a sneer: "Maybe you're too small to see it."

Mia brought out a step-ladder and David shakily climbed to

its top step, bringing him level with Portmaster. Up close, his eyes looked like rotten nectarines. "Do you see?" he asked.

At first David couldn't make any sense of the carvings: they were just endless twisting vines, a mad jungle. But then he saw one little human figure, then another, and another—and standing above them with a threatening stick in his hand was a giant twice their size. There were other scenes too—a ship landing on a beach; little humans dragging carts; newly-built Concordia House; a brother-hood of giants sitting on thrones while the little humans gathered at their feet.

"The others in the company thought I was overdoing it with this house. My lovely Concordia. They cared more about their plan-tations." Portmaster pointed at another panel a few meters away. David was an accountant at one of the fiercely-protected govern-ment-owned plantations, and had to pass through three layers of security just to get to his office, but no one seemed to remember why they were all so afraid. "I just didn't want this house to forget me. It took you all so long to build it." He stroked the wooden carv-ing of himself, the looming giant man, and then looked at David with something remarkably close to sympathy. "It's a credit to you that you forgot. Forgetting is a strength, you know. Just look at you. Forgetting let you flourish, in spite of all the ..." he clicked his tongue against his teeth, "unpleasantness."

David's parents didn't talk about the past; Mia's parents were dead, and she remembered only the smell of her mother's hair, the texture of her father's cotton shirts. "Unpleasantness?"

Portmaster waved it off. "The past is past. I just wanted to see my beautiful—*this* beautiful—house, one last time. My palace, my tomb." His eyes soared up to the cathedral ceiling as if to drink the house. "So peace, please. I'm an old man."

For several minutes they sat in the patio in mock peace, the silence interrupted only by Portmaster's hacking. David could not stop thinking about the little wooden people in the walls, wondering if that was why his mother was so neurotic about locking doors and windows, and why, when he brought his parents over from the nursing home for holidays, she would look up at Concordia House in fear. He didn't notice Mia hyperventilating beside him until she spoke:

"So why did you leave?"

A long-suppressed viciousness sprang up in Portmaster's eyes. "Because you chased us out," he snarled, "with sticks and stones. Very bloody affair. Very ugly. You killed yourselves by the thousands just to be rid of us." He hissed and looked away, but when he looked back at them he seemed to have regained his composure. Phlegm dripped between his jagged teeth, but he wiped his lips. "Of course, that was your right. It was *your* land."

That was something David's father liked to go on about—"our land," and the lengths he'd go to protect it. He spoke about it with such trembling passion that it seemed to border on pain, and David always listened, if only in pity that his father was so consumed by his love for their land, whatever that was. His father had taught him that phrase, *through hell and high water*, but he had never understood the urgency of such love until he met Mia.

Portmaster rambled on, his voice once again soft: "I only wish I could have stayed. The meat here was so ..." he looked at Mia with wanting, tear-shaped eyes, "... sweet."

Extreme cold dropped over David like a wet curtain, but he didn't know what to do about it, just like he didn't know what to do in school when the soccer team would make aggressive passes at Mia. The thought occurred to grab his wife and pull her behind him, or whatever it was that men were supposed to do—*through hell and high water*—but Mia was already pointing her finger at Portmaster. "You're sick," she said, and who was throwing out bullshit explanations now? Who was trying to hold together their understanding of reality with duct tape and a prayer? "You're a sick old man, and I think you'd better leave."

Portmaster glanced away, as if bitten by shame. "Yes, I'm sick," he whispered. "I'm old. But you don't know what the hunger is like. When you haven't had your chosen meat in years."

Mia jerked back. David was very aware of his innards plummeting between his bones.

"I went to therapy," Portmaster's words were fading in and out of earshot. The sea, just sixty meters away, had grown very loud, and the tide was bringing in monsters: leviathans, krakens, giant squid. Man-eaters, all. "Our clergy helped me realize that what we did to you was cruel. You're sentient beings, just like us." He smiled at them sloppily, showing off double-rows of arrowhead teeth. David saw now that they were stained and guilty and oddly blunted, like their points had been purposefully worn down. "It would be wrong to eat you, I know that now."

The grandfather clock in the corner of the room chimed twice. David and Mia ran into the hallway and slammed the door on Portmaster, though they couldn't let go of the giant, Portmaster-sized handles because there was no lock on this door. Through the wood they could hear their visitor shuffling around his favorite room, humming to himself, breathing deeply.

2:00 a.m. was hell hour. They sat there under the awful carnival of wooden carvings until fatigue and adrenaline combined to make their eyes cross. David was still hanging on to the door handles when 3:00 a.m. came, but Mia had moved on to another phase of panic. Her breathing had steadied—she seemed to be looking through walls.

"Do you think he killed my parents?"

David had been thinking about his own parents—about the abscess in his mother's right leg that made her drag it along the floor. It was from a wound that never healed. She told him that a big dog had bitten her, when she was a girl. Now he was thinking: big dog or big man?

"Maybe he knows what happened to them." She sucked in a deep, trembling breath. "Since everybody else forgot them." In the orphanage she had tried to make her peace with plausible explanations: they died in a car crash; they died of a plague; they abandoned her. She pretended that they satisfied but in the dead of night she still longed for closure. She used to have nightmares that they were locked in a dungeon; that they cursed their child for forgetting them.

"I'm going to ask him."

"No. No, honey, I don't think so."

But God, she was resolute. Fifteen minutes later they nudged open the door to the patio and found Portmaster sitting calmly, looking through the pile of newspapers on the coffee table. "I have to say," said Portmaster, "you people have really progressed since we left. You know none of you would have even known how to read if we didn't teach you. You were speaking some gobbledy-gook nonsense." He smiled and folded up the paper. "It's nice to know you put all our old technology to good use. We weren't sure if you'd ever learn how to use ..."

"Did you kill my parents?"

Portmaster looked up at Mia innocently. She was brandishing a walking cane, a piece of old wooden brutality that the orphanage had taught her how to use. Anger was an easier place to be than fear, and much more comfortable than sorrow. Yet Portmaster kept his ever-patient eyes on her, not the cane—as if he did not think that she could hit him, much less hurt him. What would he have done if she'd been one of his workers, back in the day? *Go back to sleep, David.*

"I don't know," said Portmaster. There was a faint hint of amusement at the back of his throat. "I have no idea which ones your parents were."

"They were from Crocodile Gap." At least that was the tin-roofed neighborhood the orphanage said Mia was from.

"Oh, well, I wouldn't know," said Portmaster, shrugging. "I wasn't in charge of that area. That was Rudderhall's territory. He was fond of ..." His voice trailed off. "But Rudderhall died a few years ago ... leukemia. Very sad."

Mia's shoulders sank a little. Her lips ran over the name "Rudderhall" repeatedly, but any chance for revenge was gone. What remained was hard and empty—the hollowed-out canoe that was Mia's heart. "What did he do with the dead?"

A moment of hesitation from Portmaster was all Mia needed to justify thwacking him in the head with the cane. Portmaster flinched and so did David, but for different reasons.

"Tell me," Mia's voice trembled, "where they are buried."

"We always threw the bones into the sea," said Portmaster. "Burial's a waste of land. But a big bag of bones always sinks."

Chains and padlocks had washed up on the beach last summer. A few children hunting for crabs stumbled upon them, nested in seaweed, seemingly vomited up by a sea that could not hold such iron anymore. The children's grandparents had quickly taken the children away and David and Mia overheard them telling the children not to play at that beach because it was haunted. They couldn't begrudge them. The sea was indeed noxious. It hurled up bridles and scythes and cattle yokes too. "Must have been a lot of wrecks over the years," Mia had said.

At 3:20 a.m., Mia retched and threw up on a potted kentia palm. David rubbed her back but kept glancing at Portmaster, who was wrinkling his nose in disgust.

"I can't imagine my parents ... jumbled up with all those *strangers*," Mia whispered hoarsely. Her forehead glistened with sweat. "In a *bag*. Like trash. What if there were ..."

Teeth marks on the bones? What if her parents had been eaten, and the tough parts thrown away like leftovers from a picnic? Had luminescent bristlemouths nibbled their way into the bags of bones at the bottom of the sea and finished off what the colonists started? Did they leave behind neck bones connected to leg bones, arm bones pushed inside skulls, human souls ground down into cartilage? Mia looked over her shoulder at Portmaster and doubled over in psychosomatic pain, howling. Portmaster, in infinite grace, was cleaning between his teeth with a fingernail. David tried to shush her.

"What if they were conscious!" she shouted. Portmaster was silent.

"Listen, why don't you go back to bed. Take a downer. I'll make him leave."

But she was pushing him away, flailing her arms like she couldn't see. Like she didn't know him. It hurt to throw his arms around her when she was in such a state but he had seen the damage she could do in a panic fugue—she punched walls; kicked doors; got into a car accident, once. He clamped down on the hurricane. The pressure of his weight stilled her, then crumpled her. With both of them safely on their knees, he petted her hair.

"It's okay," he promised, numbly—as if finding out one's parents had been enslaved and eaten was just the same as getting fired or fighting with a friend. "It's okay."

She was covering her face with her hands, struggling to slow her breathing. David tried to press into her the thoughts they'd always used to get each other through rough patches: the world was just the two of them. Nothing else mattered. Nothing could interfere. Not Concordia House. Not Portmaster. Not his atrophied parents in the nursing home. Not hers, wherever they were (at the bottom of the sea). Not Tropical Storm Suzanne. Nothing. *Breathe this, breathe us.*

Portmaster loudly slid his galoshes across the floor tiles. David looked up, annoyed; the giant was rearranging the throw pillows, like a little girl playing house. "Don't mind me," Portmaster said. "I'm just straightening up."

Mia used the interruption to push David off her and go running to the nearest floor-to-ceiling window. She had to paw her way through the drapes on her knees to get to the locks.

The blood rush nearly leveled him when he jumped up. "What are you doing?"

When she looked at him with those wild, dilated eyes he knew that none of his reassurances, none of the promises he had ever made her, had made a difference. "Trying to let a little life in here," she answered. Her pitch was so high, so artificial. "This place smells like a hospital. Like a damn morgue." Her hands got caught in the drapes again. She swore and tore them down with such force that she unhinged the rod from the window frame. The windows hadn't been cracked open in years—the patio (solarium) was supposed to be protected. But Mia kicked the window open and let in the void. The great dead sea was at a full-blown roar, louder than it had ever been. Was it asking for something?

Portmaster clapped his hands over his ears. "Close that window!"

"What?" Mia shouted back at him. "I thought you liked to look at the sea!"

Insects were flying in, hungry for the ceiling light, and geckos were crawling in after them. His mother's sensibilities kicked into gear and David lunged over the mess of drapes to pull the window shut, then tried to recapture Mia. She didn't run from him but by the limpness of her shoulders he felt that she'd been lost; she didn't run from him because she didn't see him anymore. Mia was gone. This was the husk that she'd left behind. "Come on, babe," he pleaded. The anxiety was starting to bleed into his voice. "Stop this. You're going to hurt yourself."

"No, David. You don't understand."

A lump formed in David's throat, because she had always told him that—said that he didn't understand the gaping hole inside her when his parents were sitting in a nursing home watching television just twenty miles away. He tried to tell her that what Portmaster said didn't matter; that those bad times, whatever they were, were over; that Concordia was their house now. He swore he could hear Portmaster chuckling, but when he glanced over his shoulder the giant was watching them with impassive, divine calm. Less giant than Nephilim.

"No, David. Nothing here is ours. They are in the walls. Didn't you hear what he said? We slept in *their* beds. We sat at *their* tables and drank *their* wine. We looked in *their* mirrors and saw ..." She touched his face with a warm hand, a cold wedding ring. Her unfocused eyes raced around his face in worry for a good minute; he could not see what she was seeing.

"What? What?"

"They're in *us*."

Her hands slapped against her own face and down her neck. Any last trace of control was going, David knew it, and he grabbed for her as if she was going over a cliff. But he'd barely touched her sleeve before the world slipped and tipped and Mia turned and bolted out of the solarium. She ran down the hall under the little eyeless wooden figurines, turned a corner toward the light, and rushed to the front door, her bare feet clapping against the polished floorboards.

"Mia!"

The look she gave him as she paused at the door was wretched in the depths of its suffering. *She's only twenty meters away. She's just right down the hall.* But it felt like whole oceanic leagues coursed between them. As he ran toward her the walls pulsed like massive hearts, pumping a rich, oaken blood that drowned the sound of Mia swinging open the door.

The sea was throwing itself against the beach. The moon peeked through a hole in the cloud cover like a celestial blinded eye, but the night was no longer bright. Mia was running like a woman possessed. David called and ran and called again, but she did not look back. Mia had always been the faster of the two of them. His knees were weak; she'd laughed at him as they ran for tour buses and trains on their honeymoon. She ran past Portmaster's motorboat and went splashing, wading, in the water. A great wave from the dead city swelled up in the distance, rising as it came until it was a full foot taller than her head. Most waves, clean waves from the amnesiac Pacific, were pure and frothy—this wave was tar. Opaque. Unforgiving. Its roar was so long and sustained, like the dull moan of a tanker's foghorn, that it seemed nearly silent. Mia held her hands out to it and the wave took her into itself. For a brief moment, David saw one of her sweet human hands emerge from the black avalanche, limp, accepting—and then the wave flattened out, and the sea was empty. David collapsed, weeping.

He heard a noise from the house. Portmaster stood in the open doorway, framed by the golden light of the foyer—he really was a perfect fit. With a sudden rush of long-forgotten strength he slammed the door on David, as if to say: *mine now.*

But David and Mia had made plans for that house. The bedroom next to theirs would be a nursery; Mia was going to host holiday parties for the neighborhood on the back deck. Their future was wound up and down those brutal spires like ribbons. And like hell was he going to let that cannibal freak take it from them.

David tore through the sand so hard his hands burned and forced himself to run toward Concordia House. *Through hell and high water,* he told himself.

Inside, Portmaster was cleaning the kitchen table with a contented smile and lemon glaze. David peered in a window and scowled at him once while following the trail of mice and centipedes scurrying toward the light of the Palace Beautiful—that lovely solarium, glowing in the night. He knelt in the dirt and pressed his hands against the windows until he found the one Mia had unlocked: the one with just a little bit of give. As he took a deep breath and pushed, he could almost feel her inside, curled in one of the oversized armchairs with its back to the windows, waiting for him. Maybe she hadn't been lost after all. The window gave way and the little creatures, miscreants from the Wild Wood, slipped into the light eagerly—animals had always liked her—and David followed soon after.

She wasn't inside. She wasn't inside because she lived on the outside now; in the void outside Concordia House, the beyond-the-beyond. It momentarily crushed David to see this, but a cold reality kept him from collapsing: *You have a job to do.* He thought he heard the clunk-clunk of Portmaster's galoshes coming down the hall but it might well have been the beating of his own heart, lodged where it was in his throat. He drowned it out. He had to.

When David dragged the antique leather trunk out from under the bench, layers of dead leather came off in his hands like skin cells. But it had kept well: the gun he'd inherited from his father was safe inside, tucked between his baby blankets. It started beeping when he picked it up, and a ring of green lights confirmed it was still loaded. It was so heavy and awkward that he'd only fired it once—on a milk bottle, when he was sixteen—but he could still remember its kick.

He felt vibrations in the floor. Oh, so not his heart after all. He slid his fingers against the trigger and turned around—there was Portmaster, holding a duster and looking shocked.

"I want you to get out of this house. Right now." David lifted the gun, arms shaking. It was like handling a bazooka, and his weak knees had gotten him out of mandatory military service. Somehow he steadied the cannon in Portmaster's general direction. He didn't even know where to aim. Shooting at a human man's heart would have hit Portmaster in the knee.

Portmaster squinted. "Is that my gun?"

Well, of course it was. The oversized gas-guzzling tanks they all drove were probably revolutionary loot as well. David now assumed that everything he took to be his was in fact *not* his, and everything he took to be eternal was in fact twenty, maybe thirty years old. Their city was a refugee camp. He was living in his parents' dungeon. At least Mia was real. She'd always been the truest thing in his life. And the gun was real too. "Well, it's my gun now," he said, gnawing the insides of his cheeks. "Finders keepers, losers weepers."

Portmaster shook his mighty head. "I'm sorry, but you look like a monkey with a nuke."

David nearly threw out his back lifting the gun to Portmaster's torso. "You wanna bet?" But he was slurring through his sweat and Portmaster looked taller and stronger than ever. He kept telling himself that *he can smell your fear* and for the first time he saw Portmaster as he really was: a sniffing, over-evolved Doberman.

"Poor child. You're angry, aren't you?" Portmaster's face became a simper, and his massive hand stretched toward David as if to pat him on the head. "You need to let it go. That's how you survived the first time—you let go. You forgot. You moved on. The past is past, son."

"Like hell." He thought of Mia—getting out of the car yesterday afternoon, taking in the dry cleaning, smiling back at him. Her long dark braid beating against her back, easily. And then Mia running into the ocean, and her hand emerging from the waves. His eyes stung. He was trying to stand his ground but his feet kept slipping back, slipping into retreat because Portmaster wouldn't stop his approach. "Leave now or I'll blow your head off. Stop. Stop!"

"Violence isn't the answer, my child."

Then Portmaster took a swing at the gun. David hoisted it away but accidentally tapped the trigger and fired a shot that skimmed Portmaster's ribs. It might have been Portmaster's property but unlike Concordia House, the weapon was a neutral force. It would kill anyone. Two seconds later it beeped, ready for another go.

The blast had torn open the wall and made a gnarly little breezeway connecting the solarium to the parlor. The room was scorched with soot and filled with the itchy dust of insulation. A mouse of the Wild Wood lay dying on the coffee table. David had been thrown back against the bench and his head jerked back over the edge in violent whiplash, but he never let go of the gun. Someone was moaning—it wasn't him. When he focused his eyes he saw that Portmaster was still standing, but barely. The giant was pressing both hands to his side, dark dank blood dripping through his fingers. Portmaster suddenly looked very old, feeble as a gangly tree in a monsoon. David had never even run a possum over and a part of his own mental architecture caved in when he saw Portmaster suffering, his rain slicker shining with blood.

"I told you!" David cried. "I told you I would! You better leave before I do it again!"

But Portmaster sank instead. He clung to the remains of a chair like a shipwrecked sailor and then curled up, trying to suck the injury back into a body that was beginning to look like a large chunk of petrified wood. "So this is how it ends," he sighed. "Killed in my own home, with my own gun." He snorted and set off another coughing fit. "I thought you'd become *civilized*."

"You wouldn't *leave!*" David yelled.

"We never should have had you educated," Portmaster rambled on, no longer padding his wound. Blood dripped onto the tiles and Concordia House drank it in. "Look what you do. You're still wild animals. Wild pigs. Wild … pigs."

"My wife is dead because of you." He hadn't wanted to say it. He'd wanted never to say it, because as soon as the words slipped out of his throat he felt all of his bones surrender. All his dreams—the nursery, the deck parties—went flooding out. His future was forfeit, and he had to hug the gun to stay standing. "She is dead! And I don't give a fuck about your wound or your house! I don't care …" And then he looked up at Portmaster and his voice stopped.

Sickness and age had already weakened him, but the gunshot had really pared Portmaster down. He looked thinner, more harrowed. This was not the giant-king carved into the hallway reliefs. No, what remained at his bony core was ancient and needful with the eyes of a starving dog. "Pigs," he drawled, and then his jaw unhinged. Like a python's.

Portmaster bound across the patio on all fours with the loping gait of a wolf. The room shook. He reached David in two heavy paces and David closed his eyes.

Maybe if Portmaster had been at his prime, in full health, he would have lunged up and torn David's throat out. Instead he sunk his double-decker blunted shark teeth into David's calf. The pain was vicious and uncompromising and it saturated David's brain: *This is how you were conquered. With the gun but also the teeth. Look. Look.* David opened his eyes a smidgen and through his tears saw pieces of his own leg in the giant's mouth, bloody and shredded like a ravaged sirloin. He also saw the barrel of the gun. He tapped the trigger, and that time the blast hit Portmaster in the chest.

Man and giant went down. This time, David recovered first. The bitten leg was an ugly mess of blood and muscle and had, thankfully, gone numb—the other leg, the good leg, was shaking uncontrolla- bly. He helped himself forward, leaning on the good leg, and tried to shoo Portmaster with the gun. The giant human-Doberman was alive, but only barely. His mighty rib cage had caved in. His hands, at last, had stopped reaching. "Get out," David whispered.

"I'm sorry," Portmaster gurgled. He was trying to let the blood on his lips dry. Trying not to lick it. "I lost control. I've just been so … hungry."

David saw his mother again, limping across the room. "Get out," he repeated.

"Please let me die in this house." Portmaster's voice was down to a whisper. "All I wanted was to die here."

Concordia House seemed to bend inward as if to console him; the antique ceiling fan reduced the beating of its blades to a soft, comforting hum. But outside the sea churned like stomach acid. David didn't know how it could still be hungry—hadn't it eaten Mia whole? He thrust the industrial-caliber gun barrel under Portmaster's chin.

"You can't always get what you want," he said.

He drove Portmaster out of the house on hands and knees. Crabs followed man and giant's blood-trails to the sea. The gray water washed over Portmaster's knobby hands and David just shoved him forward. How strange; Portmaster no longer looked gargantuan.

"Swim," said David. "Swim back to wherever you came from." Of course he knew there would be no swimming. Instead the riptide carried Portmaster out, a twitching and bleeding piece of driftwood, until at about fifteen meters off-shore the ocean opened up and swallowed him. The froth surged up the beach, nibbling broken shells, looking for David—it didn't care who the blood belonged to—but David hobbled back onto dry sand, pointing the gun at the water. The ocean backed away. By then the sun was rising, and as usual no sea-birds came.

David contemplated lighting the match while he was still inside the house. His feet would burn first, since they were covered in petrol. Then the fire would consume his legs—maybe it would heal the bite, swiftly and brutally turning the tainted flesh to ash?—and then his torso, and it would probably jump to his hands since they'd been holding the petrol can, and meanwhile the fire would be working its way up to his chin and there it would draw tight around his head like an infernal scarf. Like a blanket, a baby blanket. It seemed cathartic. But he thought about heat and pain and finality and chickened out. So it was from the safety of the beach and its wild grass and tumbleweeds that he watched Concordia House burn.

The mansion howled. Wood planks burst off as if the house was trying to pick up and run. Flaming curtains thrashed like vanquished ghosts from the frames of the upstairs windows. People always said that Concordia House was grotesque. Not right for the landscape, they said. Mia said she didn't think people ought to live in houses that big when she first laid eyes on it.

David leaned forward onto the gun—Portmaster's gun, his father's gun. It was the only thing he had saved.

He stood there, motionless, until he saw a shape in the water—something dark and steady, like a beaching dolphin coming in to die. It brought a strange subterranean pressure that swept over the beach and silenced the palms, the ever-restless sand. David blinked. Mia stood on the sand a few meters from him, flickering, draped with seaweed and looking unwell. He blinked again and she was right beside him, smiling and peeling in the hazy sunshine. A barnacle was growing on her cheek. He felt light-headed. She pointed.

Over the green, gently swaying hills, other seaside mansions perched on cliffs. They too were waiting for their rightful owners to return.

"Burn the rest," Mia whispered. "Burn them all."

The pressure reached a breaking point, and his ears popped. Then David started down the road, gun and petrol can in hand. He passed several sunburned villagers sitting in the beds of slow-moving produce trucks. Some of them shouted to him, but all he could hear was the sea. The asphalt scorched his feet. He had his mother's limp.

I SHALL BUT LOVE THEE BETTER

SCOTT EDELMAN

Do you remember the day I died?

Of course you do, Rhys. I feel foolish for having doubted you. I feel foolish for having asked.

I felt foolish as well on that final day we shared, during the few moments I had enough strength to take note of my surroundings, to open my eyes and look up at the freshly painted ceiling of our bedroom, to tilt my head slightly and see the new wallpaper. How long ago that last time together was, and how silly we were to have bothered!

We'd thought I'd bounce back, didn't we, thought for a long time we'd beat this thing—or why else would we have spent so much of our precious moments together during those dwindling months … redecorating? We could have done so much more with the days we had left than preparing our home for a future we'd never share. Eventually, though, we had to accept we were nearing the end, and let those fantasies go. But by then … it was too late to do all the things we'd promised we'd do.

Yes, you could have, had you wished, headed off and done them alone, but … no, you couldn't, since my world had by then shrunk to only our bedroom. You'd never have left me. I believed that then, with all my heart.

I remember what it was like to be trapped in that bed, how while I lay there, bound within each thought, a second thought ran in parallel. Which meant I was continually asking myself:

Was that it?

The thought that just went by—was it the last thought I'll think? And was that the last breath I'll ever take?

But no … my days were full of constant surprise, for there were always more of each. More thoughts and more breaths. For a little while, at least. Enough for us to have that eventual final conversation.

I'd felt a squeeze on my hand that singular morning, a hand I'd forgotten was even being held, so out of it was I, and turned to see you sitting beside me, your face lined beyond your years. Oh, how I remember that face, so smooth, so fine, from when first I saw it that day on the beach. I'd put those lines there, me and my damned disease, and after each time I'd drift away and drift back, I'd notice there were more of them. They were my calendar, and I'd count them with sadness. But the guilt I'd feel upon each waking could not be counted. It was beyond measure.

We were supposed to have had more months together, more years, more decades, but because of me, because of what had been written in my genes before birth, I was to leave you, and you were going to spend those years, those decades, every pledged moment, alone. Still, I had faith that after death, after first mine and then yours, there would be a reunion. There'd have to be.

But you knew that, too, didn't you? That's the only way we got through our farewell. Your faith, I sensed, wasn't as strong as mine, but though my body was failing, my belief was sufficient to carry us both. And so, even as the time of our first lives ran out, even as my flesh fought against me, I struggled to buoy you one last time.

"Don't be so sad," I remember whispering, way back in the before. I'd tried to raise my other hand, the one you weren't holding tight so you wouldn't drown, to your cheek, but couldn't successfully fight gravity and lift it from where it lay leaden and useless on the topmost of my blankets. The strength I needed to move it had long since faded. "Try to think of it as if … as if I'm just catching an earlier train. You'll join me when it's time. Be patient, my love. We'll be together again soon."

"You can't know that, Teeg," you'd said. I saw the worry on your face, hated what it meant for the worry on your heart, and offered words I thought would extinguish it from both.

"No, I can't," I said softly, weakly. "But I choose to believe it anyway. Now promise me …"

I paused to catch my breath, then paused some more, sensing that the catching of it would soon be beyond me, sensed the coming pause which would stretch and separate us.

"Promise you?" you said. You feared my silences, however brief.

"That you'll take the next train," I said, ending that short string of words with a gasp.

"There's no train, Teeg," you said, a sentiment you'd offered many times before, in different words, in response to different metaphors. "If only there were. Besides, will there even be trains in the future? And would you want to be in a future without them? Remember that overnight train to Edinburgh? And the haggis you ate—or tried to eat—in the dining car? There probably won't be haggis in the future either. But then, I don't think you'll mind."

You tried to smile, I could tell, as you attempted to distract me with your rambling from the promise I was aiming to pull out of you, but failed at both.

"I know that," I said. "I know there's no train, not really. But it will make it easier for me ... to go on ahead ... if I can manage to think of it that way. Think of it ... like a train ... that will only separate us ... for a few stops. So promise me ... you'll call the number ... when it's time. We worked so hard to ... to earn the right to that number, Rhys. Promise me ... you'll let them do ... what needs to be done .... Promise me you'll follow."

"Teeg, I—"

"Promise," I said, summoning all my strength, wondering if that would be the last word I ever spoke in my God-given lifetime. If it was, I knew I'd be happy in that choice.

You leaned forward then, eyes closed, and pressed your forehead to mine. I felt your tears as they dropped to my cheeks. I felt them then. I still feel them now as I prepare to do what needs to be done so I may see you again.

"I promise," you said. And I believed you.

And then, because I believed you, because your promise lay soft upon my ears, upon my soul ... I died.

Or came as close to death as one can travel without being truly dead to one's core.

What happened next I can only imagine, because only you remained behind to see, while I did not—at least not the part of me in any condition to witness.

You'd made the call we'd agreed the one who'd be left behind would make—I know that, since if you hadn't, I wouldn't be speaking to you now—and so the team of doctors who'd been waiting for that summons rushed over, accompanied by technicians and scientists, bringing with them a cold they swore I'd never feel as I slept. They took me away from you so they could prepare my body, and the essence of me that remained within, for what would happen next.

It hurts me so to imagine you there after I was gone, in the bedroom we'd hoped to occupy together until time itself ran out. It hurts to picture you alone, mourning, waiting for the next train.

Or the next elevator.

Or for that carousel to complete its revolution and bring our souls back together again.

Oh, the metaphors I'd tossed your way over the years as we planned for this step were endless, weren't they?

Yes … they were. And it's painful to think of you thinking of them, mulling over first one then another then back again, seeking one you can accept. One which will help you carry on without me. So I will not.

I will only think of that time after which neither of us will have to be alone ever again.

I wish I'd been better able, over the years, to keep hidden from you how worried I was about the dreams in which I was sure I'd be trapped—tortured by memories, chased by fears, unable to wake— even though they'd told us, when we first visited the facility for those exploratory conversations and I shared with them and you that the possibility of them filled me with terror—there would be none. I'd tried to hide that terror from you. I knew I couldn't … but still, I tried.

I'd often had bad dreams in my first life, as you came to know better than anyone, and it was only your presence beside me each night—ready to shake me, ready to hold me, ready to make me forget them—that allowed me to not shrink from sleep as I had in the years—few though they were—before you came into my life. So the idea I might dream endlessly, stuck in my own head while those who remained in the outside world ignored my frozen form as they continued their hunt for a cure, and know that if in distress I would not, could not, be woken by your hands, and was beyond the comfort of your embrace … that frightened me.

As it turns out, when it came to dreaming … they were wrong. All of them. And why not? None of the ones who'd made me those promises had yet gone on to where I was to go, and none of the others who *had* gone on had yet returned to tell tales of their journeys—so how could they know?

They called themselves scientists, they called themselves doctors, they called themselves engineers, and yet they knew no more than any of us. They were only guessing. About the dreams. About whether there would someday be a cure. And about, even if there were to be a cure, whether any of it would work—whether a life beyond the one we were first given was even possible.

Luckily, when I found myself in dream, it was a *good* dream, it was a comforting dream, and that filled me with relief. And yet— even though I was relieved that they'd been wrong, it also worried me during the initial moments. After all, if they had been wrong about the dreaming, who knows what else they might have been wrong about?

No matter. Because when the dream came, there was no reason to be afraid, and I no longer cared about their failed predictions. It pushed all my fears away. For the dream was a familiar one, letting me know by the way it began that I was wandering under the influence of one of my happy ones.

And not just *a* happy one—*the* happiest one.

I was on that beach again. You know which one—the one I always dream about—the one where we'd first met. The sand was there, as it always was, with more grains than I could count, though in my earlier dreams I'd sometimes tried. The ocean was there, too, bluer this time than it had ever been, bluer than it had any right to be, and stretching to infinity. And you were there in the distance, walking in my direction, and not yet seeing me.

In the dream, as in our original lives, as in every time I recreated the moment in my sleep, I'd spotted you first. And you were as young, while I slept and waited my waking to a second life, as you had been that real-life day when I'd initially lived it, and in the dream, I knew as surely as I had that first true moment that our futures would inevitably entwine, even though our eyes had not yet met.

Only this time, for the first time, I found myself walking a spot that was far more than the beach where we'd first met.

This time, we were not alone as we had been when we'd been young. Oh, how I wish you could have seen it with me!

Over there were capybaras rolling in the surf, chittering with joy.

And there—all the children we'd spoken of having, but which we'd never had, occasionally splashing among them, occasionally turning to look at us, gazing on us only with love, and without approbation for us never not having allowed them to be born.

I could see your parents trailing behind you in the distance, and sensed that if I turned, if I then gazed past my footsteps back to where I'd started my morning walk, I'd spot my own parents far behind me as well.

And their parents, and their parents' parents, too.

And above us, all the meteor showers we'd ever seen, overlapping with all the fireworks which had ever formed curtains over our heads, producing colors found only in dream.

As they etched the sky simultaneously you turned to me and smiled, a smile which told me you saw all the things I saw, you knew what was to come next after the moment in which we'd close the gap between us, you were ready to join me in inviting our future to overtake us. And so I hurried toward you, reached out my hands to that future, to our twinned past which would be followed by a single future, all the while knowing, as the impossible paraded around us, that it was only a dream. And not caring that it was only a dream.

And then I felt ice in my veins, and you faded, it all faded, the capybara, the fireworks, the ghosts of the future and the ghosts of the past, and I closed my eyes on that perfect beach only to open them once more on our bedroom's freshly painted ceiling and new wallpaper, occupying yet again a time and space we'd never inhabited until nearly forty years on from our original moment walking that sand.

All seemed as it had been the previous instant I'd closed my eyes, when I'd made you promise, as I'd so often made you promise, to do the work of sending me on ahead, the work of following after. I was as I had been, and all the strength I'd felt in dream was gone. I was once more weak, too weak to lift my head and look about for you.

I was back in my bed, our bed, sure I was again in the prison of my body, again waiting for my end. I was certain that if I could turn my head, I would certainly find you still beside me, find fresh lines across your face, written there during yet another moment when I'd drifted away from you, for I'd obviously not died as I had thought, and no team of strangers had yet harvested my body, protected my soul, plunged me into a decades-long dream.

But then a strange man—at least I thought it was a man, at first I couldn't be entirely sure—leaned into my field of vision, his bald head framed by a high collar. He was smiling, but it was not your smile, so it did not comfort me.

"Welcome back, Tegan," he said to me. "Call me Mikal. It's been far too long."

Certain I was still in the before living my first life, my heart sank to see a face not yours. Why were you not watching over me, alert for the breath which would be my last, ready to make the call which would eventually bring us more time, bring us *all* the time? Where could you possibly have gone during the brief moments I'd drifted away? I couldn't think of a reason why anything but death would separate us, and yet there I was again, alive, and right where I'd always been. So I looked at the man, then past him to all we had done to restore our bedroom, then at him again, bewildered.

And what had he meant by "too long"? Did we meet before, and I'd forgotten? I struggled to place his face, remember when we could have last seen each other, but came up blank.

Forgive me, Rhys, for not immediately realizing the real reason you were absent, the only possible reason you could be absent, would be absent, but even with all our planning, all our conversations about what was to happen next, what had actually occurred was still so unexpected as to be unimaginable. In that moment, I simply could not conceive of what we'd spent the final years of my life conceiving.

(I've been asking for your forgiveness a lot lately, I see, but since we had so little need to apologize to each other in our first lives, as we'd miraculously committed so few acts which required the asking of forgiveness, my recent requests, born of discomfort, leap out of me almost before I can even think them.)

"Did something go wrong with the procedure?" I asked. I didn't recognize Mikal's face, or his name, as belonging to any of those we'd met during our interviews, but I assumed that was why he had to be in *our* room. My planned preservation must have been put on hold, and he needed to visit us to explain the problem. "Why am I still here?"

I truly didn't know the state of things in that moment, Rhys. I should have, I know, but didn't. Not even when he smiled at me the curious way he did. It was only when he spoke that I began to understand. And not just because of the meaning of the words he said, but because of the precise way he said them.

His words were careful, oh, so careful. And he wasn't just being careful about me, about the effect those words would have. His diction was clipped, precise, and he was over-enunciating in a way I'd later learn was because the words he needed to use to communicate with me … they were not really his, and no longer anyone else's either. Ours was a dead language. Just as I had been dead. Just as, I would later find out, were you …

"I understand," he said, and looked away from me for the first time since I'd opened my eyes, turning to the walls which enclosed us, our room, the sanctuary we'd made, as if he'd forgotten they existed. Then he looked back, his crooked smile unwavering. "There's nothing to worry about, Tegan. You're here. You're alive. You've made it. You're where you wanted to be. You're in the future. And you've been cured. Your body is no longer your enemy. You'll have many more years ahead of you, far more than you had behind."

"So … it worked?" I said. I was breathless, Rhys, and not in the old, weakened way. Not like during what was our final conversation. It wasn't that I was too feeble to shout. It's that I was amazed. And I sensed … I was changed. Once Mikal told me the truth of things, once I began to listen to my body, I could tell. A strength I'd almost forgotten was returning to me.

"It did," he said. "And all this—"

He waved at the walls, the ceiling.

"—is not actually your room. Obviously, that room no longer exists. It's … been a while. And we've learned a few things over the years from those who preceded you. We've found it's best not to shock people when they come back. To allow them to come slowly to the realization of where they actually are. When they actually are. So we make sure to surround them with the familiar. And for you, that was this room. At least we think it was this room. That's what the records say, anyway. Were we right?"

Oh, how he was right, Rhys. This room was as familiar as my own skin. I remembered pasting on the wallpaper, rolling on the paint, with you by my side. I remembered the hard work, remembered getting covered with paint, with glue, remembered the fun of clean-up after. I remembered … everything. But without you in that room … being there was pointless.

"Thank you for the memories," I told Mikal. "But I don't think I need this illusion any more. I'm ready to understand. I'm ready for reality."

He tilted his head, and the false past which had surrounded us faded away. With the recreation gone, I then saw where we really were—in a featureless cube, its walls white, presumably to make it easier for them to be painted with a mask which would let us believe we were anywhere. I saw, too, Rhys, that I was not truly in the bed we had once shared, but instead on a pallet made from half of one of the cylinders they'd shown us so long ago, split open when I was reborn. And I saw at the same time—the two of us were not alone.

Over the man's shoulder, I could spy three others, a team previously hidden by whatever bit of tomorrow's technology had given me a projection of the home I'd made with you. But I didn't care about them or why they were present, even though I supposed I owed them my new life. Because as soon as the familiar room disappeared, leaving me with no touchstone to the past, all I cared about, all I longed for, was a return to what was most familiar to my heart—you.

"Where's Rhys?" I said, sitting up and sliding my legs off the bed. I did it without thinking, because if I'd thought about it, I wouldn't have done it. In the life which to me seemed but moments past, I couldn't have done it. As the soles of my feet hit the floor, I became slightly woozy, which was to be expected, after what I'd endured without knowing I'd endured it, but—

I did it, Rhys. I did it! I wish you could have seen, you'd have been so proud of me. It had been months, I'd thought to myself then, since I'd been able to do it at all. And as the certainty I had indeed been reborn overtook me, I realized—it was more likely years. Or perhaps even decades. Or … more?

Regardless, I was sitting up—which was proof that what we'd wanted to happen *had* happened. That knowledge made me far dizzier than the movement itself ever could.

It made me know you were out there somewhere waiting for me. If a miracle had transformed me, then surely you, whose genes had not started out mangled, were already out there waiting.

"My husband," I said. "Please."

The man's smile faded, and I was afraid then that I'd lost you. That some unimagined horror had damaged you beyond the point of return. And you know I could not bear to go on without you. But Mikal quickly reassured me.

"Don't worry, Tegan," he said, obviously correctly reading how I'd reacted to his change in expression. "It's not what you're thinking. It's only that your husband's time has not yet come. Oh, he'll join you eventually, but his case is a bit more complicated than yours. Even we haven't yet figured out a way to bring someone back, not from disease, but from old age. That knowledge will come, though, we promise you. It may take years. Maybe more than years. But it *will* happen. You *will* be reunited."

I thought of you, and was happy at first that no accident or virus had struck you down, that you'd been allowed the fullness of a life, and yet, the thought of you withering away alone until death took you …

Tears came at the thought of our separation, one that seemed moments for me, but would have seemed decades, or so I gathered, for you. Those tears were my first in a long while. But to think of you like that, in pain, beyond my reach, while I lay locked in a cylinder …

I promised you then, Rhys, that when we saw each other next, when we were together again, I would hold you and never let you go. And sitting in that strange room on the edge of the cylinder that saved me, my feet on solid ground again, I knew we *would* be together again, just as I'd always known, even without proof.

You didn't always believe it was possible, but how could it not be? The universe would never be that cruel, not to us. I looked forward to seeing your face when you woke, to being the first face you saw when you woke, rather than a stranger from a time beyond my own.

I dried my eyes and looked at the man from the future, my voice so choked with emotion I could barely get out the words. But …

"I'd like to see my husband now," I said.

Mikal nodded, and opposite me, the outlines of a door appeared where before there had only been an expanse of white. Knowing that somewhere beyond the promise of that door, you waited, I stood without thinking. I stood, Rhys! I was whole again, and you would soon—but never soon enough—be whole again, too. Our friends had scoffed at us, but they were long dead, I presumed, while everything we'd hoped for, it seemed, was coming true.

I teetered for a moment as I stood there, and the other members of the team to whom I'd yet to be introduced reached out toward me, but I held up a hand. I had this. There was no need for them to help. I stretched, raising my hands to the blank ceiling, no longer *our* ceiling, and felt my stubborn muscles come alive.

I'd been reborn. And soon, you would be, too.

"This is amazing," I said. "This is remarkable. How long have I been … away?"

Mikal mentioned a year way further ahead by far than when I'd thought I would end up waking. I hadn't expected a quick cure, but I also hadn't expected lifetimes. I considered the date, then decided … it didn't matter. As long as the two of us would inhabit that year together, Rhys … nothing else mattered.

"Let's go then," I said, walking toward the door, which opened without any of us touching it. I turned to see if anyone would follow, because I needed them to lead me to you, and could see the others, instead of tagging after, looking down at their palms, which were now cupped around flashing lights I hadn't noticed before. They were checking my vitals, I presumed. I could understand their worries, but as far as I was concerned, no diagnostics were needed. They'd cured me, brought me back better than I'd been before, and I couldn't wait for you to see the new-old me. "Do you like what you're seeing?"

"All is as it should be," said Mikal. "We are pleased. You're not the first we've been able to bring back. Just the first to return who suffered from your particular disease. But we can tell—you are as you were before it struck you down. Better, in fact."

"Thank you for this," I said, knowing even at the time I should have said so much more in the face of so miraculous an act. It occurred to me later that by my few words, I perhaps seemed ungrateful, but in that moment I had no spare thoughts for anything but you.

As we exited into a long corridor equally as featureless as the room in which I'd woken, there were many things I was still too overwhelmed to have room for in my thoughts, concerns that were suppressed by what really mattered. I only realized later that I'd never sought out a window so I could peer through and see what this world of the future had become. I'd never bothered asking for the names of the others who were helping Mikal, or where I was, whether the city where I'd been reborn had been the same as the one in which I'd died. I never asked for the exact year you'd left the world behind, starting your own frozen sleep, so I could know how long you'd been alone without me.

So many questions unasked, unthought of then. But nothing filled my mind save what waited for me somewhere down that corridor. You.

Eventually, a door opened just ahead, one I stepped through without waiting for an invitation. Inside a massive room which seemed to have no end to it, row after row of tall cylinders, similar to the one on which I woke, except vertical, and not yet split open, stretched as far as I could see, a dizzying number waiting to be reborn. After the falseness of the room in which I'd returned to consciousness, I was uncertain whether the seeming endlessness of the space was real or illusion. Regardless, I scanned my eyes across what cylinders I could see, then stepped into the midst of them.

You waited for me within one, Rhys, I knew that, and I felt I should have been able to tell which, but could not. I grew disappointed then, and not just in general, but in myself. Should not I have been able to sense your essence, track you down? My love for you told me … yes. I should not have needed help to find you. And so I felt at the time as if I should apologize to you for my failure.

(Ah, yes … more apologies. And now I feel I should apologize for that. But now I also know better. There's no need for apologies between the two of us. Never were and never will be.)

I felt suddenly weak then and placed a hand against the cylinder closest to me, hoping whoever slept inside would not mind.

"Which one is he?" I asked.

"Let me show you," said Mikal. The others stood in a line behind us, watching silently.

I let Mikal take my arm and lead me on, even though I felt I should have protested on behalf of my new body, which was fully capable of moving without his aid. As we walked on, I looked around and tried to guess from which cylinder you would eventually be decanted, wanting to feel it before Mikal paused and revealed you to me, but I had no sense which one held my future. Our future.

We finally stopped before a cylinder that looked no different than the others, and as we did, a narrower cylinder slowly began to rise out of the floor before it until it reached just the right height for me to use as a stool if I wished.

"Here we are," Mikal said. "Rhys is in here."

I needed to clear my throat before speaking, which was entirely due to the nearness of you and had nothing to do with any faulty repairs during my revival.

"May I see him?" I asked, circling slowly around the cylinder, frustrated by its opaque surface. "Is there any way? Please."

Mikal shook his head.

"I'm sorry," he said. "Isolation is a must, I'm afraid. Until his time comes, until we are ready for him, he must remain sealed just as you were. Being preserved in there is the best thing for him. Any change in temperature, anything to dilute the darkness, and he could become infected, or become too damaged to revive. Believe me, this is for the best."

"Can he hear me?" I asked. I so hoped you could, Rhys.

"You are free to think so."

Those weren't the most hopeful words, but still, I hoped.

"How long will it be, do you imagine?" I asked him. "How long will I have to wait?"

"I wish we could give you an exact answer. No one can predict these things. Every revival has been different. But I assure you, we're working on a cure, the same way we were with you. His time will come. A time will come for all of them. And we'll do our best to keep you happy and distracted until then."

Perhaps they could distract me—I could only imagine what wonders the future would hold once I emerged from the blank walls of the facility—but keep me happy? No one could do that but you.

"May I please be alone now?" I asked.

"Certainly," he said, and backed away. The others followed.

I waited until the echoing of their footsteps vanished to say to you the things I needed to say, the things meant for your ears only. Oh, I knew I was fooling myself about this, that the reason they hadn't lingered to watch over me was likely because they were tracking my vitals from a distance anyway, and could hear my words as well as my pulse, listen to my tears as well as my brainwaves, but somehow, in that large room, even with their distant monitoring, even though there were thousands there just as you, I felt as if there was just the two of us alone.

I sat before you, and as I looked toward you, squinted as if that would pierce the barrier between us, I saw myself reflected in the shiny exterior of the cylinder, saw me as you had seen me. Not, though, as you had last seen me. I looked not so different then than when we'd first met. They'd restored me, as they would restore you. I closed my eyes, leaned forward and pressed my forehead against its curve. Its surface was cool as it would have to be to keep you live, or almost alive. As I felt the chill I had not felt in dream, I hoped you did not feel it as you dreamt either.

I stretched out my arms, hugged you as best as I could, but did not make it even halfway around. I wished I knew which direction they had you facing as you slept. Were you turned toward me, I wondered, as I in life was always turned toward you? But … in the end, it didn't matter. Whether our positions meant we were hugging or whether they meant we were spooning was meaningless. That we were together was enough.

I hoped as I held you that you could sense I was there waiting for you to follow me. I hoped you were dreaming, as I had been, of our pasts, of the future we'd left trailing behind us, of the future to come. We'd been waiting so long—how long for you I had no idea, because though Mikal had told me the year of my rebirth, I'd never asked the year you … you passed … and I wanted the time we'd be separated ahead to be shorter than the time that split us behind.

I looked away from you then, wanting to ask that of those who'd revived me, and realized, as I gazed about at the forest of cylinders … I didn't know the way back to where my saviors were waiting. There were so many cylinders, so many souls in stasis. I had no idea there could be so many. We were thought foolish by most back in the old days when we decided to do what we eventually did. I guess the world changed its mind about that as the world began to change.

Before I could rise and go seek them, they were beside me again, alerted, I assumed, by a change in my pulse or an alteration in my brainwaves. Seeing them there, I no longer wanted to ask them when you had died, but only …

"Is there any way I can help?" I said, hoping a hope which even as it grew within me, I knew I had no right to feel. But I missed you so, Rhys! "Help speed up the process?"

"With this?" said Mikal. "No. I'm sorry to disappoint you a second time, Tegan. But I'm afraid whatever scientific knowledge you've brought with you from your time is insufficient. I hate to disparage my ancestors, but if what you know could help to bring him back, it would have helped in the first place so that he'd never have left."

"Oh," I said, unsurprised by what he'd said, even though a small, flickering part of me had so wanted it to be different. But with his words that flickering faded, and I knew I'd have to resign myself to years of loneliness as you had done. I hoped I could be as strong as I knew you must have been. But I didn't know if that was possible.

"But don't worry," he continued. "There is a way you can help us, Tegan, and it will help you at the same time. You did bring back one thing with you that we need."

I left you then, and it was hard, Rhys, almost harder than it had been the first time. Because dying, you see, meant I had no choice in the leaving of you, while this time, stepping away almost felt like a betrayal. But somehow, now that I'd found you, I'd have to also find the trust that I'd never lose you again.

So I followed Mikal and his parade of helpers from the cavern of cylinders to another room, a smaller room, though again one with walls equally as white and featureless as all those I'd already seen. Stools rose from the floor as we entered, filling the otherwise empty cube, and yet, for all I knew, I was once again in the spot where I'd woken. The sameness was such that I'd grown uncertain about where I was and where I'd been. I honestly had no idea. My whereabouts were as confused as they'd been during those first moments after rebirth.

And when we sat, and Mikal told me what they hoped I would do for them during my time spent waiting for you, I was even more confused.

"You just want me ... to talk?" I said. "To remember? I don't understand. How will talking about the old world help you? How is that going to pay my way through the new one?"

"No one needs to pay their way through the world any more, Tegan," he said. He smiled in that strange way he had when I first saw his face, as if he'd forgotten how and was trying to learn all over again. "The world doesn't work that way now. Within these walls, the machinery built by those who came before meets our needs, and just like the rest of us, you've earned your place within them merely by being alive. You see, Tegan, not many records remain here in this world of the world that once was, and you're the first to be revived from your period. We want you to help us understand how we got from there to here."

The initial shock of finding myself alive once more had started to fade by then, so I had the presence of mind to ask him the question I should have asked him at the very beginning of this new life. The question I know you would have asked him at the beginning.

"And where *is* here exactly?" I said.

"Here," he answered, "is wherever you want it to be. That's why we've constructed the environment this way. It's a blank canvas that can be whatever brings anyone the most comfort, as you saw when we revived you. And with your knowledge, you'll be able to help people even see them as the world you once knew. That's information we do not have. And, you see, these walls can be *any* walls. They can be what you need."

"That's a wonderful thing, it truly is, but ... what's *outside* these walls?"

I'd made it to the future, Rhys—a future we were soon going to inhabit together. I wanted to dive into it, to start learning all about it so I could share it with you when you arrived. Arrived on that next train.

"That will come, Tegan," he said. "But not just yet. Be patient. You feel strong, I know, but that's only the pink cloud which follows waking, one others before you have experienced. It may fade. You need time to recover. And we need time, too. Time for us to make sure you won't be infected out there, won't infect us. And until then, until you are reunited with your Rhys, all we ask of you is that you talk to us. All we ask is that you tell us of what came before."

It seemed so little for them to ask of me considering the magnitude of what they were willing to do for us, and so I let Mikal lead me down winding corridors as white and narrow as those I'd already seen to others—historians, educators, technicians—with whom I spent my days talking, telling them every little thing I could remember, and then after, reminiscing with you over the same events, alternating between them and you until my voice was sore. Funny that they could bring me back to life, but couldn't stop that from happening.

They pushed me to recall all I could of what it was like in the old days down to the smallest details, like what it was like to walk the aisles of a supermarket, or what traffic sounded like at night as I fell asleep, even though all I wanted to talk about was you, was us, and how we moved through those days together. They explained they wanted to be able to recreate all of the old world on the new world's walls, just as they'd done with our bedroom, so they pushed me to walk through my memories and feed them every little fact, even seemingly inconsequential ones. I think I pleased them, but I was never sure, since as I told you, they were not quite like us. I think they'd forgotten us, Rhys. But I did my best, and talked to them ... and then I'd talk to you.

Oh, how I hoped you heard me late at night when I'd whisper to you—as I'd fall asleep beside the cylinder they'd led me to rather than in the room they'd prepared for me—that it all didn't make sense, Rhys. I didn't mean the constant telling of the past. I could understand an historian wanting to know about that. But it was a feeling that they were hiding something while trying hard to pretend they weren't. Because somehow, without ever actually saying no, they'd never get around to letting me see the real world they'd promised to show me. There was always some excuse which made sense in the moment, yet when all of them were strung together ... no.

Like—no one could be found that particular day to be my chaperone. Or—there were new diseases I had no immunity for and so it wasn't safe for me to leave the facility. And—I had become too famous due to my storytelling, which was being shared with all, and would be mobbed if I did step outside. They were very creative, Rhys, and I, I was very gullible, because I wanted so much to believe.

So as the months went by, I never got to see the world outside those white walls, only the world they'd project onto them for me, the world they said was waiting. And though it was a good world, with beautiful buildings and flying cars and amazing vistas, even though it was a good recreation, too, it wasn't the real thing. It was an illusion, Rhys, and it bothered me, it really did. And maybe I should have spoken up and called them out on it as you would have—you were always a better skeptic than me—but I did not push them as I should have for fear that might cause them not to continue working to bring you back to me. And closing the gap between us was the only thing that was important. I was willing to put up with a few lies—or lie to myself that there were no lies at all—if in the end that would bring us together.

But then came the day when I'd had enough. I knew even as it was happening I was putting our future at risk, but I couldn't control myself, and I hoped you'd forgive me.

It happened while on a break from my telling of tales, during an afternoon they allowed me to use their walls to see what they would not let me yet see for real. And that day I didn't want to walk the recreated streets of their recreated cities. I'd tired of them, did not want to experience them again until I could walk the real streets of real cities.

I wanted to see one of our old places. I didn't care that it would be an illusion—at least that's what I told myself at first—as long as I could still feel closer to you. So I had them conjure up the beach where we first met. I'd told them all about it before so often they'd surely grown tired of it, but it meant they had enough information to program one of the rooms to appear like the spot we met. And for a moment, I felt comforted. Felt loved. Felt the presence of you. But only for a moment. Because—

Though the sun was the right height in the sky, its rays did not warm my face.

Though the surf sliding up the sand was the right distance from my feet, the spray that spat from it did not wet my cheek.

And as for you, dear Rhys—though you were off in the distance, heading my way, approaching me as you always did, not seeing me until I saw you, you did not fill my heart to overflowing.

I broke down then, waved away the pretense of the past, screamed at my distant minders that, though they were not in the white room with me, all they had shown me was false.

"Where is the real world?" I demanded when they came running. Some I recognized. Some I didn't. But all filled me with anger at that moment. "You've shown me nothing but white walls. Nothing but lies. Let me see what's outside of them. Let me see *now*."

No one answered me. Most wouldn't even look at me. Not until Mikal arrived and finally told me the truth.

"I'm sorry we lied to you," he said. "We thought it would be easier for you that way, easier for you to hang on until your partner was returned to you. We didn't know whether you were strong enough at first for us to tell you the way things really were, and thought you'd be better able to handle the truth together, to understand. For that we are sorry. *I* am sorry."

He sat then, made small cylinders rise, and waved for me to sit beside him, but I did not. I could not. And then he told me the horrible, terrible truth, a truth I hated to think I'd someday have to tell you.

"You've asked to see the world outside these walls, Tegan. But there no longer is any world outside these walls. At least not one in which we can live. What we project on these white walls is all of the world we have left. But we've lied to you long enough, so I will let you see the world as it is now."

He tilted his head then, and the walls went away, replaced by—

Oh, it was terrible, Rhys.

Buildings toppled. Forests burned. People gone. No life of any kind, not even a bird in the sky. And the sky red, oh, so red.

I could barely get out the words to ask what had happened.

"We don't really know," he said. "There's a gap between your time and ours. But I can tell you this—no one has been outside in generations. Centuries. Listen, though—you can have a good life here. Those who remain, those who live here, do. We know it's not the kind of life you had before. We can bring any world back, the way we did with your room when we first met. And with all you've been telling us, we'll eventually be able to give you *your* world back. The illusion of it, anyway. You can still be happy here. You may not be able to have the real world. But you can have any world."

I was almost too shocked to speak. Almost.

"Any world without Rhys in it," I told Mikal, "is not one worth having."

"And you'll have that world someday, Tegan. I promise you, we're close to finding him a cure. And we're getting closer every day. He'll be with you soon enough, and then you'll see the world we have is quite livable. You two can have a new life together. No, not the life you had. But a good life nonetheless."

He looked at me then, expecting some kind of answer. But I had no answer. I only had hope. The hope of seeing you again. The hope your presence would make it better.

And that was how I hung on day after day, Rhys, fighting my feelings about this claustrophobic future by serving up thoughts of you, distracting myself with stories of our shared past, until the time came, after far too long without you, when they revealed a cure had been found which would bring you back to me.

"It's done," Mikal said to me with that crooked smile of his one day, interrupting my recounting to an historian of a vacation you and I had taken to Peru. The telling of it had made me melancholy, for as the words poured out, I wondered whether the ancient wonders we had seen there, which had seemed so magical, had survived until the time I then occupied, or whether it was all gone. But hearing Mikal's words, I knew what he meant without him having to say any more, and because I was so happy in that moment, all sadness fled, and I began to cry.

I could tell that made Mikal uncomfortable, for he had no way of telling my tears of sadness from my tears of joy. But you would have been able to tell. You knew me, Rhys. And that was why I needed you back.

He led me down those all-too-familiar endless white corridors, corridors which would not seem so bleak once you were there to walk them with me, and took me to the room, our room, or rather, a room which they'd readied so that when we rejoined each other it would be exactly as it was when we'd parted. Would you be confused at first, as I was, and think yourself not yet dead, and then not yet back alive, on seeing those familiar walls? At least you'd have me there, Rhys. At least the first face you see would not belong to a stranger.

I was ready to see your smile again, ready to once more count the passage of time by the creases in your face. Only when I turned to the pallet made to look like our bed ...

The body there was not yours. The hair was the wrong color, the nose bent the wrong way, the limbs too gangly.

"What did you do?" I shouted. "That's not Rhys. You revived the wrong man."

I could see in Mikal's face that he was about to ask me whether I was sure, then wisely choosing not to. He turned to the others, who looked at me, then at the man they believed to be you, then down into their hands at the flashing of those colored lights.

The silence as they studied them was unbearable.

"I don't know what to say, Tegan," he said. "According to the records, the cylinder we decanted was the one assigned to your husband. And this is who we found inside when it was opened."

"There must have been some kind of mix-up. You've obviously made a mistake. Don't look at me that way! Are you telling me that even though you have no idea how we got from my world to yours, the cylinder records are perfect? You must have opened the wrong one somehow."

"I assure you, we didn't," he said, and I saw no doubt on his face. If only I had! "Could your husband have gotten plastic surgery? Grown a new face? Maybe there's a reason you don't recognize him."

I shook my head. Oh, Rhys. Even if you'd grown yourself an entirely new body, I'd still have known if it was you within it.

"He's coming around," said Mikal. "Maybe once you hear his voice …"

As the man's lids lifted I looked into those eyes, eyes which were not yours, and had to restrain myself from screaming at whoever it was behind them who'd just woken from a decades-long sleep.

Mikal was wrong. The stranger did not have to speak for me to know … this was not you.

This was not you.

"Who are you?" I asked, grinding my teeth so hard my jaw ached. "And where is my husband?"

"Oh, Tegan," he said, with a soft tone that told me he knew who I was even though I did not know him. And that told me you probably knew him, too. "I'm so sorry."

"You know me," I said flatly. It was not a question. It was the beginning of understanding. Oh, Rhys, Rhys … how could you?

"I do," said the stranger I wish I'd never met. He sat up slowly. I could see his strength returning, the way mine had. Strength that was supposed to be your strength.

"Do I know you?"

"You do not. But Rhys … he did."

On hearing your name coming from that man's lips in the past tense, I dropped to the floor in an instant, before a cylindrical stool could rise to support me. I had no control over my spasming muscles, and did not try to catch myself, landing hard. I cried as I lay there, convulsive sobbing overwhelming me. Where were you, Rhys? Why were you not beside me once more?

What had you done?

The man who was not you rolled off the bed, *our* bed, Rhys, and knelt beside me. He reached out and attempted to touch my arm, but I slapped him away.

"Listen to me, Tegan. You have to listen. Rhys would have wanted you to listen."

"No," I told him, spitting tears. "Don't say his name. And don't tell me I have to listen."

Oh, Rhys … that I'd been reborn, I could believe.

That the world had shrunk to nothing more than underground tunnels, that I could believe.

That I'd never again feel the real sun on my face, or real wind against my skin, or real sand between my toes, only fabrications of them all, that I could believe.

But that you were not there beside me once more, ready to continue what we'd only just begun … that I could not believe.

I lay there weeping, my body stilling, slowly retreating from its violence against itself, as the stranger whispered into my ears. A stranger, Rhys!

"The first thing you need to know is that your husband loved you," he said.

"I know he loved me," I said, making several attempts before I could successfully speak. "But if he loved me, why isn't he here? And whoever you are, whatever you were to my husband, why are you the one here telling me that? Why isn't he? *Why isn't he?*"

I skittered away from the man, pressing my back against the wall. Our wall, seeming fresh and new, though really centuries old. Centuries old and long gone.

The design was too painful to look at any longer, that wallpaper we'd so carefully applied, even though it was but a illusion, so I tilted my head the way I'd been taught, and returned our surroundings to blankness.

It did not make the stranger any less alien to me.

"Who are you?" I demanded. "Why are you here? What were you doing in my husband's cylinder?"

"I'm here because he loved you," he said. He spoke slowly, kindly, but that made his words no easier to take. "Loved you enough to make sure someone made it to this time to tell you what he wasn't going to be around long enough to tell you. Loved you enough to make you happy, and keep you happy, during the time you were together. He knew you wanted this thing, a thing he did not want, this being sealed up and frozen, rather than going into the ground, so he let you think he wanted it, too. But Tegan, listen. He was a man of his times. He knew, even if this rebirth were to have worked—"

"But it did work!" I shouted.

"He couldn't have known that. No one could have known that. It had never been done. In our time, this was only promises. Promises, and wishes, and as far as some were concerned, maybe even lies. In any case, Rhys knew, in his heart, that tomorrow was not for him. Only yesterday. Even if he'd survived, he'd never have survived, he knew that, and if you think about it, you'll realize you know it, too. As for me, as for who I am … just a friend of his, a friend he made after you died, a friend who stayed by his side as long as he could, a friend who grieved the same way he did."

"Grief?" I said, followed by a whimper, feeling a grief I'd sworn I'd never have cause to feel knocking at the door of my heart. But I wouldn't let it in, Rhys! I wouldn't. "What was there for him to grieve? We were going to see each other again."

"There was plenty to grieve. We met because of grief. I'm only his friend in the first place because he joined a grief-counseling group after you … well … died."

"But I didn't die," I said, weeping. "All I did was … catch an earlier train."

"Ah, the trains. Yes, he mentioned the trains. And the elevators, and all the rest. But see, the metaphors only work if you believed this thing would work. And this thing, yes, it did work. I can see that now. I can feel it. But Rhys, he didn't buy that it would. So when the time for him to make his own call eventually neared, decades on, and I was nearing the end of my time as well, he made the call for me instead, and had me take his place. It had already been paid for after all. *Someone* had to go into the cylinder. He just didn't want it to be him. He wanted to end during the time where he began. He wanted to end life the way nature intended. He wanted that closure. But as for me, I figured … why not? If it works, it works, and if it doesn't, I'm no worse off."

"So he … he died?" I shouted, feeling a rising panic and terror. "He lied to me and died? He didn't have to do that! He didn't have to do either of those things."

"Rhys didn't see it that way. He never felt he was lying. All he did, he told me, was keep to himself his feelings that the impossible was impossible. He really didn't think either of you would live to find that out. He was the last face I saw, you know, Tegan, and as everything faded away, and I had no idea whether that was my last ever moment of consciousness, he told me that if I saw you, I was to tell you he loved you, and that he was sorry. But I realized then, and I'm certain now, he only believed two of those three things. That he loved you, and that he was sorry, those were true, yes. But his saying of it, the idea that he was actually sending a message, well, he didn't think either of you would live to see ... wherever we are now."

Wherever we are now.

He didn't know, Rhys. I was so caught up by the shock of the man's message, I didn't even pause to think that he didn't know about this world and these walls and what lay beyond them. Mikal and the others, they hadn't had a chance to tell him, not even the same lies they'd told me, since I'd broken down in front of him before they could.

So I took a deep breath, gave one last shudder, pulled myself together, and numbly told him everything I'd learned during my time spent waiting for you. I told him where we were.

And where we were ... was the place without you.

I was in shock for a long while, Rhys. I'd spent my earlier time in this new world by distracting myself imagining you at my side. I'd never once considered you'd instead be under the ground. Or had your ashes been scattered? You friend did not know. He was not around to see. So no one would ever know.

And once I was no longer in shock, the pain was far worse, because I could feel your absence more sharply. But then, you already know that.

Or do you?

I was willing to believe, able to believe, back when we were last together, that I could die and see you again. But can I find it in myself to believe I could die for the final time and still see you again in a world beyond science? I guess I must, or else I wouldn't be talking to you like this. But the part of me that believes in that third life is so small it's overwhelmed by the part of me that believes … no, this world is all we have.

This is all we could have had.

So I can't yet go on. But I can't yet stay either.

There is nothing in this world for me anymore, not in the tunnels, and not even if, beyond these walls, a habitable corner could be found which has somehow survived.

You felt the future world had no place for you in it? Then it has no place for me either.

I'm going to sleep now, the sleep about which they told the truth when they said I would feel no cold, but lied when they claimed I would not dream.

I can feel the one true world fading now, the one without you in it, as I settle for a second time within my cylinder. I am already beginning to feel the sand between my toes. Soon, there will be capybaras prancing in the surf, and fireworks painting the sky, and our children, and our parents, and you off in the distance, growing closer, ever closer.

Can you see me yet, Rhys? I can see you.

Take my hand.

And we will walk that beach forever.

ALSO AVAILABLE

ANTHOLOGIES BY MICHAEL BAILEY

Pellucid Lunacy

Chiral Mad

Chiral Mad 2

Qualia Nous

The Library of the Dead

Chiral Mad 3

You, Human

Adam's Ladder
(co-edited with Darren Speegle)

Chiral Mad 4: An Anthology of Collaborations
(co-edited with Lucy A. Snyder)

Miscreations: Gods, Monstrosities & Other Horrors
(co-edited with Doug Murano)

Chiral Mad 5